REQUIEM FOR A DREAM

A NOVEL BY HUBERT SELBY, JR.

THUNDER'S MOUTH PRESS

NEW YORK

*This book is dedicated, with
love, to Bobby, who has found
the only pound of pure—
Faith in a Loving God.*

*Preface © 2000 by Hubert Selby, Jr.
Foreword © 2000 by Darren Aronofsky
Foreword © 1988 by Richard Price*
*Published in the United States by
Thunder's Mouth Press
841 Broadway, Fourth Floor
New York, NY 10003
Grateful acknowledgement is made to the
New York State Council on the Arts and
the National Endowment for the Arts
for financial assistance with
the publication of this work.*

Library of Congress Cataloging-in-Publication Data

Selby, Hubert.
    Requiem for a dream: a novel / by Hubert Selby, Jr.
        p.   cm.
    ISBN 1-56025-248-0
    I. Title.
PS3569.E547R4 1988
813'.54—dc19   87-25366
                                                          CIP

Manufactured in the United States of America

Distributed by Publishers Group West

FOREWORD

When I was in high school, I thought you had to be dead to be a novelist—dead, and from somewhere else: England, the Midwest, France.

One of the more profound, if peripheral, epiphanies hitting me upon reading *Last Exit to Brooklyn* by Hubert Selby, Jr., was that my working-class Bronx world was valid material for Art; that the voices, the streets, the gestures that I knew so well were as human, as precious, and as honorable as any found through the centuries and civilizations of literature.

Which is to say that I set down *Last Exit to Brooklyn* with the terrifying realization that if I had the will and the talent to go with the eye and ear, I could grow up to be a writer.

It wasn't until I was much older that I realized that talent and material mean nothing without something else that Selby possesses and projects on every page of every book he has written: Love—a forgiveness and compassion that elevate all the bottom dogs that populate his world, the lost, the depraved, the cold-blooded, and the insensate. His art is his ability to humanize the seemingly inhuman, and by extension to humanize the reader.

No one can convey the visceral experience of the suffering of people like Selby—the cruel hallucinations of grace, of peace, of love, of Easy Street; the wracking ache of junk sickness; the choking rage of parental/marital/sexual claustrophobia; the tightening screws of paranoid delusion; the pathetic grandiosity of walk-around dreams; and the dread of the inevitable dawn.

Selby burrows under the skin and into the brains of the urban underclass to deliver infernal monologues seething with tragically skewered delusions, short-term ecstasies, and obsessive furies that crash and boil across the page, ceaselessly. At his best, he can literally *stun* us into empathy.

Requiem for a Dream tracks the destruction of four people—three young, and one older. Here, Selby reports from the marrow of those addicted: to dope, to hope, to tragically childish visions of heaven on earth. Even as its characters ascend to the heights, their nightmarish plummet can be foreseen, but this foreknowledge doesn't protect the reader from experiencing the almost unbearable suffering, the degradation and oblivion, that is the price of dreams among the powerless.

Requiem for a Dream is quintessential Selby, fueled by moments which make the reader feel like the unwilling newscaster witnessing the *Hindenburg* disaster who sobbed, "Oh, the *humanity!*"

It is Selby's gift to us that once again we find ourselves aching for his people—which is to say we find ourselves loving the unlovable.

—Richard Price
New York City
January 1988

PREFACE TO THE NEW EDITION

Requiem for a Dream was originally published in 1978. It is extremely gratifying to know that it is still in print and going into another edition. Also, it is being made into a film, production scheduled to start the middle of April this year. So the book still lives and breathes (as do I).

For me there is something beautiful and ironic in the fact that all this is happening now, during a time of "unparalleled prosperity." The Great American Dream is coming true for many. Obviously, I believe that to pursue the American Dream is not only futile but self-destructive because ultimately it destroys everything and everyone involved with it. By definition it must, because it nurtures everything except those things that are important: integrity, ethics, truth, our very heart and soul. Why? The reason is simple: because Life/life is giving, not getting.

I am not suggesting we need to give everything to the poor and homeless—the millions of them who are still here in the midst of plenty—put on a hair shirt and go through the streets with a begging bowl. This, in and of itself, is no more nurturing than the pursuit of "getting." I am not afraid of money and what it can buy. I would love to have a house full of stuff—of course I would need a house first. I have been hungry and see nothing noble in hunger. Neither do I see anything noble in eating high on the hog, though eating is certainly better. But to believe that getting stuff is the purpose and aim of life is madness.

It seems to me that we all have a dream of our own, our own personal vision, our own individual way of giving, but for many reasons we are afraid to pursue it, or to even recognize and accept its existence. But to deny our vision is to sell our soul. Getting is living a lie, turning our back on the truth, and Visions are glimpses of the truth: Obviously nothing external can truly nurture my inner life, my Vision.

What happens when I turn my back on my Vision and spend my time and energy getting the stuff of the American Dream? I become agitated, uncomfortable in my own skin, because the guilt of abandoning my "Self/self," of deserting my Vision, forces me to apologize for my existence, to need to prove myself by approaching life as if it's a competition. I have to keep getting stuff in an attempt to appease and satisfy that vague sense of discontent that worms its way through me.

Certainly not everyone will experience this torment, but enough do and have no idea what is wrong. I'm sure the psychologists have a term for this free-floating anxiety, but the cause is what is destroying us, not the classification. There are always millions who seem to get away with doing the things that we think abominable, and thrive. It certainly appears that way. Yet I know, absolutely, from my experience, that there are no free lunches in this life, and eventually we all have to accept full and total responsibility for our actions, everything we have done, and have not done.

This book is about four individuals who pursued The American Dream, and the results of their pursuit. They did not know the difference between the Vision in their hearts and the illusion of the American Dream. In pursuing the lie of illusion, they made it impossible to experience the truth of their Vision. As a result everything of value was lost.

Unfortunately, I suspect there never will be a requiem for *the* Dream, simply because it will destroy us before we have the opportunity to mourn its passing. Perhaps time will prove me wrong. As Mr. Hemingway said: "Isn't it pretty to think so?"

—Hubert Selby, Jr.
Los Angeles
1999

FOREWORD TO THE NEW EDITION

I was a public school kid from Brooklyn facing my first exams during freshman year of college, and I was terrified. High school was a joke. The only thing I learned was how to get away with cutting class. So, when college came around I wasn't very prepared. I hit the library and tried to learn.

But Selby fucked everything up.

Out of the corner of my eye I saw the word "Brooklyn." Now when you're from Brooklyn and you see anything related to Brooklyn you're immediately interested. I pulled a worn copy of *Last Exit to Brooklyn* off the shelf. This was before the movie, and I had no clue what I was holding. From sentence one I was done, and so were my finals. I blew them off and I read. I read and I read and I screamed and I connected and I recited and I rejoiced. This was storytelling. This was understanding. This was a deep yet simple examination of what makes us human. I now knew what I wanted to do. I wanted to tell stories.

Storytelling took me to L.A. and film school. Before school started they told us to prepare three short scripts for projects to be executed during the year. So, I figured I should read short stories from my favorite authors. That led me to Selby's "Fortune Cookie," which I shot right away. The story follows the rise and fall of a door-to-door salesman who gets addicted to the fortunes in fortune cookies.

After film school I figured it was time to make a feature, so I turned to novels of my favorite authors. I found *Requiem for a Dream* in a book store on Venice Beach. I was excited to start it. I did, but I never finished it. Not because it wasn't good. Rather, the novel was so violently honest and arresting that I couldn't handle it.

It was on my shelf for a long time. Then, years later, my producer Eric Watson was heading off for a ski trip with his family in Colorado. He needed something to read, and he grabbed the book off my shelf and asked if he could borrow it. When he returned he said *Requiem for a Dream* ruined his vacation and that I *must* finish it. I did, and I knew we had to make it next.

This book is about a lot of things. Mostly it's about love. More specifically it's about what happens when love goes wrong.

When it was time to write the script I rented an apartment in South Brooklyn, out by Coney Island. The novel had amazing structure and it translated very well into three acts. But something was strange. While breaking it down I realized that whenever something good was supposed to happen to a character, something bad happened. Because of this, I couldn't figure out who the hero of the novel was.

After sketching out all the character arcs I realized they were all upside down. So I flipped them over, and suddenly I had a "Eureka!" The hero wasn't Sara, it wasn't Harry, not Tyrone, not Marion.

The hero was the characters' enemy: Addiction. The book is a manifesto on Addiction's triumph over the Human Spirit. I began to look at the film as a monster movie. The only difference is that the monster doesn't have physical form. It only lives deep in the characters' heads.

Ellen Burstyn, who knocked it out of the park as Sara Goldfarb, told me Hinduism has two main gods—Shiva and Kali. Shiva is the god of creation and Kali is the god of destruction. They exist as a team. One cannot exist without the other. Just like the Christian God and the Devil. Good and evil. There is a balance. Selby writes about Kali. He writes about the darkness.

It is in this darkness where Selby flips on his flashlight and searches for our humanity. It is that tiny but priceless diamond of love lost in a universe of evil that he cherishes. And by leading us to it he reveals everything—our beauty and our vanity, our strength and our weaknesses. He shows us what makes us tick, what makes us hate and what makes us love. He reveals what it is to be human.

I needed to make a film from this novel because the words burn off the page. Like a hangman's noose, the words scorch your neck with rope burn and drag you into the sub-sub-basement we humans build beneath hell. Why do we do it? Because we choose to live the dream instead of choosing to live the life.

You won't ever forget this read.

—Darren Aronofsky
May 1, 2000

Except the LORD build the house,
they labor in vain that build it. . . .

Psalm 127:1

Trust in the LORD with all thine
heart; and lean not unto thine
own understanding.

In all thy ways acknowledge him,
and he shall direct thy paths.

Proverbs 3:5,6

Harry locked his mother in the closet. Harold. Please. Not again the TV. Okay, okay, Harry opened the door, then stop playin games with my head. He started walking across the room toward the television set. And dont bug me. He yanked the plug out of the socket and disconnected the rabbit ears. Sara went back into the closet and closed the door. Harry stared at the closet for a moment. So okay, stay. He started to push the set, on its stand, when it stopped with a jerk, the set almost falling. What the hells goin on here? He looked down and saw a bicycle chain going from a steel eye on the side of the set to the radiator. He stared at the closet. Whatta ya tryin to do, eh? Whats with this chain? You tryin to get me to break my own mothers set? or break the radiator?—she sat mutely on the closet floor— an maybe blow up the whole house? You tryin to make me a killer? Your own son? your own flesh and blood? WHATTA YA DOIN TA ME???? Harry was standing in front of the closet. YOUR OWN SON!!!! A thin key slowly peeked out from under the closet door. Harry worked it out with his fingernail then yanked it up. Why do you always gotta play games with my head for krists sake, always laying some heavy guilt shit on me? Dont you have any consideration for my feelings? Why do you haveta make my life so difficult? Why do— Harold, I wouldnt. The chain isnt for you. The robbers. Then why didnt you tell me? The set almost fell. I coulda had a heart attack. Sara was shaking her head in the darkness. You should be well Harold. Then why wont you come out? Harry tugging on the door and rattling the knob, but it was locked on the inside. Harry threw his hands up in despair and disgust. See what I mean? See how you always gotta upset me? He walked back to the set and unlocked the chain, then turned back to the closet. Why do you haveta make such a big deal outta this? eh? Just ta lay that guilt shit on me, right? Right????—Sara continued rocking back and forth—you know youll have the set back in a couple a hours but ya gotta make me feel guilty. He continued to look at the closet—Sara silent and rocking—then threw up his hands, Eh, screw it, and pushed the set, carefully, out of the apartment.

Sara heard the set being rolled across the floor, heard the door open and close, and sat with her eyes closed rocking back and forth. It wasnt happening. She didnt see it so it wasnt happening. She told her husband Seymour, dead these years, it wasnt happening. And if it should be happening it would be alright, so dont worry Seymour. This is like a commercial break. Soon the program will be back on and youll see, theyll make it nice Seymour. Itll all work out. Youll see already. In the end its all nice.

Harrys partner, a black guy name Tyrone C. Love—Thas right jim, thats mah name an ah loves nobody but Tyrone C.—was waiting for him in the hallway, chewing a Snickers candy bar. They got the set out of the building without any trouble, Harry saying hello to all the *yentas* sitting by the building getting the sun. But now came the hard part. Pushing that damn thing the three blocks to the hock shop without it getting ripped off, or getting knocked over by some dumb ass kid, or being tipped over by running into a hole in the ground or bumping into a lump of litter, or just having the goddamn table collapse, took patience and perseverance. Tyrone steadied the set as Harry pushed and steered, Tyrone acting as lookout and warning Harry of the large hunks of paper and bags of garbage that might prove hazardous to the swift and safe completion of their appointed mission. They each grabbed an end as they eased it off the curb and up onto the other side of the street. Tyrone tilted his head and looked the set over. Sheeit, this mutha startin to look a little seedy man. Whats the matta, ya particular all of a sudden? Hey baby, ah dont much care if its growin hair just sos we gets our braid.

Mr. Rabinowitz shook his head as he watched them push the set into his pawn shop. So look, the table too already. Hey, what do you want from me? I cant *schlep* it on my back. You got a friend. He could help already. Hey mah man, ah aint mah lepers *schlepper*. Harry chuckled and shook his head, Whatta jew. Anyway, it makes it easier to get it home. Thats mah man, always thinkin of his moms. Oi, such a son. A *goniff*. Shes needing you like a moose needs a hat rack. Come on Abe, we/re in a hurry. Just give us the bread. Hurry, hurry. All the time in a hurry, shuffling around behind the counter, inspecting the pencils carefully before picking one out to use. You got such big things to do the voild is falling apart if everything isnt dont yesterday. He clucked his tongue, shook his head, and slowly counted the money . . . twice . . . three times— Hey, comeon Abe, lets get with it. You dig this dude jim? Hes lickin them fingers and countin that braid ovah and ovah like its gonna change numbers. He dont even trus his ownself. Damn.

Mr. Rabinowitz gave the money to Harry and Harry signed the book. Do for me a favor and veel it over there?

Sheeit. You know somethin jim, evertime I see you I work mah pretty little ass off. They pushed the set to the corner and split.

Mr. Rabinowitz watched, shaking his head and clucking his tongue, then sighed, Somethingks wrong . . . it just aint kosher already, it just aint kosher.

Sheeit. Why you wanna go there man? Why do I wanta go there? Because they give blue chip stamps with the dope. You know somthin Harry? You is simple minded. You shouldnt fuck aroun when you talkin about somethin serious like dope man. Aspecially when you be talkin about mah dope. Yours I'm not carin about. Just mine. And whats so great about the dope here? O man, what you mean? Theys just as many connections right here as there. We could even try somebody new. New? Yeah baby. We could jus ease on down the street and see who have the most fingers up their nose and noddin out an we know where the *good* dope be, ah mean the outta sight shit jim. An anyways, we save the cab fare. Cab fare? Who died and left you rich? This moneys goin for dope man. It aint goin for no cab. Ya gotta take care a necessities before ya fuck with luxuries.

Sheeit. You aspect me to ride them mutha fuckin subways with all them poiverts and winos? Damn. You outta your mine. They rip you off before you gets anywheres. Hey man, dont go pulling that lazy ass ol black joe shit on me. Tyrone chuckled, Man, if ah gotta do some travelin then let me call mah man Brody and see what he got. Gimme a dime. Goddamn it man, since when do you need a dime to make a call. Hey baby, ah dont fuck with no phone company. Harry leaned against the phone booth as Tyrone hunched himself around the phone and spoke conspiratorially. After a minute or so he hung up the phone and stepped forth from the booth, a huge grin on his face. Hey man, close ya mouth, its hurtin my eyes. You pale-assed mutha fucka. You shure wouldnt make it in no cotton fields. Tyrone started walking and Harry fell in alongside him. So whats happenin? Mah man got some dynamite shit baby an wes gonna get us a spoon. They walked up the stairs from the subway separately. Harry looked around for a moment as Tyrone continued down the street, then went to the coffee shop a few doors away. The neighborhood was absolutely and completely black. Even the plainclothesmen were black. Harry always felt a little conspicuous in the coffee shop sipping light coffee and eating a chocolate doughnut. This was the only drag about copping from Brody. He usually had good shit but Harry couldnt go any further than the coffee shop or they would blow the whole scene, or what was almost as bad, he might get his head laid open. Actually the smart thing to do, the really smart thing to do, would be to stay uptown, but Harry couldnt bear to be that far away from the money and the shit. It was bad enough sitting here feeling his stomach muscles tighten and that anxiety crawl through his body and the taste twitch the back of his throat, but it was a million times better than *not* being here.

He ordered another cup of coffee and doughnut and turned in the stool slightly as a cop, blacker than his doughnut and bigger than a goddamn Mack truck, sat next to him. Jesus krist, just my fuckin luck. Try to relax and enjoy a cup of coffee and a fuckin baboon has to sit next to me. Shit! He sipped his coffee and looked at the gun in the holster wondering what would happen if he suddenly yanked the gun out and started shooting, pow, pow, and blow the mother fuckers head right the fuck off then toss a bill on the counter and tell the chick to keep the change and stroll out or maybe just ease the gun out and then hand it to the cop and ask him if it was his, I just found it on the floor and I thought maybe you misplaced your gun, or what would really be a gasser would be to sneak the fuckin thing out and mail it to the commissioner with a little note how a couple a guys got burned with it and maybe he should take better care a his toys . . . yeah, that would be a gasser and he looked at the huge son of a bitch sitting next to him as he fat mouthed with the chick behind the counter and laughed his big black ass off and Harry chuckled to himself and wondered what the cop would think if he knew that his life was in Harrys hands and then Harry noticed the size of the hand holding the coffee cup and realized that it was bigger than a fuckin basketball and he stuffed the rest of the doughnut in his mouth and swished it down with the coffee and strolled out of the coffee shop, slowly, still feeling that mountain of a fuzz behind him, as Tyrone bebopped his way down the subway steps.

Tyrones pad wasnt much more than a room with a sink. They sat around the small table, their works in a glass, the water tinged pink with blood, their heads hanging loose from their necks, their hands hanging loose from their wrists, their fingers barely holding their cigarettes. Occasionally a finger probed a nostril. Their voices came low and weak from their throats. Sheeit, thats some boss scag baby. I mean *dyn a mite*. Yeah man, its really somethin else. Harrys cigarette burned his fingers and he dropped it, Shit, then slowly bent over and looked at it for a minute, his hand hanging over it, then finally picked it up, looked at it, then gradually worked a fresh cigarette out of his pack and into his mouth and lit it with the old one, dropped the butt in the ashtray, then licked the burned spot on his fingers. He stared at the tip of his shoes for a moment, then another . . . they looked good, sort of soft the way they—a huge roach attracted his attention as it belligerently marched by, and by the time he thought of trying to step on it it disappeared under the molding. Just as well, that sonofabitch mighta put a hole in my shoe. He tugged his arm up and then his hand and took a drag of his cigarette. Harry took another long drag on his cigarette and inhaled it slowly and deeply, tasting each particle of smoke and savoring the way it seemed to titillate his tonsils and throat, krist it tasted good. There was something about smack that made a cigarette taste so fuckin good. Ya know what we oughtta do man? Huh? We oughtta get a piece a this shit and cut it and off half of it, ya dig? Yeah baby, this stuffs good enough to cut in half and still get you wasted. Yeah, we/d just take a taste for ourselves and off the rest. We could double our money. Easy. Thas right baby. An then we buys a couple a pieces an we got somethin else goin man. It sure would be righteous baby. All we gotta do is cool it with the shit, you know, just a taste once in a while but no heavy shit—Right on baby—just enough to stay straight an we/d have a fuckin bundle in no time. You bet your sweet ass. Those bucks would just be pilin up till we was ass deep in braid jim. Thats right man, and we wouldnt fuck it up like those other assholes. We wont get strung out and blow it. We/d be cool and take care a business and in no time we/d get a pound of pure and just sit back and count the bread. No hustlin the fuckin streets. You goddamn right mutha fucka. We get it right from the *eye*talians and cut it our ownselves and get us some runy nosed dope fiens to hustle it for us an we jus sit back countin them bucks and drivin a big ass pink mutha fuckin El Dorado. Yeah, and I/ll get a chaufers uniform and drive your black ass all over town. An you better hold that mutha fuckin door jim or I/ll burn your ass. . . . O yeah, mah names *Tyrone* C. Love and I loves *nobody* but Tyrone C. Well, it ain't no Tyrone C. Im gonta love. Im gonta get me a fine pad by Central Park man and

just spend my time sniffin all that fine quiff walkin by.
Sheeit . . . what you gonna do with that man. You done
doogied out your dong. Im just gonta lay down beside it and
pet it man and maybe just sort of nibble on it once in a
while. Damn. Now aint this a muthafuckin shame. This
dudes gonna lay up in some fine pad with some fine fox and
hes gonna go stickin his nose in that nasty thang. So what do
you want from me, I like to knosh. A little chopped liver, a
little smoked fish, a— Gawddamn, but you a nasty mutha
fucka. Thas the trouble with you ofays man, you dont know
what to do with a fox. Shit man, we know what to do. Its you
fuckin Africans who dont have any table manners . . . why
do ya think the Jewish guys get all the broads? It aint got
nothing ta do with money. Its because we/re knoshers. Sheeit,
you just a missin dick fool man. Afta ah has mah tailor
measure me for a few more suits ahm goin back to the pad
and have me a stable of foxes jim that make your knees
buckle. Ah mean theys gonna be real fine. An Im gonna have
a different color for everyday in the week. How long ya
figure itll take us before we can go for a pound of pure?
Sheeit man. That aint nothin. We get out there an hustle up
a couple a yards for a piece an we on our way. By Christmas
we be sittin back countin those bucks and talkin that trash.
Merry Christmas man. Harrys cigarette burned his fingers,
Shit, and he dropped it, son of a bitch.

Two young kids from the neighborhood went to the hock
shop with Sara. Mr. Rabinowitz shuffled around the counter,
Good evening Mrs. Goldfarb. Good evening Mr. Rabinowitz, though I'm not so sure how good it is. And you? Uh,
he half closed his eyes, hunched his shoulders and tilted his
head, so vat could I say? Im alone in the store all day and mine
wife is shopping mit our daughter Rachel for little Izzy

something and still not home yet. For lunch Im having cold tongue, mit out da rye. . . . Im having some mustard and harseradish, but mit out da rye already, oi . . . he shrugged, tilted and peered again, but for supper maybe Im having cold soup if she still not home, are you vanting your TV? How old is little Izzy now? O, hes so cute I could just take hunks and bits out of those chubby little legs. Yes, if you dont mind. I have these nice young boys to push it home for me—such nice boys to help a poor mother—thank God he took the stand too so it makes it easier to get back. I only have three dollars now but next week Im— So take it, take, shrugging and tilting his head, and veal hope he doesnt take it again before you pay for this time, not like the time he stole already the set three times in vun month and it vas how long before youre paying it off? Izzy is being a whole year next week, Tuesday. Oooo, Sara sighed long and deep, it seems like only yesterday Rachel was playing dolls and now . . . Sara gave the three dollars, that had been folded and carefully tucked in the corner of her blouse, to Mr. Rabinowitz, and he shuffled behind the counter and put it in his cash register and carefully made an entry in a small book with the title, SARA GOLDFARB'S TV, on the cover. There were endless pages of entries and dates, covering the last few years, of money given Harry for the set and the payments his mother made after redeeming it. The two kids had started pushing the set, and the table, out to the street. Mrs. Goldfarb, can I ask of you a question, you vont be taking git personal? Sara shrugged, How many years we know each other? He nodded his head up and down up and down up and down, Whos to count? Vy dont you tell already the police so maybe they could talk to Harry and he vouldnt be stealing no more the TV, or maybe they send him somewhere for a few months he can tink and ven hes coming out hes already a good boy and takes care of you and no more all the time taking the TV? Oooo, another long and deep sigh, Mr. Rabinowitz, I couldnt, clutching her breast most fervently, Harolds my only child, and only relative. Hes all I have. Everyone else is dead. Theres only Harry and me . . . my son, my boobala. And who knows how much time I have left— Ah, a young voman—she waved away his remark, to help my son. Hes the end of the line. The last of the Goldfarbs. How could I make him a criminal? They would put him with such terrible people where he could learn such terrible things. No, hes young. Hes a good boy my Harold. Hes just a little mischief. Someday he/ll meet a nice young jewish girl and he/ll settle down and make me a grandmother. Goodbye Mr. Rabinowitz, waving as she walked toward the door, say hello to Mrs. Rabinowitz. Be careful going out the door boys. Abe Rabinowitz nodded as he watched her go out, the two boys pushing the set, then watched them go slowly up the street, past his cloudy windows, and then out of sight. He stopped nodding and shook his head, Oi, such a life. I hope she gets home already. Im not vanting cold soup. A man my age is needingk hot food for his stomach and hot water for his feet. Oi mine feet. Ahhhhhhh . . . such a life. *Tsouris . . . tsouris . . .*

After the young boys left Sara Goldfarb chained the TV to the radiator again. She turned on the set, adjusted the antenna, then sat down in her viewing chair and watched a series of Proctor and Gamble commercials and parts of a soap opera. She pulled her lips back as people brushed their teeth and ran their tongues over their teeth to be sure there was no telltale film, and felt a joy when that cutie pie little boy didnt have any cavities but he seemed so thin, he needs more meat on his bones. He shouldnt have any cavities, thank God, but he should have more meat on his bones. Like my Harold. So thin. I tell him, eat, eat, I see your bones. Fa krists sake, thats my fingers. Whatta ya want, festoons of fat hanging from my fingers? I just want you to be healthy, you shouldn't be so skinny. You should dring hamalted. Malted, schmalted, eh? I wonder if Harold has any cavities? His teeth didnt look so good. He smokes so many cigarettes. He pulled his lips back from his teeth again. Such nice white teeth. Maybe someday he/ll grow up and smoke and have yellow teeth like my Harold. They should never have cavities, and she continued to stare at the set as boxes of detergent exploded into dazzling white clothes and bottles of household cleaner exploded into exotic fag characters who wiped all evidence of humanity off walls and floors and the tired husband comes home from a tough day on the job and is so overwhelmed by the dazzling clothes and sparkling floor that he forgets all about the worries of the world and he picks up his wife—O, is she thin. Youd have to be careful she doesnt break. But shes so sweet looking. A nice girl. Keeps a clean house. My Harold should find such a girl. A nice young jewish girl like that. The husband picked up his wife and spun her around and they ended up stretched out on the sparkling and dazzling bright kitchen floor and Sara leaned forward in her chair thinking that maybe something interesting was going to happen but all they did was look at their reflections in the linoleum; and then the TV dinners were artistically arranged on the table and the wife smiled at Sara, that sly, we have a secret kind of smile, when the husband exclaimed enthusiastically what a great cook she is and Sara smiled and winked and didnt tell that it was a TV dinner and the happy couple looked into each others eyes as they ate their dinner, and Sara was so happy for them, then checked her money and realized she would have to go without lunch for a few days, but it was worth it to have the TV set. It wasnt the first time she gave up a meal for her set; and then the scene changed and a car drove up to a hospital and a worried mother hurried through the antiseptic and quiet corridors to a grave countenanced doctor who discussed the condition of her son and what they would have to do in order to save the boys life and Sara leaned forward in her chair looking and listening intently, empathizing with the mother and feeling more and more anxious as the doctor explained, in painful detail, the possibilities of failure, O my God, thats terrible . . . so terrible. The doctor finished explaining all the alternatives to the mother and watched her as she wrestled with the decision of whether or not to allow the doctor to operate and Sara was leaning as far forward as she could, clutching her hands together, Let him. . . . Yes, yes. Hes a good doctor. You should see what he did for that little girl yesterday. Such a surgeon. A crackerjack. The woman finally nodded her assent as she wiped at tears streaming down her face, Good, good. You have a good cry dolly. He/ll save your son. Youll see. Im telling you. Such a surgeon. Sara stared as the womans face got larger and larger and the fear and tension were so obvious that Sara trembled slightly. When the scene changed to the operating room Sara quickly looked at her clock and sighed with relief when she saw that there was only a few minutes to go and soon the mother would be smiling and happy as she looked at her son with the doctor telling her its all over and hes going to be alright, and then a minute after that we would see the outside of the hospital again but this time the boy would be walking with the mother—no, no, he would be in a wheelchair—to the car and everybody would be happy as he got into the car and they drove off, the doctor watching them from the window of his office. Sara sat back and smiled, and relaxed with the inner knowledge that everything would be alright. Her Harry is a little mischief some times, but hes a good boy. Everything will be alright. Some day he/ll meet a nice girl and he/ll settle down and make me a grandmother.

The sun was down which made it night time, but Harry and Tyrone were bugged with all the lights that stabbed and slashed and skewered their eyeballs. They hung tough behind their shades. Daytime is a drag, when the sun is shining, the sunlight bouncing off windows and cars and buildings and the sidewalk and the goddamn glare pushing on your eyeballs like two big thumbs and you look forward to the night when you can get some relief from the assaults of the day and start to come alive as the moon rises, but you never get the complete relief you look forward to, that you anticipate. You start to feel the apathy of the day start to seep away as the lames and squares all make it home from the 9 to 5 and sit down to a dinner with the wife and kids, the wife lookin like the same beat up broad with hair in her face and her ass saggin, dumpin the same old slop on the table and the goddamn house apes yelling and fightin about whose piece of meat is bigger and who got the most butter and whats for dessert and after dinner he grabs a can a beer and sits in front of the tube and grunts and farts and picks his teeth thinkin that he oughtta go out and get a good piece a ass but too tired and eventually the old lady comes in and flops on the couch and says the same thing every night. Never changes. Watch ya watchin, hon???? By the time that scene is played all over the apple there's a little life in the streets, but theres still those damn lights. Yeah, the lights are a drag, but its a lot better than the sun. Anythings better than that. Especially in the middle of summer. Now you have just said a mouthful, mah man. Ah feels like slidin mah pretty little ass to some nice dark corner and groove behind some fine sounds and maybe lay a bad dick on some groovy fox, and ah mean a *bad* mutha fuckin dick jim. Jesus krist man, you really got pussy on the mind. Cant you ever think above your navel fa krists sake? Sheeit. What the fuck you talking about man? Jus cause they cut the bone outta yours dont mean diddly to me. Mines still moren just a pee pole. Gahd damn, give me five. Harry slapped the palms of Tyrones hands and Tyrone slapped Harrys. Well man, we gonta stand here all night and count the cars goin by, or should we try to drum up a little action? O man, what you mean? you know ah caint count. O krist, man, why dont you cool it, eh? You think they cut that shit with laughin gas? Anyway, lets go where theres some life. Whatta ya say? Hey baby, Im down. Why dont we make it crosstown to the morgue? Hey, yeah, Angels on duty tonight. Theres always a little action at the morgue. Lets make it baby.

Harry Goldfarb and Tyrone C. Love got on the crosstown bus. Harry started to sit in the front, just behind the driver, and Tyrone grabbed his arm and dragged him out of the seat and shook him, his eyes Step-n-Fetch-It wide, yawl outta yoe mine man? shaking Harry as his body shook, darting glances everywhere at once, yawl tryin to get us killed? Yawl tryin to get us lynched from the lamppost? Yawl outta your gawd-damn mine? Hey man, lighten up. Whats with you? Whats with me—the bus lurched to a stop and they knocked into the railing around the driver and Tyrone jerked them back as he tried to hide behind his shoulder and peer at the people boarding the bus—whats with me? Is you crazy? This here is the south Bronx man, ah mean the *south*, S O U T H, you dig? O shit. Lets make it man. They slunk down the aisle, bouncing off the seats, bowing and scraping, Sorry, sorry. No offense man. . . . The other passengers continued reading their papers, talking, looking out the window, reading the advertisements, straining to see the street signs, blowing their nose, cleaning their glasses and staring straight ahead at nothing, as they lurched by. When they reached the rear of the bus they sat down with a long, loud sigh. Hey massa Harry, how come you is a sittin back chere wit us black foke? Well, ahll tell you brother Tyrone, cause under it all ah feels that we is all brothers and under this white skin beats a heart just as black as yours, hahahaha, lay it on me, and they gave each other five. Sheeit baby, you aint white, youse just pale . . . and you got to remember baby, beautys only skin deep, but uglys to the bone, and they gave each other five again. Harry made a telescope with his hands and peered through it at the ads along the side of the bus. What the fuck you doin man? Its the only way to look at an ad, man. You really get to peep the broads without distractions. Harry deepened his voice: Dont be half safe, put Arried under both your arms. Sheeit man, Mums the word. You think Im putting ya on, eh? Go ahead, try it. Its the only way, man. Im tellin ya. All those lovely ads up there and you never noticed them. Harry scanned the ads as a lookout the horizon. Hey, look at that one. I bet you missed it. Does she or doesnt she? Only her gynecologist knows for sure. What he doin peepin at her thang. Yeah, it dont mean a swing if you aint got that thang. They stretched out and continued rappin and gooffin on their way to the morgue.

They eased themselves out of the bus and stood on the corner for a moment as the bus roared slowly away and the

diesel fumes floated unnoticed around them. They lit cigarettes and savored the deliciousness of the first drag as they
looked around before crossing the street. They went down
the dimly lit street, around the back, over the low fence and
quickly dropped down to the runway leading to the tunnel,
then quickly through the tunnel and off to the right in a
small, narrow recess and rang the bell with the opening movement of Beethovens Fifth, DA DA DA DAAAAAA. There
was an old serial named Spy Smasher, and the opening music
for each chapter was the beginning of Beethovens Fifth as a
huge V appeared on the screen and the morse signal for v
appeared under it, dot dot dot dash. Angel loved that serial.
He thought it was real hip havin Beethoven help them win
the war. That was his secret signal for everything. Angel
peeped at them for a moment, then opened the door slightly,
Hurry up before fresh air gets in here. They slid in and
Angel closed the door, shut. The warm, humid summer air
was left behind and it was suddenly cool, very cool. They
walked past the machinery, up the steel staircase to an office.
It was dense with smoke that whirled as the door opened and
closed and looked exotic in the blue light. Tony, Fred and
Lucy were sitting on the floor, listening to the music from
the radio on the desk. Whatta ya say, man? Hey baby, whats
happenin? Hows it going sweetheart? Hey, mah man, what's
happenin? Things are pretty good Harry. Whats happenin
baby? Groovy baby. Harry and Tyrone sat down and leaned
against the wall and started to move slightly in time to the
music. Any action tonight Angel? Hey man, theres always
action here. This is a lively joint when the Angels around,
eh? You straight? Not yet. Itll be here soon. Gogit is on his
way. Hey, groovy man. He always got some good stuff. The
Spy Smasher ring got Angel to his feet and out of the office.
He came back in a minute with Marion and Betty. Hey, whats
happenin man? Im cool baby, what goin on? Whatta ya say?

Whats shakin baby? Makin it, makin it. You know, same old thing. They joined the others on the floor, Marion sitting next to Harry. Tyrone looked at Fred, You lookin good man. You know me man, strength and health. Watch you do, change embalmers? Sheeit man, theys got stiffs out in them boxes that looks betteran you. Ooooo, thats some deep shit man. O sheeit. That dude walk in that room an he scare them stiffs outen here. O man, thats rank. Dont letim shit all overya man, open ya mouth. You know somethin baby, yawls a degenerate. The giggling was becoming laughter and becoming louder and louder. Hey man, who let you out without a leash. Oooo, thats—DOT DOT DOT DAAAA-AAAASH. Angel spun around and out of the room and the silence maintained itself as effortlessly as it had started as everyone felt that it was Gogit and waited to see him bebop his way through the door. He did. Hey mah man, whaz happenin? Hey baby. Lay it on me jim—*slap*. You straight baby? Sheeit, ahm ah straight? What the fuck yoe think ahm doin here, lookin at the scenery? Yeah, its kindda dead, eh? Ah got some boss shit, man. Ah mean its dy no mite, right from the *eye*talians. Everybody started taking their money out and Gogit put the heroin on the table and scooped up the money. Lets go git it on. Everyone left the office and started roaming around the dimlit refrigeration room, reaching down cracks, crevices, under floorplates, behind machinery, between loose bricks, for their works. No matter how many other sets they might have stashed around town, everyone always had a set stashed in the Bronx County Morgue. They went back to the office, got paper cups filled with water and each one staked out a small portion of the floor for themselves. The radio was still playing but the concentration was so intense that no one heard the music or was aware of anything but their own cooker as they carefully dumped the heroin in it, then added the water and heated it until the dope dissolved, then drew

the liquid up through the cotton in the cooker into the
dropper, then tied up. Each knew they were not alone in the
room, but paid absolutely no attention to what was going on
around them. When their favorite vein was ready they tapped
the needle into it and watched the first bubble of blood pulse
through the fluid and streak to the surface, their eyes glued
to it, their senses aware only of the fact that they got a good
hit and that their stomachs were churning with anticipation
and then they squeezed the bulb and shot the shit into their
vein and waited for the first rush and then let the dropper fill
with blood again and squeezed that in and then booted again
and went with the flow as they flushed and felt the sweat ooze
from their skin then filled their droppers with water and let
their works set in the cup of water while they leaned back
against the wall and lit a cigarette, their movements slow,
their eyes half closed, everything inside them quiet and
mellow; the air smooth, their lives free from all concerns;
their speech slower, quieter. Harry started picking his nose.
Hey man, this shit is somethin else. Gogit mah man, you is
alright. Yoe gahddamn right ah is. Yoe seen the rest now you
sees the best. The laughter and giggling was low and slow,
and oooo, so cool. Hey man, pick me a winner. Harrys right
pinky was still buried deep in his nose, his brows knit in
deep concentration as he probed, his entire being involved in
the sensuous pleasure of the search, the near orgasmic satisfaction of finding a solid substance to be picked and pried
from the drying sides with the nail, then extracted with care
from the darkness of the cavern to the caressing blue light
to be deliciously rolled between the tips of his fingers. The
sound of his voice was soothing to his ears as it reflected an
inner peace and contentment. Be cool man. Different strokes
for different folks, eh man? Marion kissed Harry on the
cheek, I think youre beautiful Hare. I like to see a man
enjoy himself. There was a little more intensity to the laugh-

ter, but still low and, ooooo, so slow. Sheeit, whyent chuall leave the dude alone and letim do his thang in peace. It got to be a drag, man, to be a booger freak. Yeah, anytime he wants to lose ten pounds he just picks his nose. I should tell my sister that. She makes two of me. She really gets up tight when she sees me. Well baby, yawl just turn her on to some smack and her butter ball ass go right down the drain and ah mean right now. Hey man, you sure you aint finger fuckin yourself? Hey Harry, yawl wanna borrow a finger? Sheeit, whyent chuall get offen his muthafuckin ass? Sheeit, thats as good as pussy, right Harry? Go git it on man, git it on!!! Harry grinned as the others laughed and took time out to take a poke on his cigarette, then rubbed the tip of his nose with the back of his hand. I should have you all locked up for interferin with religious freedom. Betty made the sign of the cross at him, In the name of the father, the son and the holy booger. Harry joined the laughter and Angel turned the radio up a bit and they gradually started nodding and finger poppin in time to the music. Hey Angel, any interesting customers out there? Na, theyre all a bunch of stiffs, har, har, har. Angels head was nodding up and down as he continued to laugh, and when he spoke the words sputtered through his laughter, theyre all a bunch of dead beats. Sheeit, I bet they look better than you baby. Dont say that. I think Angel is cute. Yeah, haha, like Count Dracula. I bid you velcome. Drink you blood before it clots. Lucy giggled for a few seconds, shaking her head, Ah wonder what that dude would do here, hehehe, hed be one hungry mutha. You aint shitin man. Alls he gotta do it bite into Gogit and hed o.d. Thats a funny scene, a strung out vampire. Harry put his arms around Marion and pulled her close to him, Be cool baby, or I/ll biteya on the chroat, and started nibbling her neck. She giggled and squirmed and soon they both tired and just leaned against the wall, smiling loudly. No kiddin Angel, do

ya ever get anything special in here, like some young good
lookin heads? Sheeit, this muthafuckas a ghoul man. Everyone
was giggling and scratching. Thats okay man, I understand.
Some likeim hot and some likeim cold. Hey Gogit, watch
you put into Freds stuff? Marion was giggling and gagging on
a mouthful of smoke, Hey Fred, go over to the other side of
the room. Id feel a lot safer. They were all laughing and gig-
glin an rubbing their noses between taking pot shots at Fred
and drags on their cigarettes. The smoke was becoming so
thick that the blue light made the room look as if a small part
of light blue sky had somehow fallen into the room. Sheeit,
ah dont care what was in the stuff, ah wants to know whats he
gonna do with it? He got to find it first. There was one here
yesterday that was a real doll, man. I mean gorgeous. A real
knockout. A redhead. A real redhead, and built like a brick
shithouse. She had a pair like this and a ass that didnt quit.
Fred looked and spoke as eagerly as the dope allowed him, No
shit man? How old was she? Hey, what could I tellya? About
nineteen or twenty. Sheeit, aint this a bitch? This mutha
worryin how old she is. Hes got scruples man, he dont wanna
get caught with anyone underage. Right Fred? Everyone was
grinning as broadly as possible and chuckling, their heads
bouncing and bobbing. Where is she? Maybe Fred/d like to
meater, M E A T? Betty was shaking her head and chuckling,
You know something, you guys are sick. Hey, dont knock it.
Its ecologically sound. Ya gotta recycle everything man. The
faces still grinned and the heads still bobbed and the laughter
got a little louder. Sheeit, yoe honky ass mutha fuckas is
weird jim, ah mean weird. Yawl sound like a bunch a guhddamn cannibals. Hey man, whats all the static? I was just
askin a friendly question. The laughter was getting a little
louder and a little more energetic. Watch she die of? Who
said she was dead? She was a visitor, har, har, har. The heads
stopped bobbing and started shaking. Thats pretty good, eh?

Really had ya goin, didnt I? Yoe know somethin jim? youse got the right job cause yoe haid is daid baby, an ah means daid. A hand reached up and turned the volume of the radio up and the music worked its way through the blue smoke and over the chuckling and laughter. Hey, that's mah man wailin. Everyone was nodding at the lyrics. Yeah, tellem baby, we sure do need someone to lean on. O, lean on me baby, *lean on me!* You dig what that mutha say about her breas be always open? What kind a weirdo is that, she close her legs? Hey Angel, why dont you be cool man. Everyones eyes were half closed from the smoke and dope, and their faces kept twisting and grinning as they leaned into the words. Hey baby, you got some space for me in your parking lot? Fred grinned and made a few clacking noises, and Lucy continued to keep her attention on the stream of smoke bending up from her cigarette, digging the difference between the color of the smoke coming out of the lit end and the other end. Lay some of that coke and sympathy on me an fine out sucker. There was some giggling, Oooooo, that one bad bitch jim. They were all suddenly silent as they listened through the *dream on* lines, each in their own way thinking they didnt need anyone to dream on, that this boss shit did the job just fine. . . .

Then they all twisted into the next lines and giggled and snickered and grinned, Yeah, now youre talkin man, I need someone to cream on. Yeah, do it *to* me baby, uh huuuu. Lucy squinted in Freds direction, Doan look at me baby, betta see your mammy. The others worked into a slight giggle. Oooooo, she bad jim. Fred giggled as loud as he could, but still couldnt hear it himself. He tried to look at Lucy but couldnt raise his head, saving his energy to poke at his cigarette. The singing continued and they listened and savored each word and rolled it around in their heads. Harry put a new cigarette in his mouth and reached over to take Tyrones to light it, but

Tyrone moved his head away and tossed him a pack of matches. Harry looked at them for a moment, then slowly picked them up and went through the process of taking a match out, igniting it, raising it as high as he could and lowering his head as much as possible, then lighting his cigarette. O yeah, take it all baby, jus doan fuck with mah haid. O what pleasant *com pan eee*. Hey man, play that again. Why, who do you want to bleed on now? Sheeit, ah doan care just sos it aint mah blood. Man, the only blood I wanna see is in my dropper just before I shoot the son of a bitch back in my vein. Sheeit, you got a one track mine jim. Yeah, and the tracks are all up and down his arm. The giggling and snickering was approaching laughter as they nodded in time to the up tempo music, taking an occasional drag on a cigarette, seeing the drab gray of the concrete floor they were sitting on but not noticing it, involved with how they felt, and baby they felt gooood. The last notes were still in their heads when another tune started. Hey, you dig what they playin? Damn, ah aint heard this since befoe I started shootin stuff. Sheeit, aint no record that ol jim. Marion leaned comfortably into Harrys shoulder, her eyes and face soft in a smile. Remember when we used to dig this cat downtown? Yeah . . . The voice so filled with nostalgia that you could almost see the memories floating through the blue smoke, memories not only of music and joy and youth, but, perhaps, of dreams. They listened to the music, each hearing it in his own way, feeling relaxed and a part of the music, a part of each other, and almost a part of the world. And so another swinging night in the Bronx County Morgue slowly drifted toward another day.

The phone rang a second time and Sara Goldfarb leaned toward the phone as she continued to adjust the rabbit ears on her set, torn between the need to know who was calling and to get rid of the lines that darted, from time to time, across the picture, and she ooood as she tensed and squinted, leaning more and more toward the phone as it rang again, one hand reaching for the phone while the tips of the fingers of the other hand continued to tap the antenna over one centimeter at a time. Im coming, Im coming. Dont hang up, and she lunged at the phone, almost falling down in the middle of the sixth ring and flopping on the chair. Hello? Mrs. Goldfarb? Mrs. Sara Goldfarb? Its me. Speaking. The voice was so bright and cheery and so enthusiastic and real that she turned toward the TV set to see if the voice was coming from there. Mrs. Goldfarb, this is Lyle Russel of the McDick Corporation. She looked at the phone. She knew for real that his voice was coming from there, but it sounded just like a television announcer. She kept at least one eye on the television as she listened and spoke to Lyle Russel of the McDick Corporation. Mrs. Goldfarb, how would *you* like to be a contestant on one of televisions most *poignant,* most *heartwarming* programs? Oooo me? On the television???? She kept looking from the phone to the television, and back again, trying to look at both at the same time. Hahaha, I thought you would Mrs. Goldfarb. I can tell just by the warmth in your voice that you are just the kind of individual we want for our programs. Sara Goldfarb blushed and blinked, I never thought that maybe I would be on the television. Im just a— O haha, I know how you feel Mrs. Goldfarb. Believe me when I say I am just as thrilled as you to be a part of this fantastic industry. I consider myself one of the luckiest men in the world because every day I get a chance to help people just like yourself, Mrs. Goldfarb, to be a part of programming that not only are we proud of but the entire industry—no, the entire nation is proud of. Harrys mother was clutching the top of her dress, feeling her heart palpitate, her eyes blinking with excitement. O, I never dreamed . . . Lyle Russels voice became earnest. Very earnest. Mrs. Goldfarb, do you know what programs I am referring to? Do you have any idea? No . . . I a . . . Im watching an Ajax and Im not sure . . . On the television???? Mrs. Goldfarb, are you sitting down? If not, please sit down immediately because when I tell you what programs I am talking about you will be dizzy with joy. Im sitting. Im sitting already. Mrs. Goldfarb I'm talking about none other than . . . his voice suddenly stopped and Sara Goldfarb clutched even tighter at the top of her dress and stared wide-eyed at the phone and the television, not sure from which instrument his voice would come. When he spoke his voice was deep, low and full of feeling—Mrs. Goldfarb, we represent the quiz shows on television. Ooooooo . . . He waited dramatically as Sara Goldfarb composed herself, her breathing audible over the voices from the television. Lyle Russels voice was authoritatively dramatic, Yes, Mrs. Goldfarb, plus—plus the brand new, I said, brand new, shows that will be on next season; the shows millions of Americans want to be on; *the* shows that are looked forward to anxiously by millions— Me . . . me . . . on the—O I cant— Yes, Mrs. Goldfarb you. I know how you feel, you are wondering why you should be so lucky when so many millions would give anything to be on one of these shows— O, I cant tell you . . . Well, Mrs. Goldfarb, I cant tell you why you are so lucky, I guess its just that God has a special place in his heart for you. Sara Goldfarb fell against the back of the viewing chair, one hand clutching desperately at the phone, the other the top of her dress. Her eyes bulged. Her mouth hung open. For the first time in memory she was unaware of the television. You will receive all necessary information in the mail Mrs. Goldfarb. Goodbye and . . . God bless. Click.

Visions of heavenly angels passed before Harrys mother as the psalmist sang so soothingly to her, before the buzzing of the phone in her hand, and the exploding of a bottle of cleaner into a white tornado, dispersed them. She breathed. Then exhaled. The phone. Yes. The phone goes on the hook. Gets hung gup. Aa haaaaaaa. Clunk, clunk. She missed the cradle. She looked at the phone for a minute then picked it up and put it gently on the cradle. On television. O my God, television. What will I wear???? What do I have to wear? I should be wearing a nice dress. Suppose the girdle doesnt fit? Its so hot. Sara looked at herself then rolled her eyes back and up. Maybe I/ll sweat a little bit but I need the girdle. Maybe I should diet? I wont eat. I/ll lose thirty pounds before Im on television. Then with a girdle Im looking like Spring Boyington . . . a little . . . sort of . . . Hair! I/ll get Ada to do my hair. Maybe they do it. Special. O . . . I should have asked . . . asked who? What was his name? I/ll remember, I/ll remember. It will come. He said they send me everything in the mail. I look good in the red dress with— No! Red doesnt come so good on the set. Isnt just right, kind of funny and blurred. And shoes and a pocketbook and earrings and necklace and a lace handkerchief O O O O, Sara nodding her head, grabbing her temples and rolling her eyes and lifting her arms, her palms turned upward, then closing her hands in a loose fist and tapping them against each other, then suddenly stopping all movements, sitting stiff in the chair for a moment, I/ll look in the closet. Thats what I/ll do. The closet. She nodded her head affirmatively and got up and out of her chair and went to the bedroom and started rummaging through her closets, taking dresses off hangers and holding them up in front of her then tossing them on the bed; crawling around on her hands and knees as she investigated the darkest and remotest corners of the closet, finding almost forgotten shoes and singing in a wordless and tuneless monotone as she dusted them off and tried pair after pair on, wobbling on some as her callused feet oozed over the sides,

attacked the straps, then posed in front of the mirror looking
at her shoes and her blue striped and stippled legs. . . . O,
how she loved her gold shoes, all of them. Finally she couldn't
resist. She put on the red dress. I know red doesnt come in
so good on the set, but the red dress I like . . . I love. She
posed, looked over her shoulder into the mirror . . . then the
other shoulder, adjusted the length to various heights, started
to try to zip it up but after half an inch and many minutes
of exertion and squeezing and stuffing and adjusting she gave
it up so she stood with it unzipped in front of her mirror,
liking what she saw as she looked through eyes of many
yesterdays at herself in the gorgeous red dress and gold shoes
she wore when her Harry was bar mitzvahed . . . Seymour was
alive then . . . and not even sick . . . and her boobala looked so
nice in his— Ah, thats gone. No more. Seymours dead and
her— Ah, I/ll show Ada how it looks. She held the unzipped
back of her dress tightly as she waited for a station break, then
went next door to her friend Ada. So wheres the party? Party,
schmarty. This is like all the parties. When I tell you youll
jump out the window. A basement window I hope. They sat
down in the living room, strategically, so each could keep an
eye, and ear, tuned to the television set while discussing the
momentous occasion that brought Sara Goldfarb forth in the
gorgeous red dress and gold shoes she wore the day her Harry,
her boobala, was bar mitzvahed, an event so important and
undreamed of that Sara was in such a state of shock, though
ambulatory, she turned down a piece of halvah. Sara told Ada
about the phone call and how she was going on television.
She, Sara Goldfarb, was going on the television. Ada stared
for a moment (with one ear she caught the end of the scene
of the soap opera). For real? You wouldnt kid me? Why should
I kid you? What am I dressing for, the supermarket? Ada
continued to stare (the music told her they were fading out
on the scene. She knew instinctively that a commercial was

coming on even before there was that sudden increase in volume and explosion on the screen). You want a glass tea? She got up and started for the kitchen. Sara followed. The water was quickly boiled and each had a glass of tea when they returned to the living room, just at the end of the commercials, and sat in the same strategic positions, their ear and eye still tuned to the television, as they discussed and speculated on the enormity of the coming event in the life of Sara Goldfarb, an event of such prodigious proportions and importance that it infused her with a new will to live and materialized a dream that brightened her days and soothed her lonely nights.

Harry and Tyrone C. were walking through the park, spending most of their energy in trying to avoid the kids who were running around screaming or flying by on skates or a skateboard, never knowing from which end or side the attack might come. Sheeit, I dont know why they got to have a summer vacation. They oughtta keep those little muthas in school *all* the time. You kiddin? theyd tear the school down. This way it saves the taxpayers money. Now aint this a bitch, this muthafucka aint worked in his natural life an he worried about taxpayers. Hey man, ya gotta worry about those things. Whats the matta with you, aint ya responsible? Oooooo, listen to this shit, this stud has gone and blew his cool. Comeon baby, lets get somethin to eat, youse in serious trouble. They strolled over to a hot dog pushcart and got a couple with onions and mustard and red pepper, and a bottle of soda. When they finished they walked as far as possible from the playground and stretched out on the grass. Ya know man, I wasnt bullshit about gettin a piece. Hey baby, Im down. Well, then lets stop fuckin around and get with it. Sheeit, get with what? We aint got no braid. No shit? I thought we had money up the gazoo. That the only place we got it. Well lets stop fuckin the duck and figure out how we can pick up the bread. How much do we need? Ah dont know exactly. Couple hundred. Best be going up there with four hundred that way you knows you got enough no matter what comes down. Are you sure Brody can cop a piece for us? Man, what the fuck you talkin about? Course Im sure. Even after he take his tase we got enough to cut it in haf and double our braid and have a nice tase for us. Im hip. He sure does have some dynamite shit. But I dont want to get into it heavy man. I dont wanta blow the whole thing by getting strung out. You damn right. You be cool an we have a whole string of runny nosed dope fiens offen our shit for us. Yeah, thats the only way to go man. Ive seen cats get strung out and they blow their whole scene and end up in the slammer. Sheeit, we too smart for that baby. Yeah, they slapped palms. So where do we get the bread? Ah dont know baby, but ah dont want to go rippin nobody off. Ah aint been in no joint an ah wants to keep it that way. O man, be cool. What am I, a ganggester? The old ladys TV is one thing, but a robberys something else. We could sell hot dogs. Yeah sure, whos gonna push the cart? Doan look at me baby, ahs a salesman. Hahaha, what a scene that would be . . . jesus, I could see you openin the bun and me floppin a hot dog in an then we flip a coin to see who puts the mustard on. Well, lease we wouldnt be hongry. Well man, I aint worried about that. Comeon, Ty, think. There must be a way we can pick up a couple a yards in a hurry. They smoked, and squinted and scratched, then Tyrone flipped his butt away and rubbed his head, sort of stroking it to activate the gray matter . . . and relieve any itch he might have. You know, theres a couple of dudes that goes down to the newspaper like four or five in the mornin and shapes up to load trucks. How much they get? Ah doan know man, but ah do know that theys always wearin some fine threads an driven some really pretty shorts. Yeah? Harry

looked at Tyrone for a minute. Hmmmmmmm. Whatta ya
think? Tyrone was still rubbing his head, but now he was
more or less caressing it. Well man, ah tellya, ah aint so hot on
that workin shit, ah mean ah dont like it any more than you.
Yeah . . . five oclock in the mornin. Jesus. I thought even bar-
tenders were asleep at that time . . . but . . . Harry continued
to stare and Tyrone C. Love continued to rub. Whatta ya
think? Ah doan know baby. . . . But ah guess we could sort
of maybe go see whats happenin down there. Harry shrugged,
Shit, why not? Tyrone stopped rubbing his head and slapped
Harrys hand then Harry slapped his and they got up and
strolled from the grass to the path, then along the path
through the park to the street as a couple of sparrows swooped
down to claim a few Crackerjack crumbs. Harry figured he/d
go home while they were working so he/d be sure to get up
on time. If I tell the old lady I got a job she/ll be sure to
get me up. I guess we/ll have ta get up about four, eh? to be
sure to get there on time . . . four oclock in the morning, that
seems impossible. Then jus think a that piece a pure shit
baby, thatll get your ass up. Then you come by mah crib an
get me up. You bet your sweet ass. If I have to get up youre
gonta get up. They laughed and slapped palms and Harry
was about to turn to go and get ready to start the new routine
that would make them big time dealers, when they spotted a
friend rushing along the street. Hey, whats happening baby?
You look like the man is afta you. Whats the rush? You know
Little Joey, the cat with the ripped ear? Yeah, sure. From
across the avenue. Yeah, thats the dude. He an Tiny an some
other cat just copped from Windy and before Joey emptied
the dropper he was gone jim. O.d. just like that. They say he
just had a tase an he was out. So Tiny horns a little just to be
cool, ya know, an he gets wasted jim. No shit? You straight? Ya
goddamn right. Why ya think Im hustlin my ass over to
Windys? I wanna get there before he finds out what he has

jim. That mutha fucka got a habit thats so long even mule piss wouldnt get him high. Harry and Tyrone joined in the rush to Windys. They could always go to work some other time, but you dont always get a chance to score for some dyn a mite shit like this.

The next night they still had some stuff left, it was that good. Man, somebody sure did screw up. That stuff shoulda been cut at least a half dozen times. Sheeit, there better not be too much around jim or theres gonna be a lot a daid dudes in this town. Man, whats a couple a more stiffs in this town? Sheeit, they drive the man nuts tryin to figure whats goin down.

They were feeling mellow and realized that there was no point in thinking of going to work tomorrow morning, which was only a few hours away. There was no sense in ruining a good high with work. They decided to fall by Tonys pad to see what was happening.

The streets were filled with the actions and sounds of a summers night. The stoops and firescapes were filled with people and there were hundreds of games of dominoes and cards, the players surrounded with onlookers, cans of beer and bottles of wine being passed around. Kids would burst past the games and the players would automatically yell at them without taking their eyes off the game or missing a drink. It was a nice night. A pleasant evening. There seemed to be stars somewhere and it was easy to avoid stepping in the garbage and dog shit on the streets. A truly beautiful night.

Tony lived in a converted loft in an old industrial building. Actually what was meant by converted was that there was a bed at one end and a stove and refrigerator at the other end. In between was a lot of space. Usually the space was dotted with people getting high, getting higher, or wondering why they werent high yet. When Harry and Tyrone got there there were a few people sitting around on the floor. Tony sat

in the only chair, a large, overstuffed, ripped and torn chair
that had huge wings that made it look as if it was going to
close itself around Tony and somehow swallow and digest
him and he would end up on a shelf somewhere in the dark
and dusty corner of a secondhand furniture store staring back
at the cat sitting on the floor staring up at him, a not-for-sale
sign hanging from his chest. He was watching television, the
set a large old console that was the perfect companion for
the chair and fit in perfectly in the loft. Tony had a Chinese
water pipe hanging from a cord around his neck. The bowl
was filled with hash and he took a poke, from time to time,
always staring at the set. A few people were sitting around a
hookah that had been filled with wine, the bowl filled with
pot, a piece of hash on top. Marion had just taken a poke
when Harry and Tyrone walked in. They squatted next to
the others. Whats happenin man? Hey baby, whats goin down?
Whats happenin? Same old thing man. The stem was handed
to Harry and he sucked on it for a minute then handed it to
Tyrone. When Harry finally exhaled he leaned back a little
and looked at Marion. Hows it goin? O, the same old thing.
Harry nodded toward the hookah, Thats some nice hash.
Uh huh. Its really doin a number on my head. Just smoothed
it right out. Harrys eyes were closed slightly and his face was
relaxed in a smile. I figured that. Youre sure lookin good.
Marions face burst into a sudden grin and she chuckled, Is
that supposed to be a compliment, or you playing the dozens?
Harry spread his arms and shrugged, his face still in a sleepy
grin. Sometimes Im not too swave when Im ripped. Marion
chuckled a little louder, Maybe not, but youre a lot more
sociable. You know, you have a really nice smile when you
relax, like you are now. Harry laughed then leaned a little
closer, I aint got no choice baby, I feel so relaxed I think Im
going to melt. Marion laughed and squeezed Harrys hand,
then took the hose and took another poke from the pipe then

passed it to Harry. He laughed, This is just what I need now . . . you know, to sort of help me get rid of the tension, right? Marion shook her head and strained not to laugh as she held the smoke in her lungs. Tyrone pushed the hose closer to Harrys face, Comeon mah man, you can talk that trash later. Jus take your hit an git on with it. Harry took a poke, concentrating as hard as possible, then passed the hose to Fred. Tyrone watched as Fred sucked on the hose in one long continuous breath that seemed to last five minutes, that threatened to force the hashish to burst into flames it glowed so brighly under the force of air. Damn, this muthafucka goin to suck up that hash right through the pipe. Look see if he dont have a hole in the back of his haid, all that air gotta be goin somewheres. Fred finally took the hose from his mouth and passed it to Tyrone, a broad, dumb smile on his face, and still holding his breath he grunted, Dont get greedy baby. Tyrone started laughing, clutching the hose in both hands, and the others started giggling, and Tyrone looked down at the floor and shook his head then looked up and at Fred who still had a big shit eatin grin on his face and Tyrone started laughing harder and harder and the others started laughing and shaking their heads, unavoidably drawn to looking at Fred sitting there with that dumb grin that kept getting larger and dumber and now a momentum had been built up and no matter how hard they tried they could not stop laughing and Fred continued to hold his breath although he felt like he was suffocating and his face was flushing more and more and his eyes were bulging and Tyrone kept pointing at him and shaking his head and laughing and sputtering, Shee . . . Shee . . . and finally Fred blurted the air out and quickly sucked in some more and shook his head back and forth, Gahddamn, and the others laughed uncontrollably and Tony took another hit on his pipe and frowned at the television set as the story was interrupted for a commercial, and

then a few more, and then a station break and then a few
more commercials and Tony took another hit and fidgeted
in his chair and started grumbling under his breath about the
goddamn bullshit, he wanted to see the goddamn show not
some bullshit dog eatin horse meat, and then he started
yelling at the set, Go ahead ya fuckin hound, stick ya nose
up her drawers. Whats the matta, donta ya like fish? Eh? Ya
don't like fish ya faggot dog bastard. The others had stopped
laughing, and were finished smoking the hash for a while,
and were just leaning back and listening to the music and
rapping and then they started to half watch and listen to Tony
and the giggles started again. Hey baby, yawl shouldnt talk
about faggots like that when Harrys aroun, he get his feelings
hurt. Fred stuck that dumb countryboy grin on his face, How
you know hes a faggot. Maybe its just a bulldike, and he
suddenly started to fall apart laughing, damn, that tickles the
shit outta me, hahahahahaha, a bulldog, bulldike, hahahaha-
ha, damn, hahaha; and Tony was still grumbling incompre-
hensibly and the others were giggling and laughing as they
watched Fred laughing and shaking his head and whenever his
laughter started to subside he/d start blithering about bulldog, bulldikes and everybody started giggling again and Tony
got up, his water pipe hanging from his neck, and went to the
dresser and took something out of a drawer and plopped back
into his chair and disappeared from sight behind the enveloping wings and put a fresh piece of hash in the bowl and lit it
and took a couple of long pokes, as the show came back on,
then settled back and silently and motionlessly watched the
show. Fred finally exhausted himself and was incapable of
any more laughter although he continued to shake his head
and grin and the others avoided looking at him because when
they did they started laughing and everyone had pains in
their sides from laughing and so looked everywhere except
at Fred, and Harry and Marion drifted away from the others

and were sprawled on a few old cushions and half leaning against a wall, half listening to the music and directing most of their attention toward each other. You living alone now or do you have a roomie? No, Im alone. You know that. Harry shrugged, Hey, how do I know? The last time I remember bein at your pad you had a roomie, right? My God, that's months ago. Wow, is it that long ago? Tempus really fugits, eh? Sometimes. Sometimes it seems to stand still. Like youre in a bag and you cant get out and somebodys always telling you that it will get better with time and time just seems to stand still and laugh at you and your pain. . . . And then eventually it does break and its six months later. Like you just got your summer clothes out and then its Christmas and inbetween there are ten years of pain. Harry smiled, Jesus, all I said was hello and you give me ya fingerprint classification. But Im glad youre alright. Marion laughed and Harry lit a joint and took a couple of quick pokes and handed it to Marion. Tony started to jerk slightly, his movements involuntary as he sensed a coming disaster. He was absorbed in the show as much as possible and wondering how the heavy was going to cool that bad dude and rip off the broad, pullin for the cat just as hard as possible, but something in him knew that that goddamn television set was plotting against him, that it was just layin back and waiting to getim. He lit his pipe again and took a couple of long pokes then snuffed the hash and stared at the television, Youd better not fuck with me ya son of a bitch. Im warnin ya. He stopped twitching and settled back into his chair and disappeared once again from sight. Marion chuckled, He really has his own S&M scene going on with that thing, doesn't he? Yeah. Hes like a guy with a broad who wont giveim a little. The others were half watching Tony too, and smiling, enjoying him, as they had many times before, more than anything on the tube he was watching. You know somethin man, he think thats his ol lady. Shit, he aint never talked to his ol lady like that. They laughed and went back to their listening, talking and smoking. Harry was sort of leaning against Marion as she slowly stroked his head and played with his hair as they listened to the music. From time to time he would leisurely reach up and rub the nipple of a boob with his fingertip, or caress a boob with the palm of his hand, ever so gently, not through design, but a kind of reverie. He would watch his fingertip rubbing the protruding nipple and imagine it under her blouse and think of opening her blouse and kissing it, but it seemed like too much of an undertaking at the moment and so he postponed it and just listened to the music and moved with the flow of the stroking of his head, surrendering deeper and deeper into the sensual currents it stoked. You know somethin baby, that feels better than a fix. It really turns me on. I like it too. I have always liked curly hair. It feels good around the fingers. You cant just push through like straight hair. It resists. Like it has a life of its own and it feels exciting when you defeat it, and Marion watched her fingers going through Harrys hair, watching the ends twist and bob as her fingers worked their way through, and then she would twirl the hair with a finger, watching it snap and bounce, then let the hair caress the palm of her hand then close her fingers and raise her hand slowly feeling the hair slowly slide between the fingers, her fingers, aware that she was creating a rhythm to her caressing that was governing her breathing and then she became a part of the breathing and flowed into the ripples that tingled through her as Harry rubbed the nipple of a breast between fingertips, imagining her rosy nipple and how it would feel between his lips, when Tony started yelling at the goddamn television again, Youd betta not do it prick. Im warnin ya ya lousy bastad, Ive had enough a ya shit, and he squirmed in his chair and peered defiantly at the television screen and Tyrone giggled his giggle, Ah doan mind him fat

mouthin that set, but I sure hope the muthafucka doan start
talkin back toim cause when that happens ah gotta cut loose
this shit and split jim, and he took another good poke and
turned his head so he wouldnt be lookin into the dumbass
grin of Freds who was always doin that, tryin to get him to gag
and spit out the smoke; and somebody broke out some amyl-
nitrite and popped it open and held a finger over one nostril
and sniffed deeply until the popper was grabbed from his
hand and the person shoved it up their nose and squeezed
the other nostril shut and the both of them fell on the floor
giggling and laughing and roaring and Tony leaned forward
in his seat, I knew it, I knew the rat bastads were gonna do it,
Jesus krist they gripe my shit the rotten bastads, the dirty
rotten bastads; and Harry and Marion suddenly stopped,
simultaneously, fondling each other as the smell of the popper
titillated their noses and they sat up and leaned into the
aroma and looked at the people sitting and lying around,
giggling and roaring with laughter, Hey man lay one on us,
and a yellow popper came floating through the air and Harry
grabbed it and he and Marion lay down, side by side, their
bodies almost penetrating each other, and Harry snapped the
popper and they both breathed deeply and held tight to each
other as their bodies started to vibrate and their heads whirled
and for a moment it felt as if they would die, but then they
started to laugh and push even harder against each other,
grinding with their laughter, the popper jammed between
their noses; and Tony leaned forward even further, You scum
bag muthafuckas I got ya fuckin strawberry douche ya douche
bag pricks, and he raised his right hand and aimed the old .22
target pistol he was holding at the set, you aint fuckin with me
any more ya rotten pricks, cockteasin me along with ya
goddamn shows an then shove it up my ass wit that fuckin
bullshit when Im waitin ta see what happened; and everyone
had a popper up their nose and were rolling and scratching

and sweating and laughing and Tony peered even harder at
the set, Ya been fuckin wit me long enough with ya fuckin
dog food, and douche bags, and under fuckin arms an no
smell shit paper, he was yelling louder and louder, his face
as red as the others who were sweating behind the poppers,
and they watched and listened to him as they stared through
sweat stung eyes, hysterical with laughter, YA HEAR ME?
EH? IVE HAD YA BULLSHIT YA FUCKIN PRICKS, and
he squeezed the trigger and the first slug hit the tube dead
center and there was a mild explosion that momentarily
covered the hysterical laughter and Tonys screaming and
sparks and flames burst out at an angle and huge hunks of
thick glass assailed the room as smoke drifted up and around
the set and Tony stood up screaming hysterically, I GOT YA
NOW YA MUTHAS CUNT, HAHAHAHAHAHAHA-
HAHAHAHA, and he fired another shot into the dying
television set, YA GONNA GET EVERYTHINS THATS
COMMIN TO YA, HAHAHAHAHAHAHAHAHA, and
another shot went into the crumbling body, HOW DO YA
LIKE IT? EH? HOW DO YA LIKE IT YA PUNK ASSED
MUTHA FUCKA, and he kept edging toward the set and
fired another shot into the smoking remains of the once
noble set, YA THOUGHT YA COULD GET AWAY WIT
IT, EH? DIDN YA? EH? and the others continued to watch
and laugh and shake as he put one more slug into the body
as he continued walking toward it and then he stood over it,
savoring the last slug, glaring, grinning, and gloating at the
shattered and smoldering remains, watching the spastic sparks
leap and crawl then shoot along the electrical cord and burst
and fizz as they reached the socket and smoke curled from the
burned wire and plug, and Tony started to drool slightly as
he watched the set tremble under his gaze, as it shook and
begged for mercy, for one more chance, I/ll never do it again
Tony, I swear on my mudders head, Tony, *pleeze, pleeze,*

give me anotha chance, Tony, I/ll make it right, I swear, I swear on my mudders head I/ll make it right for ya Tony, and Tony sneered at the set as it begged and pleaded, Tonys whole being filled with contempt for the sniveling sonofabitch, CHANCE??? CHANCE???? I GOT YA FUCKIN CHANCE, SWINGIN, HAHAHAHAHAHAHA, YA CANT EVEN DIE LIKE A MAN YA PUNK SON OF A BITCH, pleeze, Tony, pleeze . . . dont shoot, pl— SHAT UP, PUNK, and Tonys expression was bulging with contempt as he twisted and looked the set right in the eye and told it in a soft, vicious voice, Suck on this, and fired the last shot into the trembling and still pleading body of the television set and it shivered slightly from the *coup de grace* and one last spark jumped across a foot of burned space and fizzled away into eternity as the final wisp of smoke whirled into the atmosphere and commingled with the smoke from the pot and hash and cigarettes and the popper scented air and sought freedom from various and sundry cracks and crevices to disperse itself in the atmosphere. Tony shrugged and jammed the gun into his waist, I toldya not ta fuck wit me, and he shrugged again, nobody fucks wit Tony Balls, eh? and he joined the others and took the popper offered him and did it in and fell on the floor laughing with the others as somebody offered up a prayer for the deceased, between giggles, and Harry and Marion had another popper jammed between them as their bodies continued to grind into each other as they laughed and clung like skin to each other and the music continued to drift through the smoke and laughter and through ears and heads and brains and minds and somehow came out the other side undisturbed and unchanged and everyone felt good man, I mean real good, like they just beat a murder rap, or made it to the top of Mt. Everest, or got heavy with sky diving or floating through the air like a bird, yeah, soaring and floating on the currents like a bird, just like

a big bird man . . . yeah . . . like they were suddenly cut loose,
like they were suddenly free . . . free . . . free . . .

Sara Goldfarb sat in her viewing chair polishing her nails
as she watched the television. Her conditioning had been long
and thorough and Sara was able to do anything while watching the television, and do it to her satisfaction, without missing a word or a gesture. Maybe it wasnt perfect, maybe a
little polish got on the fingers and it looked a little lumpy,
but who would notice? From a few feet away it looked like
a professional job. And even if it didnt, whats the big deal?
Who did she have to polish her nails for? Who did she have
to worry would see its not so good? Or the sewing or the
ironing or the cleaning? No matter what she is doing one and
a half eyes on the television makes the job, the day and life
pass bearably on. She held a hand out in front of her and
looked at the nails while looking at the television screen
between her spread fingers. She stared at her fingers indulging
herself in the optical illusion that made it look like fingers
were piled on top of each other and that she was looking
through them. She smiled and inspected the other hand. Such
a nice red. Gorgeous. Goes so nice with the dress. Lose a few
pounds and the dress would fit like new. The top started to
fall away from her shoulders as she moved and she pulled it
together in the back and leaned back in the chair so it wouldnt
fall again. She loved the red dress. She should be able to lose
weight. She could always let the seams out a little maybe. The
library will have books. Tomorrow I/ll go and get the books
and go on a diet. She put another chocolate covered cream
in her mouth and let the chocolate slowly melt and savored
the flavor of the chocolate mixing with the cream center then
slowly squeezed the chocolate between her tongue and the
roof of her mouth and smiled and half closed her eyes as her

body tingled with tiny shocks of delight. She tried desperately to allow the candy to slowly dissolve by itself but as hard as she fought the urge to bite and chew it was useless and her eyes suddenly opened wide and her expression stiffened into one of seriousness as she chewed the candy with intensity and rolled it once or twice then gulped it down, wiping the corners of her mouth with the back of her hand. They have plenty of books in the library. I/ll ask for the one I should get. The one that does it quick. Maybe soon I/ll be on the television so soon I need to fit in the red dress. She stared at the screen aware of the action and the words, but her mind was still centered on the box of chocolates on the table next to her chair. She knew exactly how many were left . . . and what they were. Four. Three dark chocolate, one milk chocolate. The milk chocolate was a chocolate covered cherry with the cherry juice filling. The other three was one caramel, one brazil nut, and one nougat. The cherry was last. That was already pushed to the side of the box so she wouldnt pick it up by mistake while watching television. The others were first. Maybe she wouldnt even look what one she was taking. But the schedule was made. Just like always. The nougat, the brazil nut, then the caramel. Then wait as long as possible before eating the chocolate covered cherry with the cherry juice filling. She always played a game. For how many years the same game? ten? Maybe more. Since her husband died. One night she let it sit in the box alone . . . all alone for the whole night. Even the million dollar movie and the late show. She went to bed and it was still there alone in the box with the empty brown papers that all the other chocolates had been so sweetly nestled in. She had looked defiantly at the candy before going to bed. She snapped her head at the box and felt so ipsy pipsy as she undressed and nestled between the sheets and fell almost instantly asleep. Her sleep was restful, as far as she remembered, void of dreams of troubles, then she suddenly bolted up in the middle of the night, her forehead pitted with cold sweat, and for endless seconds she sat there staring into the darkness, listening, wondering why she was awake and what had awakened her and wondering if someone had broken into her apartment and was about to hit her and she strained her ears but heard nothing and sat perfectly still, barely breathing, for many seconds, then jerked the covers off and rushed to the living room, going unerringly through the dark to the table with the piece of chocolate and scooped it up as if her hand had been divinely directed and almost fainting as the first rush of flavor assailed her brain and she folded in her viewing chair and listened to herself chomp the milk chocolate covered cherry with the cherry juice filling, then staggered back to her bed. The next morning she awoke early and sat in the soft filtered light, trying to remember something, but not know-ing what. She vaguely sensed that something had happened and assumed it had been a dream, but as hard as she tried she could not remember the dream. She rubbed the soles of her feet and then her temples but still she could not remember the dream. She hit her head for many seconds with her knuckles trying to stimulate her memory, but still . . . nothing. She got up and wandered, unthinkingly, into the living room instead of the bathroom, turned on the television, and sud-denly became aware of herself as she was standing over her viewing chair looking at the empty chocolate box. She stared for many long moments, then she remembered her dream and almost collapsed in her chair and shook slightly as she fully realized that she had eaten the chocolate covered cherry with the cherry juice filling the night before and couldnt really remember eating it. She tried remembering biting into it and feeling the cherry juice oozing onto her tongue, but her mind and mouth were empty. She almost cried as she remembered how she had fought so hard to make the box of chocolates last two days, something that had never happened before, twice as long as ever before, and she was going to save the last for morning so she could say it was three days and now it was gone and she didnt even remember eating it. That was a bleak day in the life of Sara Goldfarb. She never let that happen again. Never again was she so foolish as to try and make it last or save it for later or the next day. Tomorrow would take care of itself. God gives us one day at a time, so one day at a time shes eating her chocolates and knowing she ate them. She smiled at the handsome announcer and reached over and gently picked up her final chocolate, the milk chocolate covered cherry with the cherry juice filling, and placed it on her tongue and sighed as she teased it with her tongue and teeth, feeling the tingle of anticipation in her body and the slight knot in her stomach and then she could fight no more and started to ease her teeth into the softened chocolate covering and continued to exert pressure as the flavors of the chocolate and the cherry juice twitched in her mouth and then the covering was parted like the red sea and the captured cherry floated to freedom and Sara Goldfarb rolled it around her mouth filled with flavors and fluids that she allowed to slowly trickle down her twitching throat and then she rolled her eyes back as she bit into the cherry, but didnt roll them back so far that she would miss any of the action on the screen. She licked her fingers and then held her hands, one at a time, in front of her and inspected the cherry red nail polish then stared through her spread fingers at her television set, and snuggled into herself as she walked from the rear of the stage to the front, wearing her cherry red dress that fit so good since she lost the weight, and the gold shoes that look so rich on her feet, and her hair was such a gorgeous red like you wouldnt believe— O, I almost forgot. The hair. It should be red. Its so long since it was red. Tomorrow I/ll ask Ada to dye my hair. So who cares if red doesnt show so good. Im wearing red. Except the shoes. Except the shoes Im all red. When they ask my name I/ll tell them Little Red Riding Hood. Thats what I/ll say. I/ll look the television camera right in the eye as the little red light is winking and blinking and tell them Im Little Red Riding Hood.

Harry walked Marion home. The night was warm and humid, but they werent too aware of the weather. They knew it was warm and humid, but it remained a fact outside themselves and not something they were experiencing. Their bodies still tingled and tensed slightly from the poppers and the laughing, and they also felt loose and cool from all the pot and hash. It was a delightful evening, or morning, or whatever it was, for walking the streets of that part of the Apple called the Bronx. There was a sky somewhere above the tops of the buildings, with stars and a moon and all the things there are in a sky, but they were content to think of the distant street lights as planets and stars. If the lights prevented you from seeing the heavens, then perform a little magic and change reality to fit the need. The street lights were now planets and stars and moon.

Even at this time of the morning the streets were fairly active with cars, cabs, trucks, people and occasional drunks. A block away two staggered vaguely in their direction. The woman kept tugging on the arm of the guy, I gotta pee. Fa krists sake stop so I can pee. Cantya wait five minutes fa krists sake. Its just anotha couple a blocks. No. I gotta pee. Back it up the ladder. Whatta ya think Ive been doin? My molars are floatin. Jesus krist, your some pain in the ass, ya know that? Yeah? Well it aint my *ass* thats buggin me. She grabbed him and they stopped and she lifted her skirt and hung on to his belt and squatted behind him and started to

pee, Hey, what the hell ya doin ya crazy bitch?— Ahhhhhhhh
that feels so good— You some kindda nut or— Stop wigglin,
ahhhhhhhhhhhhhhh— Aintya got no shame? He spread his
legs tryin to avoid the ever widening and ceaseless flow of an
evenings beer drinking as she continued to sigh with life
saving relief easily ignoring the gentle splashings that tingled
her legs, her eyes closed in absolute ecstasy as she swayed back
and forth, tugging at his belt as she reached the end of the arc
in either direction, he trying to maintain his own precarious
balance and tug her back in the other direction while doing
a quick pantomime to avoid the results of the opening of the
floodgates, Let go fa krists sake, but she continued to tug
and sigh and pee, Ya gonna pullus—suddenly he noticed
Harry and Marion and he jerked himself to attention, smiled,
and spread his arms out to hide his crouching lady friend of
the emptying bladder. Harry and Marion adroitly, though
sleepily, avoided the stream and stepped over it with aplomb
and Harry smiled at the guy, Your old ladys a pisser man, and
then laughed, and he and Marion continued down the street
and the guy watched them for many seconds and then an
emergency bell went off in his head as he felt his body lurch
to one side and he tried to resist and maintain his balance,
but lost the valiant but short battle and found himself floating in the air toward the rapids below, Hey, what the fuck
ya doin ya crazy—and he hit the surface of the stream with
a splat and floundered around, HELP! HELP! while his
lady friend lay sprawled on her back continuing to sigh,
ahhhhhhhhhhhhh, and to add volume and speed to the rivers
flow as her defender and companion of the evening splattered
and splashed, I CANT SWIM, I CANT SWIM, and finally
through grim determination and pure grit reached shallow
ground and pulled himself ashore and knelt, with his head
hanging, catching his breath as his lady of the evening rolled
over with another long sigh and curled up in a fetal position

and went to sleep in the sheltering bushes of the rivers head-
waters. Harry was chuckling and shaking his head, Juice
heads are too much, aren't they? They really have no class, no
class at all.

He and Marion continued along the streets aware of the
dryness in their throats and a yearning in their stomachs.
They stopped in an all night diner and got a piece of pie
with a couple of scoops of ice cream, chocolate and strawberry
syrup and whipped cream, with an egg cream on the side.
Marion paid the check and they continued to her place. They
sat around the kitchen table and Marion lit a joint. Harry
suddenly started to chuckle, That broad was somethin else.
That guy needed a canoe. Marion passed the joint to Harry,
then slowly let the smoke out. They should have *pissoirs* on
the streets. Then she wouldn't have to degrade herself just
to urinate. Men can go in an alley or behind a parked car
and its perfectly acceptable, but if a woman does it shes
ridiculed. Thats what I loved about Europe, theyre civilized.
Harry tilted his head as he looked at her and listened then
half smiled and half smirked as he passed the joint back to
her, I dont know if youre talkin to your shrink or a judge.
There was still a little bit of the joint left and she offered it
to Harry and he shook his head so she carefully put it out and
placed it on the edge of the ashtray. Well, doesnt the whole
thing stink? I mean its utterly ridiculous. Women arent supposed to piss or shit or fart or smell or enjoy getting laid—
excuse me, I mean having sex. Hey baby, Im innocent, okay?
Remember me? I didn't say a word. Thats okay, I need to
practice on someone. Well, go practice on your shrink. He
gets paid for it. She smiled, Not anymore. You cutim loose?
Not exactly. Im seeing him, but not as a patient. Harry
laughed, You ballin him too? Occasionally. As the mood hits
me. My folks ask me if Im still seeing him and I tell them
yes so they keep giving me the fifty dollars a week for him.

Marion laughed loud and long, And I dont even have to lie to the clods. Werent you ballin your last shrink too? Yeah, but that got a little tacky. He stopped writing for me and wanted to leave his wife and straighten me out . . . you know, a real chauvinist. This guy is different. I see him once in a while and we have fun and theres no pressure. We just have a good time. And he still writes for tranks and downers. A couple of weeks ago we flew down to the Virgin Islands for a weekend. It was a ball. Hey, crazy. Sounds great. Yeah. So your folks are still footin the bills, tilting his head toward the rest of the apartment, for the pad and so forth? Yeah. She laughed out loud again, Plus the fifty a week for the shrink. And sometimes I do a little freelance editing for a few publishers. And the rest of the time you just lay up and get high, eh? She smiled, Something like that. You really got it made. But how come youre so hard on your folks, I mean like youre always coming down so heavy onem. They bug me with their middle class pretensions, you know what I mean? Like they're up there in that big house with all the cars and money and prestige and collect money for the UJA and B'NAI BRITH and KRIST knows who else—howd he get in there? He/d better watch out, we gotim once we/ll getim again. Marion joined Harry in laughing, Yeah, they would too. I mean, thats the way they are. Theyll cut anybodys throat to make money then give a few dollars to the NAACP and think theyre doing the world a favor. You see how liberal they are when I come home with a black guy. Eh, theyre no worse than anybody else. Harry leaned back and stretched and blinked his eyes, The whole world is full of shit. Perhaps, but the whole world doesnt embarrass me. They have everything but culture. Theyre gross. Eh, gross, schmoss, and he shrugged and smiled, his mouth hanging loose and his eyes sleepy. Marion smiled, I guess youre right. Anyway, no point in letting them bring me down. Thats the whole trouble with pot. Sometimes I get a little paranoid behind it. Yeah, ya gotta learn how to hang loose, and he smiled his sleepy grin and snapped his fingers and bebopped his head and they both laughed, Whatta ya say we get to bed? Okay, but dont fall asleep right away. Hey, what am I? some kindda nut? They chuckled and Harry splashed some cold water on his face before getting into the bed. He hadnt finished stretching and getting comfortable when Marion was leaning over him, her face close to his, a hand rubbing his chest and abdomen, I dont know if its the pot or talking about my parents, but Im horny as hell. Whatta ya talkin about? Its me. I have that effect on broads. Im irresistible. Especially since the plastic surgeon hung me, and he started to laugh and Marion looked at him and shook her head, Dont you ever get tired of that old joke? Talk to your shrink about it. Maybe its a wish fulfillment, and he laughed again and Marion chuckled then kissed him and rolled her mouth from one side of his to the other, thrusting her tongue as deeply as possible into his mouth, Harry reacting with his and putting his arms around her and feeling her nice smooth flesh under his hands and caressing her back and the cheeks of her ass as she rubbed the inside of his thighs and gently ran her fingertips around his balls as she kissed his chest and stomach then grabbed his joint and stroked it for a moment before wrapping her lips around it and caressing the tip with her tongue, Harry continuing to fondle her ass and crotch as he squirmed and stretched, his eyes half closed, streaks of light shattering the darkness of his lids and when he opened his eyes he could vaguely see Marion hungrily gobbling his bird, his mind electric with ideas and images, but the drugs and the pleasure of the moment created an inertia that was delicious, absolutely delicious. The inertia was suddenly broken as Marion sat up and nested his bird and for hours, or perhaps seconds, he just lay there with his eyes closed listening to the exciting squish of joint against snatch—*Ride a cock horse to*

Branburry Cross—then opened his eyes as he reached up to grab her boobs, then pull her down so he could tease them with his tongue, nibbling, chewing and sucking on them as he slid his hands up and down her back and Marions eyes were rolling back in her head from time to time as she moved and rolled and sighed and groaned and they continued their lovemaking until the dawns early light started seeping through the shades and curtains and the heat of their love-making cooled in the warmth of the sun and they were suddenly, and completely, asleep.

Sara lovingly spread the cream cheese on her bagel, an eye and a half on her set that glowed in the early morning light in her living room. She took a generous bite out of the bagel then slurped a little hot tea. From time to time she smoothed and evened the cream cheese on the bagel before taking another bite and slurping more hot tea. She tried to eat the bagel and cream cheese slowly, but still it was gone before the next commercial. I/ll wait. No more before the commercial. The next one should be a kitty litter. They got such nice pussy cats. They purr so nice. She sipped a little tea from the glass and watched the set thinking that maybe she wouldnt have anything else until after *all* the commercials. After all, its no big deal. And after breakfast I/ll go to the library and get the diet books. Dont want to forget. The library first then to Adas so she can dye my hair. A lovely, gorgeous red. O hello puss. O, youre a sweetie little puss. So cuddly like a baby. She reached over and picked up the cheese danish and started dunking it in her glass of tea before she realized what she was doing. She awoke to her action as she chewed and rolled the danish around in her mouth. She looked at the pastry in her hand, and the indentation her teeth made on the edge where she had bitten, then realized why her stomach and throat were smiling. She almost ignored the commercials completely as she continued to bite and chew as slowly as possible, taking short, jerky sips of tea. When she finished the delicious cheese danish she licked her lips again, then her fingertips, then wiped her hands on the dish towel on her lap, then gently rubbed at her mouth before sipping more tea. She looked at the wrapping that had been around the danish and wiped the glazed moisture with her fingertip and licked it. Waste not and want not. Hmmmmmm, it tasted so good. It seemed to be extra special this morning like it was made for an affair. Maybe she should get another one. I/d miss the end of the program. I dont need any more. Eh, who needs it. I/ll forget all about it. I/ll watch the show and not think of the cheese danish. She continued to wipe the wrapping then lick her finger. She finally crumbled all the wrappings up in a little ball and tossed them into the garbage and forgot all about the bagel and cream cheese and the cheese danish that seemed so extra flaky today. A special. She watched the show and sighed, as always, at the happy and humorous ending, then finished her tea and readied herself to go to the library. She washed the plate, the knife and glass and put them on the drain board, brushed her hair and neatened herself, put on her nice button down sweater, then looked at her set for another moment then turned it off and left the apartment. She knew it was too early for mail, but she would check anyway. Who knows?

The library was two blocks to the left, but she automatically turned to the right and was unaware she had turned in the wrong direction until the girl behind the counter in the bakery handed her her danish and change, Here you are, Mrs. Goldfarb. Take care. Thank you dolly. Sara left the bakery trying to believe she didnt know what was in the bag, but the game didnt last long because she not only did know what was in the bag, but she couldnt wait to get it out and eat it.

But she ate it slowly and with deliberation, just teensy little nibbles that titillated her palate and enabled her to make it last all the way to the library. She asked the librarian where the diet books were. The librarian looked at the bakery bag Sara was still clutching then escorted her to the section containing the many diet books. O, so many. I/d lose weight just looking at all the books. The librarian chuckled, Isnt it pretty to think so. But dont worry, Im sure we can find just what you want. I hope so. Im going on the television and I thought maybe I should lose a few pounds so I look svelte, and Sara rolled her eyes and the librarian started to laugh then contained it to a chuckle. You dont have to worry about all these books in this section. This deals with nutrition and proper diet and health and improper diet and disease. Disease I dont need, thank you. And weight I dont need. Sara Gold-farb smiled at the librarian who returned her smile. Then Saras eyes twinkled, Maybe a little more than some. Well, the books you would be interested in are here, these deal with losing weight. Sara tried to look at all of them at once, They look so fat, if youll excuse the expression. She twinkled again at the librarian who had to control her laughter and keep it down to a chuckle. I think a skinny book is better. I dont have too much time. The time I need to lose weight, not to read a book. I could get muscles lifting books that big. The librarians eyes were tearing slightly from controlling her laughter. Well, heres the slimmest volume on the shelf. Suppose we take a look at it. The librarian glanced through it quickly, nodding her head, Yes, yes. I think this will fit your needs perfectly. Theres a minimum of reading, the regimen is clearly laid out in easily understandable terms and, this is the part I think you will really like, it says you can lose up to ten pounds a week, or even more. I like it already. Also, I happen to know that this is a very popular book. We have three copies and we have a difficult time keeping one on the shelf. I assume it is a good book from a reducing point of view. She chuckled again, Of course I wouldn't know personally. Im noticing. I hate you already. Just dont tell me you eat ice cream and cake every night. The librarian was still chuckling and put her arm around Saras shoulders, No, just pizza. You should *plotz* already. They were both chuckling and the librarian kept her arm around Saras shoulder as they walked to the check out counter. After the librarian checked her out and handed Sara the book she asked her if she wanted to throw the paper bag away. Sara looked at it in her hand and shrugged, Why not? It worked hard. It needs a rest. The librarian tossed it in the wastepaper basket, Have a good day, Mrs. Goldfarb. Sara smiled and twinkled, Take care dolly. She held the slim volume tightly in her hand as she walked home. The sun felt so nice and warm and she found joy in the yelling of the children who ran along the street and between cars, jumping on each others back ignoring the honking of horns and the screams of drivers. Just feeling the book in her hands she could visualize the pounds melting off. Maybe this afternoon, after Ada fixes her hair, she/ll get a little sun and feel thin. But first the hair.

Ada had everything ready. For twenty-five years she had been dyeing her own hair and in her sleep she can turn anyone into a redhead. Maybe not knowing always ahead of time exactly what shade of red, but red. She first made each a glass tea because, believe me, youll need it to wash out the taste and smell, then she got to work. She set everything up on the kitchen table and worked in such a way that they could watch the action on the television. Ada wrapped a bath towel around Saras neck and started stripping her hair. Saras face twisted and wrinkled like a prune, Ech, what a smell. Thats the Gawanus Canal? Just relax dolly, you got a long way to go. Youll get used to it. Get used to it? Im almost losing my appetite. They both chuckled and Ada continued the slow stripping process as they listened to, and watched, the television. After an hour or so, Sara became accustomed to the smell and her appetite returned and she wondered if they would be finished before lunch time. Sweetie, we/re lucky if we/re finished before supper. So long? Thats right. With you we/re starting from scatch one. And I thought I would catch a little sun today. In a box youll catch it. You just relax and think how gorgeous youll look with your red hair. Today the hair tomorrow the sun.

The heat and the sun awakened Harry and Marion in the afternoon. They each tried to convince themselves to go back to sleep and not let the other one know they were awake, but after a few minutes the game became tedious. Especially for Harry thinking of the nice taste he had saved for now. He sat on the side of the bed for a moment, then went to the bathroom and threw some cold water on his face, rubbed it with a towel, then filled a glass with water. Hey baby, get up and get your works, I got a little somethin here. Marion sat up and blinked for a moment as she stared at the bathroom door. You putting me on Harry? Hey, I dont play those kind of games. Me and Ty scored for some way out dynamite shit yesterday and I still got a good taste left. Marion got her works and joined Harry in the bathroom, Here. She put the cooker on the sink and Harry tapped some heroin in, then the water, and cooked it up. He drew all the fluid up in the dropper then squeezed half of it out and passed it over to Marion, Ladys first. Well, thank you kind sir. Marion wasnt fully awake, still feeling the grogginess that comes from a long party and sleeping during a hot afternoon, but she was alert enough to tie up and pump up a good vein in a couple of seconds and get a good hit. She started to nod almost immediately and Harry took the works from her hand and cleaned them then tied up and got off himself. They sat on the side of the tub for a few minutes, rubbing their faces and smoking. Harry tossed his butt in the toilet and got up, Whatta ya say we get dressed for a while, and went back to the bedroom and put on his shirt and pants. Marion continued to sit on the side of the tub, rubbing her nose, until the heat from her shortening cigarette forced her eyes open and she tossed the butt in the toilet and washed her face, slowly, hanging over the bowl looking at the water and the face cloth, smiling at them, thinking of how she would pick up the cloth and soap it and then scrub her face and rinse it and splash on cold water then pat it dry . . . while just spinning the cloth around, dreamily, with the tip of her finger. Eventually she picked up the cloth and lovingly caressed the water from it and rubbed her face then stood up and looked in the mirror . . . then smiled. She let her face air dry and enjoyed the tingling sensation, then cupped her hands under her breasts and smiled with joy and pride as she turned and posed in various angles admiring their size and firmness. She thought of brushing her hair but just fluffed it with her hands, luxuriating in its feel and sheen, then posed for a few more minutes before putting on her robe and joining Harry at the kitchen table. O, you finally got out, eh? I thought maybe you fell in. She smiled, I thought you were trying to, and she grabbed his breasts and squeezed. Hey, take it easy. You wanta give me a cancer? He slapped her on the ass and she smiled again and sat down and lit a cigarette. Jesus, thats some good stuff. Harry leered at her, What are you talking about? She smiled, Animal. Yeah. You love it. I didnt hear you complaining. Hey, you know me, Im a happy go lucky clod. Well, I dont know how happy you are, and they both chuckled, almost inaudibly, their faces in wide grins and their eyes partially closed. Marion poured a couple of glasses of Perrier water and Harry stared at the bubbles for a minute then asked if she had any soda? No, but I have some limes. Harry giggled. They sat smoking and drinking Perrier water until the nod started to wear off and they settled in with a fine, mellow feeling as their eyes started to open a hair at a time. After a second glass Marion asked Harry if he wanted something to eat, Yeah, but not until ya take a bath, and he giggled. Animal. Will you settle for some yogurt? Harry started laughing, Yogurt??? Wow . . . and you call me an animal, and he continued laughing. Marion chuckled, Sometimes I think youre sick. Sometimes? Yes, sometimes. The rest of the time theres absolutely no doubt. She took a couple of containers of yogurt out of the refrigerator and put them on the table, along with two spoons. Well, Im glad that at least some of the time you have no doubts. Indecision is a terrible thing. Still on the pineapple yogurt kick, eh? Yes. I love it. But dont you ever get the hots for strawberry or blueberry or any of them? No. Just pineapple. I could live on it the rest of my life. Well baby, if eating pineapple yogurt every day will get you looking the way you do Im all for it. Marion pulled her shoulders back and turned slightly in a pose, You like the way I look? Hey, you kiddin? Youre sensational baby, Harry leaned across the table, Youre good enough to eat. Well, maybe you had better start with the yogurt. Its very nourishing. O yeah? You mean it puts lead in your pencil, eh? Okay, take a letter, and he started laughing. Marion shook her head as she smiled and put a spoonful of yogurt in her mouth then licked her lips. How can you laugh at those jokes of yours, they are positively terrible. Yeah, but I lovem. If I dont laugh, who will? Marion continued to smile as she finished her yogurt. They had another glass of Perrier water and were really enjoying their high even though they were sweating from the heat of the day and the dope. Harry closed his eyes and started breathing deeply, a serene smile on his face. What are you doing? Sniffing. Sniffing? Sniffing what? Us baby. Us.

It smells like the Fulton Fish Market in here. Marion smiled and shook her head, Don't be so *gauche*. At least its better than being crass, and anyway, Im lovable. Harry laughed and Marion chuckled, then he got up, Why dont we take a bath? Marion smiled, I didnt think you knew how, and then she started laughing, I like that. That was a good one. They both laughed and he took off his pants and shorts and tossed them on the bed as they went back into the bathroom. Marion put some bath oil in the water and they plopped in the tub and luxuriated in the smooth, scented water and washed each other slowly, as they worked the soap in to a lather and caressed the lather over each others body, then slowly dripped water over each other, floating away the heat of the afternoon.

Sara continued to stare in the mirror, blinking. Thats red? Ada shrugged, Well its not exactly red but its almost, maybe, in the same family. The same family? Theyre not even distant cousins already. Well, maybe a poor relation. Not even welfare. How poor is poor? How poor is poor? How high is up? Its a red. Not a red red, but a red. Red? Youre telling me this is a red? Yeah. Im telling. Its a red. Youre saying a red? Yeah. Im saying. Then whats orange? If this is red I want to know whats orange? I want to see an orange thats not even a poor relation of this. Ada looked at Saras hair, then her reflection, her hair, reflection, then pursed her lips and shrugged, Well, it could be a little orange too. A little orange? Ada kept nodding as she stared in the mirror at Saras reflection, Yeah, it looks like it could be, maybe, a little orange. A little orange? Its a little orange like being a little bit pregnant. Ada shrugged again. So whats to worry? Itll be alright. Whats to worry? Someone may try to juice me. Relax, relax, dolly. It just needs a little more dye. Itll be alright for the television. I look like a thermometer. Thats what I look like. Like an upside down thermometer. So dont blow your top. Relax. We/ll have some smoked fish and bialy. Come, come, sit down. Ada led Sara away from the mirror and sat her down at the table. I/ll get you a glass tea and youll feel better. Ada put the water on and got the fish out of the refrigerator and the bialy from the bread box, and the plates and utensils. All day long Im getting my scalp scraped, and burned and smelling like dead fish and I look like a basketball. You should learn to relax. Thats your trouble, you dont know how to relax already. Im telling you its alright. Tomorrow we/ll do it again and youll look like Lucille Ball. Here, have a piece of smoked fish and bialy.

Tyrone fell by Marions pad shortly after sunset. They sat around smoking a joint for a while then Marion decided they should eat, Im starving. Yeah, me too, get me a Snickers. Damn Ty, dont you ever eat anything except Snickers? Yeah, Chuckles. Ah digs Chuckles. You sure as hell dont know anything about eating, man. What you need is some good chicken noodle soup. Sheeit, Pepsi and a Snickersll take care of anything. Well, I hope you wont be offended, but I am not going to get any TV specials. When I am hungry I eat food— and no remarks from you Harry, chuckling as he grinned broadly. I didnt say a word. No, but you are thinking very loudly. Sheeit, if he ever had a thought it/d be his first one. They all chuckled and Marion left for the store and came back a short time later with a large loaf of crisp French bread, cheese, salami, black olives, caponata and a couple bottles of cheap chianti. Hey baby, lookit that, soul food. Youd better not let the M A F I A hear you say that Theyd get very bugged. Whats that? The Militant Association For

Italian Americans. They would burn your ass man. Sheeit, the onlyest difference between them and me is that ah smell better. Why dont one of you *bon vivants* open the bottles while I get some plates. Groovy. Here ya go man. Harry tossed the corkscrew to Tyrone and went over to the stereo and turned on a music station. In a matter of minutes Marion had set the table with plates, silverware, knife and cutting board. Harry poured the wine then sniffed his glass, sipped it, rolled it around in his mouth then smacked his lips. Great bouquet. Full rich body. Hearty yet smooth. A magnificent wine. Must be at least a week old, right? Sheeit I sure as hell dont care how old it is. Just so long as they dont wash they dirty socks in it. Where this wine comes from Tyrone, they dont wear socks. Oooo, this chick is bad jim, ah mean bad, and they continued to laugh and chuckle as they cut hunks out of the salami, the bread and the cheese and wash them down with the wine, sopping up some caponata with their bread or rolling it up in a slice of salami and stuffing it in their mouths, the guys wiping their mouths with the backs of their hands as Marion dabbed at hers with a napkin, then Harry picked up his napkin and started using it. Marion ate slowly and leisurely and Harry slowed his pace to hers. When they finished there were only bread crumbs and salami skin left on the plates. They made coffee and lit a joint. When the joint was finished Marion brought out the dessert, three cannolis. Tyrone dug into his with enthusiasm and Harry battled his trying to duplicate Marions cool way of eating it without the cream squirting all over, by gently breaking off small pieces with her fork and putting them ever so delicately into her mouth and waiting the appropriate length of time after slowly chewing and swallowing before sipping her coffee and dabbing her mouth genteelly with her napkin. When they finished Tyrone leaned back, patted his stomach,

Guhddamn . . . now that was somethin else. They refilled their coffee cups and lit another joint and luxuriated in the feeling of deep and all pervading satisfaction, a feeling of knowing absolutely that all was well with the world and them and that the world was not only their oyster it was also their linguine with clam sauce. Not only were all things possible, but all things were theirs. Harry gazed at Tyrone C. Love through half closed eyes, I think maybe we/d better forget about goin down and shapin up tonight, eh? O man, ah dont even want to talk about work right now, not that ah ever am too hip on it, but right now ah just wants to think of Tyrone C. Love an how *goooooood* he feel. Tyrone looked up in the air for a minute, then smiled, Well maybe ah feels like thinkin about some fine fox, but ah damn sure dont want to have anythin to do with work in any way, shape or form, uh uh. Marion opened her eyes as wide as possible and raised her eyebrows. What is this about work? You lose a bet? Tyrone started giggling, Damn, this a righteous chick, jim. Harry chuckled for a minute then ran down their idea about working for a short time, a very short time, and getting enough bread together to get a piece of Brodys shit and cut it and off it. When he finished Marion was actually listening. She agreed that it was a good idea, But I just cant see you guys getting there at that time in the morning. Well, we/ll make it. You may make it there, but how long are you going to last? Hey baby, dont be a bring down, ah feels too good. We figure we/ll cop some bennies and thatll get us through. They all smiled and nodded. Well, if thats all you want I can take care of that. I always have a supply of dexies and downers. Sheeit, dont rush it now. We needs time to think about this, right man? Harry laughed, Dont panic Ty, we aint goin to work tonight. You bet your sweet ass ah aint. Uh uh. No way ahm gonna blow a nice high like this. They laughed, then Harry got serious for a moment. How about tomorrow? We/ll cool it during the day and when we/re ready to go we/ll drop some dexies and take a few with us just in case. Whatta you say Ty? Sheeit, ahm down jim. But remember, tomorrow. Mah sainted mutha always tole me dont never do today what you can put off till tomorrow. An there be a fox ahm goin to see tonight that aint about to let me go before tomorrow. You have enough dexies to keep us working? You know we aint about to make it on the natch. Of course. I told you I have a couple of doctors writing for me. Then we/re cool. Tomorrow night we make it, right? You got it baby, and they slapped palms. We is on our way.

Sara was in her viewing chair, watching the television, reading her diet book and rationing the chocolates to herself. She read the introduction and then skimmed and skipped through the various chapters dealing with the need to be the proper weight, the charts that showed the proper weight for each height, the charts that showed the incidence of various disease with pounds and percentage of overweight. It was a case of lose weight or suffer a lingering and ignoble death. Then came the chapter that proved why this method was superior to all other methods and how the chemical balance created in the body from this diet would force the body to burn its fat and the pounds would melt away like ice in the sun. That sounds nice. Maybe tomorrow I/ll get some sun. She continued to read and finally started skipping pages, I believe already, but wheres the diet???? At last. After almost a hundred pages she came to the diet. FIRST WEEK. She took the entire page in at once. She blinked, then sectioned it off and looked at it. It didn't change. Then she read it. Line by line she read the entire page. It remained the same. She rummaged around, without looking, in the chocolate box for a chocolate covered caramel and chewed and sucked on it as she continued to stare at the page in disbelief.

BREAKFAST

1 hard boiled egg
½ grapefruit
1 cup black coffee (*no* sugar)

LUNCH

1 hard boiled egg
½ grapefruit
½ cup lettuce (*no* dressing)
1 cup black coffee (*no* sugar)

DINNER

1 hard boiled egg
½ grapefruit
1 cup black coffee (*no* sugar)

NOTE: Drink at least 2 quarts, 64 oz., 8 8-oz. glasses of water each day.

Sara continued to stare and chew. She looked very carefully between the lines having heard that that was where the real information was. Every night on the news that nice young man with the mustaches and glasses, always said, "Reading between the lines it becomes obvious that what was really said is . . ." She looked. She stared. She held the book at various angles, but all she could see was white paper. Then it finally penetrated. She slapped her forehead. Such a *klutz*. If this is the first week then there's something different for the second week. Of course. They keep adding food. Thats what it is. She quickly turned the page and stared . . . it was the same. Exactly the same. Why would— Ach, so thats the difference. She looked very carefully at the luncheon menu for the second week and it was different. The egg was replaced with a 4 oz. meat patty, broiled. She quickly looked at the third week menu. The meat patty was replaced with 4 oz. of fish, broiled. She dropped the book on her lap and reached over for another chocolate. Any kind of chocolate. She stared at her set. How could that be? How could you eat only that? A mouse would starve already on that. She felt hollow inside. A profound sadness started to pervade her being. Her head started to hang forward and she had to raise her eyes in order to see the screen. She felt forlorn, utterly devastated and alone. Absolutely alone. Completely alone. Her throat was constricting and tears were rapidly building up behind her eyes. She kept blinking them back and then she noticed herself dressed in her red dress, her hair a gorgeous red, walking across the screen, so slim, so trim, so sexy. Such curves. How many years now since she had such curves? Who can remember? When she first met Seymour she had curves. She was firm then. Thats right, firm. Curvy. O how Seymour used to look. And touch. He used to tell me how all his friends envied him I was so beautiful. *Zophtic.* Thats what I was, *zophtic.* She watched herself stand with the announcer as she was introduced to the audience and she could hear the applause and the wolf whistles. She smiled at the audience. Maybe they want me for a regular TV show when they see how I look? Maybe a Ziegfield girl. She tilted her head this way and that as she watched herself on the screen, and her face widened in an appreciative smile. So whats the big deal about only eating a few eggs for awhile. I/ll drink lots of water and think thin and the weight will melt off . ... just like that. Eh, big deal. Who needs a danish? She finished the chocolates so they shouldnt go to waste, then went ipsy pipsy into the bedroom, eagerly looking forward to getting up in the morning and starting the diet that would melt pounds off like that, and lead her to a new life. She even sang a little "By Mir Bist

Du Schön," as she undressed. The sheets felt cool and refreshing, the darkness friendly. She sighed into her pillow and squirmed into a soothing position and watched the little pellets of light bounce off her closed eyelids until they finally disappeared and her mind was filled with Seymour and their many years of joy. She breathed and smiled a prayer for Seymour . . . and Harry. He was always such a good boy. How she used to love to make over him. She could still see those chubby little thighs and take bites out of them. Such joy, such joy, in the carriage along the boulevard and in the park . . . O, if only they could stay babies forever . . . mommy, mommy, looky. . . . O Harry, God should bless you so you don't have pain. . . . Ahhhhh, my boy. . . . Be well and happy and make a good wedding. . . . Ahhhhhhh, a good wedding. . . . And the summer before the wedding. Remember Seymour? The Mardi Gras. My first time in Coney Island. Clowns, and dragons and floats and confetti . . . the sun . . . remember the sun that day Seymour? I can feel it now. And we went on the carousel . . . I can hear it . . . it was somehow different that day. O, Seymour, so many days were different for us . . . and you used to grab me, Sara chuckled and squirmed slightly, and say such things. . . . Im going on the television, Seymour. What do you think of that? Your Sara on television. Adas fixing my hair. Red. Like the dress. Sort of. Remember, I wore it for Harrys bar mitzvah? Well, the hair isn't so good but Ada will make it nice. Can you imagine, your Sara on the television? Did you ever think it could be? Maybe I/ll stay a long time. They might want me for some other show too. Remember, they discovered Lana Turner in a drugstore? Remember? I think Swabs? Who knows? Its like a new life Seymour. Its already a new life . . . and Sara Goldfarb, Mrs. Seymour Goldfarb, nuzzled her cheek into her pillow and smiled such a nice smile that even in the dark it glowed with the joy that flowed from her heart and through her entire being. Life was no longer something to endure, but to live. Sara Goldfarb had been given a future.

Harry and Marion got off on the last of his stuff and made it on the couch grooving behind the high and the music. There was a softness in the music that they automatically focused on, a softness in the light that glowed from the top and the bottom of the shades and glowed in widening circles, and filtered through the multicolored sides of the shades and ever so gently pushed the darkness into the far corners and soothingly coated the room with a hint of color that was friendly to their eyes; and there was a kindness and tenderness in their attitudes as they held each other and turned their heads to avoid blowing smoke in each others face; even their voices were low and gentle and seemed a part of the music. Harry was brushing the hair back from Marions forehead, noticing how the dim light reflected from the perfect blackness of her hair and made the outline of her nose and high cheekbones seem to shimmer. You know something? Ive always thought you are the most beautiful woman Ive ever seen. Marion smiled and looked up at him, Really? Harry nodded and smiled, Since the first time I met you. Marion reached up and caressed his cheek with the tips of her fingers and smiled tenderly, Thats nice Harry. Her smile broadened, That really makes me feel good. Harry chuckled, Good for your ego, eh? Well I cant say that it does it any harm, but thats not what I mean. It makes me feel good all over, like . . . well, you know lots of people tell me things like that and its meaningless, completely meaningless. You mean because you think theyre putting you on? No, no, nothing like that. I dont know or care if they are. I guess maybe they really mean it, but from them, Marion shrugged, it just doesnt mean anything to me. They can be the most sincere person in the world and I feel like asking them what that has to do with the price of coffee, you know what I mean? Harry nodded and smiled, Yeah. . . . She looked into Harrys eyes for a moment, feeling the tenderness in her look, But when you say it I *hear* it. You know what I mean? I really *hear* it. It has meaning to me. I mean, like its important and I not only hear it, but I believe it with all of me . . . and it makes the inner me feel good. Harry smiled, Im glad. Because you make me feel good. She turned excitedly, You know why? Its because I feel that you really know me, the real me. Youre not just looking at the outside, Marion looked even more intently into Harrys eyes, but youre looking at my inner being and seeing that there is a real *person* inside. All my life Ive been told Im beautiful, a, quote, Raven Haired Beauty, unquote, and I was told that because that was supposed to make everything alright. Dont worry honey, youre a beauty, everything will be alright. My mothers an absolute nut like that. Like thats the Alpha and Omega of existence. Like if youre beautiful you dont feel pain or have dreams or know the despair of loneliness. Why should you be unhappy, youre so beautiful? My God they drive me nuts, like all I am is a beautiful body and nothing else. Not once, never, have they ever tried to love the real me, to love me for what I am, to love me for my mind. Harry continued to stroke her head and caress her cheek and neck and gently rub the lobe of her ear, smiling as she moved her head and softened her smile as he caressed her. I guess we/re kindred souls and thats why we can feel so close to each other. Her eyes glowed even more intensely as she turned and leaned on an arm and looked at Harry, Thats what I mean. You see, you have feelings. You can appreciate the inner me. Like right now I feel a closeness between us that Ive never felt with anyone before . . . *anyone*. Yeah, I know what you mean. Thats how I feel. I don't know if I can put it into words, but— Thats just it, it doesnt need words. Thats the whole point. Like whats the use of all those words when the feelings arent behind them. Theyre just words. Like I can look at a painting and tell it, youre beautiful. What does it mean to the painting? But Im not a painting. Im not two dimensional. Im a *person*. Even a Botticelli doesnt breathe and have feelings. Its beautiful, but its still a painting. No matter how beautiful the outside may be, the inside still has feelings and needs that just words dont fulfill. She nestled into his chest and Harry put an arm around her and held her hand, Yeah, youre right. Its not just the outside thats beautiful, but they dont know. Its hopeless. Thats why you cant be worried about the world. Theyll just do you in anyway. You cant depend on them because sooner or later theyll turn on you or just disappear and leave you there alone. Marion frowned for a moment, But you cant shut everyone out. I mean you have to have someone to love . . . someone to hold on to . . . someone— No, no, I don't mean that, Harry pulled her back to his chest, I just mean that bunch of lames out there. Someone like you could really make it alright for me. With you with me I could really do something. Marion almost sighed, Do you really mean that Harry? Do you really think I could inspire you? Harry looked into her eyes, then at her face and gently glided the tip of a finger over her cheek and traced the outline of her nose, his face and eyes in a soft and tender smile, You could really make my life worth while. A guy needs something to give his life a reason or whats the point of living? I need more than the streets. I don't want to be a floating crap game all my life. I want to be something . . . anything. Marion hugged him tightly, O Harry I think I really can help you be something. Theres something in me thats crying to come out but it needs the right person to open the lock. You can unlock it Harry. I know it. Harry put his arms around her as she cuddled into him. Yeah, I bet we could. He stroked her head for a moment as he looked up at the ceiling, Thats why I want to get some money and buy a piece. I dont want to spend my life hustling the streets and end up like the rest of them. If I can just get some money I can go into a business and settle right into it. He looked at Marion and smiled, I never told anybody this, but Ive always wanted to open a coffee house theater sort of place. You know, it would have good food and pastries and different kinds of coffee and hot chocolate and teas from all over the world, Germany, Japan, Italy, Russia, all over. And it could be sort of a theater group where youd have performances at night and maybe mimes doing little skits from time to time. I don't know, I havent really got it all straight, but— Marion sat up, O, that sounds fantastic. Thats a great idea Harry. O, you could even have paintings by young painters on the wall. It could be sort of a gallery too. Sculpture. Harry nodded, Yeah. That sounds good. O Harry, lets do it. O lets. Its a terrific idea. I can get the painters without any trouble. O, and we could have poetry readings a couple of nights a week O Harry its so exciting and it could work, I just know it could. Yeah, I know. I figure it may take time, but I could probably open up a couple of them. You know, after the one here gets going we could go to Frisco and open one. O, you would love San Francisco, Harry. And I know enough people there to get it going, the mimes, the poets, the painters, I know them all, and who knows what could happen after that. Harry smiled, Yeah. But we have to make sure its goin right here before we go spreading our wings. O, I know. But we can still plan. How long do you think it will take to get the money? Harry shrugged, I dont know. Not long. Once we cop the first piece it will be pretty easy after that. She hugged him, O Harry, Im so excited. I cant tell you. Harry chuckled, I never would have guessed. They laughed and put their arms around each other and kissed, first

gently, then more passionately, and Harry pulled his face
back a few inches and looked lovingly at Marion, I love you,
and kissed her on the tip of her nose, her eyelids, her cheeks,
then her soft lips, her chin, her neck, her ears, then nuzzled
his face in her hair and caressed her back with his hands and
breathed her name in her ear, Marion, Marion, I love you,
and she gently moved with the flow and felt his words and
kisses and feelings flow through her, easing away all her problems, her doubts, her fears, her anxieties and she felt warm
and alive and vital. She felt loved. She felt necessary. Harry
felt real and substantial. He could feel all the loose pieces
starting to fall into place. He felt on the verge of something
momentous. They felt whole. They felt united. Though they
were still on the couch they felt a part of the vastness of the
sky and the stars and moon. They were somehow on the crest
of a hill with a gentle breeze blowing Marions hair flowingly;
and walking through a sunlit woods and flower studded field
feeling the freedom of the birds as they flew through the air
chirping and singing and the night was comfortingly warm as
the soft filtered light continued to push the darkness into the
shadows as they held each other and kissed and pushed each
others darkness into the corner, believing in each others
light, each others dream.

Sara smiled her way into wakefulness. It was early but she
felt completely refreshed. She wasn't sure if she had dreamed
or not, but if she had it was a beautiful dream. She thought
she heard birds chirping. She got up and went ipsy pipsy
into the bathroom and showered and got ready for the new
day. She looked in the mirror at her hair and shrugged and
smiled. Big deal. Its beautiful. Its in the family, and she
giggled. Flash, bam, alexkazam, its an orange colored sky.
She giggled again and went ipsy pipsy into the living room,

turned on the set, then into the kitchen and started boiling her egg then went out to the mailbox to see if her television papers had come yet. She knew the mailman wasn't due for hours, but you never can tell. There might have been a special delivery of some kind or maybe theres a different mailman whose delivering the mail early. Her mailbox was empty. So were the others. She went back to her apartment and started fixing the grapefruit and wondered if she should eat first the grapefruit or the egg. She sipped her black coffee, thinking, then ate part of the grapefruit, then the egg and then finished the grapefruit. And then it was all gone. It seemed like she just got up and already the breakfast was gone. She shrugged and filled an eight-ounce glass of water and drank it, visualizing the weight melting off. She sat at the table drinking her coffee, but her hands kept reaching for something so she got up and washed the dishes, then dried them and put them away, then looked at the clock wondering how long before lunch time and realized it wasnt even breakfast time yet and a feeling of panic started in her stomach, but she went back to the bedroom and made the bed and straightened the room and told her stomach to stop already, Youll feel better in the red dress than a cheese danish. She sang and hummed and fluttered about as she cleaned the living room, waiting until it was time to go to Adas for another treatment on her hair. As she cleaned she became more and more interested in the program on television and so she finally stopped and sat in her viewing chair to watch the remainder of the show. The ending was not only happy, it was funny and heartwarming and her heart was even more joyful as she got her towel and left the apartment. She checked the mailbox again then went to Adas. At least todays not so bad. Just some more dye. Did you get the letter? No mail yet. I think maybe its coming today. You think its telling which show? Sara shrugged, I hope. What

are you winning maybe? What am I winning? a weekend with
Robert Redford, how should I know? Maybe when I find
out the show I/ll know the prizes. Ada wrapped the towel
around Saras neck as they adjusted themselves in front of the
television set, I saw yesterday a lady from Queens on a show
she won a brand new car, a six piece set of luggage with
already a cosmeks case, o such a gorgeous blue. You know
Ada, thats just what I need. A new car and luggage. For
when I drive to Miami. I always have new luggage when I go
the Fountainblew. Make sure you have the car waxed and
not a cheapie, but solomized. In that sun you need protection
on the car. Tell me, was the car big enough for a driver and
the luggage? Ada started applying the dye, You should have
seen that lady, she almost fainted. I think she lives near
the Katzes. The Katzes? Yeah, remember? Rae and Irving
Katz. They used to live over Hymies delicatessen. When was
this? Maybe ten years ago. Who knows? Im supposed to remember ten years ago the Katzes from over Hymies delicatessen. Thats when my Seymour died. O, I know, I know. But
you remember. They had such a nice young boy. Hes a big
doctor now. In Hollywood. Oh yeah, I remember. So they live
near the lady with the car and luggage? Ada shrugged. Could
be. They moved to Queens. Maybe they know each other.
Anyway, its a nice prize. Just what I need. I saw yesterday a
couple win a swimming pool. A swimming pool? Yeah. With
already a filter and heater and all kinds things. Now thats
what I need. I could move out the couch and they could put
it in the living room. It wouldnt work Sara. Theyd raise your
rent. Raise it over what? Everything. I/ll give them the
luggage. Let them take a trip and leave me alone. Careful,
dont move while I get this. Youre not needing a red nose. Ada
carefully applied the dye as they continued to talk and specu-
late, and when she finished Sara looked at the clock, Good.
Just in time for my lunch. For a change, I think I/ll have a

egg, grapefruit, black coffee, and a little bit letttuce. Bone appetite.

Harry and Marion slept in each others arms on the couch. The music was still playing and the light from the lamp in the corner blended with the sunlight that eased through the drawn shades. There was a stillness in the room that somehow ignored the noise of the Bronx streets, cluttered with people and vehicles grumbling, yelling and rumbling. Their skin was moist from the hot, humid air yet they slept undisturbed and restful. The apartment, and everything in it, seemed isolated and insulated from its surroundings, and reflected the attitude of the sleepers. Occasionally a truck would rattle windows and shake floors and walls, but the sound was muted by the stillness of the air; and, from time to time, something would disturb the air and the dust motes that floated in the diffused sunlight danced as the air gentled by in caressing waves. The summer sun continued to rise in the sky and propel shocks of heat down on the city and the heavy moisture moistened bodies and clothing, and people fanned and wiped at sweating faces trying to survive another bitch of a day as Harry and Marion peacefully passed the day sleeping in each others arms oblivious to the reality surrounding them.

Sara checked the mailbox after a hearty lunch in which she had some extra lettuce. Well, actually you couldn't call it cheating because it was only half a cup of lettuce. . . . Well, it really depends on how you measure: loose or tight. If youre just putting a little lettuce in the measuring cup theres already more air than lettuce. All Sara did was push out the air between the pieces of lettuce . . . very hard, and got almost a half a head in half a cup. So whats the big deal? Youre not needing a toothpick no matter how much lettuce you eat. She drank two glasses of water, rapidly, then tried to convince herself that she was filled, but who you kidding? Nobody believes a story like that. Im not full, Im starving. She rechecked the book again and it assured her that after the first day or two (two! you got to be kidding!!!) you will be feeding off your own fat and wont be hungry. Im waiting. The book also suggested that she visualize herself at her perfect weight and concentrate on that to avoid thinking of any hunger she may have *(may* have? Whos kidding who?!) and she did and again she saw herself in her gorgeous red dress and red hair with golden shoes looking so *zophtic* as she walked across the television screen, but even at a perfect weight and looking so ipsy pipsy nifty she was still hungry. Im not hungry because Im thin and beautiful? I dont eat just because Im so gorgeous? She looked at the book, Eh, you should *plotz* already? She didnt bother with her coffee but went out to the mailbox. Still no mail yet. She went back to the apartment and stood in the middle of the kitchen staring at the refrigerator and could feel herself leaning forward slowly, but continuously, and she became fascinated and hypnotized by the action and wondered how far forward she could lean before she fell flat on her face and she leaned further and further until she suddenly put her arms out and stopped herself from falling by pushing on the refrigerator. This I dont need. She turned her back on the refrigerator and walked sideways past it into the bathroom. She fluffed her hair and looked at it carefuly. Still not the red she wanted, but red it is. Sort of carrot, but a red. Definitely its part of the family. Tomorrow she/ll get another treatment and maybe then its perfect, but for now its alright. Maybe she/ll go out and get a little sun while she waits for the mailman. Theyll all want to see how gorgeous her new hair is. She stopped in the doorway to the kitchen and turned her back and tossed her head at the refrigerator, So whats the big deal, and picked up her folding chair and went ipsy pipsy out to the street, checking the mailbox first. She joined the others sitting alongside the building, getting the sun. A few had reflectors that they held under their chins as they stared up at the sun. Sara could feel how her hair glimmered in the sun and shook her head a little as she waited for the first comment. Ada told us. Its gorgeous. Thank you. We/re making it a little darker tomorrow. To match the red dress. So why darker? Now its looking like Lucille Ball. But Im not. But soon . . . Im on a diet. One of the ladies lowered her reflector for a moment, Cottage cheese and lettuce, then raised the reflector again. The women continued to keep their eyes closed and their faces stretched toward the sun as they talked. What diet you on? Eggs and grapefruit. Oi vay. I was on once. Lots of luck dolly. Its not so bad. How long you been on already? All day. All day? Its one oclock. All days forever? So? All day is still all day. Im thinking thin. My Rosie lost fifty pounds like that almost. Like that? Like what? Like that, that. Poof. You put her in a sweat box? A doctor. He gave her pills. It makes you not want to eat. So whats so good about that? Who wants not to want to eat? You mean Im sitting here not thinking about chopped liver and pastrami on rye? With a slice of onion and mustard. Herring. Herring? Yeah, herring. In sour cream. With matzoh. A nosh. When the sun goes behind that building Im having a nosh, she squinted at the sun, maybe another twenty minutes. You shouldnt talk like that already when someones on a diet. Eh, big deal. I/ll sneak an extra piece of lettuce. Im thinking thin. The women continued to sit on the chairs, pushed up against the building wall, faces thrust at the sun, and talking until the mailman came. Sara picked up her chair and followed him into the building. Ada and the other ladies followed. Gold-

farb. Goldfarb. I know you have a big important mail for
Goldfarb. Well, ah dont know. Aint much of anythin here
but a couple a things, and he continued to put mail in the
boxes, aint much aroun here cept on the beginnin a the
month wit them social security checks. But Im expecting
something— Here somethin for Goldfarb, Sara Goldfarb,
and he handed Sara a thick envelope. So lets see. Open it,
open it. Sara carefully opened the envelope, not wanting to
injure anything on the inside, and took out a form letter and
a two part questionnaire with a return envelope clipped to
them. So whats the show? The mailman closed the boxes then
worked his way around the knot of women around Sara, So
long, have a nice day now, you hear? and whistled his way out
of the building. The women nodded and automatically said
a goodbye or two, then leaned, intently, toward Sara. It
doesnt say what show. What? How can you know if theyre
not telling you? They decide after you send them this form.
So why a big mystery already? Ada took the letter from Sara,
and Sara pointed to the paragraph, See? Ada nodded her
head as she read, ". . . as the promotional agency for several
of the shows on television utilizing contestants, as well as
proposed shows, we want to take this opportunity . . ." A
lot of words to say nothing. Its like the soap opera, tune in
tomorrow for the next chapter. They chuckled and went back
to the chairs to get the last bit of sun before it went behind
the building. Sara shrugged and went back to her apartment
to puzzle over the questionnaire. She flipped on the television
and sat in her viewing seat and read the questionnaire several times before going into the kitchen. She turned her back
on the refrigerator and made a glass of tea, then sat down at
the kitchen table to complete the form. Actually, Sara had
not filled in too many forms in her life, but whenever she
was faced with the ordeal they always seemed impossible at
first. This one was the same. She just sat, with her back to

the refrigerator, and sipped her tea for a moment knowing
that soon it would start to make sense. She looked at the form
out of the corner of her eye then slowly slid it across the table
until it was right in front of her so it was almost touching her
nose. So, big deal. A piece of papers going to bug me? Ask me?
Go ahead Mr. Smartypants, ask me a question? Uh. You call
that a question? That kind I take six at once. She started to
fill in the form, carefully printing each letter. Her name. Address. Telephone number. Social security number. Huh, like
a breeze, and she glided from one question to the next, then
stopped abruptly. So now youre getting personal? Does Macys
tell Gimbels? She squinted at the form out of the corner of
her eye and sipped her tea. Okay, you want to know so I/ll
tell you, and she quickly put down a few numbers after: Date
of Birth. The next question was: Age. So now they want me
to count for them. An Einstein Im not, but I can figure that.
She looked at the next question and smiled then chuckled and
shrugged before answering it. Marital Status: wanting, needing. Maybe theyre sending me Robert Redford . . . or maybe
even Mickey Rooney. Sex: So why not? She giggled and continued talking to the form, putting in the answers carefully
and clearly. When she finished, she reread it several times
making certain that every answer was exactly right and that
nothing had been overlooked. She couldnt be sloppy or lazy
with something as important as this. How many dreams
could come true through this form? Where can it lead? Every
day on the television she saw things suddenly work out for
people. People get married. Sons come home. Everybody is
happy. She sat with her eyes closed for a moment then ever
so gently folded the form, in its original creases, and put it
in the self-addressed envelope, sealed it pressing hard for
many long seconds on the flap, then putting it on the chair
and sitting on it for extra insurance. If that doesnt seal it
then it doesnt have to be sealed. She tossed her head and

shoulders at the refrigerator, Who needs you? and left to
mail the form. A few of the ladies were sitting in the shade.
Sara waved the envelope, Its ready to go on its way. They
walked with her to the mailbox on the corner. I wonder when
youll hear? Maybe theyll send you for a week to Grossingers,
thats where they send all the stars. Im eating eggs and grapefruit at Grossingers? The ladies smiled and chuckled as they
walked down the street. Their own friend, Sara Goldfarb,
for twenty years, for some more, their friend and she was
going to be on the television. Theres sorrow and pain in
everyones life, but every now and then theres a ray of light
that melts the loneliness in your heart and brings comfort
like hot soup and a soft bed. That ray of light was shining
already on their friend Sara Goldfarb and they were par-
taking of the light too and sharing her hope and dream. Sara
pulled down the panel on the mailbox and kissed the envelope before dropping it in. She closed it then opened it
again to make sure it had dropped down into the box, and
entrusted her dream to the United States Postal Service.

    The nine to fivers, the brown baggers, the strap hangers,
the working stiffs, the squares were at home, or on their
way, by the time Harry and Marion slipped into a new day.
Whenever their eyes opened, even partially, the shadows
seemed to attack them and force them shut so they rolled
over as best they could on the narrow couch, groaning unconsciously, and tried to go back to sleep, but though their
eyes were heavy and their bodies sluggish, additional sleep
was impossible so they hung between wakefulness and blackness until the blackness became too uncomfortable and they
forced their stiff bodies up and sat on the side of the couch
for a moment orienting themselves. Harry massaged the back
of his neck, Wow, I feel like I've been playing football for

krists sake. He pulled at his shirt, I'm soakin wet. Take it
off and put it on the back of the chair. It will dry out pretty
fast. I/ll make some coffee. Harry watched Marion walk
across the room, her ass grinding gently from side to side.
He put his shirt on the back of the chair, stared out the window for a moment, holding the shade just a few inches from
the window, staring at the action on the street so blankly that
everything seemed to split up into many images and eventually he had to blink everything back into perspective. He
rubbed his head and stretched his eyes open wider for a
second. He gradually became aware of the noises coming from
the kitchen then released the shade and joined Marion as she
put two cups of coffee on the table. Good timing. Yeah. They
sat and started sipping the hot coffee as they smoked. Jesus,
I dont even remember falling asleep, do you? Marion smiled,
I only remember you rubbing the back of my neck and
whispering to me. Harry chuckled, The way my hand feels I
must have been rubbing it all night. Marion looked and
sounded almost shy, It was nice. I love it. Last night was the
best night I have ever had in my life. You putting me on?
She smiled softly, sweetly, and shook her head, No. After
sleeping with you with our clothes on how can I put you on?
Harry chuckled and shrugged, Yeah. That is a little weird,
isn't it? But it was kindda groovy. Marion nodded, I think its
beautiful. Harry yawned again and shook his head, Man, I
cant seem to get it going this morning, or today or tonight or
whatever it is. Here, Marion passed him a spansule, take this
and youll be awake soon enough. Huh, whats this, putting it
in his mouth and swallowing it, then chasing it with coffee. A
dexie spansule. You can take another one before you go to
work. Work? Oh yeah, we/re supposed to make it down to
that newspaper gig tonight, eh? Jesus. Dont worry, by the
time you finish the next cup of coffee youll have a different
attitude toward it. Especially when you remember why youre

working. Harry scratched his head, Yeah, I guess so. But right
now it all seems impossible. Then dont think about it. She
refilled their cups, When we finish this we/ll take a shower.
That always works. Yeah. She smiled, Like walking in the
rain.

Harry was not only wide awake by the time Tyrone called,
he was chomping at the bit and had been talking for a couple
of hours without stop, taking the edge off the dexies with a
couple of pokes off a joint once in a while. He was more
actively a part of the music, his body moving energetically,
his fingers quietly snapping, his head seeming to be in the
midst of the chords as they were absorbed by him. When he
stopped talking long enough to take a drink of coffee, a drag
on his cigarette, a poke, or just to breathe, his jaws kept moving as he ground his teeth. Jesus, I could listen to that all
night. That son of a bitch has an incredible sound, really
something else . . . yeah, baby, blow . . . Harry closed his eyes
for a moment, nodding in time to the music, his head tilted
toward the radio, You hear that? eh? You dig the way he
comes down and flattens it? You dig those changes? Man! thats
too much . . . yeah, go get it baby, hahaha, blow your ass off,
jesus hes great. The way he just sort of glides into the up
tempo really knocks me out, you dig? Like no sudden change
with a funky ass drum roll and snare shots but just a nice
easy glide into the up tempo and before you know it hes got
you finger poppin. Hes outta sight man, just really outta
sight. . . . The piece ended and Harry snapped his attention
back to Marion after finishing his coffee. Marion refilled his
cup. You know, after we cop the piece and have the bread we
should go downtown and fall by one of the joints and dig
some music. I/d love to. Theres a lot of things we/re going
to do when we make that bread. We/re going to move on
out. We/re going to get it all together and turn things upside
down. We/ll have that coffee shop going in no time and then

we/ll go to Europe and you can show me all those paintings youre always talking about. We can even get you a studio and you can go back to painting and sculpting. The coffee houses will take care of themselves with the right people running them, and we can just make it around the world for a while and lay back and dig the scene. Youll love it Harry. Walking through miles of Titians in the Louvre. You mean the *Lou ver*? hahaha. A place I always wanted to go was Instanbul. I don't know why, but Ive always wanted to go to Instanbul. Especially on the Orient Express, you know? Maybe with Turhan Bey and Sydney Greenstreet and Peter Lorre. Krist, cant forget him. Remember him in *M*? Marion nodded her head. I always wondered what it was like to be like that, you know a child molester. I dont know, but Ive always felt sort of sorry for those dudes, I mean I feel sorry for the kids too, but the guys, krist thats really got to be something to have to pick up little kids and con them into going down some cellar or someplace and then making it with them, jesus . . . I wonder what goes on their heads, like what do they think about? It must be a drag when they wake up alone and know what they did . . . jesus. And in the joint all the other prisoners hate them, ya know that? Marion nodded her head again, They're the most despised guys in the joint. Everybodys on their case and when some con dumps them nobody does anything about it even when they know who did it. They just turn their back and go the other way and in some joints they punk them and if they dont go for it they rape them. Man, its got to be a tough bit. Im sure glad thats not my *shtik*, leaning forward and looking even more intently at Marion, his eyes straining from their sockets, his chest vibrating from the beating of his heart, Im glad its us and we dont need nothing or anything else, just us, he grabbed her hands in his and caressed them for a moment then kissed her fingertips then the palms of her hands then held them tight against his mouth for a moment then caressed her palm with the tip of his tongue and looked over her hands at her and she smiled from her mouth, her eyes, her heart and her entire being, I love you Harry. We/re going to do great things, baby, and show this world where its at because I can feel it in my bones, I mean I can *really* feel it, theres nothing I cant do, nothing, and Im going to make you the happiest woman in the world and thats a promise and a fact because Ive got something in me thats always been trying to come out and with you baby its going to come out and nothing can stop me, its right to the top and if you want the moon then its yours and I/ll even wrap it up for you—Marion continued to hold his hands and look into his eyes, her expression soft and loving—Im telling you I feel like Cyrano, and he stood up and waved his right arm around as if holding a sword, Bring me giants, not mere mortals, bring me giants and I/ll chop them up in little pieces and— The doorbell rang and Marion got up and went to the door, chuckling, I hope its not a very big one. She opened the door and Tyrone dragassed in. Harry stood in the middle of the living room waving his imaginary sword, This is a giant? On guard! and he started fencing with Tyrone who just stood there trying to raise his eyes, My father was the best swordsman in Tel Aviv, and he continued to go through his fencing number lunging forward, parrying, thrusting, bending at the knee and suddenly, while bent low, he thrust forth his trusty rapier and struck his enemy a mortal blow, touché! Harry bowed, his fighting arm at his waist, and ushered Tyrone into the kitchen. Marion laughed. Hey man, what the fucks wrong with *you*. Wrong with me? Nothings wrong with me. I never felt better in my life. Its a great day. A momentous day. A day that will go down in the annals of history as the day Harry Goldfarb turned the world around, upside down, and on its ass, the day I fell hopelessly and completely in love and give to my betroved my white plume, and he bowed deeply again and Marion curtsied and accepted the plume and he knelt at her feet and kissed her extended hand, Arise, Sir Harold, royal knight of the garter, defender of the realm, my beloved prince— Sheeit, alls ah did was askim whats wrong with him and ah gets television on the hoof—Marion and Harry were laughing and Tyrone seemed to be held up by invisible strings that threatened to snap at any moment—Yawl is crazy. You alright Ty? you look a little pale, and Harry broke up laughing. Now aint this a shame? aint this a mutha fuckin shame? Youd better close your eyes man, youll bleed to death, and Harry laughed louder and Marion giggled as she shook her head. O sheeit. Ah feel like Im in the middle of a mutha fuckin comic book jim. Harry was still laughing, You got to get with it man. Dont be a drag, feed your dog flag. Tyrone flopped at the kitchen table and looked up at Marion. Whatch you feedin this cat, baby? Love man. Shes feeding me love. Ive finally found the diet Ive been looking for all my life. Dont you know that its love that makes the world go round man. Ah aint worried bout the world baby, jus you. Harry and Marion laughed as Tyrone smiled weakly and Harry twirled Marion around in a circle then put his arm around her waist and kissed her delicate throat ever so lightly as she bent slightly on his arm. Ah been up all night and day ballin till ah feel like mah ass be in mah shoes and you stand there with your big ugly face flappin in the breeze an tell me love make the world go round. Sheeit. It make me wanna sleep for thirty-seven years. Tyrone giggled and Harry and Marion laughed and she gave him a dexie and Tyrone popped it and gulped at a cup of coffee. Ah dont know why Im here. Ah swear ah dont. If that fox didn't wake me up and say ah got to go cause I make her promise me she/d get mah ass out . . . sheeit, ah could sleep on a picket fence. Its the power of love Ty. Thats what got you here. We sent out vibrations of love so your pale, but

sweet little ass could get over here so we can go make that
bread to get that piece. Sheeit. What do love have to do with
bein greedy for a piece? Harry bent Marion over as he held
her with a hand on her back and sang, ala Russ Columbo,
Ah but you call it madness, but I call it love. Ah just hopes ah
survives long enough for that funky ass cap to work before
yawl drive me bananas. Thats not much of a drive, thats a
short put, and Harry broke up laughing as Marion giggled
and shook her head, O Harry, thats awful, and Tyrones eyes
flashed open, briefly, and he looked at Harry, a mock expression of disbelief on his face, Somebody oughtta shoot this
dude, jim, he be in *baaaad* pain, and Tyrones giggling joined
Harrys laughter and Marion started laughing and they all
sat at the table and when Marion stopped laughing she refilled
the coffee cups and Harry finally slowed enough to take a
couple of deep breaths and got hung up in a tune and his
consciousness was absorbed by, and involved in, the tune and
he half closed his eyes and nodded and finger popped as he
listened, Sheeit, he may look like a fool but he shure do
sound betta this way . . . damn, that tickles me, and Marion
started laughing and Tyrone continued giggling and Harry
looked at him with his cool expression, Be cool man, and
went back to nodding and finger popping and Tyrone C. Love
finished his second cup of coffee and the hinges on his eyes
sprung the lids open and he started sipping on his third cup
of coffee and lit a cigarette and leaned back in his chair, Blow
your ass off, baby, and started nodding and finger popping
and Harry, with his eyes still half closed, extended his arm
out to the side, the palm up, and Tyrone slapped it, Sheeit,
we/s gonna make it baby, and Harry slapped his, Yeahhhhhh,
and Marion leaned against Harry and he put an arm around
her as they listened and felt the strength of determination
pound through them, occasionally nodding toward the clock,

waiting for the time, the time that was now going fleetingly by, to step forth to a new dimension. . . .

The first day of the diet was over. Well, almost. Sara sat in her viewing chair, sipping on a glass of water, concentrating on the show on the screen and ignoring the refrigerator which was whispering enticingly to her. She finished the water, her tenth glass, thinking thin. She refilled the glass from the pitcher on the table, the pitcher that replaced the chocolate box. If eight glasses of water was good, then sixteen is twice as good and maybe I/ll lose twenty pounds the first week. She looked at the glass of water and shrugged, If I stay up all night I cant make sixteen. I drink any more Im going to be up all night anyway. She sipped the water, thinking thin. The refrigerator reminded her of the matzoh in the cupboard. Without looking at it she told it to mind its own business. What do you have to do with the cupboard? Its bad enough you have to remind me about the herring you got but the cupboard is too much already. She sipped some more water and stared at the screen and shut her ears to the refrigerator, but he managed to penetrate the barrier and tell her that the herring, the beautiful and delicious herring in sour cream, will go bad if she doesn't eat it soon and it would be a shame to let such good herring tidbits go to waste. So listen to Mr. Concerned. Youre worried so much about the food going bad why do you do it? Thats your job *meshuggener*. Youre supposed to keep the food from going bad. You do your job an the herring will be fine thank you. She sipped some more water—*thin, thin, thin, thin*. Too bad I dont have a scale. I could weigh myself and see how its working. Eh, right now it would groan. All this water. Anymore and I/ll float away. The program ended and Sara yawned and blinked her eyes. She thought briefly of staying up and watching the late show, but quickly ignored that thought. Her body was aching and was crying for sleep. It was a day. The hair is getting closer to *the* red. At least now theres a nodding acquaintance. She drank more water—*thin, thin.* The form . . . eh, a nothing. Zipping through like a whirling dervish, youll excuse the expression. And the eggs and grapefruit, one, two, three, and some lettuce thank you. A long, tiring day. Almost too tired to go to bed. She suddenly remembered the refrigerator, If he tries to grab me I/ll hit him, and not in the *tuchis.* She finished her water— *thin, th— zophtic, zophtic, zophtic.* She stood up and listened to the sloshing, I feel like a goldfish bowl. She turned off the set, put the pitcher and glass in the sink and, with head high and shoulders back, she walked past the refrigerator swerving neither to the left nor right, her eyes fixed steadfastly ahead at her goal, knowing that she had conquered the enemy and that he shook with fear—listen to him grumbling and rumbling, shaking in his boots already—and she walked like a queen, a television queen, to her bedchamber. She slowly, and luxuriously, lowered herself onto the bed and stretched out, thanking God for such a nice bed. Her worn nightgown felt so silky and smooth and cool and softness seemed to surround her, and a feeling of peace and joy gently spread out from her stomach, like small ripples in a pond, through her body and rested ever so lightly on her eyes as she floated off into a joyous and refreshing slumber.

Marion hustled them out of the house early so Harry and Tyrone were among the first to show up for work. Actually it didnt make any difference because so few shaped up that everyone was put to work. They took another dexie before leaving so they were very quick and ready to go. It was a hot and humid night and the sweat poured off them as they tossed bundles of papers into the trucks, but they just tossed and laughed and giggled and talked, doing as much work as any six men there. When their first truck was loaded they went over to another one to help, and the guys stood back and shook their heads as Harry and Tyrone tossed the bundles of papers around like it was a privilege and a game . . . a fun game. One of the guys told them to cool it, Youll fuck this thing up man. Like how? Shit, they push us hard enough as it is, if you guys start racin like this theyll expect this every night. One of the other guys handed each of them a can of cold beer, Here, take it easy and cool off. We come here pretty steady, you know? an we want ta keep it like it is. Sheeit, I dig what you say baby. We be cool. We doan want the man to lay a heavy han on nobody jim. Yeah, Harry nodded an swallowed half the beer then wiped his mouth with the back of his hand, goddamn thats good. Cuts through the blotter I got in my mouth. The other guys slapped Harry and Tyrone on the back and everybody was happy, and when the trucks were finished Harry and Tyrone bought the next dozen cans of beer and passed them around while they waited for the next line of trucks to back in. Later on a few bottles of wine were passed around and Harry and Tyrone were feeling pretty good, the alcohol taking the sharp edge off the dexies. They worked a couple of hours extra and were as happy as hogs in shit figuring out just how much they would make that night. The kick in the ass came when they found out they wouldnt get paid that night, but would have to wait until the end of the week to get their checks. Sheeit. Now aint that a shame? Aint that a mutha fuckin shame? Ah fuck it man. What the hell. This way we/ll get our bread all at once an wont have to worry about pissin it away before we get enough for the piece. Yeah, maybe so, but workins weird enough, but workin without getting the braid is some-

thin else jim. Dont sweat it, Ty my boy, just go home an take
those downers Marions gave ya an get some rest. A couple
more nights an we got our piece. Harry extended his hand
and Tyrone slapped it, You goddamn right baby, and Harry
slapped his and they left the newspaper plant, hurrying to get
home before they got caught in the early morning rush hour,
and the sunlight.

Marion languidly tidied up the apartment after they left,
humming and singing to herself. The apartment was small
and there wasnt much to do other than clean the cups and
coffee pot and put them away. She sat on the couch, hugging
herself as she listened to the music. She had the strangest
feeling inside, a feeling that was unfamiliar but not threatening. She thought about it, tried to analyze it, but she couldnt
quite identify it. For some reason she kept thinking of the
many, many madonnas she had seen in the museums of
Europe, especially in Italy, and her mind was filled with the
bright blues and brilliant light of the Italian renaissance and
she thought of the Mediterranean and the color of the sea
and sky and how, as she looked at the isle of Capri from the
restaurant on the top of the hill in Naples, she suddenly
realized why the Italians were masters of light and why they
could use blue like no one before or since. She remembered
sitting on the patio of that restaurant under the net awning,
the sun warming a new life into her and firing her imagination and experiencing what it must have been like to sit
there a few hundred years ago in that light and color and
listen to Vivaldis strings singing and vibrating through that
air, and Gabrielis brass canzones pulsing from the nearby
towers, and sit in a cathedral with the sun bursting through
the stained windows and gleaming on the carved wood of the
pews listening to a Monteverdi Mass. It was then, for the first

time in her life, that she felt alive, really and truly alive, like she had a reason for existing, a purpose in her life and she had realized that purpose and would now pursue it and dedicate her life to it. All that summer and fall she painted, mornings, afternoons, evenings, then walked around the streets that were still echoing the music of the masters, and every stone, every pebble seemed to have a life and reason of its own and she somehow felt, though vaguely, a part of that reason. Some nights she would sit in the café with other young artists and poets and musicians and who knows what else, drinking wine and talking and laughing and discussing and arguing and life was exciting and tangible and crisp like the clear Mediterranean sunlight. Then as the grayness of winter slowly seeped down from the north the energy and inspiration seemed to ooze from her as paint from a tube and now when she looked at a bare canvas it was only a bare canvas, a piece of material stretched over a few pieces of wood, it was no longer a painting waiting to be painted. It was just canvas. She went further south. Sicily. North Africa. Trying to follow the sun to the past, the very recent past, but all she found was herself. She went back to Italy, gave away all her paintings, equipment, books and what nots. She went back to that restaurant on the hill in Naples and sat there for endless hours for a week, looking at Vesuvius, Capri, the bay, the sky, trying, with the desperation of the dying, to reawaken those old feelings, trying with jewels of sparkling wine to rekindle the flame that half fired her imagination just a short lifetime ago, and though the wine sparkled in the sunlight, and the moonlight, the once blazing fire was extinguished and Marion finally succumbed to the stone coldness within her. She shivered as she remembered leaving Italy and coming back to the States, back to the grossness of her family, back to the dulled brilliance of her life. She shivered again, involuntarily, as she sat on the couch, looking back through so many miserably unhappy yesterdays, then smiled and hugged herself tighter, not from coldness nor fear nor despair, but joy. All that was in the near and distant past. Over with. Gone. Once more her life had reason . . . purpose. Once more there was a direction for her to follow. A need for her energies. She and Harry were going to recapture those blues of the sky and sea and feel the warmth of desire that had been rekindled. They were going to a new renaissance.

Sara slowly awakened in the middle of the night and though she tried for many long seconds to fight it, eventually she got out of bed and stumbled to the bathroom to relieve the urgent pressure of her bladder. She tried to blink her eyes open, but they were unyielding to her attempts and so she kept them almost completely closed as she sat thinking thin. Though still partially asleep, her mind clouded and fogged, she was still aware of the water passing through her body and the reason for its abundance—*thin, thin, thin*— she suddenly straightened up—*zophtic, zophtic, zophtic*— Why should I settle for second best? Still half asleep she stood for a few seconds watching and listening to the whirling water in the bowl with joy because she knew that not only unwanted pounds were going down the drain and ultimately to the ocean, but an old life, a life of loneliness, a life of futility, of being unnecessary. Sometimes her Harry needed her, but . . . She listened to the music of the water filling the flush tank and smiled through her haze of partial wakefulness, knowing that freshness was filling her and soon she would be a new Sara Goldfarb. The fresh water in the bowl was crystal clear and looked cool and refreshing, even in a toilet bowl it looked cool. Clean is clean and new is new. . . . Still I/ll drink from the faucet, thank you. Sara went back to bed, a slight bounce to her step. The sheets felt cool and refreshing as she lay down and rubbed her fingertips up and down on the silky smoothness of her nightgown, sinking deeper into a smile, a smile that she saw reflected on the inner surface of her eyelids. She breathed slowly and deeply then sighed long and happily as she floated in the weightless joy between sleep and wakefulness and dozily felt the sensations tingle through her body and then seem to disappear somewhere in her toes as she cuddled into the light fluffiness of her old pillow and kissed herself goodnight and sailed eagerly into the comfort of her dreams.

Harry was still wired when he got back to Marions pad. She gave him a couple of sleeping pills and they sat on the couch for a while, smoking a joint, until Harry started to yawn and then they went to bed and slept through the dreary heat of the day.

Today the hair was perfect. Such a color. It was so gorgeous it makes you want to jump out a window. Now you should hurry up and get on the show before the roots grow out. Believe me, I want to, but Im glad theyre waiting until I lose more weight. When I walk across the stage its a hush youll hear. I/ll look over my shoulder and say I vant to be alone. So now youre Swedish American? They chuckled and Sara went back to her apartment to see how her red dress would look, now, with her red hair. She put it on, and the gold shoes, and posed and twisted and turned in front of the mirror, holding the back of the dress as close together as possible. It seemed to come a little closer. She could feel that she lost weight. She wiggled and squealed and smiled at her reflection, then threw herself a kiss, Youre gorgeous, a living doll. She wiggled and squealed again, kissed her hand then grinned at her reflection, A Greta Garbo youre not, but youre no Wallace Beery either. She looked over her shoulder in the direction of the refrigerator, See, Mr. Smarty-pants, Mr. Fancy Dancy Herring Tidbits? Already its almost fitting. A few more inches, more or less, and I/ll fit in nice and snug thank you very much. Keep your herring. Whose needing? I love my egg and grapefruit. And lettuce. She posed and pranced for a while longer, then decided to eat her lunch and go out and get some sun. She took the egg, grape-fruit and lettuce out of the refrigerator, an expression of smug superiority on her face. She tossed her head contemptuously at the refrigerator and hit the door with her *tuchis*. So, hows by you Mr. Big Mouth? You see how I look and youre speech-less. She vamped in front of the refrigerator then proceeded to fix her lunch, humming, singing, wiggling, feeling safe and cocky. When she finished her lunch she washed the dishes, put them away, got her chair and, before leaving the apartment, kissed her fingertips and patted the refrigerator, Dont cry, dolly. As my Harry would say, Be cool. She chuckled, turned off the television, and left the apartment and joined the ladies sitting in the sun. She put her chair in a good spot and closed her eyes and faced the sun like the others. They didnt change positions as they talked, but continued to look straight ahead in the direction of the sun, turning their chairs occasionally so the sun would always be shining directly on their faces. Know yet what show? Are you hearing anything? How could I hear? I just mailed it yesterday. Maybe tomorrow. It might even be longer. So whats the difference what show? Thats how I feel. Its the television thats the important thing. Theyll let you know ahead of time? What are they going to do, tell her after the show? You can bring friends? Sara shrugged, So how should I know? They should let you bring at least a *schlepper*. Whose going to carry all those prizes? Believe me I/ll get them home. Especially Robert Redford. For him I dont need a *schlepper*. The women chuckled and nodded as they continued to stare at the sun, and women who were walking by stopped to talk with Sara and by the time she had been sitting there for half an hour all the women in the neighborhood were knotted around her talking, asking, chuckling, hoping, wishing. Sara felt warmed not only by the sun but by all the attention she was suddenly receiving. She felt like a star.

Marion bought some sketch pads and pencils and charcoal. She also bought a sharpener and a spray can of fixit. She wanted to buy some pastel chalks, but for some reason what they had didnt appeal to her so she let it go for now. She could always get them later. Maybe in a few days she would get down town and roam around the large art supply stores and smell and touch the canvas, the stretcher strips, easels and brushes and just sort of browse. She had no intention of buying any oils until she had a studio, but she did want to do some watercolors. Thats where her head was really at right now. She could feel that light, delicacy within her that she knew she could transform into beautiful and fragile water-colors. Yes, that was what she liked most about watercolors, their fragility. She couldnt wait. She had this incredible urge to paint a single rose standing in a slender vase of trans-lucent blue, Venetian glass, or perhaps lying on a piece of velvet. Yes, that would be lovely too. With just a hint of shadow. So delicate and fragile that you can smell its fra-grance. Well we/ll see. Perhaps in a few days. But for now some sketching to help to re-animate the eye and hand. She felt an almost uncontrollable urge to draw everything she saw as she walked the street, everything had such a vibrance, such a life. She quickly noticed the shapes of noses, eyes, ears; the planes of faces, the cheek bones, chins; the curve of necks; and hands. She loved hands. You can tell so much from hands and the way the fingers are shaped and primarily the way people hold and treat their hands. She was quite young, a child, the first time she saw a picture of Michelangelos Creation and when she saw the detail of God giving life to Adam the image was immediately and irrevocably implanted in her mind. The more she studied painting in the later years the more impressed she was with the simple conception behind that image and the incredible story in the attitude of the two hands. It was an attitude that she tried to incorporate in her work and every now and then she felt she had succeeded, at least to some degree. She wanted to simply, and directly, tell the viewer something about the painting with the attitude of the object whether human or otherwise, to transpose her inner feelings to the surface of the canvas . . . to express her attitude through her art, to have her sensitivity seen and felt.

The following days were pretty much the same for Marion, Harry and Ty. Harry and Ty got wired at night and worked their asses off, slowing down as much as possible when the other guys got on their cases, and then taking a few sleeping pills and sleeping through the day. Just once being a habit with Harry he was accustomed to the routine by the second night so when he got home in the morning he made love to Marion for a couple of hours before taking a couple of her sleeping pills and crapping out. Now I know why you lose weight on these things, you ball the weight off. You know, its just the opposite for some men. Yeah? Thats right. It makes them completely impotent and in some cases indifferent. Tougha lucka joe. That aint my problem. Comere, and Harry pulled her down on the bed and Marion giggled as he kissed her on the neck. What are you doing? Harry snapped

his head back and looked at her, If you dont know I cant
be doin it right. They laughed and Harry kissed her on the
neck, the shoulder and the breast and moistened his lips and
kissed her stomach, I want to see if I can wear it out. Which
one? How many ya got? and they both laughed and giggled
and passed a loving morning until it was time to sleep the
day away.

At night, while Harry was at work, Marion sat on the
couch with her sketch pad and pencils and charcoal. She
crossed her legs under her and hugged herself and closed her
eyes and allowed her mind to drift into the future where she
and Harry were together, always, and the coffee house was
always full and a feature article had been written about it
in the NEW YORKER and it became an *in* place and all
the art critics came to sit and drink coffee and eat pastry and
look at the paintings by the great artists of tomorrow that
had been discovered by Marion; and artists and poets and
musicians and writers sat around talking and discussing and
from time to time Marion would display her paintings and all
the other painters loved them and even the critics loved
her work and praised its sensitivity and awareness, and when
she was not at the coffee house she could see herself in her
studio painting, the light from the paintings dazzling the eye,
and then she would pick up her sketch pad and look around
for something to sketch and nothing seemed to be exactly
what she wanted to do and so she tried to set up a still life
with objects from the kitchen or living room, but nothing
seemed to excite or inspire her so she went back to her fan-
tasies and enoyed the comfort and reassurance they gave her
and they were more real than sitting on the couch looking at
the pencils, the charcoal and the virgin sketch pad.

Each day Sara checked the mailbox very carefully, but still no reply from the McDick Corp. But she stuck to the diet anyway, but it was becoming harder and harder even with eating a whole cup of lettuce. She spent the day with Ada and the ladies getting the sun and still they came and asked and she showed them her red hair but still nothing new happened. When the sun went behind the building some of the ladies went in the house, especially those with the reflectors, but Sara and a few others stayed outside enjoying the cool shade. Even then it was not easy to forget about the food and just enjoy the special attention she got as a soon to be contestant on a quiz show, her mind drifting to images of lox and bagels and delicious cheese danish that were so sharp she could smell them and actually taste them and the ladies voices drifted by as she smiled and licked her lips. But the nights were worse as she sat, alone, in her viewing chair, watching the television, with her back to the refrigerator hearing him murmuring to her, spasms of fear knotting her stomach and a heaviness squeezing her chest. It was bad enough him bugging her, but then the herring started too. A couple of *yentas* already. Never stop. All the time talk, talk. Her ears started to feel like they were under water. I feel good, so why dont you go haunt Maurrie the butcher. Bite his thumbs off. Youll do everybody a favor. —*in sour cream with onions and spice, hmmmmmm*—I dont hear you—*with a hot bialy . . . or onion roll*—I like Kaiser, thank you, and anyway Im not hungry—*and that growling in your stomach keeps me awake*—growling, schmowling, thats just my stomach thinking thin—*and the lox is red like your hair with the cream cheese and bagel*—who needs it? One more day and I/ll have a meat patty for lunch and you can drop dead, thank you very much, and Sara drank another glass of water—*zophtic, zophtic*—and put the glass in the sink and tossed her red head at the refrigerator, shook her *tuchis* in his face, and went to bed. She was getting up a couple of times a night now and was almost tempted to stop, or maybe cut down, on the water, but she kept thinking of all the pounds that were going down the drain and she continued to drink, drink, drink, water all day long, not too disturbed by the nocturnal visits to the bathroom. But now she was dreaming. Sometimes a couple of dreams in one night. Like seeing chickens flying through her room, but they were neatly plucked and roasted to a golden brown with little balls of kasha on their backs. And then that roast beef. It kept rolling down the hill threatening to crush her but somehow it just whirled by, just missing her by a few inches, dragging behind it a gravy boat filled with rich brown gravy, and bowls of mashed potatoes and chocolate covered cherries with cherry juice filling. A couple nights of dreaming and Sara decided enough already. She got the name of the doctor from her lady friend and made an appointment. I dont know from diet pills, but eggs and grapefruit I/ve had up to here thank you.

Harry had a hollow, sinking feeling in his gut, which was reflected on his face, when Marion told him she was seeing the shrink for dinner and a concert. Why do you have to see him for krists sake. You can cut the son of a bitch loose. I dont want him mentioning to my parents that I have stopped therapy. I want that fifty dollars a week. Marion looked tenderly at Harry and spoke as gently as possible, with feeling and care. Sweetheart, I am not going to sleep with him— Harry shrugged and threw a hand up in the air, Yeah, youre just—I told him I have the curse so hes planning on going home after the concert. Harry tried, desperately, not to show his feelings, but he failed and his chin kept getting lower

and lower and he started getting bugged with himself for not
being able to stop himself from sulking. Whats that supposed
to mean? Marion smiled, then started chuckling slightly hoping to snap Harry out of it, but Harry was unyielding. Suddenly Marion hugged him and squealed with absolute glee,
O Harry, youre jealous. Harry halfheartedly tried to push
her away, but stopped trying after a moment. Marion kissed
him on the cheek and hugged him, Come on sweetheart, put
your arms around me . . . come on . . . please??? please????
She lifted Harrys arms and placed them on her shoulders
and he grudgingly left them there for a moment then did not
resist as she pushed them down around her and snuggled into
him. Eventually he exerted a little pressure and held her
closer and Marion sighed and nestled her head into his
chest then kissed him on the lips, the cheek, the ear, the neck
and forced him to squirm and giggle, and continued until he
was laughing and begging her to stop, Comeon, stop . . . stop,
you crazy bitch or I/ll biteya on the chroat, and he started
kissing her on the neck and tickling her and she joined him
in laughing and they were both panting and begging the other
one to stop until they eventually laughed themselves into
submission and they stopped, Marion sitting on Harrys lap,
both hanging loose like rag dolls, tears of laughter tickling
their cheeks. They wiped their eyes and face and took a
couple of deep breaths, breaking out in chuckles from time
to time. Suppose he doesnt believe you about the curse? O
Harry, tapping him on the nose, dont be so naive. What do
you mean? I mean simply that I know how to handle the
situation. He will accept whatever I tell him whether he
believes me or not. He wouldnt think of forcing the issue.
Hes not the type. Suppose he was the type? Then, my dear, I
would not be going out with him. Harry sweetheart, I am
not a fool. She chuckled, I may be crazy but Im not stupid.
Yeah??? Harry looking at her with a dubious expression on

his face, Why doesnt he take his wife to the concert? Shes
probably at a meeting of the PTA, Marion shrugged, how
should I know? He likes to be seen in fashionable places with
a beautiful young woman. Hes a typical john. It makes him
feel good. Yeah???? Well, personally I think anybody who sees
a shrink ought to have his head examined. O Harry, thats
dreadful, chuckling, giggling. Then why are you laughing?
I dont know. Out of sympathy I guess. Anyway, I have to get
ready to go. She got up and started for the bedroom, then
turned around and came back to Harry, who had gotten up
too, and put her arms around him and hugged him tightly
and put her head on his shoulder, closed her eyes and
sighed. . . . O Harry, Im so glad you were upset, not because
it makes you feel bad sweetheart, but it makes me feel good
to know that you care that much for me. Care for you? Now
whos insulting who, eh? You think I was playing games when
I told you I love you? No, no, sweetheart, I believe you. With
all my heart I believe you. But I guess I like the way it looks
on your face. Okay, okay, we/ll cool it. She smiled up at him
for a few long moments, then kissed him on the lips and went
to the bedroom to dress, I promise I/ll think of you the entire
evening. Thats great. I/ll think of you too eating and drinking wine and listening to the music as Im working my ass off.
Harry laughed, I guess thats better than you working your
ass off, and he continued laughing. O Harry, thats dreadful,
and she chuckled and laughed with relief as she dressed for
the evening.

Marion met Arnold at the small bar of an intimate con-
tinental restaurant on the east side. He stood as she approached and extended a hand. She took his hand and his
seat. How are you Marion? Fine Arnold, how are you? Well,
thank you. The usual? Please. He ordered a Cinzano with a

dash of bitters and a twist for her. You look exquisite, as usual. Thank you. She smiled and let him light her cigarette. Soon they were advised that their table was ready and the maitre d' led them to the table and asked Monsieur and Madam how they were this evening and they smiled and nodded politely, as one does to a maitre d', and told him they were fine. Marion relaxed into her chair and felt her body absorb the atmosphere. The thing she enjoyed about Arnold was his taste in restaurants. They were always small, intimate and chic, with exceptional food, something you very rarely find in America. The elegance of her surroundings had more to do with the glow she felt than the aperitif she sipped almost continuously. Im disappointed that you are indisposed. Well, theres nothing much I can do about that, she smiled, Freud notwithstanding. Is Anita out of town, or something? Why do you ask? No reason, really, just curious. He looked at her for a moment before answering, No, but she will be involved in something most of the night. Newsmen were there yesterday taking her picture, along with a few other "members" in the garden. Can I ask you a personal question Arnold? Certainly. How did you and Anita ever manage to have any children— She held up her hand, Im not trying to be facetious, honestly, its just that the two of you always seem to be in different places at the same time. Arnold sat a little straighter, Well, actually theres no mystery about that. I didn't mean about the children, Marion was smiling, I *do* know about that. Why do you ask these questions, its very curious. What, exactly, do you mean by all this? Marion shrugged and finished chewing her escargot, Nothing other than what I said. Im curious. Marion sipped a bit of the white bordeaux he had ordered as he scrutinized her, O, this is marvelous. She took another sip then went back to her escargot. Arnold was still frowning slightly, When people reach a particular point in life, when they have attained a certain degree of success . . . a substantial degree, their interests broaden and their perspective widens. I imagine with Anita its an inner need for fulfillment, her civic work, a need to find her own identity. But what really interests me is why you should be asking a question like that. Its so obvious that you are trying to vicariously fulfill the lack in your life by playing a substitute role, substituting yourself in the role as my wife. O Arnold, dont be gauche. She finished her wine and immediately the waiter was there to refill her glass. Arnold nodded politely at him. And anyway, Im not in the least worried about my identity, she smiled at him and patted his hand, really Im not. She had finished her escargot and dabbed at the garlic butter with a piece of roll. Ive started painting again and I feel marvelous. You have? She had finished and the waiter took the empty plates and she sat back and smiled at Arnold. Thats right. I havent actually finished any canvases yet, but Im working. I can feel the paintings just welling up within me, begging to come out. Well . . . I would very much like to see your work. It would give me, I feel, a tremendous insight into your subconscious. I should think that you would be familiar enough with that by now. Well, its not exactly a stranger to me, but this would be approaching it from a different angle, a different point of view so to speak. You see here most of your defenses would not only be down, but the symbols would be far more obvious than in the dreams and it would give wonderful corroboration to the conclusions formed from analyzing the free association. Well, maybe sometime I/ll invite you up to see my etchings, and Marion chuckled, but not too loudly, as she forked a little meat off her frogs legs.

After the concert they stopped in for a nightcap. Arnold didnt drink his scotch with any particular interest, but Marion loved to roll the chartreuse around in her mouth before swallowing it. That was a marvelous concert, just marvelous, and she had a reflective look on her face as if she were still hearing the music, especially the Mahler. Whenever I hear his Resurrection Symphony, more than any other, I start to understand why they say he took romanticism to its ultimate in music. I feel all welled up inside like Ive just run up a flower covered hillside and the breeze is blowing my hair in the wind and Im whirling around and the sunlight is glancing off the wings of birds and the leaves of trees, and Marion closed her eyes and sighed. I agree, it was a definitive performance. I think he really got to the heart of Mahlers ambivalence and understands how he unconsciously projected it into his music. Marion frowned, What ambivalence? The basic conflicts in his life. His compromise with his jewish heritage and his willingness to renounce it to further his career. His constant conflict as a conductor when he wanted to compose, but needing the money to live. Its obvious the manner in which he changes keys that he was unaware that these conflicts were responsible for those changes. Just as they were responsible for his changes in attitude toward God. But that was over by the time he wrote the second symphony. Ostensibly, but I have listened very carefully to his music, and analyzed it thoroughly, and there is no doubt that though he may have said certain things, and perhaps even believed them in his conscious mind, that his subconscious had not as yet resolved the conflict. Arnold breathed deeply, Mahlers music is extremely interesting from an analytical point of view. I find it very stimulating. Marion smiled and put her empty glass on the table, Well, I still love his music. It sort of makes me happy to be sad. She sighed and smiled again, I really have to be going Arnold. I have been very busy lately and am tired. Fine. He drove her home and before she got out of the car he smilingly smirked, I/ll give you a call in a couple of weeks. That should be about right. He kissed her and she kissed him back and left the car. He waited until she was in the building before driving away. Marion lit a joint as soon as she got in the apartment, then changed her clothes, then put Mahlers Kindertotenlieder on the phonograph and sat on the couch with her sketch pad and pencils. She continually adjusted the pad on her lap, taking another poke of the joint until it was half gone then put it out, and tried to work up some sort of image to transfer onto the sketch pad. That should be easy enough to do. Mahler . . . good pot . . . it should all come together. She realized she was pushing too hard and so she just sat back and relaxed and waited for it to come. Still it was a blank. If only she had a model. Thats what was needed. A model. She could feel the drawing begging to come out, her need to express herself giving her energy, but she couldnt seem to unloose the gates and organize that energy. She jumped up and grabbed a couple of womens magazines from the table and started rapidly thumbing through them marking all the ads and articles with pictures of babies and mothers and, finding a few that suited her, tore them out and used them as models and started sketching, at first tentatively, then with increasing speed and assurance. The mothers and babies were placed in various positions and juxtapositions, with varying expressions, the expressions becoming more and more melancholy. She very rapidly did a sketch of a child in a contorted position, a look of silent pain on its face, and the mothers expression quickly began to look like the man in the Edvard Munch woodcut and Marion looked at the sketch very carefully from every angle and felt excited and inspired by it as she felt a deep identification with both figures. She looked very carefully at the babys pained face then drew another baby next to it, about a year older, yet the expression remained the same. She continued to draw the child, in each drawing the child was a year older and as she progressed the drawings became more skillful, more lifelike, more filled with emotion and she began to sketch little birthday candles under the drawings showing the age of the child and then the features became more distinct and the hair long and black, the same silent pain on her face, and then she started to blossom and become a woman and she was slowly transformed from a pretty child to a lovely girl and then a beautiful woman but always that haunted and pained expression on her face, and then she stopped drawing and looked at the beautiful woman on the pad looking back at her, a woman of long flowing lines and curves, classic features, dark shining hair, her inner pain reflected in her dark and penetrating eyes, and then she left a wide space and sketched another figure, a figure of uncertain age, but certainly much older than the last figure, but the lines and curves the same, the body the same, the features of the face the same until it suddenly turned into the anguished expression of the Munch figure. Marion stared at the figure and suddenly became aware of the silence. She got up and played the record again, then sat back on the couch and looked at her drawings. They excited her.

When the time came for Harry and Tyrone to stop working and collect their money they were in such a habit of popping the dexies and making it through the night, then crashing behind the downers, that they felt they could work forever, but they had too much sense to allow that feeling to become a thought no less a reality. Because of their energy, and the compulsive need to work that the dexedrine generated, they had put in a few hours overtime, wanting to make as much as possible in as short a time as possible. They had declared twenty-five dependents so their checks were for the maximum amount. They cashed them in the bar across from the plant, had a few beers as they counted the money a few times, grinning and slapping each other on the palm, Sheeit, aint

that some pretty lookin braid? and Tyrone fanned the bills
and waved them back and forth. Harry punched him on the
arm, We did it man, we fuckin did it. We got the bread for a
piece. You fuckin well right, baby, sos lets not sit in no bar
with it. Lets take care a business. Right on man, and they gave
each other five again and split. They stopped at a phone booth
on the corner and Tyrone called Brody. Harry leaned against
the booth, smoking and watching the smoke being absorbed
by the air, humming an up tempo tune, nodding his head
and snapping his fingers in time to the music, occasionally
mumbling, Yeah baby, go, but be cool an— Sheeit! Aint that
a mutha fuckin shame!!! Whats happenin man? He say a
piece of good shit gonna be about five bills. Balls! That means
we need about another hundred. Thas right jim. He say
maybe four fifty, but, and Tyrone shrugged. Well man, lets
not panic. We can always scrounge up a hundred bucks.
We/ve been around long enough for that. Yeah, but you
knows what happens when you picks up a buck here and a
buck there. The first one gone by the time you gets the
second. Harry nodded his head and agreed. An Brody say
they got some fine shit now too jim. Real fine. Fuck! and
Harry flipped his cigarette out onto the street, then jerked
his head back for a moment, Hey, whats the matta with me
fa krists sake? I know where we can get the bread, Marion.
You think she give us the braid? Sure. No sweat. An we/ll be
able to pay her back by tonight anyway, right? Right on baby,
and they gave each other five. Lets go. They went to Marions
pad and Harry quickly ran down what had happened. So all
we need is another hundred and we/re in business baby, and
by this time tonight we/ll not only pay you back, but we/ll
be on our way to that coffee house. Marion smiled, Im sure
my broker would say that it is a good investment. Now that Im
working again I need a gallery. I/ll cash a check in the market.
Groovy baby. Ahll call Brody an tell him wes on our way. No,

not from here Ty. Lets wait till we get to a phone booth.
Tyrone shrugged, Okay jim. Marion left and was back in
about fifteen minutes with the money. Harry hugged and
kissed her, See you later baby, after everythings straight. I
dont want to come around here carrying any weight. I dont
want your place to be hot. You sure as hell doan feel that way
bout mah pad. Hey man, you are not Marion. Ah know, she
even paler than you. Krist, I have to hear this for the rest of
the day. Marion laughed, Hes as bad as you. They all laughed,
I thought you were on my side. Marion kissed him on the
cheek, Next week is love your buddy week, remember? Hey
baby, lez go: Okay, okay. Harry kissed Marion and he and
Tyrone split. Tyrone went downtown to Brodys while Harry
bought a supply of glassine bags and milk sugar and went
to Tyrones pad to wait. This was just the beginning.

The refrigerator snickered as Sara spread a large piece of
cream cheese on the bottom half of the bagel. Go ahead and
laugh Mr. Smarty Pants. We/ll see who laughs last. She stuck
her tongue out at the refrigerator and took a large, slow, very
slow, bite out of the bagel so richly smothered with cream
cheese, and smacked her lips and licked them, And Im telling
you something else Mr. Chuckles, for lunch I/ll eat the
herring, and maybe I wont eat it all, but save some for a nosh.
Sara hummed out loud as she lovingly spread cream cheese on
the other half of the bagel and raised her eyebrows and looked
disdainfully at the refrigerator who was still smirking, thinking he had won the contest, that he had defeated Sara Goldfarb in the war of the calories, but Sara just shook her head,
A poo, poo on you Mr. c.i.a. You think maybe you won a war
but I outfoxed you Mr. Know It All. The refrigerator laughed
and told her he was too old to believe her con job and Sara
dismissed his words with a wave of her hand, I know youre old,

I hear you grind and grunt and groan all the time, but youre
not such a big shot you think you are. The refrigerator
laughed out loud as Sara dunked a corner of her cheese danish
and carefully placed it in her mouth so as not to drip any coffee
on the table, That doesnt look like an egg or grapefruit to me,
and he laughed even louder. So enjoy, enjoy, Mr. Empty
Head. I/ll finish my breakfast and then I/ll go out to my
public. Maybe youd better sew the seams on your dress,
theyre splitting, hahahaha. So haha to you. When Im *zophtic*
and on the television I wont even talk to you. I/ll have
someone else throw you out with the junk. I wont dirty my
hands. Huh, and she tossed her head and went back to humming as she finished her danish then washed the dish and cup
and got ready to join the ladies on the street getting the sun.
She passed by the refrigerator, who was abashed by her last
remark, in triumph. The other ladies were waiting for Sara
and when she arrived they gave her the special place, the
place where the sun shone the longest. Sara sat and immediately the speculation about what show she would be on continued as they all anxiously waited for the mailman to see if
today would be the day she would get something in the mail.

Harry knew that Tyrone would be a few hours so he settled
down with a couple of joints, cigarettes, and the rinkydink
radio Tyrone had on the table. He sure as hell didnt dig being
away from the action for so long, but he knew he couldnt
wait in the coffee shop that long. He was too conspicuous. He
carefully placed the envelopes and sugar on the table then
frowned and thought for a moment about what would happen
if the man came in and saw the "paraphinalia" and looked
around for some place to stash it, but gave up in a couple of
minutes because there just didnt seem to be a good place and
then it all seemed unnecessary, And what the hells the big

deal, ya cant get busted for having a pound of milk sugar and some stamp envelopes. He took a few pokes of a joint then put it out, lit a cigarette then sat back to listen to the music. After a few minutes the music didnt sound as fuzzy as it had, and the longer he listened to that radio, and the more pot he smoked, the better the music sounded. As a matter of fact it wasnt half bad. Well . . . half of what? When somethings as bad as that sonofabitch, any improvement is something. Half bad of that is terrible, but, Harry shrugged, eh, its somethin. I guess its better than nothin. Anyway, itll help pass the time. Wont be long Tyll be back and we/ll be baggin the shit and rakin in the dough and we/ll have a couple guys peddlin the shit for us and then we can go for weight . . . yeah, a pound of pure right from the italians and we can have some fuckin operation goin man, GOLDFARB & LOVE INCORPORATED, none a that Inc. shit, and we/ll have everything in black and white, hahahaha, an equal opportunity employer. Shit, who knows how far we/ll be able to go. We/ll be cool and stay straight and we/ll have it knocked. In no time we/ll be coppin that pound of pure. . . .

Harry had just finished counting the money and Tyrone double checked him, Right on baby, seventy-five Gs. Good. I sure as hell dont want to make any mistakes with those cats man. They dont believe in honest mistakes. Not less theys their own. They can get very bugged. Okay, lets get it packed. I gotta get goin. I dont wanta be late. They packed it neatly in an attaché case, locked it, and Harry put on a light brown top coat and a dark brown hat, See ya later man. Okay baby, be cool. Harry locked the car doors and made sure the windows were closed before starting the drive to Kennedy. He kept the music low so it wouldnt be distracting, and glanced at the briefcase beside him with the seventy-five grand, smiling smugly and shrugging slightly in his tan top coat, wondering if the people on the streets and in the other cars were looking at him and wondering who he was and what he was up to, and then he realized that they didnt pay too much attention to him because he was being so cool he just melted into the traffic unnoticed. That was the way it should be. Never be noticed. Thats why he was driving a Chevy instead of a Mercedes. Thats why he made the contacts with the white guys and Tyrone made them with the black guys. Always blending in. Thats why they were successful. Thats why they were on the top and would never get busted. The man didnt know them from any other dude walking the streets. He drove cautiously but not overcautiously. He didnt believe in playing scared pool. Thats when you really get them down on you. No, you just move along with traffic and dont do nothin to attract attention. He merged easily with the traffic, looking from time to time at the people in the cars around him, wondering what the people would do if they knew he was Harry Goldfarb, one of the big drug distributors in the city, and that he had an attaché case with seventy-five grand in it on the seat beside him and he was going to pick up a pound of pure???? Theyd shit a brick. Thats what theyd do, theyd shit a brick. Probably wouldnt believe it. Bet they think Im just another successful business man. Maybe a stock broker . . . an investments counselor. Yeah, thats what I am . . . sort of, an investments counselor. I bet I could go up to anybody on the streets and tell them Im a big time drug distributor and theyd laugh and say, Yeah, and Im Al Capone, hahaha. Yeah, bet I could go into a police station with the pound of pure and hang around and ask some questions about something and theyd never flash to what I was or what I was holding. Maybe I/ll go into the station house and ask them if they have much of a problem with drug addicts in the neighborhood . . . that might be a good way to find out about some new neighborhoods, let the man tell me where they are, as if you couldnt smell them a mile away. Might be a gas. He slowed for the toll booth then accelerated and watched the sunlight bounce off the cables of the bridge, fascinated by the brightness, thinking that they were a thousand spotlights and that he was the star. He eased into the traffic for the parkway and though there was a lot of traffic it moved freely and smoothly and he relaxed behind the wheel keeping his eyes on the road and glancing from time to time at the attaché case and then looking at the people in the cars around him from the corner of his eye, knowing they were either going to or coming from some job, trapped in some box in the suburbs or rat trap in the city, never knowing what was going on and never knowing what its like to be free, free man, and go where you want when you want and to have an out of sight old lady on your arm so when you walk into those uptown joints all the dudes dig your action and wish they were you . . . yeah, they wish they was in my shoes. . . . Look at them the poor bastards. Twelve o'clock and theyre beat already. He felt like lowering the window and yelling out to them to hang loose. From time to time he glanced, quickly, at the gulls gliding over the water and the sunlight twinkling on the rippled surface. It looked gray and cold, but that didn't phase him. Nothing did. Everything in his life was going great. He and Marion were grooving together. The coffe house was going great, his legitimate investments were doing great, and a few more deals like this and he would retire and just spend his time taking care of his business interests and traveling. He and Marion hadnt had a chance to do the traveling they had planned, except for a few brief trips to the Bahamas, and with all the bread he had here, and in Switzerland, he wouldnt need this anymore and he would cut it loose before it soured out. He wasnt going to be like those other guys who stayed in the business too long and got busted for heavy time or ended up in somebodys way and got burned. No, not me man. We/re going to make it. Lay on the beach on the Riviera for a while, then sit around those cafés in Paris and Rome, and then good old Istanbul and if Turhan Bey gets in the way thats just too bad. Hey, thats a great tune, man. He started nodding his head in time to the music and started singing, If Turhan Bey gets in the way, it's just too bad. If Turhan Bey gets in the way, its just too bad. He smiled and chuckled inwardly, Not bad. Maybe I should become a song writer in my spare time. He exited from the parkway and joined the slow and heavy traffic to the airport. He glanced at his watch and smiled as he realized he had plenty of time and there was no need to rush around finding a parking space. Thats why he always left early so he wouldnt have to worry in case he got tied up in traffic or somethin. Sometimes some poor sucker gets a flat or his car conks out and it ties up traffic for a while and he never wanted to blow more than half a million dollars on some jerks flat tire . . . or worse that that. Those peope dont take too kindly to being hung up with a pound of pure out there in the wide open spaces like that and then having to *schlep* it back. Harry always planned ahead. Thats one of the secrets of success, careful and meticulous planning. He parked the car and leisurely walked to the terminal. He had some time so he stopped in the coffee shop and had a cup of coffee and a piece of pie ala mode. He kept the attaché case on his lap as he ate, smiling smugly to himself thinking of how the people around him would shit if they knew he had 75Gs in the case. He paid the check and walked, slowly, to the cocktail lounge and sat at the far end near the large windows overlooking the field. He put the case on the floor, a few inches from his left foot, and toyed with his drink, sipping it from time to time, and watching the planes take off and land, then taxi to the ramps. He continued to watch the planes as a guy dressed in the same style and color top coat and hat and suit sat on the stool to Harrys left. He had an attaché case just like Harrys and he put it on the floor a few inches from his right foot. He ordered a drink and finished it before Harry finished his. He put his empty glass on the bar and picked up Harrys attaché case and left. Harry continued to toy with, and sip, his drink, and watch the planes on the field. Ten minutes later he picked up the attaché case and left. He walked directly, but unhurriedly, out of the terminal and to his car. He didnt bother looking around to check people out to be sure the man wasnt somewhere, he knew everything was cool. He trusted that gut feeling and it said swing baby. He opened the door of the car and tossed the case inside, almost laughing, and got in and locked the door behind him. That was it man. The last pick up. The last pound of pure he would ever cop. When he and Ty finished running this down to the streets they were closing up shop and kissing the streets goodbye but for good. The traffic out of the airport, and almost all of the way back, was clogged and slow, the same old stop and start, but he was used to it and he just sat back in the seat, vaguely aware of the music, his mind alert and on the traffic, and relaxed. The traffic was one of the safeguards they had set up. They knew that no one would expect people to make a meet in the middle of the afternoon at a place like Kennedy. It was all wrong. Too public. Too open. Too many cops of all kinds checking people coming into the country. And if you get rousted where could you go? You couldnt run. You couldnt drive. You couldnt swim. Hahaha, shit, I cant make it across the pool for krists sake man and thats a big mother fuckin ocean. It was all wrong. Everything about it was wrong. Thats why it worked so good. But today the snarls in traffic were worse than usual. There seemed to be flat tires and tapped bumpers all over the parkway. It seemed like everywhere he looked: in front, behind, he saw those flashing red and yellow lights, but he was cool and didnt panic and realized it was either a tow truck or ambulance and it had nothing to do with him, even when he saw a cop waving traffic around an accident he stayed nice and calm—Shit! No man. Thats all bullshit. Who the fuck wants to go through all that. Even if the man dont getya the goddamn traffic will. Good old Bob Moses and his biggest parking lot in the world. The really cool thing, the really way out place for a meet thats so great it just tickles the shit outta me. Yeah. Nobody man, no fuckin body, would flash to Macys. Hey, I like that. Too fuckin much man. The toy department . . . Yeah . . . By the trains. Maybe I/ll pick up some when we/re straight. Be a real fuckin groove to have a room all fixed up with those trains . . . houses, bridges, rivers, trees, cars, trucks, lights for day time and night time, the whole fuckin *megillah*. Yeah, by the train display. Just hop in a cab and sit back while the cabbie fights with the traffic and bitches and moans about all the fuckin assholes drivin aroun the city and why dont they leave their cars at home and stop cloggin up the streets fa krists sake an looka that creep tryin ta cut me off, Hey, get back where ya belong ya fuckin ape bitch, and he turned to look at Harry, Must be onea those fuckin lezies the way she drives, and he suddenly swerved in the other lane and there was the screeching of brakes and screams and curses and he gave them all the finger out the window and continued to weave his way through the traffic, giving his perpetual finger to the horn blowers as he pounded his own, and yelling to them, What else ya get fa Christmas besides a new horn, harhar har, and Harry just sat back in the cab, smiling, chuckling, nonchalantly holding the case on his lap thinking it would be a gas to open the case and pour all that bread out on the seat and watch the cabbie shit a brick, but he was cool and nodded at the cabbie and handed him the fare when they stopped at Macys and told him to keep the change and waved to him as he walked away from the cab and into the department store. He was early so he stopped at the lingerie department and looked at something he thought Marion would like, but didnt buy anything, he always takes care of business first. You have to concentrate on what you are doing, thats how you beat the man and the world. Concentrate. He strolled through the ground floor and took the escalator up to the toy department, enjoying looking down at the floor below as the escalator ascended. The train display wasn't too tough, but they did have some nice trains on display, and then when it was exactly the time he moved in front of the display set up with a few accessories and a few trains constantly moving around, and put the case on the floor a few inches from his right foot and the guy came like before and they switched cases and all that and he strolled out of the store and took a cab uptown, walked a block, took another cab further uptown, another walk and then another cab a short distance downtown then walked a few blocks to the cutting room where Tyrone was waiting. Here it is baby, the last pound of pure we/ll be messin with. Yeah, an its never been touched by human hands. Jesus, Ty, youre somethin else. Whatta you gonna do when we retire, just sit around and giggle all day? Sheeit. Not me man. Ahm gonna do a little scratchin too. They carefully cut the shit, and bagged it, then got it out to their people who took care of the street people. They didnt deal with anybody who used, anybody who wasnt cool. Tyrone took most of the stuff because he dealt with the blacks, and Harry took the remainder to the honkys. When the last of the shit was finally gone they celebrated. Harry and Tyrone took their old ladies not only out on the town, but all over the town and ended up riding around Central Park in hansom cabs and watching the sun come up. The next day Harry spent some time with his business manager discussing the acquisition of some additional income property and then made arrangements for he and Marion to start their trip around the world. Think we/d better stay away from Africa, doesnt seem to be too cool there. Except North Africa. Maybe start at Algiers, Casablanca,

Yeah, play it again Sam. Then go east. See whats hapening in Cairo and some of those places and then good old Istanbul. Good old Istanbul—Jesus, with a passport in the name of Goldfarb? Maybe I should change my name to Smith or Turhan Bey, and Harry chuckled and leaned back in his chair and half listened to the music coming from Tys rinkydink radio and emptied the end of a cigarette and stuck the roach from the last joint in it and smoked it as he heard steps on the stairs, then a key in the lock, and Tyrone C. Love bebopped into that two by four with a big ass shit eatin grin on his face and dropped a little package on the table. There it is baby and Brody say it be dynamite, that we/d betta cut it at lease, at lease, three times, an he say if we get off we betta just take a pinch. He wouldnt let you take a taste there? Not even a snort to check it out? Uh *uh*. He doan let no body get off in his pad. Noway. How can we tell if we/re gettin burned? He doan burn nobody man. Thas why he still be alive an dealin. He say it dynamite, then its dynamite. Ah told him we wasnt goin to get into it anyway, that we goin to be cool and not fuck up. Yeah, but how can we tell what we have an how to cut it if we dont take a taste? Thas right, eh? Well, just a little tase aint gonna hurt nothin. Right. But we/ll just take a pinch. We could jus horn it. Hey, if Im gonta get off Im gonta get off. Im not gonta waste no good dope by hornin it man. Or any other kinda dope. Harry chuckled and they got out their works. But lets really be cool man. Hey baby, ahs always cool. No, no, all shit aside, Ty, lets really be cool. This is our chance to make it big and I mean really big. We dont have to be dealin in no petty ass pieces all our lives. We play it right an we can get that pound of pure, but if we get wasted we/ll fuck it up. Hey baby, ahm not jivin you. Ah doan want to be runnin no streets the res of mah life in no ripped sneakers, mah nose runnin down to mah chin. Groovy, and Harry held out his hand and Tyrone slapped

the palm and Harry gave it back to him. Okay, lets just put
a taste in. Harry tapped a small amount in the cooker, started
to tap in some more, then stopped. Thats enough. Cant take
care of business with our fingers up our nose. They got off
and with the first wave from their gut up to the flushing of
their faces they knew that Brody wasnt bullshittin them and
they could cut the shit out of this stuff an still put a good
bag on the streets. Sheeit, we be cutting this four times an
still wont be nobody gettin on our case about burnin them.
Yeah . . . this is too fuckin much man. He say there still some
more a this aroun so we betta turn this ovah as fas as we can
and get us some more jim cause this be out of sight. You know
somethin man, we hustle our asses off and we can cop a couple
a pieces tomorrow. Solid! and they gave each other five then
got to work carefully mixing the heroin with the milk sugar,
not smoking for fear of blowing some of the precious powder
into the air or coughing or sneezing and blowing it into
oblivion. They were aware that they were high so they concentrated very strongly on what they were doing, all their
movements slow and precise. From time to time they took a
break and moved away from the table to have a much needed
cigarette. When they finished they each took fifty bags and
went out to the streets. They didnt like the idea of walking
the streets holding so much weight, but they had no choice.
They had to let people know where they were at, and Tyrone
didnt have a phone in his pad so the only way they could
make any contact with the junkies was by going out there
amongst them. Harry called Marion and told her everything
went fine and what they were going to do and she told him
that they could use her number for a while. You sure? Yes.
Just use discretion. I mean dont give it to every junkie in the
streets. You know, just people like Gogit. People you really
know. An you can keep the stuff at Tys. Okay sweetheart,
we/ll do that. That sure as hell would make it a lot easier

until we get set up with a pad and a phone. I just didnt want to get you involved, you know? I understand Harry, and appreciate your concern. But its alright. Great. Okay, I/ll see you later. O Harry? Yeah? Save a little for us? Hey, dont worry. Im way ahead of you. Not much. You know. Right. We/ll get straight later. Seeya. Bye. Harry hung up the phone and then told Tyrone that they could use Marions number for a while, We can take the calls there an then meet later with the stuff. We/ll leave it at your pad. Thas great man. But be cool with the number man. I got it baby. Okay, seeya back here later. Yeah baby. They split, Harry going in one direction and Tyrone in the other, the operation being in black and white.

Things went well. Tyrone ran into Gogit almost immediately and he gave him Marions number and Gogit made his usual rounds finding out who wanted to cop and pretty soon Tyrone was out of stuff and had to go back and replenish his supply. By the time he got back to the neighborhood there were a lot of anxious junkies waiting for his stuff, the word having gotten around that he was putting out a good bag. Tyrone felt the excitement run through him but he stayed cool and didnt feed that incipient hysteria within him while fighting the urge to take another taste. He was glad that he had a tase though so that he could stay cool and he told himself to hang loose and take care of business and then worry about having another tase. He knew the streets and the scene and knew how to hang tough and trust those instincts that he developed through his twenty five years of living that enabled him to survive the streets from the Bronx to Harlem and he figured if he could survive those streets baby he could make it any fuckin where an that aint no boolshit jim. An instincts were razor sharp tonight. They had to be. He had to let people know he was holding, but as soon as the word was out that meant there would be people tryin to rip him

off and theyd just as soon cut your throat as light a cigarette.
Ones the same as the other to those cats jim. Theys some
down and dirty dopefiens baby, so Tyrone distributed his
stash in a few places and made sure no one was following him
when he took the bread and went to get the stuff. He was
extra sharp and extra alert because he believed that this was
his chance, his one chance and didnt think there would be
another one. Twenty five years was a long time to live in the
world he lived in and he knew that the chances to get out
of it rarely, if ever, came along and this was one and he wasnt
going to let it go. He wasnt sure how all this happened, how
he happened to be holding so much stuff and takin in the
bucks, it seemed like it came out of some sort of dream, but
it was here and he wasnt going to let it go. And he knew if he
didnt stay sharp jim it would be more than the dream that he
would lose. And he was tired of losing. These streets were
made for losers. These streets were ruled by losers. He was
on his way up and out. An he didnt so much care about having a big ass El Dorado and a stable of fine foxes . . . sheeit,
one ol ladys enough for me. What Tyrone wanted more than
anything else was not to have any hassles. Thas it baby, no
hassles. Thas all ah seen all mah twenty five years. Somebody
always hasslin somebody. Somebody always gettin up side
somebodys haid. If it aint the man its a brother. Aint nobody
ever satisfied. That scag get into your blood jim, or that
juice, and you go scufflin and beggin for a fix or a drink.
Sheeit, that jus aint for me baby. Uh uh, no way. An ah aint
no greedy ass mutha fucka. Jus enough to lay back with a
little store—sheeit, ah doan even care what kind jim, a dry
cleaners, a television, just somethin to keep me an mah old
lady doin fine an not have any hassles. You know, a nice little
place outta the city. In the suburbs somewhere. Ah dont
know, maybe Queens or even Staten Island. Jus a house and a
car and some fine threads and no hassles. Sheeit, we doan even

need no garden or no nothin man, just be free an easy jim like ah loves you and you loves me . . . sheeit, you doan have to love me jim, you can hate mah black ass, I jus dont want no hassles.

Harry strolled around the neighborhood, letting a few people know he was holdin, then sat around a candy store for a while, drinking egg creams and reading stroke magazines. He did some business from the store and when they closed he stood around the streets with a few guys he knew for a while, then moved on to a bar, then to another one, never staying in one place too long. When he sold out he stayed for a while seeing who wanted what. A guy he had known for a long time, Bernie, told him he was going to cop for a bunch a guys and hed be back in an hour so Harry went back to the pad and picked up another load and offd that too before going to Marions. Tyrone called him later an told him how much he had offd and when they added up their sales they had enough for a piece already and things were just starting to move. Sheeit baby, now that a couple a cats knows what we got wes gonna be outta shit before tomorrow night. Im hip. As soon as we off enough to get two more pieces we/ll cop, eh? You gawddamn right jim. Ah wants to get as much of that shit as we can. Groovy. Give me a call later if I dont fall by first. Later baby, and Tyrone hung up the phone and bebopped to his pad. It was a long assed night jim an he sure would be glad to get his pretty little ass in bed. He could feel the sweat runnin down his back. He had spent a lot of time in the streets, but these past hours had been the worst of his life. He had never thought too much of the streets except to know he wanted to get away from them. But they had never been such a personal threat before. He could roam the streets day or night and it didnt make any difference who might walk by or pull up behind him, but now it was different. You bet your sweet ass it was. He never had anything to lose before. He never had anything anyone else wanted. He was just another black cat, another brother, scufflin and tryin to make it through one more day in this honkys world. Nobody feared him and he didnt fear nobody. He just giggled and scratched his way through the streets. When you know the streets an stay away from the nuts, those drunken madmen who run around with butcher knives and guns, then theys just streets that you got to beat, but when you got somethin that somebody elses is wantin then you got trouble jim. Then its more than just concrete and tar you got to fight . . . you got to be fightin the fuckin crazies that those streets put into dudes. One of those cats by himself is alright. An the streets by themselves aint no big deal. But when you puts them together you got the mutha fuckin crazies jim an then you got to look out for your ass. An when you got somethin somebody else wants you got some trouble and when that somethin is shit an you walkin those streets you got some serious trouble. Sheeit. Its a bitch jim but the only way to beat those streets is to make them work for you. You just got to out hustle them mutha fuckas man.

Harry picked Marion up by the waist and spun her around after he hung up the phone, We/re on our way baby, we/re really on our way. At this rate we/ll have that pound of pure in no time and then watch our smoke. O Im glad Harry, hugging and kissing him, Im so glad. I didnt think it would bother me, but I was worried the whole night. I guess I never thought of it before but all of a sudden everything out there seemed so threatening. You want to know something sweetheart? I was sweatin it too. You get busted with that much weight and you got a heavy beef, theyre going to lay some heavy time on your head. Are you going to have to go through this every night? Naw. Marions face was wrinkled with concern and Harry smiled at her. We just wanted to push it as much as possible so we could turn over enough stuff to cop two more pieces tomorrow while we could still get that great stuff. Then we/ll cool it an get some place where we can lay it off. I hope so sweetheart. Last night was one of the loneliest nights I have ever spent. Harry hugged and kissed her again, Dont worry, in no time we wont be goin near the streets. We/ll off the stuff to the dope fiend pushers and just lay back—but lets forget all that, eh? Lets take a little taste an lay back and talk about our coffee house and those trips to europe. They got off and stretched out on the couch, listening to the music, and went over their future once more, making more specific plans for their first coffee house, Marion getting her sketch pad and pencils and sketching the ideas as they came up with them and soon they had a complete floor plan for the first one, complete with hanging plants, small stage for performances, a small aviary in the open air garden that had grapevines growing over it, and all the walls constructed specially for paintings up out of the way of harm; and then Marion started to describe the place she had in mind for the coffee house in San Francisco and sketched that too and showed him what could be done with it and how much he would love Fishermans Wharf and the mimes that perform there and the great restaurants and you know their theater is really excellent and theres always something happening there just like in New York as far as music and art are concerned, or anything for that matter, and she put on the Kindertoten-lieder and played that a few times as they sat side by side on the couch drawing, talking, leaning against each other and suddenly laughing or chuckling and hugging each other and kissing and dreaming and believing. . . .

The waiting room was crowded. Sara didn't know anyone there, but they had a familiar look, even the young thin ones. She filled in the form and handed it back to the nurse and shortly after was led to one of the examining rooms. The nurse weighed and measured her and asked her how she was, Fine, thats why Im here, and they both laughed. She took her blood pressure and asked her how her hearing and vision were and Sara told her she had both, and the nurse laughed again then left the room. In a little while the doctor came in and looked at the chart the nurse had prepared, then looked up at Sara and smiled, I see youre a little overweight. A little? I have fifty pounds Im willing to donate. Well, I think we can take care of that without any trouble. He listened to her heart for a second, tapped her back twice with with his fingers, then went back to the chart. You seem to be in good condition. The nurse will give you a package of pills to take with a pamphlet of complete instructions. She will also give you an appointment for a week. I will see you then, and he was gone. Sara got her package of pills and the nurse explained the instructions so that Sara understood them completely. Okay, this I understand, but tell me dolly, how much does the doctor charge? He said to come back in a week and I don't have any money. O, dont worry about that Mrs. Goldfarb, we/ll arrange it so that Medicare will take care of the bill. O, good. Thats a relief. So a week I see you again. Right. Goodbye, Mrs. Goldfarb. Goodbye, dolly. Take care.

Sara sat at the kitchen table, the pills and directions in front of her. So lets see, the purple one I take in the morning and the red one I take in the afternoon, the orange one I take in the evening, she turned and smirked at the refrigerator, thats my three meals Mr. Smarty Pants (the refrigerator frowned in curious silence) and the green one at night. So, just like that. One, two, three, four, ipsy, pipsy and the pounds come falling off. So I/d better take the purple one now, its almost time for my red one, and she chuckled as she pranced over to the sink to get a glass of water and take her breakfast pill. She hummed as she opened the refrigerator and took out the cream cheese and pushed the door closed with smug superiority and opened the bag on the table and took out a large onion roll and unwrapped a piece of smoked fish. So look Mr. Ice Box and eat your heart out. Im splurging. Soon I/ll be saving lots of money on the food bill. She shrugged her shoulders and tossed her head at the refrigerator and smeared the roll with cream cheese and picked up loving tidbits of fish, Hmmmmmmmmmmm, smacked her lips, and turned in her chair so Mr. Smarty Pants Ice Box could see her devour the delicacy.

She made a second pot of coffee. She never had more than one cup of coffee in the morning and the rest of the time she drank tea. But this morning she drank an entire pot, six cups, and now she was making another pot and not thinking about it, aware only of how she felt . . . good, exhilarated, expansive. And then she became aware that it was lunch time and she wasnt even hungry. Not a tiny bit. She drank more coffee. Lunch time already and I dont want anything, she stuck her tongue out at the refrigerator, not even a herring tidbit in sour cream, thank you. Such magic. No little tickle thinking of a nosh. A hot fudge sundae I dont want. A pastrami on rye with mustard and potato salad I dont want. Nothing I want. Since breakfast I/ve had one pill and a cup of coffee and—she looked at the pot and her cup and realized that she had had more than one cup, that she had made a second pot and that was almost empty . . . Eh, she shrugged, big deal. A pill and a pot of coffee and Im being already *zophtic* so whos complaining? She finished her coffee and refilled the cup, Im looking at you, and she winked at the refrigerator, and now its time for lunch, and she picked up the red pill and daintily dropped it on her tongue and washed it down with coffee and wiggled and shimmied in her chair for a moment thinking about this incredible miracle that had taken place in her life. If only she knew about this before.

She was feeling so young, so full of energy like she is climbing mountains. She thought maybe she would wash the floors and the walls, at least the kitchen walls, this afternoon, but decided to postpone that and go sit with the ladies and get some sun and tell them how she felt. She couldnt wait to tell them that she found the fountain of youth and Im telling you, its not at the Fountainblew.

She took her chair outside and joined the ladies, putting her chair in the place of honor that was always kept in reserve for her. There was at least a dozen ladies waiting and when she came out they right away started the same old thing about the show and where and when and she just smiled and waved her hands in her best regal fashion and looked up and down the street for the mailman and bounded with unbridled energy and flitted about and around the ladies, sitting for a moment then getting up and walking around again, and when the lady who had given her the name of the doctor joined them she hugged her and kissed her and told her forever shes loving her, that what is happening is the most wonderful thing in the world and she cant believe it but shes not even thinking about food, that even if a big bowl of chicken noodle soup was put in front of her she wouldnt eat it, not even if it was smothered in borscht, and how good she feels since shes not making herself so tired with all that food and now shes feeling free like a bird and wants to just fly and flutter her wings and sing songs "O by Mier Bist du Schön" and it doesnt even cost, hes making it on the Medicare, and maybe I/ll go dancing and she tried to sit and get some sun but she kept bouncing up as if some unseen force continually propelled her off her seat and sent her bunny-hopping amongst the ladies and looking up and down the street for the mailman who soon will have something for her from the McDick Corp. telling her what show she is on and how much longer before getting into the red dress and the ladies shook their heads and nodded and told her to sit, sit already and relax, get some sun, feeling good is alright but dont let it wear you out, and they laughed and kidded and Sara sat and walked and hugged and kissed and looked up and down the street until the mailman came and as she started walking toward him, her retinue behind her, he shook his head, Aint nothin today, and went into the building with a few pieces of mail but Sara didnt despair, she just kept telling them how good she felt and how soon she would look like Little Red Riding Hood.

Sara was the last to leave the street. She didnt have to prepare dinner so there was no rush. The first thing she did was to turn on the television, then make another pot of coffee and thumb her nose at the refrigerator who still sulked in silence as he smelled the scent of defeat. Sara busied herself in the kitchen rubbing, wiping, swiping, continually looking at the clock to see if it was dinner time. Eventually the hands of the clock formed a straight line and Sara excitedly sat down at the table with her orange pill. She dropped it in her mouth, drank some coffee, and then went back to sweeping and cleaning and scrubbing while humming, talking to herself, the television, and pointedly ignoring the refrigerator. From time to time she reminded herself about the water and she drank a glass thinking thin and *zophtic*. Eventually her energy started to wane and she became aware of the fact that she was clenching her teeth and grinding, but that was easy enough to ignore as she settled in her viewing chair, or at least tried to. She continually fidgeted and squirmed and got up for this or that, or another cup of coffee or glass of water, feeling a hint of squirming under her skin and a slight and vague feeling of apprehension in her stomach, but not quite strong enough to be really disturbing. She was only aware that she didnt feel quite as good as she had in the afternoon, but she still felt better, more alive, than she had in many years. Whatever might be off a little was worth it.

A small price to pay. She kept thinking of the green pill and though the program she was watching was only half over, she got up out of her chair and took her green pill and went back to her viewing chair. She drank a few more glasses of water and decided that tomorrow she would drink less coffee. Its no good that coffee. Tea is better. If something is wrong its probably the coffee. She drank some more water visualizing it dissolve the fat in her body and washing it out and away . . . away . . . far, far away. . . .

    Tyrone had copped two more pieces and by night he and Harry were ready to do some heavy business. They continued to cool it with the stuff, just taking a small taste, just enough to keep them cool out there on the streets, but not enough to dull their senses. They had to hang cool, but tough. Phone calls had been coming in during the day and they were ready to off at least half their stuff before they had even cut it. After making several drops Harry called Marion to find out who else had called and what was happening. It became such a hassle that Marion suggested they just keep the stuff there until they got a phone in Tyrones pad. All this running around and taking messages is absurd. And it seems like youre taking unnecessary risks, Harry, the way you are operating now. Harry quickly agreed with her suggestion and they operated out of her apartment until the phone was installed in Tyrones pad a few days later. Now everything went easier and smoother. They were still very careful with how much they used themselves and the stuff they were copping was still so good they could cut it four times and still off a good bag. Cats were waiting for their shit. They started cutting it five times and made even that much more money. The bucks were piling up by the thousands and they got a safety deposit box, under assumed names, and stashed the money there.

They were making over a thousand dollars a day and decided it was time to lighten up a bit and get themselves some decent clothes to wear when they went out. But it seemed like they never had time to go out so they started fronting a couple of guys like Gogit with some stuff to off through a night and getting the bread the next day and splitting it down the middle with the guys. All of a sudden, or so it seemed, the world had turned around and they were coming up roses. Now, instead of the bottle being half empty it was suddenly half full, and getting closer and closer to the top.

One night Harry and Marion were sitting on the couch listening to music, after having gotten off, going over their plans for the coffee house as usual, when Harry leaned back, with a pensive expression on his face, then nodded his head as he reached a decision, Yeah, thats what I/ll do. Marion smiled, Do for what? Or should I say whom? The old lady. Ive been thinking of getting something for her, you know, some kind of present, but I didnt know what to get, you know it aint easy to think of something for someone like that. Like what could she use or want? Every woman loves perfume. You can get her something exquisite with a crystal bottle. Naw, that wouldnt make it for her. You know my old lady. Yes, I guess youre right. But I hope you take the hint, and she chuckled. Later for you, and he kissed her on the cheek and brusquely rubbed the back of her neck. I finally figured the perfect thing. Its right there in front of my nose and I miss it the whole time. I finally asked myself, whats her fix? and I told myself, television, right? If ever theres a TV junkie its the old lady. And I figure maybe I owe her a new new one anyway with all the wear and tear her set got from being *schlepped* back and forth to old Abes. Dont use that word. What? *schlep*? Yes. It reminds me of my father and his garment center vocabulary. Harry shrugged and laughed, You sure do have a thing with him, eh? Marion shrugged it off, I can ignore it. But whats this about a television? Im going to get the old lady a new set. I figure I can go for a grand if I have to, and get her a set that will knock her out. I mean that will really spin her head. She/ll *plotz* already! O Harry! Marion pouted and Harry chuckled and put his arms around her, I'm sorry, but sometimes I just cant resist, you get so bugged so easy. Anyway, tomorrow Im going to get her a big, fat super color TV that will make her forget all about the times I borrowed her set. Marion tilted her head to one side and looked at Harry for a moment, then smiled gently, You really love her, dont you? Harry shrugged, I guess so. I mean, I dont know exactly. One time I feel one way and the other time I feel something else. Most of the time I just want her to be happy. You know what I mean? Marion nodded her head, a longing expression on her face. Id just like to see her happy and making it . . . but sometimes I just cant seem to stop myself and I want to attack her like . . . ah I dont know. Its not that I want to attack her so much, its just that I see her sitting there in that same old apartment that shes been in forever, wearing the same old house dress, you know even if it isnt the same it is, and I dont know what to do. When Im away from her its fine, like I love her and have nice thoughts about her, when I think about her. But when Im there, in that apartment with her, something happens and I get so goddamn irritated that I end up yelling at her. O, its probably simple. You love her and have a dependency and you dont know how to obtain your independence in a healthy manner by simply outgrowing the nest, so to speak, so you lash out and reject her before she can reject you. Its a classic case, really. Could be. Me, I dont care about all that. I just know that shes always lecturing me about being careful, youre a good boy, take care, dont get hurt . . . you know? like she wont let me breathe. Marion was nodding. Harry shrugged, Ah, I dont know. Its not important. Now that Im set I can take care of her and visit her once in a while an maybe now she/ll get off my back when she sees how good Im doing. Hey, maybe sometime we can take her out to dinner or something. A show, who knows what. What do you think? I/d love to Harry. Ive always loved your mother. Shes always so charming and quaint, and . . . and real. So unaffected. She lives in the Bronx and loves the Bronx and lives her life in the open. Not like some who look down their noses at people unless they live in New Rochelle or the Connecticut suburbs or Westchester and think theyre something theyre not while they still sound like theyre clearing their throat when they talk and slop cream cheese and bagels in their mouths in the morning and every Sunday night they go out to eat chinks. Theyre so disgusting. There is nothing worse than a cultural barbarian with pretensions. Hey, youre really cooking, and he chuckled. O, well, it really irritates me. Shakespeare said, This above all, unto thine own self be true. Polonius may have been a fool but there is a great deal of wisdom in that line. I think thats one of the problems with the world today, nobody knows who they are. Everyone is running around looking for an identity, or trying to borrow one, only they dont know it. They actually think they know who they are and what are they? Theyre just a bunch of *schleppers*—Harry chuckled at the way she spit the word out and the intensity with which she spoke—who have no idea what a search for personal truth and identity really is, which would be alright if they didnt get in your way, but they insist that they know everything and that if you dont live their way then youre not living properly and they want to take your space away . . . they actually want to somehow get into your space and live in it and change it or destroy it—Harry started to blink and stare as the anger mounted and flared out— they just cant believe that you know what you are doing and that you have your own identity and space and that you are happy and content with it. You see, thats the problem right there. If they could see that then they wouldnt have to feel threatened and feel that they have to destroy you before you destroy them. They just cant get it through their philistine heads that you are happy where you are and dont want to have anything to do with them. My space is mine and thats enough for me. Harry looked at her for a moment. I/ll tell you something baby, Im glad thats the way it is. I sure as hell wouldnt want to have to share your space. It might catch fire. All I did was say *schlep* and look what happened. Imagine what would happen if I said *yenta,* and Harry laughed and hugged Marion and she suddenly relaxed, allowing the dope, and Harrys attitude, and her own weariness to smooth the wrinkles from her brow and she started laughing too. You know something baby, its like Confucius said to Lei Kowan before the famous battle of Wang Ton: Letim eat cake, and they both started laughing again, O Harry, thats dreadful, and Marion got up and put the Kindertotenlieder on again and then went back to the couch and cuddled into Harry as they relaxed and listened to the music, and discussed the plans for the coffee house, as the dope continued to flow through their blood whispering dreams to every living cell in their bodies.

Harry still remembered his plan to buy his mother a new TV the next day, and still wanted to, but somehow the thought of actually getting out there in those stores and trying to find a salesman to help you and then trying to get the sonofabitch to show you what you want rather than what hes tryin to dump is a real drag . . . a big, fat mother fuckin drag. Goddamn it! If only he could just call up some joint and have them send one over that would be fine, but going in a store and talking with people and everything . . . He brooded over it for a while then realized that all he had to do was take a taste and everything would be alright. Yeah, a little taste and he could hack those stores and the goddamn salesmen. He didnt want to get off so early in the day, but what the hell, this was different. And it seemed right, after all he was always usin the old ladys set to get cop money so now he/ll use a little stuff to get her a set. Yeah, hahahaha, thats pretty good. I like that. Yeah . . . its like the goose and the gander, or some shit like that. Harry invited Marion to join him and at first she started to protest getting off as soon as they got up, but the words never came out of her mouth and so they started the day with a taste, a little more than the day before, and went shopping. Marion asked him where he wanted to go and he shrugged then suddenly snapped up, Macys. Thats the place. Why do you want to go all the way down to Macys? I like it. I do a lot of heavy business there. Especially the toy department, and he chuckled and Marion looked at him as if he were goofy, but shrugged and went along with it. I guess a cab ride through town wont kill me.

When they got to Macys Harry insisted the driver take them to the seventh avenue entrance. The driver just shrugged and looked like Harry was just another nut, Its your money buddy. Why do you want to go to seventh avenue Harry, we could get out here just as easily? No, seventh avenue. Thats the way I do it. Marion looked perplexed and Harry smiled and smirked. Marion wanted to go directly to the television department, but Harry insisted they go to the toy department first and look at the trains. Marion shook her head, again, but went along to look at the trains. When they got to the television department Harry quickly glanced around at the sets and when a salesman came over and asked if he could help Harry looked at him and spoke with self-assurance, Yes. I want a large console. Well, we have this beautiful model over here in a luxurious Mediterranean cabinet thats on sale today only. Marked down from $1,299 to only $999.99. Its a complete home entertainment system with an am-fm radio, a— No, no. Nothing like that. Just a television. Fine. Right this way. This is our finest model. It has— Is it the largest you got? Yes. And it is guaranteed, parts and labor, for one whole year, picture tube for five, it— Okay, I/ll take it. The salesman smiled and continued to describe all the outstanding features of the set as he wrote up the sale, then wrote a service contract for five years after the guarantee expires, and Harry paid him off in hundred-dollar bills and calmly waited for his change. He continued to sit by the desk as the salesman went to the register to complete the transaction, and smiled to himself as he watched himself sitting there so calmly, taking care of business just like a real people. He smirked and chuckled inside himself as the salesman came back with his change, acting almost like a servant. Harry pocketed the money carelessly and gave the guy a nod and a wave as they left.

Later that night Harry thought about being in Macys buying the set and he started to flush and get nervous and sweat started to slide down his sides. When he thought about it the guy kept asking him questions he couldnt answer and Harry continually stammered and stuttered and felt embarrassed and apologized for not wanting the complete entertainment system and the more the guy told him what a bargain it was and how his aged mother would be grateful until her dying day if he were to buy this for her the more guilty he felt until he finally realized that he would be a fool not to buy this beautiful home entertainment system and if it was too big to fit in his mothers apartment then they would make the necessary adjustments. Harry shook his head and rattled the thoughts away and he and Marion went into the bathroom and got off and got ready for another evenings work.

Visiting his mother didnt seem like such a good idea when the time came to leave, but a little taste makes all things possible. He dressed in a sharp new pair of slacks and sport shirt and casual shoes. He checked himself out in the mirror again then asked Marion how he looked. Handsome. Really handsome. You look like the son every mother has been looking for. What are they doing looking in places like that? and he chuckled then checked himself out again. Okay, guess I/d better split. See you later baby. Marion kissed him, Just relax. Its going to be just fine. Your mother isnt a barracuda like mine. Maybe that would be easier. Okay, later. Harry left and stopped at a bootblack by the subway and got a dazzling spit shine on his new shoes, then gave the kid a couple of bucks and hailed a cab.

After two weeks on the pills Sara was accustomed to their effects. She almost enjoyed the grinding of the teeth, and even if it annoyed her a little from time to time it was worth the slight inconvenience to feel so good and to see the weight dropping off. Each morning and evening she tried on the red dress to see how much closer it was to fitting and each time the back came closer and closer together, she could tell. She cut back to only one pot of coffee in the morning and drank tea the rest of the day. Sometimes her eyes felt a little bulgy, but what was the big deal. She mentioned some of these things to the doctor and he told her that that was a normal reaction and not to worry about it. Youre doing just fine. You lost ten pounds the first week. Sara beamed and forgot everything else. Ten pounds. Such a good doctor. A real crackerjack. She went each week, got weighed, a new supply of pills, signed the Medicare form and went home. Who could ask for anything better. When she joined the other women getting some sun she gave them all a treat and let them look at her gorgeous figure before sitting in her special spot. But she wasnt sitting too long. Every now and then she got up to stretch, to walk, to do something in addition to talking. Her tongue got so much exercise that the rest of her needed some too. And every day it was already the same thing with the mailman: Theyre all looking at him as hes walking up the street and hes grinning and shaking his head and telling them not today. When ah sees it ahll be wavin it all ovah, ah mean all ovah, and he would go in the building to distribute the mail he did have. But there was something that was different . . . her refrigerator didnt talk to her anymore. He didnt even seem to sulk. He was still there but had lost his personality. He was just an ice box. At first she missed being able to antagonize him, but soon she didnt give it any thought and just went about her business as quickly as possible in the kitchen and then joined the ladies getting some sun.

She was sitting in her special spot when Harry got out of the cab. He adjusted the waist of his slacks and faced the phalanx of women, his mind trying desperately to think of some way to out flank them, but a lifetime of experience proved that that was impossible, so he girded his heroin strengthened loins and walked directly toward his mother. Sara stared for a brief second, her stimulated mind instantly computing everything the senses transmitted: the cab door closing, Keep the change, the new clothes, the relaxed attitude, the smile, the expressive eyes that were filled with color. She jumped up, Harry, and wrapped her arms around him almost knocking him off balance. She kissed him and he

kissed her and she felt so excited she kissed him again and
again, Hey, take it easy ma, youll crush me, and he gave her
a quick smile then adjusted his clothes. Come, come inside
Harry. I/ll make you a pot of coffee and we/ll make a visit.
She took his arm and started walking toward the entrance,
Your chair ma, you forgot your chair, and he went over and
picked it up and folded it while saying hello to all the women
who have known him since almost the day he was born already, and some since before he was born when he was only
some smoke in his fathers eyes, and they told him how good
he looked and told him they were so happy he was doing so
well and he nodded and was kissed and squeezed and finally
escaped their clutches. Sara made a pot of coffee immediately
and bustled around and about getting cups and saucers and
spoons and milk and sugar and napkins, And how are you
Harry youre looking so good, and she checked the coffee to
see if it was ready and asked Harry if he wanted something
to eat, a little nosh maybe or a cake I/ll go get some if you
want, but I dont have anything in the house but Ada will
have something, a cupcake maybe, and Harry watched and
listened to his mother, half wondering if he was in the right
house, and finally the coffee was ready and she filled the two
cups and asked Harry again if he wanted anything to eat.
No ma. Nothing. Sit. Sit for krists sake. Youre making me
dizzy. She put the coffee pot back on the stove and then stood
in front of Harry and smiled, You notice something? Harry
blinked, still a little dizzy from all the activity. You notice
Im slimmer? Yeah, yeah, I guess you are mom. Twenty five
pounds. You believe it? Twenty five pounds. And thats just
the beginning. Thats great ma. Thats really great, Im really
happy for ya. But sit down, eh? Sara sat. Harry was still a
little bewildered and his head seemed to be ten yards behind
him. Im sorry I havent been around for a while ma, but Ive
been busy, real busy. Sara kept nodding her head and smiling

at Harry as she clenched her jaw, You got yourself a good
job? Youre doing good? Yeah ma, real good. What kind of
business? Well, its sort of a distributor like. For a big im-
porter. O, Im so happy for you son, and she got up and gave
him another big hug and a kiss, Hey ma, easy, eh? youre
killing me. Krist whatta ya been doin, liftin weights? Sara
sat down, still grinning with her jaw clenched, Who you
working for? Well, Im sort of in business for myself. Me an
another guy actually. Your own business? O Harry, and she
started to get up again to hug him and Harry pushed her
down, Hey ma, please, eh? Your own business, O Harry I
knew when I saw you that you had your own business. I always knew you could do that. Yeah, ma, you were right. I
made it, just like you said I would, and he smiled and
chuckled. So now maybe youll meet a nice young jewish girl
and make me a grandmother. I already met one—Sara
squealed and squeaked and started to jump up and down
in her chair and Harry held his hands up in front of him,
Jesus krist ma, dont go ape shit, eh? O Harry, I cant tell you.
I cant tell you. Im so happy. Whens the wedding? Wedding?
Hey, cool it, eh? Just relax. Plenty of time to worry about
getting married. Is she a nice girl? Whose her parents? What—
You knower ma. Marion. Marion Kleinmeitz. Remember,
you— O, Kleinmeitz. Of course. I know. New Rochelle. Hes
got a house in the garment center. Yeah, yeah, hes big in
womens undies, and Harry chuckled but Sara continued to
grin gleefully as she anticipated the big wedding with all
her friends watching her son get married, Harry and Marion
under the canopy, the rabbi, the wine, the grandchildren . . .
She was so excited she couldnt sit still so she got up and
refilled the coffee cups and sat down. Before you go bouncin
all over again and make me forget, what I want to tell ya is
that I got you a present and— Harry, I dont want a present,
just make me a grandmother, and she continued to grin and

grin— Later for that, eh? Will you let me tell you what I got, eh? will ya? Sara nodded, grinning, grinding, clenching. Krist, youre really something else today. Look, I know . . . well . . . Harry rubbed his neck, scratched his head, and searched for words and cloud feel the embarrassment flushing his face so he lowered his face and drank some coffee, then lit a cigarette and started all over again. What Im trying to say is that . . . well, he shrugged, well . . . I know I aint been the best son in the world— O Harry, youre a good— No, no! Please ma, let me finish. I/ll never get it out if you keep interrupting me. He took a deep breath, Im sorry for being such a bastard. He stopped. Breathed. Sighed. Breathed. Sara grinned. Clenched. I wanta make it up. I mean I know I cant change anything thats happened, but I want ya to know Im sorry and I love ya, and I wanta make it right. Harry, its— I dont know why I do those thing. I dont really wanta do them. It just sort of happens, I guess. I dont know. Its all kindda goofy somehow, but I really do loveya ma and I want you to be happy so I got ya a brand new TV set. Its gonta be delivered in a couple a days. From Macys. Sara was squealing again and Harry warded her off by raising his hands and she sat back down and grinned at her son as she clenched her jaw and ground her teeth, her happiness vibrating from her entire being. O Harry, youre such a good boy. Your father would be so happy to see what youre doing for your poor, lonely mother. I got ya a five year service contract that takes care a everything after the guarantee runs out. Its guaranteed for five years and one year. I dont know which is for what. Its a long time. Its the best they got. The top of the line. You see that Seymour? You see how good our son is? He knows how lonely his mother is living all alone, no one to make her a visit even th— Hey ma, come on, eh? Dont go laying any heavy guilt trips on my head, eh? Saras eyes stretched even wider than they were as she clasped her hands

to her breast, I wouldnt do a thing like that to my son. Never.
I swear I want nothing but the best for my son, I wouldnt
want him to feel bad for— Okay, okay, ma, lets just cool it,
eh? I just wanted to give ya the set and tell ya Im sorry and
I want ya to be happy, okay? and Harry leaned over the
table and kissed his mother for the first time since he couldnt
remember when. He hadnt thought of it, hadnt planned it,
it just seemed to happen as a natural result of the conversation somehow. Sara beamed and blinked her eyes as her son
kissed her and she put her arms around him and kissed him
back and he kissed her again and put his arms around her
and found a strange feeling going through him, a feeling
something like a high, but different. He couldnt identify the
feeling but it was a good feeling. He looked at his mothers
smiling, beaming face and the feeling increased, flowing
through him with an unexplained power and energy making
him feel sort of . . . yeah, I guess thats it . . . sort of whole.
Harry, for a brief moment, felt whole, like every part of
him was united with and in harmony with every other part
of him . . . like there was just one big part of him. Whole.
The feeling lasted for the briefest moment as he sat there
blinking at his mother and his own actions and feelings, then
a feeling of puzzlement seeped through him and he found
himself trying to identify something and he didnt know what
it was he was trying to identify, or why. O Harry, Im so
proud of my son. I always knew youd make good and now
youre making— Harry heard her words but his mind was
completely preoccupied with the question of identifying
something. Then it slowly started to come to him. He had
been bending over his mother, kissing her, when he heard a
familiar sound . . . yeah, thats what it was he was trying to
identify, that sound. What in the hell could it be???? Your
father and I used to talk so long about you and how he
wanted you to be happy— Thats it! Thats what that noise

is. He stared at his mother at first bewildered not knowing what it meant and then it all started to fit in and a lot of pieces suddenly fell into place and Harry could feel his face folding into an expression of surprise, disbelief and confusion. The noise he heard was the grinding of teeth. He knew he wasnt grinding, he was on stuff, not speed, so it had to be his mother. For many long moments his head fought against the truth, just as it had fought against recognizing the obvious since he had first stepped out of the cab, but now he was overwhelmed with the facts and his eyes were still blinking as he leaned across the table, Hey ma, you droppin uppers? What? You on uppers? his voice starting to rise involuntarily. Youre on diet pills, aint ya? Ya dropping dexies. Sara was completely bewildered and befuddled. All of a sudden her sons voice and attitude changed and he was yelling at her and saying things she didnt understand. She looked and shook her head. On, on, what is on? How come ya lost so much weight? I told you, Im going to a specialist. Yeah, sure. What kindda specialist? What kind? a specialist. For weight. Yeah, thats what I thought. Youre makin a croaker for speed, aint ya? Harry, you alright? Sara shrugged and blinked, Im just going to a doctor. I dont know from croaker, making . . . she continued to shake her head and shrug, Whats wrong Harry, we/re sitting and making a nice conversation and you— What does he give ya ma? Eh? Does he give ya pills? Of course he gives me pills. Hes a doctor. Doctors give pills. I mean what kind of pills? What kind? A purple one, red one, orange and green. No, no, I mean what *kind?* Saras shoulders were hunched up around her ears, What kind? I told you. And theyre round . . . and flat. Harry rolled his eyes back and his head shook slightly, I mean, like whats in them? Harry, Im Sara Goldfarb, not Doctor Einstein. How should I know whats in them? He gives me the pills and I take them and I lose weight so whats to know? Okay, okay, Harry was fidgeting in his chair and rubbing the back of his neck, So you dont know whats in them. Whered you get this jokers name? From who? From Mrs. Scarlinni, where else? She got it from her daughter. Harry was nodding his head, It figures. Rosie Scarlinni. Whats wrong? Shes a nice girl and such a cute figure. With all the speed that broad drops the weight cant stay on. It shakes itself off. Harry, you confuse— Look ma, does that stuff make you feel good sort of and give ya lots of pep and maybe you talk a little more than usual, though with you *yentas* its pretty hard to do that, eh? Sara was nodding her head and pursing her lips, Well, I guess maybe a little. Harry rolled his eyes back again. A little. Jesus, I can hear ya grinding ya teeth from here. But that goes away at night. At night? When I take the green one. In thirty minutes Im asleep. Poof, just like that. Harry kept shaking his head and rolling his eyes, Hey ma, ya gotta cut that stuff loose. Its no good. Who said its no good. Twenty five pounds I lost. Twenty five pounds. Big deal. Yeah, big deal. Do ya wanta be a dope fiend fa krists sake? Whats this dope fiend? Am I foaming at the mouth? Hes a nice doctor. He even has grandchildren. I saw the pictures on his desk. Harry hit himself on the forehead, Ma, Im tellin ya, this croakers no good. Ya gotta stop takin those pills. Youll get strung out fa krists sake. Strung, schmung. I almost fit in my red dress, Saras face softened, the one I wore at your bar mitzvah. The one your father liked so much. I remember how he looked at me in the red dress and gold shoes. The only time he saw me in the red dress. Its not long after that he got sick and died and youre without a father my poor boobala, but thank God he saw you bar mitzvahed and— Whats with the red dress? What does that— Im going to wear the red dress on television. O, you dont know. Im going to be on the television. I got a call and a application and soon Im on television— Comeon, ma,

whose pullin ya leg? Leg, schmeg. Im telling you Im being a
contestant on the television. They havent told me yet what
one, but when Im ready theyll tell. Youll see, youll be proud
when you see your mother in her red dress and golden shoes
on the television. You sure someone aint puttin you on? On,
schmon. I got an official form. Printing and everything. Harry
was nodding and shaking his head, Okay, okay. So its official.
Youre goin to be on television. You should be happy Im going
on television. All the ladies theyre happy. You should be
happy too. Im happy ma, Im happy. Look, Im smilin. But
what does that have to do with takin those goddamn pills
fa krists sake. The red dress shrunk, Sara was smirking and
giggled slightly, and its a little tight, so Im losing some
weight, what do you think? But ma, those pills are bad for
you. Bad? How can they be bad? I got them from a doctor.
I know they are ma, I know. How come you know so much?
How come you know more about medicine than the doctor?
Harry took a deep breath and almost sighed, I know ma, believe me I know. And theyre not medicine. Theyre just diet
pills. Just diet pills. Just diet pills. Those just diet pills took
off already twenty five pounds and we havent stopped yet. But
ma you dont have to take that shit to lose weight. Sara was
hurt and perplexed, Harry whats wrong? Why you talking
like this? All I want is to fit in my red dress. The dress for
your bar mitzvah. Your father loved the dress Harry. Im
going to wear that dress. I/ll wear it on the television. Youll
be proud of me Harry. But ma, whats the big deal about being
on television? Those pillsll kill ya before ya ever get on fa
krists sake. Big deal? So who do you know thats been on
television? Who? Harry was shaking his head in frustration.
Who? In the whole neighborhood whos been on the television. Whos even been asked? You know who Harry? You
know who the only one whos been even asked. Sara Goldfarb.
Thats who. The only one in the whole neighborhood whos

been even asked. You drove up in a cab— Harry was nodding
and shaking his head, Yeah, I drove up in a cab— You see
who had the sun seat? You notice your mother in the special
spot getting the sun?—Harry was still nodding and shaking—
You know who everybody talks to? You know whos somebody
now? Whos no longer just a widow in a little apartment
who lives all alone? Im a somebody now Harry. You see how
nice my red hair—Harry blinked rapidly and muttered a holy
shit under his breath. Her hair was bright red and he hadnt
even noticed. It still didnt make much sense but he figured
that her hair must have been a different color before, but he
couldn't remember what it was—so guess how many of the
ladies are going to get red hair? Go ahead, guess? Ma, whatta
my goin to guess? Six. Six ladies. Before I got red hair people
on the street, little kids, maybe they say something, but now
they know, even little children, Im going on the television
and they like the red hair and they like me. Everyone likes
me. Soon millions of people will see me and like me. And
I/ll tell them about you and your father. I/ll tell them how
your father liked the red dress and the big party he made
for your bar mitzvah. Remember? Harry nodded, feeling defeated and worn out. He didnt know what was defeating him,
but he sensed it was something he could not cope with, something that was far beyond his power to control or even at
this point in time comprehend. He had never seen his mother
so alive, so involved with anything in her life. The only time
he had ever seen anybody so enthused and excited was when
somebody told an old dope fiend about some good shit and
he had enough money to cop. His mother had a light in her
eyes when she talked about the television and her red dress
that he couldnt remember seeing there before. Maybe when
he was a little kid, but he couldnt remember back that far.
Something in her attitude was so strong that it simply over-
powered him and made any continued resistance or attempt to

change her mind impossible. He just passively sat and watched and listened to his mother, part of him confused, and part of him happy that she was happy. And who knows what I might win? A new refrigerator. A Rolls-Royce maybe. Robert Redford. Robert Redford? So whats wrong with Robert Redford? Harry just blinked and shook his head, bewildered, and went with the flow. Sara looked at her son, her only child, with a tangible earnestness, the grin and grinding gone, replaced with a plea that softened her eyes and calmed her voice, Its not the prizes Harry. It doesn't make any difference if I win or lose or if I just shake hands with the announcer. Its like a reason to get up in the morning. Its a reason to lose weight so I can be healthy. Its a reason to fit in the red dress. Its a reason to smile already. It makes tomorrow alright. Sara leaned a little closer to her son, What have I got Harry? Why should I even make the bed or wash the dishes? I do them, but why should I? Im alone. Seymours gone, youre gone—Harry tried to protest but his mouth hung silently open—I have no one to take care of. Ada does the hair. Anybody. Everybody. What do I have? Im lonely Harry. Im old. Harry was completely flustered, his head shaking, eyes blinking, hands fidgeting with each other, voice stammering, You got friends ma, what— Its not the same. You need someone to make for. How can I shop when I dont cook for someone? I buy an onion, a carrot, an occasional chicken, a little nosh, Sara shrugged, for me how can I cook a roast? a special . . . special . . . anything? No Harry, I like how I feel this way. I like thinking about the red dress and the television . . . and your father and you. Now when I get the sun I smile. I/ll come visit ma. Now that Im straight, my business is going good, I/ll come. Me and Marion—Sara was shaking her head and smiling— honest ma. I swear. We/ll come for dinner. Soon. Sara shook her head and smiled at her only child, trying hard to believe,

Good, you bring her and I/ll make your favorite borscht and stuffed fish. That sounds great ma. I/ll give ya a call ahead a time, okay? Sara nodded, Good. Im glad. Im glad you got a nice girl and a good business. Im glad. Your father and I were always wanting only the very best for you. I see on the television how its always alright in the end. All the time. Sara got up and put her arms around her son and hugged him close to her, tears gently caressing her cheeks, Im glad Harry that you have someone to be with. You should be healthy and happy. And have lots of babies. Dont have only one. Its no good. Have lots of babies. Theyll make you happy. Harry did the best he could to hug his mother and allow her to hug him without trying to pull away, and he held on to her with desperation, the reason why completely unknown to him, something impelling him to hold, and be held, for as long as possible, as if this were some momentous event. He felt cramped and crowded, but he hung on somehow against his will. Eventually, just when he thought he would dis-integrate, his mother backed off slightly and looked into his face and smiled, Look, Im crying already. Im so happy Im crying. Harry forced his face into a tight smile with the utmost of effort, Im glad youre happy ma. I really love ya. An Im sorry—Sara shook her head and waved away his apologies, tosh, tosh—I really am. But Im goin ta make it up now. You should just be happy. Dont worry about me. Im used to being alone. They looked at each other for a moment, silent and smiling, and Harry thought his face was about to crack open and he moved and looked at his watch, I got to go ma. I have an appointment downtown in a couple a minutes. But I/ll be back. Good. I/ll make for you. You still have your key? Yeah, I got it ma, shpwing her his key ring. I/d better hurry. Im late now. Goodbye son, and Sara gave him another hug and kiss, and Harry left. Sara looked at the door for many minutes, time seeming to have no meaning, then poured herself another cup of coffee and sat at the table nurturing her feeling of sadness. She thought of Harry as a little baby with chunky legs and cheeks and dressing him warm and wrapping three blankets around him when she took him out in the cold weather, and when he started to walk, and how he loved the playground, and the slide, and the swings, and then the coffee started to stimulate the chemicals in her body and her heart started beating faster and she started grinding her teeth and clenching her jaw and a feeling of elation started to pump its way through her and she started to think about her red dress and the weight she was losing and the television—*zophtic, zophtic*—and her face started to squeeze itself into a grin and she decided to finish the pot of coffee and then go out and tell the ladies about how good her Harry was doing with his own business and a fiancée and how she/ll soon be a grandmother. It was a happy ending.

Harry felt confused and bewildered when he left his mothers. He was not only confused and bewildered, he was aware of it. He knew he always had a hard time being around his mother, she always seemed to know how to push his buttons and drive him up the wall, but something happened this time that was different and unexpected, and he didnt know what in the hell it was. He didnt feel like lashing out at her but rather he felt like crawling up inside himself. Or maybe he always felt like that. He didnt know. Shit! It was confusing as hell. Red hair. Red dress. Television. It all seemed so goofy yet there was something happening, a feeling of some kind, that seemed to make it alright. Maybe it was because his mother was happy. That was a gasser. He never realized how much he wanted his mother to be happy. Never thought of it like that before. It was just that she was always a drag to be around. But she sure as hell was up today. Yeah,

on those goddamn pills. Jesus, he didn't know what in the
hell to do. His old lady on those goddamn diet pills and
dyeing her hair red . . . Harry shook his head as the words
and thoughts and feelings bombarded him, increasing his
confusion and bewilderment. He didnt know what was happening with his mother, but he sure as hell knew that he
needed a fix. Yeah, a little taste and everything will be
just fine.

For many weeks Tyrone was able to cop that dynamite shit
that they were able to cut four times and still put a boss bag
on the streets. That safety deposit box was filling up with
bucks and they were nosing around to see where they could
get a pound of pure. They had to be as quiet as possible so
that the wrong people didnt get ideas and rip them off. There
seemed to be some new people peddlin the shit and they
were the people they were trying to get in contact with because they were the ones putting out that dynamite. They
handnt made the contact yet, but they were getting close, real
close. And things were going great. Theyd lay off the stuff to
the street guys and just lay back and let the business take
care of itself. The demand was always there. It was definitely
a sellers market and they just waited for them to come to them.
They realized they didnt have to sweat it so they dipped a
little more into the merchandise. They didnt have to get
worried about being strung out when they were the connection, not that that was a real problem. They knew they could
stop any time they wanted to. If they should ever want to.

Another couple of weeks passed and Sara still hadnt heard
from the television people, but that didnt bother her at all
until today. Today she got up and tried on the red dress and

she could actually zip the back closed. The last few inches were tucking and tugging, tucking and tugging, with also a little grunting and a lot of deep breathing, but it closed. Soon she would be able to wear it and breathe at the same time. Now she started to become concerned about hearing from them what show she would be on and when. If even they didn't tell her when, if she just knew the show she could watch it and know what to expect, sort of a rehearsal, and she could tell the ladies and she could maybe have them in to watch the show on her gorgeous new set that her son Harry gave her now that he is doing so well in business, his own business, and she wished he would come with his fiancée to dinner and she could make the borscht and stuffed fish that Harry likes so much just like his father who used to always smack his lips and ask for more . . . Sara sighed . . . but Harry called the other day to ask how she was and say hello and tell her again he would soon visit but he couldnt do it now because he was all tied up with business. But couldnt you come? If even for only a little while? Ma, I toldya, I'm tied up. I got a lot of irons in the fire and I have ta be around ta take care a them. Your own mother? Not even a little visit? What did I do Harry that you should not want to see me? Whatta ya talkin about for krists sake? I aint doin nothin to ya. You could come with your fiancée and let me give her a hug and a kiss. You oughtta lay off those pills. Theyre makin ya goofier than usual. So now Im crazy? Who said anything about crazy? Hey ma, will you lighten up and stop playin those guilt games with my head? Games? What games? Just cool it, eh? I just called ya up to tell ya I love ya and that I/ll see ya soon and you start laying guilt trips on me and I dont need it, okay? Okay, okay. I dont know what you dont need, but okay. I guess maybe you dont need me, but okay. Harry breathed deeply and shook his head and squeezed the phone, hard, and thanked God he had sense enough to get off before making

the call, Look ma, I dont wanta hassle you, okay? I love ya
an I/ll see you soon. Take care. Be well Harry. He hung up
and she shrugged and poured herself another cup of coffee
and sat at the table waiting expectantly for the coffee to
reactivate the diet pills and send that flush of euphoria
through her system and soon she was grinning and grinding
and went back out to the street to join the ladies and get
some sun. And if she didnt hear from the television by Monday she would give them a call.

Harry and Marion were getting off twice a day, sometimes
more, and inbetween were smoking a lot of pot and dropping
an occasional pill. They looked at Marions sketches of the
coffee house they were going to open, but with diminishing
frequency and enthusiasm. Somehow there just didnt seem
to be time for it though they spent a lot of time just lying
around and not doing much of anything in particular and
making vague plans for the future and enjoying the feeling
that everything would always be alright, just like it was now.
When Harry resigned from the business, Marion insisted
they would *not* live in the suburbs, and they would *not* live
in a house with a white picket fence, and they would *not*
barbecue on Sundays, and they would *not*— Hey, wait a
second, eh? What *are* we going to do? and he grabbed her
by a boob and put his other arm around her and kissed her
on the throat and she pushed him away and giggled and
hunched her shoulders to cover her neck, Dont, dont, Im
ticklish. Okay, so we/re not going to tickle you either. So
what else? We/re *not* going to own a Cadillac, and we/re
not going to visit my family at Passover, as a matter of fact
we are *not* going to have a Passover or even have a box of
matzoh in the house. Harry kept nodding his head and rolling
his eyes as she counted off another will not, But we will have

a nice place in the west side of the Village, and we will stop in for an occasional drink in a neighborhood bar, and we will shop on Bleecker Street and have lots of nice cheese, especially provolone, hanging in the kitchen, and anything else we want. Harry raised his eyebrows, O, anything else we want? Dont worry about it Harry, we/ll be able to have it. He smiled and pulled her close to him, I have it now, and he kissed her and slowly moved the palm of his hand over her ass, you have everything I want. Marion put her arms around his neck, O Harry, I love you. You make me feel like a person, like Im me and Im beautiful. You are beautiful. Youre the most beautiful woman in the world. Youre my dream.

As usual, Sara started her day on Monday with her purple pill and a pot of coffee, but somehow it wasnt doing what she was used to it doing. The weight was still coming off and the red dress was zipping up without too much stuffing, but there was something missing, even after a pot of coffee. She didnt feel the same like she did when she first started taking the pills. It was like they took something out of them. Maybe they made a mistake and gave her the wrong pills? Maybe she should get stronger ones? She called the doctors office and talked with the nurse and asked two, three, how many times, if she was sure she didnt give her the wrong pills? No Mrs. Goldfarb, Im absolutely certain. But maybe you gave me a smaller one the last time. That isnt possible Mrs. Goldfarb. You see they are all the same potency. The change is in the color. All the purple are the same strength, all the red, etc. But something isnt the same. Youre just becoming adjusted to them. At first you may get a strong reaction, but after a while that wears off and you just dont feel like eating. Its nothing to worry about Mrs. Goldfarb. You mean Im—

I have to hang up, my other phone is ringing. Sara looked at the phone for a second, So click. Maybe shes right. Im not eating—*zophtic, zophtic*—and the dress is going on. She sighed, Im thinking thin. She unthinkingly made another pot of coffee while looking at her jar of tea, and drank it as she puttered around the house before putting on a sweater and going out to get some sun with the ladies. It was a little chilly in the morning now, and evenings, but they still sat and in the afternoon it was warmer. She put her chair in her spot for a while and then got up, but without her usual buoyancy and smile. Sit, sit. Why you have to be all the time like a yo yo. I/ll sit. I feel a little jumpy today. Today youre feeling jumpy? Yesterday you were sitting quiet and calm? Sara, for weeks youre like a young girl thinking about Robert Redford, the ladies laughing and chuckling. You should relax. Soon youll be on the television and you shouldnt be like a jitterbug, chuckling and laughter. Im waiting, Im waiting. I think it will come today and then I can relax when I know what show and maybe theyll tell me when. Sara shrugged, Who knows. The red dress fits now, Sara still pacing around in a small circle, then walking out to the curb, looking up and down the street but not paying attention to what she was seeing, then going back to the ladies, sitting for a moment, then up again and pacing in ever widening circles, but my hair needs a touch up. So tomorrow we/ll fix it up like new and youll be gorgeous just like Rita Hayworth. Sara posed with a hand on her hip, *Zophtic,* the ladies laughing. Sara looked up and down the street again, Todays the day. I know, todays the day.

It wasnt yet three oclock and Sara was taking her orange evening pill and following it with a cup of coffee. She had watched the mailman walk up the street and he just nodded his head and went into the building. Sara followed, watched him put the mail in the boxes, stared at the emptiness of hers for many seconds before he left, then went into her apartment. She automatically made a pot of coffee then took her dinner time pill and sat at the kitchen table watching the new television her son Harry gave her. From time to time she looked at the clock. A little before three she was thinking it was almost dinner time. She took the orange pill and drank some more coffee. She made another pot. She sat. She thought. About the television. The show. About how she felt. Something was wrong. Her jaw hurt. Her mouth felt funny. She couldnt figure. It tasted like old socks. Dry. Sickening. Her stomach. O, her stomach. Such a mess. Like theres something moving. Like theres a voice in there saying look out, *LOOK OUT!!!!* Theyll get you. She looked over her shoulder again. Nobody. Nothing. *LOOK OUT!* Who's getting? Whats to get? The voice kept rumbling in her stomach. Before when it started she took more coffee or another pill and it went away, now its just there. All the time. And that nasty coating in her mouth, like old paste, it used to go away, or something. It didnt bother her. Now, ech. And all the time the trembles in the arms and legs. Everywhere. Little things under the skin. If she knew what show it would go away. Thats all she needed. To know. She finished her coffee and waited, trying to think those good feelings back into her body, her head . . . but nothing. Paste and old socks in the mouth. Squirming under the skin. The voice in the stomach. *LOOK OUT!* She stared at the television, enjoying the show, and all of a sudden, *LOOK OUT!* Another cup of coffee and she felt worse. Her teeth felt like theyre going to snap. She called the McDick Corp., asking for Lyle Russel. Who? Lyle Russel. Im sorry, but I dont have his name listed on my directory. What was it in reference to? The television. What television? I dont know. I want to find out. Just a moment please. The operator took another call and Sara listened carefully to the silence. What show did you say that was? I dont know dolly.

He called me and said I was going on a show and— Just a minute. I/ll connect you with the programs department. Sara waited as the phone somewhere rang and rang, until a voice asked her if she could help her. I want Lyle Russel. Lyle Russel? I dont think we have anyone here by that name. Are you sure you have the right number? The operator connected me. Well, what was this in reference to? Hes putting me on a show. A show? What show?—*LOOK OUT!*—Sara could feel sweat sliding down somewhere. I dont know. Hes supposed to tell me. Im afraid I dont understand, the impatience in her voice was obvious, If you cant tell me— He called me and said Im going to be a contestant and he sent me papers. I sent them back a month already and I still dont know— O, I understand. Just a moment, I/ll transfer you to the proper department. She clicked the phone, and clicked and clicked, O, come on, and clicked some more as Sara clung to the phone and wiped the sweat from her face, Can I help you? Transfer this call to contestant clearing please. One moment please. Again Sara listened to a phone ringing, her eyes rolling around in her head the sweating and squirming getting worse, her mouth almost stuck together with that old paste, Can I help you? Sara couldnt talk. Hello? The sweat burned her eyes and eventually she pried her lips apart and a shock of terror trembled through her body as she anticipated the response when she asked for Lyle Russel. Who? Sara started to sink into her chair. She thought she would come out through the bottom. She thought she was dying and—*LOOK OUT!*—she twisted around and looked from one end of the room to the other as she repeated the name. Are you sure you have the right department? Theyre sending me here. The agony was unbearable. If only she had another cup of coffee. With intense will she unglued her mouth and told her story again to the voice on the other end, somewhere, of the phone. O, yes. Finally! Finally! Recognition. Sara almost melted away with relief. He must have been one of our phone solicitors. We have so many you know. Can I help you? I want to know what show and maybe when Im— Can I have your name and address please? Sara slowly and carefully spelled her name and address, the *shiksa* on the other end not understanding English too well. Finally her name and address were written. I/ll check this Mrs. Goldfarb and we/ll be in touch with you. Thank you for calling. Click. Sara was still talking into the phone many seconds after the click had drifted away and mingled with the voices from her television set. She looked at the phone, the sweat almost feeling like tears. Theyll get in touch, she shook her head, theyll get—*LOOK OUT!!!!*

Tyrone laughed, Ahm glad ah dont have no one laying any a that kind of heavy motha shit on my jim. You honkys is too much with that guilt shit. Krist, you aint kiddin man. I dont know what it is, but I try to do the right thing with the old lady, but . . . and Harry shrugged . . . but she always comes on with that jewish mother shit. Sheeit, it aint just you jews jim, its all you honkys. You guys dont get that shit, eh? Sheeit. Moms liable to get upside your haid, but she aint about to beat her breast, uh uh. She beat your ass instead. You know, I sometimes think we/d be better off without mothers. Maybe Freud was right. Ah dont know man. Mah moms died when ah was about eight, but ah remember she was one groovy woman. She have seven kids jim an she was like one of those movie mammys, all big like an all the time singin and smilin. She have a big chest like this and she used to cuddle me jim an ah remember how good it felt in there an how sweet she smell. Seven kids man an she never hit nobody. She just love us all up and down . . . an everybody love her. An she be a singing fool. Ah mean all day an night she be singing those gospel songs so it make you believe heaven jus aroun the corner. You know, she sing an it make you feel good all ovuh, jus like dope. Harry laughed then chuckled, A regular Mahalia Jackson, eh? O she be somethin else jim. Yeah, I guess it was pretty cool in my house when I was a kid. I mean the moms was still alive and it seemed like everything was groovy. You know, like going places an doin things and sort of having fun in the house. Then the moms died an . . . Tyrone shrugged . . . Whatever happened to your old man? Sheeit, he done split a *long* time before the moms die. He probly still out there doin his own thang. When moms die we all sent to different peoples. Ah went to mah auntie in Harlem an we live there for a while. She your mothers sister? Yeah, but she be a lot different jim. But nice. She dont do no singin an she like to lay a stick on your ass, but she always see we get a sugar tit when we got home from school. Sugar tit? What the fucks that? What that? You mean you doan know what a sugar tit? I know what some sweet pussy is man, but a sugar tit beats the shit outta me. They were laughing and Tyrone shook his head, A sugar tit is some butter and sugar stuck in some cheese cloth and you suck on it like a tit. O, is that what they call that? Damn, you sure is one ignorant son of a bitch. . . . She a nice lady ol auntie . . . but ol moms was somethin else, she really somethin else. Harrys eyes were closed and he was leanin back remembering how his mother always protected him from the cold wind in the winter when he was a kid, and how warm she felt when he got in the house and she hugged the cold out of his ears and cheeks and always had a bowl of hot soup waiting. . . . Yeah, I guess the old lady was pretty groovy too. I guess its a bitch being alone like that. Harry Goldfarb and Tyrone C. Love sat loosely in their chairs, their eyes half closed, feeling the warmth of fond memories and heroin flowing through them as they got ready for another nights work.

One thing Tyrone loved was fine silk shirts. Damn! he
sure did love the way they feel so smooth an fine, just like
his old ladys ass, and she be an out of sight fox jim, ah mean
somethin kinda fine. He had a couple dozen or so shirts hanging in his closet, various styles and various colors, all kinds
of colors. He liked to stroke his shirts just like he liked to
stroke Alice, an sometimes he just stood in front of the closet
and dug all them fine shirts jim. Damn! he even liked that
closet. It had two big sliding doors and the whole front was
a mirror, one big ass mirror jim. Sometimes he would just
slide the doors back and forth getting his rocks off. What you
doin honey? Why dontcha come back to baid? Sheeit, plenty
time for that baby, I got me a big ass toy that ahm groovin
behin. Ah remember seein a movie once when I was a kid an
this dude have him a big ass closet like this with sliding doors
and the whole thang was filled with suits an behind them was
a secret passage. It was a gasser. What he need a secret passage
for? Ah doan remember, ah just remember the closet. Tyrone
closed the doors and looked in the mirror, seeing his fox
behind him, and he smiled at her. When Tyrone first came
to look at the apartment he fell in love with the closets in
the bedroom and they made up his mind for him. It was one
of the first things the super showed him. Them doors is ten
feet wide and all mirror. The closets about twelve feet I think.
Both ofem. One on each side a the room. Ya put a bed in
between and you got yaself a good show, and he laughed
and winked and poked Tyrone in the arm, harharhar. Tyrone
was naked and stood by the side of the bed rubbing his
stomach, Yes sir, mah names Tyrone C. Love and thas what
ah am, and Alice started to giggle when he jumped, kapoing,
in the bed. Doan do that Tyrone, you scare me to deth. O
little momma, ah wouldnt wan to scare you, rubbing her neck

and shoulder, gently, so soothingly, ah doan wan to scare
nobody, especially the finest fox that ever did live, and Alice
started to squirm slightly as he kissed her on the neck and
then she held him close to her as he kissed her throat and
then her breasts as he caressed her things with his hand
and she grabbed his head and kissed him and kissed him and
kissed him and hugged and squeezed and squirmed and
sighed and moaned as Tyrone C. Love made her feel so good
and so special with his lovemaking and when he finished and
was lying on his back she just sort of vibrated all over for a
second and squealed, Oooooooooooooooo, then quickly rolled
over on her side and hugged and kissed until they both lay
quietly and peacefully, arms around each other, Tyrone on
his back, Alice, his lady, on her side, her face nuzzled so
warmly in his shoulder, feeling a peace and contentment and
excitement neither had ever known before, with or without
heroin. From time to time Tyrone would open his eyes,
slightly, to reassure himself that this was real and that he
was lying on this bed, in this room, with this woman, and
then he would sigh deeply within himself and feel her
smoothness and warmth next to him and the peace and contentment within him. He allowed his head to roll slowly to
the side and he kissed his Alice on the forehead and stroked
her head, You is really here, and she squeezed him and
nuzzled harder against his shoulder and he could feel her
breath on his arm and he somehow felt and sensed that life
in her that was now a part of him, and that he wanted to be
a part of, and take care of. He wanted to keep her in his
arms all nice and safe an they would just sort of be cool and
laugh and have a ball an there would be no hassles.

The honeymoon was over. The dynamite was gone. Brody told Tyrone he didnt know exactly what happen, but it probly got somethin to do with those dudes they foun in the garbage cans. You mean those dudes with their throats cut and the signs, Keep our city clean? Yeah, Brody was nodding his head and they both chuckled. Sheeit baby, if they fuck up that dynamite scag it aint nothin to laugh at. Brody continued to nod his head for a moment, Right on, brother, but the way I heard it they fuck with the wrong people. They ripped off a couple a keys from the Jefferson brothers and wanted to make it quick so they put out that dynamite. But the Jeffersons burned their asses? Brody chuckled, Who else do that? Aint nobody fuck with the Jefferson brothers baby . . . an git away with it. Tyrone rubbed his head, back and forth and around, How this stuff? Just like it used to be? You caint do no moe than cut it in haf if you wants to put anything in the bag. Tyrone just shrugged and took the stuff back to his old pad where Harry was waiting for him. Before they did anything else they dumped some in the cooker as usual, and got off. They looked at each other as they booted a few times, waiting for that flash. It never quite happened. There was a hint of a flash,

but it didnt rush them like they were used to. Sheeit, that
mutha fucka werent kiddin when he say this aint no dynamite. You aint kiddin man. We/d better cook up some more.
That taste was a drag. They dumped more in the cooker and
got off again and this time it was a little better, at least good
enough for them to feel it in their gut and on their eyelids.
They looked at each other and shrugged. Lookit all the
money we save on milk sugar, Harry laughed and Tyrone
giggled. We/s doin alright anyways. We still be makin some
bucks.

By the time they used what they wanted there was a lot
less left to be sold now, and they didnt make a hell of a lot
more than expenses, but that was no big deal, they had some
bread stashed and pretty soon they should be able to score
for weight, and score some dynamite again, and soon theyd
be able to get their shit together and get that pound of pure.

Sara got easily into the red dress now, but still she didnt
know what show she would be on. She called two times every
week, but she always got the same answer, that they were
processing her application and she would be notified. Now
when she called and left a message the girl simply nodded her
head at the phone while looking at the others around her
and smiled. Its her again, eh? The girl nodded and had to
make a strong effort not to laugh. Sara always stared at the
phone for many minutes after she hung up, then went into
the kitchen and made another pot of coffee. She was saving
money on food, she was eating so little, but she was spending
it on coffee. And the price of coffee today, ahhhh. She tried,
from time to time, to go back to tea, but somehow it left her
with a vague yearning in her stomach, a vague dissatisfaction,
that only coffee satisfied. But the coffee no longer satisfied the
real need the way it had, but it left less of a yearning than

the tea. She felt constantly uneasy, which was bad enough, but what made it even worse was the fact that she didnt know why. Something was wrong but she didnt know what. All the time she felt like something terrible was about to happen. And sometimes she felt like crying. And not like before when she felt sad when she thought about Seymour or Harry, her boobala, and felt so lonely. Now she/d be sitting and watching the television and start to cry—LOOK OUT!—her heart rolled over and caught in her throat—and she didn't know why. When she called about her show she almost wanted to cry. She wanted to tell the girl how important it was, but her head was all confused. If she could tell her already the names of the shows they got people for she could have something, but the girl told her that that was confidential information and held her hand over the mouthpiece of the phone as she giggled and winked at the girl at the next desk. Sara spun the dial on her TV set and tried to watch as much as possible of all the quiz shows, but somehow she couldnt sit still long enough to really watch them and find out what they were like and watch her image walk across the stage. A couple of times she managed to get herself started across the stage from the far corner, but it seemed like all her energy went into keeping the dress red and the shoes gold so that the entire image faded almost immediately and she ended up just sitting in her viewing chair looking at something but she wasnt there. She wasnt in the show. She tried to sit for a whole show, but couldnt. She got up and poured another cup of coffee, or stood over the stove while she made a fresh pot, vague thoughts going through her head that some more pills would make it better. She started taking the purple, red and orange pills all at once in the morning, and that made it better for a while and she got her house cleaned in no time at all and was ready to go out and get some sun, but by noon her body was crawling and knotting and—LOOK OUT!—

and she kept waiting for a car to come up on the sidewalk, crashing through all the parked cars, and hit her; or maybe something is falling off the roof, or. . . . She didnt know, she didnt know, but something bad. She couldnt sit. She got up and the ladies laughed and kidded her, Antsy pants Sara, and she walked around thinking thin and *zophtic,* and even when Ada touched up her hair every couple of weeks she could hardly sit still and kept bouncing up, not knowing ahead of time that she was going to, and Ada pushed her down, If you want red hair you got to sit still already. She was losing, she was losing. The dress fit nice. No stuffing. No huffing. She was losing. She should be happy. The red dress fits, her hair is like Rita Hayworth, her gold shoes sparkle and she was going to be on the television, a dream, a dream, and she should be happy, she should be happy!!!!

New York was no longer a summer festival and Harry and Tyrone were hit with a cold shot . . . Brody couldnt score any more uncut weight. What! Thas right. He can get weight, but its been cut. Shit man . . . what happened? Tyrone shrugged and rubbed his head with the palm of his hand, Brody say it look like somebody trying to stretch out their dope. Stretch it out? Tyrone was still nodding, An if Brody caint get no uncut weight aint no body gettin it. Harry was staring at the package on the table, We cant do any more than pay for our own stuff this way. Well, why doan we just stop using???? They stared at each other for a moment, the implication of Tyrones question slowly, through much resistance, sinking in and registering. Harry shrugged, Yeah, I guess we/d better. But I guess we may just as well get off now an cool it tomorrow. Yeah, baggin this shit without a tase is a draig. Harry chuckled, Looks like we/re gonna end up with a supply of milk sugar. Thas okay baby, someday we be gettin us that pound of pure an we be needin it than.

Marion and Alice were all for not using and so all went to sleep that night with a grim resolve. They got up about noon, smoked a joint with their coffee, feeling good about the fact that they werent giving any thought to. not using, and sat around for a while, watched a little television, talked about maybe eating something, but not really feeling like it, then sort of moped around thinking and talking about the various things that should be done that day and making plans for doing them, then watched a little more TV, and more coffee, and more grass, spending much of the time dabbing at their running eyes and noses, and by three oclock they realized they were making a big deal out of nothing, that if they really wanted to stop using they certainly could, they were proving that right then, but it was stupid to panic and to think the world was coming to an end just because they couldnt score for any uncut weight right now, so they got back into the spoon. Their noses and eyes cleared up and they listened to music as they ate.

A week later they still couldnt score for any uncut weight so they tried again to stop using, but this time they were back in the spoon before they were dressed. They awoke earlier than usual with panic roiling their stomachs, their eyes burning and their noses running, and the magic of the dope healed all their ills immediately. It wasnt that they couldnt stop using, it was just that this wasnt the time. They had too much to do and they werent feeling well. When everything was straightened out they would simply cut the whole scene loose, but for now theyd take an occasional taste to hang loose.

Sara finally developed a morning schedule that enabled her to accomplish a few very necessary things. She took her purple, red and orange pills at once, drank a pot of coffee, then tried on the red dress and golden shoes and spun around in front of the mirror looking so *zophtic* and feeling so good and trying to force from her mind how she would be feeling by noon. She kept the dress on and sat in her viewing chair and watched the shows, no longer spinning the selector, but watching the entire show. She saw the announcer, the audience, the prizes, and heard the laughter and applause, then forced herself, with much effort, to cross the stage to where the announcer was waiting, a big smile on his face, and listened to the applause, but now she couldnt control herself and she left the screen and came into the room and walked around the apartment, looking at the old, old furnishings, the lack of light and life, then tried to get back into the set but couldnt quite make it and eventually seemed to disappear somewhere, Sara wasnt quite sure where, maybe in the back of the set or under the bed, someplace. It puzzled Sara. She looked all over the house, but couldnt find the little red riding hood. The next time she paid closer attention to where she went and asked her what she was doing and where she was going, but she just looked up at her and tossed her head and shrugged her shoulders and gave her a So who are you? look and went her merry way and again disappeared. For days she was stepping right out of the set and walking around. She didnt jump down to the floor, but just sort of stepped out of the screen and was on the floor and very obviously and noisily ignored Sara as she roamed around looking down her nose at the apartment, occasionally looking over at Sara disapprovingly and gave a huff and a humf, and continued on her way inspecting everything and finding fault with everything and giving Sara that look of looking down while looking up. Finally Sara got upset and angry and stared right back at her, Who are you to be telling me? Who do you think you are? and Sara turned her nose up at her, and when she lowered her gaze she had disappeared. For many mornings the same thing until one morning the announcer left the set too, and little red riding hood led him around the apartment showing him this and that, the both of them shaking their heads with overwhelming disapproval, then looking up at Sara, shaking their heads again, then back at the spot of inspection, back to Sara, another shake of the head and off to another area to continue the inspection and the disapproving glances and shakes. For three mornings it happened and each time Sara felt worse as she watched them look at the shabbiness of her apartment, What do you expect? You could do better all alone? Its an old building. Ten years no painting, maybe more. Im old. Alone. You do it. Im trying, Im trying, and Sara could feel a hot twisting in her gut and a wave of nausea clutch her throat, Please . . . please. I/ll explain. But they didnt stay to listen but went right back into the set and waved at the audience and then hundreds of people followed them out of the set and around the drabneses of her tiny apartment and the television followed with their cameras and other equipment, the thick cables stretched across the floor and Sara could see herself sitting in her viewing chair looking at the set surrounded by the lifeless gloom of her apartment and it seemed to be getting smaller and smaller as she watched it on the screen and felt it happening around her and she was feeling a sensation of being crushed, not by the walls, but by her shame and despair. She didnt know what they were finding and seeing, but she knew it was bad . . . o so very bad. She should have looked before they got here. What was there? She was cleaning the other day. No? She wasnt sure. She changed the channel, but the picture was the same. Every channel, again and again, the picture the same. Millions of people were watching her stand in front of her set trying to change the channel, to change the picture, and she felt something crawling within her. Everybody knew her shame. Everybody. Millions. Millions of people were already knowing, but she didnt know. The tears whirled around in her eyes and trickled down her cheeks. She didnt even know. She only knew that they knew and that she was overwhelmed with shame and despair. And now she could see the little lady in red and the announcer leading the people around her dingy little apartment, on the screen she could see them and they were looking out at her with expressions of disgust. Sara clung to the television set trying to hide the screen and slowly, ever so painfully slow, she folded into herself until she was kneeling in front of the set and leaning against it, her head hanging low, her tears staining her red dress that she wore at her Harrys bar mitzvah, curling into a ball as the screen filled with people looking down on her disapprovingly and she hugged herself as a huge wave rolled from her stomach up to her throat and she felt herself drowning in her tears, O please, please . . . let me on the show . . . please . . . please. . . .

Brody got burned. Snuffed. Tyrone couldnt find out exactly what happened—he asked a half dozen people and got a half dozen answers—but how it happened was unimportant, the fact that he was cold stone dead was. He was found in an alley either shot, stabbed, shoved off a roof, or by what they call misadventure. His pockets were empty so it was obvious he was done in. Whenever he was out of the pad he was either holding or had the bread to cop. Tyrone listened to the stories and boolshit for a while then split. All the way back to the pad he bugged himself about not having a good backup connection. They had looked around half assed, but Brody was getting such dynamite shit they knew they couldnt do better if they went to France. Then when he ran out they just couldnt seem to get around to looking for somebody else, being convinced that the dynamite would be back soon, that if there was anything good in town that Brody would sniff it out. Now they were fucked . . . s.o.l., just plain shit out of luck. Jesus krist man, thats a fuckin drag. Getting himself fuckin killed an leavin us high and dry like this. It just dont figure. Not Brody. Not after all these years. Well baby, seem like we gotta do somethin. Caint just sit aroun here. Yeah. Thats no fuckin lie. Shit! What a lousy fuckin break! Just my fuckin luck! Hey mah man, cool it. Aint gonna do no good sittin aroun here nose wipin our selves. Yeah, yeah, I know man. It just gripes my shit is all. Well it dont make me feel like doin no tip toe through the mutha fuckin tulips jim, but we gotta get our little asses out there an see what we cain do. Harry finally chuckled slightly, Yeah, I/ll go to the front of the bus an youll go to the back. Yeaahhh, ah always did like mah business in black and white. Sheeit, we/ll latch on to somethin baby. We jus be cool an somethin will break.

Sara had to go to the store. For days she had to go, but couldnt move. Couldnt get out of the house. She didnt get the sun. If there was a sun. Maybe its cloudy outside too. Inside its like night. Maybe worse. Night, you put on the light and its cheerful. Now its gray. Gray. She had to get to the store. For days she had to go. If Ada would come. Maybe then? Maybe she should call? Ada would take her. She/d ask her why she cant go? What could she say? She didnt know. Its just the store. Yes. Just the store. But she couldnt go. She knew it was wrong not to go. Something bad. She could feel inside it was bad. Crawly. How could— LOOK OUT!!!! no no no no ahhhh. hh—How could she tell her? Whats to say? Whats to say???? She had to go. For days now. No toilet paper. No sugar. Now its all gone. Now she had to go. She had to get out. Just get up and walk across the room. That's all. Up and out the door. Little red riding hood. Ipsy pip—LOOK OUT! Nothing. Nowhere. Nothing. She was going. The refrigerator was changing shape. It was nearer. With a huge mouth. Closer . . . She got up. Her pocketbook. Where? Where? She found it. She clutched it with both hands. She was moving toward the door. The refrigerator moved. Closer. Out of shape. Almost all mouth. Her gold shoes clicked on the kitchen floor. The red dress was wrinkled. She yanked at the door. The refrigerator got closer. The television was bigger. The screen got bigger and bigger. She yanked at the knob. People came out of the set. The door opened. She banged it behind her. She wobbled on her gold shoes. The high heels clicked on the tile. The breeze was a little cool. It was gray here too. Nobody by the house. She walked down the street. Swaying. Wavering. Holding on to the wall. She reached the corner. Stopped. The traffic. Traffic! TRAFFIC!!!! Cars. Trucks. Buses. People. Noise. Movements. Whirls. She was dizzy. She clung to the light post. Desperately. She couldnt move. The light turned green. She clung. Knuckles white. The light continued to click from green to yellow. To red. To green. Over and over. Many times. Many, many times. The people passed. Some looked. Shrugged. Continued. Sara clung. She looked across the street. Up and down. Waiting for the light. Safe to cross. She tried. She stopped looking. Hid face in pole. Hung on. Hung on. The noises blurred. Flashes of light stabbed her closed lids. She hung on. The pole was cold. She could feel the clicking in the pole. She hung on . . . So whats happening? Ada and Rae looked at her. Youre holding up the pole? Sara slowly moved her head. She looked at them. Sara, youre not looking so good. Sara just stared at them. They looked at each other for a moment, then each grabbed an arm and helped Sara to Adas apartment. Sara trembled slightly and they gave her a glass tea and Sara sat mutely sad gripping her glass with both hands, occasionally lowering her face to it and sipping the tea as she stared dully in front of her. I thought you were just a antsy pants, but now Im wondering. Ada and Rae smiled and chuckled and Sara started to respond, To just be antsy pantsy would be a pleasure. Maybe you got already a virus. Why dont you go to see your doctor? He can give you a anti something. My appointment isnt for two days. For two days? Whats the matter, you get sick by appointment? Whats he going to say? stay well now and get sick in two days? They all chuckled and Sara frowned inwardly because she hadnt thought of going to the doctor. She puzzled it for a second, then let it go away to some place and listened to the chuckles, felt herself chuckling, and sipped the tea until the glass was empty.

The waiting room was filled like always and Ada and Rae talked as Sara just sat. When she got to see the doctor she told him she wasnt feeling so good. And just what seems to be the problem? Your weight seems to be doing very well, and he smiled at her. The weight is fine. Im not so good. The television people are coming out and—LOOK OUT! and Sara whirled around and looked behind her, around her, under the chair, then at and around the doctor. He kept his teeth hanging out in a smile. Something wrong? Things are all funny. Mixed up. Confused like— Well, thats nothing to worry about. He wrote something on a slip of paper, You just give this to the nurse and make an appointment for a week. See you then. She was alone in the room with a piece of paper. She stared at it for a few moments, then forced herself out of the room. She handed the paper to the girl. He said one week. I have an appointment in two days. O fine. We/ll cancel that and put you down for one week from today. Lets see now, how about three oclock. Sara nodded. Good. My pills? I'll give you another weeks supply. Sara and her body sighed with relief. Good. Thank you. Now lets see what we have here. Okay. The girl got a bottle and dumped out a handful of capsules and counted twenty one and put them in a small bottle and put a label on it. You take one capsule three times a day. I have it on the label. Whats this? O, just something to help calm you down.

Sara looked at it. How you say this? Valium. Valleyum? It sounds more like a disease. The girl chuckled, See you in one week. And take one as soon as you get home. Sara nodded and left the office. They all went back to Adas and had a glass tea with a prune danish. Sara took a small piece of the danish, but couldnt eat it. Maybe tomorrow. Now . . . and she shrugged and sipped her tea. She sat with Rae and Ada, waiting for the pill to do something, but not knowing what she was waiting for. But she somehow sensed that she would soon feel better.

When she got back to her apartment the refrigerator and television set were where they should be and were acting properly. She turned on the television and put the bottle of pills on the table next to the others then noticed herself as she passed a mirror. She had on the red dress. It was wrinkled. It had already some stains. She blinked her eyes for a moment and stared at her reflection. She vaguely remembered trying on the dress, like every morning, but she never wore it out before. Only once, at her Harrys bar mitzvah. She shook her head and puzzled over it for a moment, then shrugged and smiled and changed her clothes before going back to the kitchen and taking another·one of the new pills then sitting in her viewing seat. She felt calm inside. Sort of nice. Her eyes felt a little bit heavy. Not much. Just relaxed. The chair seemed softer. She sunk down. The shows were nice. The people behaved. She sipped a glass of tea. She reached over to the table next to her chair, but it was empty. Nothing on it. Then she realized she was rubbing her fingertips on the table and she looked at it, her fingers, shrugged and then went back to looking at the show, whatever it was. Whatever it was it was nice. They all seemed nice. They stayed on their side of the screen.

Tyrone tried to be as cool as possible, but the only way to find out where the good dope was at was to get out there where it was, and when youre there theres always heat. Everybody and his brother was willing to take his money and promise him theyd be back with some boss shit; or they could get weight that was dynamite; or they could set up a meet. . . . Everybody had a story. Tyrone smiled and chuckled and told the dudes to go to Jersey to peddle that boolshit. He hung tough and loose for a few hours, staying away from doorways, hallways and alleys, and finally ran into a cat he knew and copped a couple of bundles. He was making his way down the street to get a cab when he was stopped by a couple of narcs. They frisked him, felt the dope in his pocket but didnt take it out. They took out his money and counted it, Twenty bucks. Thats a lot of money to be carryin around this time of night. They chuckled and Tyrone remained silent. He had over a hundred dollars left but said nothing. They shoved him in their car and one of them got in the back with him. Tyrone knew what he was supposed to do and he did it as quickly and smoothly as possible. He eased the dope out of his pocket and pushed it down the side of the seat. When they got to the station house they asked him if he was ready and he nodded. When they got inside Tyrone asked them what the charge was and they smiled and told him, Consorting. Tyrone nodded and waited to start the drag ass process of being booked. The holding tank was filled mostly with dope fiends, and winos. When he got his phone call he called Harry, but he was still out so he told Marion what had happened and where he was and to have Harry bail him out. He also asked her to give Alice a call before he was hustled off the phone. A short time later an old time dope fiend, who looked like he was a hundred and four, was thrown in the tank and made himself at home as if he had been born and raised in jail. He had needle tracks on the side of his neck where he had been shooting heroin into his vein. Thats why he always wore a tie. It was old and ratty and looked like shit but it served its purpose. Beautiful. Just go into a public toilet, cook up your shit, pull the tie tight and hit the sonofabitch. Cant miss it. Big as a fuckin rope. He also wore a jacket with padded shoulders that looked like a Salvation Army reject, but that too was part of his equipment. Every time he got off he shot a little dope into the pad of his left shoulder. You can always dig up a set of works in jail and so he would take some of the padding out, cook it up, and have one last fix before going wherever he was going. And I/ll still have a little somethin waitin for me when I get out. Probly get a six month bit on the Island. He bummed a cigarette from a young guy nearby and nodded to him as he lit it. Shit, I know fuckin Rikers inside an out. Been there so many fuckin times I own stock in it. The others laughed and Tyrone sat down on the floor a few feet away from the old guy and listened, along with most of the others in the cell, to the old guy tell stories about Raymond Street, the old Tombs, Rikers, all the joints upstate and especially Danamora which is really a fuckin Siberia. I been in some fuckin hellholes, but that fuckin place is the asshole of the world. Even worse than that fuckin chain gang in Georgia. Did three months on the mutha fucka too. For a couple of hours he continued about the times he made it to Fort Worth and K Y, but only made that fuckin Lexington once. Got out and started to make it back to the Apple with this dude and he wanted to stop off in fuckin Cleveland to see some relatives, the fuckin asshole. We cop for some paregoric an we/re cookin it down and cold shakin it and get off a little taste and the next thing you know the fuckin man is breakin

down the door of the hotel and we/re back in the fuckin
slammer and we get two and a half to five for fuckin traces.
Aint that some shit? That asshole started givin them some
shit—he didn't know how to do time—an he did the whole
fuckin nickel. I did a deuce and I aint never been near
that fuckin Ohio since. Aint never goin to either. The others
were laughing and chuckling, Tyrone with them. You know
something, that fuckin Ohio they got the fuckin death
penalty for dope. But I hooked up with a young guy when
I gets back here—jesus he was a good tief. He could steal ya
blind and ya wouldnt even seeim, everybody joining in the
laughter. The circle of guys drew closer to the old guy and
there was a feeling of camaraderie among them as they
listened to the man of years, of scraggly dead hair, gray skin
and a few broken and brown teeth tell of the golden days of
the past when you could stay high forever on a three dollar
cap. Shit, they used to have some fuckin stuff that was so
fuckin good it got ya high while it was still in the fuckin
cooker, hahaha, and when ya got off it tightened ya ass hole
right up man. Shit, you couldnt even tink a takin a shit. Ya
couldnt even remember what it was like. Ya tought the
shitter was fa washin ya feet, the others laughing loudly,
all the energy of their frustration and fear going into their
laughter. Before the war the fuckin Germans was sending
stuff over here that was pure stuff—you tink ya know what
pure stuff is?—an ya could get a pound of pure for fuckin
nothin practically, but thats all we had was nothin, everybody laughing louder. I guess the fuckin Germans figured
theyd turn on the whole fuckin country an win the fuckin
war like that, eh? But nobody gave much of a shit then.
Ya could cop all the fuckin p.g. ya wanted an all kinds
a shit had opium in it. Laudum. Great shit. If ya sick. Just
gulp down a fuckin bottle a paregoric and dump some
goof balls then chew some guinea bread real quick. Best

way ta keep it down. In those days it was practically legal
ta have pot. It used ta be growin in empty lots—there was
lots of empty lots then, not like now. All these fuckin
empty lots all over the fuckin city—lots a times no body even
knew what it was. Can ya imagine what would happen now
if ya had a whole fuckin lot full of fuckin pot? The fuckin
animals would break ya fuckin head ta get it, eh? everybody
laughing and straining to hear more. They used ta burnem
every now an then, but they had to notify the people—
somethin about fire laws—I dont know. So they put notices
in the paper—I aint shittin, right in the fuckin paper—that
such an such a lot is gonna be burned on such an such a
date, you know, the time an everything. I remember one, I
was just a young punk—hadnt even had my first real habit
yet, not a real one—an they was gonna burn this lot in the
neighborhood, eh? So the night before the guys pick as
much as they can, right, an the next day when theyre gonna
burn all these fuckin weeds every head in the neighborhood
and from all ova the fuckin city is standin a few yards down
wind, breathin hard man . . . whata fuckin sight man. . . .
Theres gotta be hundreds a guys standin in the street lookin
like theyre doin some kindda deep breathin exercises and
laughing their asses off and the fuckin firemen are lookin at
us like we/re fuckin crazy as we just stand there man an get
high all over, even our fuckin teet an hair was high. Everybody was roaring with laughter so much that one of the
guards cruised by to check out the cell. Tyrone found himself
hooked on listening to the old dope fiend who sat like a
guru in the corner dispensing his stories of glory and en-
lightened wisdom. Yeah, Ive known some fuckin winners
man. Guys that would—we had this one guy in Danamora
that was really sometin. He—they called him Pussy McScene
—he would fuck anythin. This here guy would fuck anythin
he could get his cock into. He was in that fuckin Siberia so

long man he forgot what a woman looked like, but you know the joints, theres always plenty a assholes ta play. So Pussy McScene gets out an he hooks up with some broad by Needle Park an—I tink her fuckin name was Hortense—so they get together—shes about fifty because Pussys gotta be in his sixties by this time, but he can still get it up—so he writes back that hes fuckin a woman. Naturally nobody believes him. Hes fucked so many guys we figure he dont know how ta fuck a woman so theyre takin bets all over the joint if Pussys really fuckin a broad so they gotta get somebody to find out to settle the bets, eh? So a guy gets paroled and he looks up Pussy and he writes back that Pussys really got himself an old broad an he takes a picture of her with Pussy holdin up her dress showin her snatch an—you know what? that old fuckin broad was turnin tricks for Pussy for krists sake. Yeah, about once or twice a month she/d get a fuckin john—outta Bickfords, eh?—an then bring the money to Pussy an tellim, Here ya are baby, everybody was laughing and giggling and slapping each other on the shoulder, Youre too much ol man. Youre one fuckin pisser pops. Yeah, Ive been around. Ive seenem come an go. A lotta big time fuckin junkies, eh? But I'm still here. Theyre all fuckin dead. Potters field or some fuckin place. Its not easy to make it in this racket, eh? Ive seen a lotta good guys get blown away or hot shotted. He bummed another cigarette. I/ll tellya how to make it. I/ll tellya why Im here an all those other fuckin guys aint. Sure, Ive had some ups and downs, but the reason I made it, and am still makin it, is because I never got fucked up with a cunt. Theyre fuckin cancer, the kiss a deat. Hey pops, whatch yoe talkin about? Aint nothin wrong with a little pussy now an thain, hehehehe. Yeah, eh? I/ll tellya somethin—I usually charge for my advise, but I/ll tellya for nothin, eh? Pussy is like quicksand, ya fall in and itll suck ya right down, an the harder ya fight the deeper ya sink until ya drown. Sheeit, whatta way to go. Im with you pops. Fuck them bitches jim. They get you *all* fucked up. Yeah, I/d rather feed my habit than some fuckin broad. The old man adopted an attitude and expression of fatherly concern and leaned forward with a grave countenance, Like I said, its not easy to make it in this world, but ya can do it. I know because Im making it. Remember that kid I told ya about, the guy who was such a good tief. He coulda been a success just like me, but he fucked up. He gets himself hooked up with some bimbo, eh? I tellsim at the time ta cutter loose, but he laughs at me, Shes a high class hooker he tells me. Brings in a lot of bread, he tells me. Keeps him in fine clothes an dope. So he gets lazy an lives off her money an that turns into a full time job, eh? Hes gotta be sure shes bringing home all the bread an not givin any free samples, eh? Right on pops— laughter—Then hes gotta protect his investment. She starts chippin with some guy—there aint no cunt in the world that wont chippie onya, take it from me—an hes gotta straighten it out, eh? So what happens? He takes three slugs right in the fuckin head. Just like that. Its a fuckin shame too. He was a good fuckin tief, he didnt need no fuckin bimbo grief. I tellya kid, stay away—shit, even poor ol Pussy got fuckin burned because a that old fuckin Hortense broad. Sheeit, yoe mean somebody wanna steal that ol woman? Hahaha, fuck no. That crazy ol broad burned a connection an told him it was Pussys idea an poor old Pussy didnt know from shit and the guy ranim down. I wasnt there but they said it knocked him from Bickfords to Needle Park, hahahaha. But I/ll tellya kid, if ya wanna make it out there an feed ya habit, ya stay away from the broads an ya dont go for nothin too big. Small stuff so that if ya get busted ya —listen, ya gotta get busted every now an then. Thats the law of averages an it gives ya time ta rest an clean up so ya

can go out there an get off with just a taste again. But stay
to the petty thefts. No felonies. The only way. You can make
it good that way. You can boost just as much that way without takin no chance of doin big time. I got some heavy
bits, but I got fucked up by the man. They fuckin framed
me because I wouldnt rat out my connection. Shit, I dont
rat out no— Tyrone was gradually leaning back more and
more, as he laughed along with the others, until he was
leaning against the side of the cell and looking at all the
other dudes listening to the old man, the young guys, like
him, leaning forward and grabbing in every word, the older
dudes sitting back and nodding their heads and slapping
their legs and laughing along with the rest. Something funny
was happening inside of him that he couldnt put his finger
on. There seemed to be something between him and the
rest of the dudes in that cell. He gradually became aware
of a sense of identification, like they had something in
common. But he quickly buried the feeling because he knew
he was different than the old man and the other dudes in the
cell. He became aware of knots in his gut and a pain in the
back of his head. He looked at the old man. He stared.
Hard . . . He look like a fuckin rat jim. Thas what he look
like. A fuckin rat. His skin be so fuckin tight an gray an he
got tracks all up an down his arms, his legs an his neck an
he sittin back fat mouthin while he gettin ready to do some
more time. Sheeit, that aint no fuckin way jim. Ah aint
gonna marry no habit. No mutha fuckin death do us part
with me an no jones. *Uh* uh. You aint gonna catch Tyrone
C. Love boostin no steaks outta no store or sneakin down no
cellar to cop their coffee. Sheeit, when ah gets out an we gets
straight we jus gonna wheel an deal an not go fuckin with
any penny boolshit. We gonna make it good jim. Things
get straight an we get us a pound a pure an we gonna be
back jus like we was, sittin back jus countin those bucks,

an me an Alice gonna live high offa that hog jim. He looked at the old man sitting in the corner, taking another butt from somebodys pack, the rest of them grouped around him. No man, ah aint gonna do no time. Even a teeny bit a time. Ah doan need to go to no fuckin joint to clean up. Ahm doin jus fine like this jim. An anyway, ah aint got no habit. Not like he be talkin about. Ah could cut it loose any time ah wanted an when the time come ah jus kiss this old shit goodbye an— LOVE . . . LOVE, TYRONE C. 735. Get your shit together an comeon. The guard opened the door and Tyrone followed him down the corridor to another room. The guard handed a slip of paper to another guard behind a counter and the process of leaving started. When he finally got all his possessions and signed the necessary papers he was let loose. Harry was waiting for him on the other side of the door. Whatta ya say man? Sheeit . . . les go jim. Harry chuckled, Im with you man. They hailed a cab and headed for Tyrones place. I got down here as soon as I got back. Ah sure do preciate that baby. He smacked Harrys hand, and Harry hit his. You got something at your place? Yeah. Ahm straight for a while. Howd you do? Nothin spectacular. You know. But some decent shit. Could only get bundles, but itll do for now. I can get weight like that so that we can do alright. But only in bundles. Tyrone shrugged, Betteran nothin jim. You aint shittin. At least until we can get back into real business. What happened with you? Sheeit, Tyrone chuckled and shook his head, Them two mutha fuckas, The Beas, bus me jim. He giggled then told Harry the story. He finished a few minutes before they got to his pad. When the cab stopped he thanked Harry again and they gave each other five, and he split. He was still feeling the closeness he felt for Harry when he saw him waiting for him as he stepped through the doorway, a closeness that increased as they shared the cab. It felt warm

and good. He wasnt going to be like that old man. He had
some good friens man. He an Harry be tight jim, real tight.
He thought of how Harry got his ass right down to the
jail, but his mind kept going back to the old man too.
Everytime he tried to keep that good feeling going through
him by thinking of how Harry got him out of the slammer,
his mind pushed that aside and filled him with a picture of
the old man. Sheeit, fuck you ol man. Ah aint no fuckin
dopefien. You is a stoned out hope ta die dopefien. Ahm jus
a dude what doan want no hassles an havin a good time an
gettin some bucks together so we can get a pound a pure
an then go into a little business. . . . Yeah, me an mah fox
jim. Alice was all over him when he got in the door, O
baby, ah was so afraid they gonna keep you there all night;
and Tyrone hugged and kissed her an they smiled and
laughed for a moment, then Tyrone started for the bathroom, Ah need a little tase baby . . . git the tase a that jail
out a mah pretty little mouth. . . .

He didnt know why, but Harry felt disturbed on the
way back to his place. He couldnt really latch on to what it
was or why. It was something like a memory that was trying
to come back but wasnt quite making it an he was trying to
push it so he could find out what it was, but the more he
pushed the more it hid behind the corner and got lost in the
darkness. He kept directing his mind to the fuckin cops
who stole their dope and their bread, but another part of
his mind, just like Tyrones, kept wanting to look at the old
man, and Harry would shake his head, inwardly, an once
again fix his mind on the fuckin cops but his head was
persistent and kept shoving the image of the old man in
front of him and Harry kept turning his back on him and
wrinkling his face in disgust, How could anybody let them-

selves get to be that low for krists sake? If I ever got to be half that bad I/d fuckin kill myself. Shit! and he frowned again in disgust. When he got back to Marions he told her about the bust and the old man, and she smiled, Well, one just doesnt get to meet a better class of people in places like that, and then she chuckled. Harrys face relaxed slightly, then he chuckled too. Marion dismissed the old man with a wave and a nod, Hes so obviously Freudian that its pathetic. I mean that business about women. Obviously he never did sublimate his oedipal complex and it made him an addict. That way he can claim not to be interested in women without accepting the fact that hes afraid of them. Probably impotent. I/ll bet you anything hes impotent and that's why hes so afraid of them. So he becomes an addict. Obvious. Really pathetic. Harry chuckled then laughed. He didnt know why, but what Marion was saying made him feel better. Maybe it was the way she looked and waved her hand around, but whatever it was he felt something draining out of him, and whatever it was was being replaced with a sense of relief. He continued to smile as he listened and watched. What really annoys me, I mean what really galls me are the cops. Typical fascist pigs. Theyre the same cops that killed the students at Kent State, that torture people in Korea and South Africa. Its the same mentality that built the concentration camps. But try and get these stuffed middle-class—ooooo, it just infuriates me. We would be watching the news and be seeing the cops beating people over the head with their clubs and my mother and father would claim it wasnt really happening or they were some sort of hippie degenerate commies. Thats the big thing with them. Everybodys a commie. Talk about freedom and human rights and youre a commie. All they want to talk about is the sacred right of the stockholder and how the police protect our property. . . . She took a deep breath,

closed her eyes for a moment, then looked at Harry, You
know, if I were to tell them about this theyd say it didnt
happen, that I just made it up. She shook her head, It just
amazes me how blind some people can be to the truth. Its
right there in front of them and they dont see it. It just
amazes me. Yeah, its weird. I dont know how they do it.
Harry got up, Comeon, lets have a taste of that new shit
before I get to work.

R osh Hashanah and Yom Kippur had passed. Sara knew it was going to be a good year. She followed a strict observance of Yom Kippur for the first time since she didnt know when. Not even a glass of tea she had. Only water. And her pills. Medicine she figured was different. It wasnt food. And it came from a doctor so it was medicine. But she fasted and atoned. She thought of Harry and a sadness flowed over her. She prayed for him. Again. How many times. She prayed she would see him. She would see him a poppa. It was a few weeks into the new year. Maybe more. Now she called the McDick Corp. a couple of times a week, sometimes in the morning after she had taken her purple, red and orange pills and had drunk a pot of coffee, and told them how they had to find her card and let her know what show she would be on. She couldnt wait, and are they sure they hadnt lost her card and maybe she should come down there and help them look and the girl she spoke to, whoever it might be, would get annoyed and feel like yelling at her but would stay calm as possible and tell her, firmly, that they didn't need her help in doing their job and that she should relax and stop calling for Gods sake and they would eventually hang up and hope and pray that she wouldnt call again; but she would, after taking her tranquilizers she would call late in the afternoon and be sweet and tell the girl, whoever it might be, Youre such a nice girl, dolly, youll please check for me and see what show, I dont want to trouble you but so many people are asking and youre like a daughter to me, its like doing a favor for your mother and I promise I wont bother you again youre so sweet, and the girl would giggle and nod and shake her head and finally hang up the phone and Sara would go back to her viewing chair.

Winter came early. It seemed like there were a few lovely autumn days where the air was clear and crisp, the sky blue with white puffy clouds, the temperature warm and comforting in the sun and cool and invigorating in the shade. Days of absolute perfection. Then suddenly it was gray and windy and cold and rainy and then the sleet and snow came and even if you could find the sun it seemed to have lost its warmth. From time to time Marion fiddled with a sketch pad, but her hand seemed to be moving the pencil while the rest of her was completely detached from the action. Occasionally they would attempt to resurrect their enthusiasm for the coffee house, and their other plans, but for the most part they spent their time shooting dope and watching television or listening to music occasionally. Once in a while they went to a movie, but with the bad weather that interested them less and less. About the only time Harry went out now was to cop the stuff, and that was becoming more and more difficult. Every time they found somebody to cop from they went out of business for some damn reason. It seemed like the fuckin gods were against them. They had long since given up the idea of a pound of pure, though they consciously mentioned it once in a great while, and of getting uncut weight. They were content to score bundles, but now that was becoming a rarity. They were just getting what they could and using it all themselves, they couldnt even get enough to off to pay for their own stuff. At one time it seemed like they had a nice pile of bucks, now it seemed like they didnt have shit. Harry and Tyrone would discuss the situation and the amount of money remaining, and try to analyze what was happening, sifting through the various reasons they had heard for the shortage of dope, all plausible and equally far fetched. Some guys said the italian and the black gangs were fightin and other dudes said that was a bunch of mutha fuckin boolshit cause I heard it right from mah man there be a big bus on a ship carryin fifty mutha fuckin keys jim an— What the fuck you talkin about? They consciskate a hundred pounds a scag man an there be all kinds a headlines an the TV be spitting that ol dope shit *all* day. Sheeit, the man rip off that much stuff an we all be in mournin baby. Right on man, and he gave him five then they passed it around and the stories continued. But in the final analysis it didnt make any difference why. There was a problem and that was that. Why didnt make a fiddlers fuck and all they could do was to hang tough and hope the scene would break soon so they could get back where they were. They knew that sooner or later there would be dope all over the city, just like before. There was too much money involved for there not to be. Harry talked about it from time to time with Marion and, of course, the conversation was as fruitless as the ones with Tyrone. Except it did keep the bond between them cemented. As long as they could share they felt close and that was important. And whenever they started to feel the chills of fear and the grinding of anxiety they simply got off and melted all the cares and concerns away with its warmth. Sometimes they would fix up new cookers just for the sake of doing it. It was part of keeping house. The entire routine made them feel a part of something. It was something looked forward to with the greatest of joy and anticipation. The entire ritual was symbolic of their life and needs. The careful opening of the bag and the dumping in the cooker of the dope, and dropping in the water with the dropper. Making a new collar from time to time for the dropper so the needle would fit snugly, Harry using a piece of matchbook cover, Marion a piece from a dollar bill. Staring at the solution in the cooker as it heated and dissolved and then stirring the cotton around with the needle then drawing the solution up and into the dropper and holding the dropper in the mouth as they tied up and found a favorite vein, usually going into a previously made hole and feeling the spurt of excitement as the needle penetrated the vein and the blood spurted up the dropper and they let go of the tie around their arm and shot the shit into their arm and waited for that first flash of heat through their body and the warm swelling in the gut and they let the dropper fill up with blood and booted and then yanked it out and put it in the glass of water and rubbed the drops of blood off their arm and sat back feeling whole and invulnerable and safe and a lot of other things, but mostly whole.

But there was less and less dope out there. It seemed like each day it was just a little more difficult to get the dope and their phone rang constantly with calls from people looking for some. Occasionally they would get enough to sell and make some bread, but it seemed like most of the time they were using most of what they got. One night they couldnt get any at all. They kept getting promises from a couple of dudes that they would have some soon, but nothing came. Eventually they fell asleep with the aid of a few sleeping pills, but their bodies were shaking slightly and inwardly they were trembling. They had never gone to bed without having dope in the house for when they woke up. They had never thought of it in those terms before. Even with the hassles they were having lately, they always had enough for themselves, but now there wasnt a thing in the house, just the cottons they had been saving. They were going to use them, but through an intense exertion of will, and the use of downers and pot, they decided to save them for morning. Their sleep was worse than shallow. It was almost worse than being awake. They could feel their bodies sweating and could smell the sweat. They seemed to be freezing. The back of their heads and their stomachs seemed to be linked in pain, working together to bring about a nausea that continually threatened to erupt, but there was nothing there but the constant pressure of the pain and nausea; and with every breath their panic increased. Their anxiety grew and grew until it consumed their bodies and swelled in their chests and threatened to cut off their air and they gasped for air and sat up in the bed and looked around in the dark trying to identify whatever it was that had awakened them. They tried closing their eyes and going to sleep, but they couldnt tell the difference between sleep and being awake. They seemed to be caught in some sort of trap, and they tossed and moaned and finally Marion bolted up in bed, gasping for breath and Harry put the light on, You alright? Marion nodded, Must have had a bad dream I guess. She was still panting, her entire body heaving with each breath. Harry put his arm around her, Maybe we should use the cottons now? Do you think we should, its so early? Why not? Itll probably help you. Yes, I guess so. I/ll get the stuff. Alright. Harry went to the bathroom, and Marion got out of bed to be by his side when he divided the cottons, both feeling justified in using them so far ahead of schedule, feeling that the weight was off their backs, and the other had really suggested it. Saving cottons had started as a game, but now they were more like a life preserver. After they got off the dope, combined with the sleeping pills, had them nodding out and they went back to sleep for a few more hours, but this time they drifted into unconsciousness. The sun was shining when they awoke and they immediately went back to the cottons before doing anything else. There was a little something left, but not much. Harry got on the phone, but nothing was happening. They sat around stiffly smoking a few joints and trying to watch the television but even though they could hear the radiator clicking with steam, there was a cold chill in the air, a stiffness that surprised them but didnt occupy them for they had only one preoccupation, waiting to get some dope. A little before twelve Tyrone called to ask if anything was happening. No man, nothin. Ah just got a call from mah man downtown, he got some stuff so ahm on mah way. Great! How long will it takeya? Depen on traffic. Maybe a hour. Or less. Ah let you know when I get back. Groovy. I/ll hang around here in case somethin happens at this end. Later baby. Harry hung up the phone with an audible sigh. The room was suddenly warm and the barriers seemed to have been dissolved. They sat around talking, smoking, watching television with a hysterical and rigid nonchalance. Neither one wanted to be obvious and look at the clock, but they kept calculating the time mentally by the progress of the television show, feeling almost nauseous from the intensity of their anticipation. When the phone rang Harry did his best to just saunter over to it and pick it up carelessly, and Marion tried to assume an attitude of indifference, keeping her gaze on the television, but watching Harry out of the corner of her eye, a sharp twist of panic turning her head as she noticed the expression on Harrys face, No man, nothin yet. Try me later. She sighed inwardly, at least it wasnt Tyrone saying he didnt get anything. Harry sat back on the couch, A lot of people out there looking for something. Marion nodded, wanting to say something, but no words formed so her mouth remained closed and her eyes continued to watch the television screen, not seeing what was happening, but allowing it to help push the endless time a little faster. Harry moved to the far end of the couch so he would be closer to the phone and when it rang he stayed seated and just sort of reached over to it, the both of them feeling the immediate hush and press of silence and anticipation, as if all life and action in the room had been immediately suspended. Marion had his face clearly in view when it widened in a grin, Seeya man. Harry stood up, Tys back and hes straight. Marion stood, trying to keep her voice as casual as possible, yet unable to deny the struggle going on within her, I think I/ll ride over with you. I could use some fresh air. The life suddenly rushed back into the room and the stillness chattered and dissolved as they put on their coats and smiled at each other, suddenly feeling something huge and heavy flow from them, leaving them free to smile and talk. They couldnt believe what was happening within them, trying to deny its existence but not telling the other one about it, trying desperately to stay involved in meaningless conversation as they rode to Tyrones pad. There was a voice, loud and clear, saying they were hooked, but good, and they tried to shrug it away but it persisted, more as a feeling than a voice, that permeated their every cell just as the dope they were addicted to had already done, and they tried combating it with another voice saying so what, it was no big deal, they could stop any time they wanted to, it was no big thing and what else was there? things would straighten out soon and they tried to interest themselves in staring through the cab windows at the people fighting the wind and the cold, thinking of how soon they would feel that loving warm flush, and when they got to Tyrones they still tried to maintain the cool attitude and smile and joke for a few minutes as they took off their coats, consciously and deliberately not asking about the dope but feeling a wave of joy when they saw Alices eyes almost closed and Tyrone looking so cool, but eventually the taste in the back of their throats refused to allow them to continue the bullshit about the weather and they asked him about the stuff and he got out two bundles and they took a couple of bags and went in the bathroom and borrowed Tys works and got off and immediately all the thoughts and nightmares and fears and terrors of the previous night, the inner battles during the short day and ride to Tyrones, were obliterated and dissolved and never existed, and the four of them sat around the rest of the day, listening to music, rapping, getting off, wrapped in the comforting warmth of their camaraderie.

Now the shit really hit the fan. It must have hit something because it sure as hell wasnt floating around the city. There no longer was any thought, or even desire, to make money, but just an unending effort to get enough for themselves. Some days it was a case of just copping enough for right now and then going out again to take care of the rest of the day and have that wake up shot nice and secure.

And the streets were getting tougher. All the neighborhood streets were filled with dope fiends, even in the snow and sleet, looking for something, anything. Every hallway was cluttered with sick faces with runny noses and bodies shivering with the cold and junk sickness, the cold cracking the marrow of their bones as they broke out in sweats from time to time. The deserted buildings that stretched for miles and made the city look like a battleground of WWII, that gave it the pathetic and devastated look that froze on the faces of the people that inhabited them, were spotted with tiny fires as shivering bodies tried to keep warm and survive long enough to get some dope, one way or another, and make it through one more day so they could start the same routine again. When someone did cop he then had to make

it safely to his pad, or some place, where he could get off
without someone breaking down the door and stealing his
dope and maybe getting killed, or killing, if he didnt want
to part with something more precious, at that particular
moment, than his life, for without it his life was worse than
hell, far worse than death, death seeming to be a reward
rather than a threat, because this process of lingering death
was the most fearful thing that could happen. And so the
city became even more savage with the passing of each day,
with the taking of each step, the breathing of each breath.
From time to time a body would fall from a window and
before the blood had a chance to seep through the clothing
hands were going through his pockets to see what might be
found to help them through another moment of being suspended in Hell. Cabbies were avoiding certain neighborhoods
and carrying guns. Deliveries werent made. Some services
discontinued. The sections were like cities under siege, surrounded by the enemy trying to starve them into submission,
but the enemy was within. Not only within the boundaries of
the cities, of the neighborhoods, the deserted buildings and
piss stained doorways, but within each and every body and
mind and, most of all, soul. The enemy ate away at their will
so they could not resist, their bodies not only craving, but
needing the very poison that ground them into that pitiable
state of being; the mind diseased and crippled by the enemy
it was obsessed with and the obsession and terrible physical
need corrupting the soul until the actions were less than
those of an animal, less than those of a wounded animal, less
than those of anything and everything they did not want to
be. The police increased their personnel on the streets as the
number of insane robberies increased and men and women
were shot as they broke store windows and tried to run down
the street with a TV set, the sets exploding as they fell to
the ground, the bodies sliding on the ice leaving a trail of

blood, and freezing, stiff, before being picked up and disposed of. For every bit of dope that was put on the streets there were thousands of eager and sick hands reaching, grabbing, stabbing, choking, clubbing, or pulling the trigger of a gun. And if you did rip somebody off and get away nice and clean you werent sure you would ever get to see it flow into your veins. And maybe you wouldnt even know that you didnt as you concentrated on cooking it up, not wanting to spill a drop, and somebody bashed in your head before the needle ever got in your arm.

Harry and Tyrone were slowly absorbed by the cesspools they were spending more and more time in. It was a gradual progression, like most diseases, and their overwhelming need made it possible for them to ignore much of what was happening, distorting some, and the rest accepted as part of the reality of their lives. But with each day more and more of the truth was impossible to ignore while the disease instantly and automatically rationalized the truth into an acceptable distortion. Their disease made it possible for them to believe whatever lies it was necessary for them to believe to continue to pursue and indulge their disease, even to the point of them believing they were not enslaved by it, but were actually free. They climbed crumbling old staircases to shattered apartments shielding shattered people where old plaster was peeling off walls that had huge holes in them with broken beams and gigantic rats, as desperate as the other inhabitants of the building, bursting from the darkened holes and corners, sniffing and attacking the unconscious bodies sprawled on the floor. Harry and Tyrone went together now, no matter what the color scheme, because a loner was an open invitation to being ripped off of your dope and your life. Everyone looked like a muskrat and smelled like a skunk, that peculiar and overwhelming junk sick smell penetrating the clothes and the frigid air. At first Harry and

Tyrone stayed on the fringes of the devastation, seeing the campfires in the hollowed buildings from a distance, but it became progressively necessary to go deeper and deeper into the desolation to fulfill their needs, the urgency of the need being the first concern of their lives. At first their forays were tentative and timid, now they were cautious but assertive, realizing the necessity of getting to where the action was as rapidly as possible before it was just no mans land with empty bags, broken bottles, unconscious bodies and an occasional corpse. Whatever chances they had to take they took automatically as their disease ordered and they obeyed, a small part of them wanting to try to resist, but that part shoved so far down that it was no more than an ancient dream from a previous life. Only the insatiable and insane need of the moment had any bearing on their lives, and it was that need that gave the orders.

They were really scuffling and barely making it from one day to the next, one hour to the next, and with each day they became more desperate. Many times they were ripped off for a hundred bucks here, a few hundred there, but that was all part of that world and all they could do was get more bread and scuffle and hustle until they got the dope they needed. Many times they could only get a couple of bags and they would shoot them up and continue to try and cop more so they could have enough for Marion and Alice, but sometimes it was a long time between fixes for them. After they got off Harry and Tyrone would affirm that they would take the next stuff back to the pad, even if it was only a couple of bags, so their old ladies could have a taste, but each time they got only two bags they shot them up immediately knowing it would be better for everyone involved if they got off and stayed up here where the action was so they could get some weight and then give the girls a real taste. They knew, and believed, that it was better to have nothing at all than to have less than enough and who knows what might come down while they were away from the scene. And when they got back to their pads the lies came out easily and believingly.

From time to time they would think of the old man but as quickly as possible they would dismiss him from their minds knowing that they would never get like that, that they would do something about it before that would happen to them. And whenever they saw cats scufflin the streets trying to sell somebody elses glasses for a fix, or dipping into a toilet bowl to get the water to cook up their stuff, they knew they would never stoop to shit like that. Shooting dope was one thing, but only a fuckin animal would do that. Yet somehow everything that was happening became progressively easier to ignore. They were walking with a few other cats to cop from a connection when some dude came out of a doorway and shoved a gun against the connections head and blew half his fuckin head off and grabbed the dope and split muttering something about no mutha fucka goin burn him. The others dropped and scattered when it happened and when the guy split they looked at the connection for a brief moment, the blood pumping from the hole in his head, then scattered. The frozen body was found eight hours later.

Sara took another Valium before going to visit Ada. They sat drinking tea, talking, and watching and listening to the television. Maybe now the holidays are over youll hear what show youre going on. Theres more holidays coming. Theres always more coming. Right now we/re between. Maybe when I call later theyll have my card. Maybe they found it and are waiting for me to call. Ada shrugged, Could be, who knows. But you should eat. And you should sit still so I can get the roots. I dont like the way you look so thin. The red dress fits nice. It fits nice, it fits nice. But you dont fit nice.

You should eat. Eh, you sound like my refrigerator. Ada looked at her with both her eyes, completely forgetting about the television, Now I sound like a refrigerator? What does a refrigerator sound like? besides rattling and groaning and sometimes just stopping like mine? Sara shrugged, They need a rest. Sara, youre alright? Of course. Why shouldnt I be? Why shouldnt you be? Because you dont look good. You look tired and— Im *zophtic* already. You should see the red dress and the gold shoes. Sara, theres something wrong. Im happy the dress is fitting, but Im worried. Your eyes dont look good dolly. Please, please, let me fix something for you . . . some soup. I just made fresh. Sara shook her head and waved her hand, No, no, no. Not now. Later. Sara got up, I have to call. I can feel they found my card. Ada looked sad as well as worried, You said that already a hundred times. I know, I know, but this time its for real . . . I can tell . . . I can feel it.

Harry and Tyrone had been scuffling the streets and alleys for many, many hours. The wind was strong and gusting from time to time with sleet and hail. Whenever they stood still for any length of time it became almost impossible to initiate movement again. Their feet were beyond numb and seemed to be frozen to the ground and the pain went from their soles up through their legs, almost shattering their knees. They tried to keep their backs to the wind, but it seemed to always be blowing in their faces no matter what direction they faced. They huddled as deeply as possible into their jackets, but they were still so cold they could barely talk, but only nodded toward each other. Their eyes and noses were constantly running and freezing, their faces stiff with a thin layer of ice. They looked at the glow from the campfires in the distance and wanted to just hang over one for a while, but they knew if they went near one they would be ripped off for everything they had, including their clothes, so they lived with their pain and the ice until they finally scored for a dozen bags and then, as rapidly as possible, split from the scene. They went to a public toilet in a subway station, locked the door and burned some toilet paper to warm themselves, then filled their droppers with water from the stained and cruddy toilet bowl and got off and just leaned against the walls of the cubicle feeling the heat of the dope crack the ice in their blood and bones, then wiped the water off their faces and smiled at each other and slapped each others hands, Thats some good shit man. Yeah baby, thas jus fine, jus fine. They left the toilet and went down the steps to the subway feeling warm and safe.

The word was out that in a couple of days there would be dope on the streets. Everybody nodded and uh uhed and went on their way trying to survive another day. But the story persisted that Harlan Jefferson had sent word to let go a couple a keys for the Christmas season, he being a good Baptist boy an not wantin anybody to be wantin during this glorious season. With the persistence of the story people started to believe, mostly because they wanted to and also because that sounded like Harlan Jefferson. There was a feeling of expectancy, a tension, in the air, a reason to hang tough and make it through till they cut loose with the shit. When the word came down that the price would be doubled and you had to cop for weight, then everybody was a believer. The word came through subway, bus and Hudson tubes that the next night, at ten, in a huge area of deserted and crumbling buildings, there would be shit but you have to cop at least half a piece and it was going for five hundred dollars. Five hundred dollars for a half a fuckin piece was insane man, but what you gonna do? The man aint goin to lay no nickel bag on you, thas for damn sure. The cats in the streets were generating steam trying, desperately, to dig up the bread to cop, but how can you boose enough to be able to go for five hundred bucks? Hustlin, scufflin and boosin enough to cop a couple a bags a day was a bitch, but five hundred???? Sheeit, aint no fuckin way ah cain do that, but the race was on anyway. If they couldnt get the bread to cop from the man, maybe theyd get enough to cop from the guys who did, but the price of a bag was damn sure goin up jim.

Harry and Tyrone wanted desperately to cop a piece but they only had seven hundred between them. They tried to think what they could hock or steal but they couldnt think of anything that would give them a few hundred bucks. Then Harry thought of Marions shrink. You mean Arnold? Yeah. I havent seen him in months. So what? Hes still callin, aint he? Yes, but I dont know. Look, tellim we/ll give it back toim in twenty-four hours. Thats all itll take ta get the bread back. Marion frowned and looked worried, upset. Harrys voice and expression were urgent, Look we get this and off some and we/re back in business. This probably means the panics over and therell be stuff on the streets again and we wont have ta scuffle and make that scene every fuckin day anymore. I/ll tellya honey, its a fuckin drag. I know Harry, I know. I dont like whats happening either. Then whats the problem? I dont know, I— Look, you can get him to part with a few hundred bucks. Whats that to him? Hes loaded for krists sake. There was a hint of pleading in Marions eyes and voice, I just wish there was some other way to get the money. Look, I dont care how we get it. If you got some other idea, great, but Im fuckin lost and we need that bread. Getting the money is not the problem Harry— Then whats the problem fa krists sake? Marion looked at him almost pleadingly, I just dont know what I/ll have to do to get it. What Marion said was obvious and inevitable, but Harrys need forced, and allowed, him to quickly sidestep the obvious before the truth registered enough to alter his desires and he shrugged the suggestion away, Dont sweat it. You can handleim. Marion looked at Harry for endless seconds, hoping something would suddenly, and happily, change the words and situation, a *deus ex machina* would emerge from the ceiling and the dilemma would be instantly solved. Either you get the money from the shrink or we dont get no stuff. Its that simple. Marion got her wish. The dilemma was solved. She nodded and called his office.

At Marions request they met in a small, quiet restaurant that had a feeling of privacy and was dimly lighted. She got there fifteen minutes late to be certain she would not have to wait for him and feel conspicuous sitting alone. Her makeup covered her complexion, but the thin haggard look was obvious even in the dim lighting of the restaurant. Are you alright? Something wrong? No, no, Ive just had the flu forever it seems like. Just cant seem to shake it. It goes away for a few days and then its right back again. Have you been under stress? You know unresolved emotional tension can precipitate viral infection. Marion could feel her insides tensing and she struggled to control herself and forced a smile on her face, No, its nothing like that. Just been very busy. Getting a lot of work done lately. Well, thats wonderful, Im glad to hear that you have been productive. Marion did her best to keep the smile on her face as she toyed with her food and sipped at her wine, Arnold commenting from time to time at her lack of appetite, and surprised at the way she was neglecting her wine, Its one of your favorites. She kept the smile in front of her and nodded, I know, reaching over and touching his hand, but this flu, or whatever it is, just seems to have killed my taste buds and appetite. He smiled and touched her hand with his other hand, To be perfectly candid, I was rather surprised to hear from you. Is there something wrong? Marion fought back the urge to shove the candle in his face and did her best to broaden her smile, No, why do you ask? O, thats usually the case when someone calls whom you havent heard from for a while, and who has been turning down dinner and lunch invitations for a few months. Marion sipped the wine, then took another drink, No, everythings fine, but I do have a favor to ask. He leaned back a few inches and smiled knowingly. Marions gut was yelling, You smug sonofabitch, but she lowered her face slightly and looked at him through half opened eyes, I need to borrow three hundred dollars. May I ask why? Its personal, Marion trying to put as much warmth in her smile as possible, not caring what he thought just as long as he didnt bug her. He looked at her for a second, then shrugged. Thats no problem. Marion gave an inner sigh of relief. I/ll have to give you cash, you understand. She nodded, That will do just fine, and she smiled a smile of genuine warmth and sincerity and found herself eating a little food and enjoying the wine and being thankful that Harry had been able to cop some good dope so she wouldnt have to go through this feeling sick. She kept reminding herself that this was no different than all the other times she had had dinner or lunch with Arnold. It was the same. It was the same. Tell me, does this have anything to do with this fellow youre living with? Marion had to fight the sudden heat of anger that inflamed her and kept the smile on her face, No. He smiled and leaned forward and touched her hand, Its not important. I was just curious. Whats he like? Marion allowed her body to relax and the dope to once more circulate through her system and fill her with its warmth and feeling of contentment. Hes very nice. Rather wonderful actually. Marion finished her wine and Arnold waited for the waiter to refill her glass before leaning forward slightly. Hes quite handsome and sensitive . . . poetic. You look and sound as if you love him. Marions face softened even more, I do. And he loves you? Yes. And he needs me. Arnold nodded and they smiled at each other. I can help him accomplish great things. We have lots of plans.

After dinner they went to the small apartment Arnold kept in the city. Marion sat in the very familiar surroundings trying to feel comfortable, trying not to feel threatened, but every time Arnold spoke she wanted to shout into his face but she just continued to stare and try to smile, trying desperately to remember how she had acted and what she had done and said all the other times she had been here with him, but nothing came to mind except the urge to scream in his face. She kept adjusting herself in the chair trying to find a familiar position, did she usually look at the bookcase when she was here or the painting over the couch? How did she hold her cigarette? It suddenly felt large and conspicuous and when she tapped the ashes into the ashtray she found herself wondering if she should have rolled the ash off instead. She sat up suddenly and stretched her neck and back, then quickly uncrossed her legs and pulled her skirt down then blinked her eyes and felt herself flush as she wondered if Arnold was appraising her behavior. She tried to talk herself into a feeling of familiar comfort, but failed. Everything continued to feel strange. She tried to scare away, or at least obscure, the feeling by telling herself it was all the same, all the same, the same as all the other times, but the feeling persisted. Arnolds voice continued over the music and she could feel her facial muscles responding, and could hear her voice answering his, but she somehow felt oddly detached from that, too, as she did from everything else. She seemed to be waiting for something, perhaps to have the phone ring and hear Harrys voice tell her to forget the money and come on home, I got some stuff, but Harry didnt know this number, or that she was here. He thought they were at a show or some such place. He had no idea she was here, waiting to go to bed with Arnold. He didnt know. If he did he wouldnt have— She tried, desperately, to continue, but an inner voice was mocking her and the truth wormed its way through every inch of her being . . . she knew and Harry knew. They were in love, but they both knew she was there waiting to go to bed with Arnold. . . .

Marion sat on the edge of the bed, her back to Arnold, agonizingly trying to orient herself. Her feeling of alienation increased—its all the same, its all the same—and she blinked as she glanced around, the sound of Arnolds voice droning in her head. She looked at the floor and knew she had to undress. The light from the bedside lamp was so dim she could barely see the wall, but it bothered her and she asked Arnold to turn it off. He frowned for a moment, Why do you suddenly want the light off? You never did before. She swallowed a scream and almost started crying. She tried to sound normal, whatever that was, but the annoyance in her voice was obvious, I just do. Please Arnold. He shrugged and turned off the light. She almost felt secure for a moment in the sudden darkness and she quickly undressed, conscious of each piece of clothing coming off her body, and felt her arms crisscross her chest as she quickly slipped between the sheets— its all the same, its all the same—they felt slimy.

In the light of the apartment Arnold noticed the pallor under the makeup and her gauntness. Having been to bed with Marion many times over a period of a couple of years Arnold was aware of the difference in her body and attitude, but more noticeable, after he was accustomed to the dim light, were the needle marks on her arms. Marion had naturally enough worn a long sleeved dress to hide her arms, but it was impossible to do so forever. Arnold almost asked her about them but suddenly changed his mind and tried to pretend that they did not exist. He rolled over on his side and started kissing her and Marion responded as warmly as she could, continually reminding herself, Its the same. Its the same. She had been in bed with Arnold before. It was all the same.

There was no difference. She went through the motions, making what she hoped were the proper movements and sounds as she tried desperately to remember what they were, but somehow everything seemed foreign and incongruous and then she tried thinking of Harry but that quickly started to destroy everything and she froze for a second until his image was out of her mind and she grabbed Arnold even harder and just flailed around hoping she was acting the same way she had all the other times she was with Arnold but no matter how much she reminded herself that it had been many times she still felt dirty and over and over she told herself *It was the same. It was the same. It was the same.* But she couldnt convince herself and all she could do was try to convince Arnold and so she chanted her mantra *it was the same* and though it did not make her feel clean it allowed her to do what had to be done and she just reminded herself, from time to time, that Harry needed the money and she was really doing it for him and not for the money and *it was the same, it was the same, it was the same.* . . .

Marion took her clothes into the bathroom with her. After she bathed she got dressed, fixed her hair and makeup then went back in the bedroom. The light was on but she felt safe. Arnold was sitting on the side of the bed smoking. She smiled at him hoping it was the smile he was accustomed to, but more concerned about getting back to her place than anything else right now. Does the money have anything to do with the marks on your arms? What? Those marks. Needle marks. Is that why you needed the money? Are you??? he shrugged— What are you talking about? her eyes flared. Arnold smiled professionally, Dont get upset. If youre in trouble maybe I can help you. Her eyes relaxed, Im not in any trouble Arnold. Everything is just fine. He looked at her for a moment, a puzzled expression on his face. May I have the money Arnold? I really have to go home. Its late. He continued to look at her for a moment, I really would like an answer. I mean are you—what are those marks on your arm? O for Gods sake Arnold, do you always have to beat around the bush? Cant you simply ask me if Im using drugs? Isnt that what you want to say? Isnt it? He nodded. Yes. Well, if it will make you feel any better, I am. He looked hurt and shook his head slightly, But how could you be? Its impossible. Nothings impossible Arnold. Remember? But youre so young and bright and talented. I mean, youre not like those . . . those people who roam the streets mugging old ladies for enough money to get dope. Youre cultured and delicate and have been under therapy—and the therapist—they looked at each other for a few moments, Arnold becoming more and more confused and pained. But why? Why? Marion stared at him for a moment, then sighed loud and long, her body responding as if it had been squeezed tighter, Because it makes me feel whole . . . satisfied. The pain and confusion in Arnolds eyes started to glint with anger. May I please have the money Arnold? I really do have to go. He got up stiffly and went into another room and came back with the money and handed it to her, I guess I may just as well give it to you— I/ll repay you in a couple of days. No, thats alright. After all, youve earned it. He walked to the bathroom and closed the door behind him. Marion stared at the door for a moment, then left the apartment. She walked down the stairs, anger and disgust building and fighting, her eyes starting to tear, and when she thrust herself out into the street, and was hit with a shock of cold air, she suddenly stopped, dizzy, and leaned against the building and vomited, and vomited. . . .

Harrys guts were squirming. The first half hour or so after Marion left he just sort of sat back and hung loose with the dope and watched the tube. He kept telling himself that she would be back in a couple a hours and that everything would be cool, but as the minutes accumulated slowly something seemed to tighten and grow in his gut then swelled and rolled up to his chest and tugged at the back of his throat so that he was resisting a vague feeling of nausea. In a way he didnt mind the physical discomfort because he could dwell on it and avoid the things that were going on in his head, the things that were progressively growing and developing into images as well as words, images and words he didnt want to see or hear. After an hour he was really getting fidgety. He looked at his watch several times in less than five minutes, each time amazed at the time, feeling certain that more time than that had passed, then directing his eyes back to the tube, then thinking again about the time, not believing that he had looked at his watch correctly and so he would look at it again and be annoyingly disappointed at the reality of the time and so go back to the tube again, repeating the same procedure many times before getting up and changing the channel on the fuckin set from one station to another, each fuckin show looking worse than the one just flicked off and so he went through all the stations several times before tuning in an old movie, and sat back on the couch and consciously fought against looking at his watch. He smoked half a joint figuring it would settle his stomach and when he finished he leaned back and unconsciously put his right hand over his watch and tried to develop an interest in the show by staring at the tube, but it wouldnt even absorb the energy in the surface of his mind, and he was becoming increasingly aware of the images and words forming in his head so he directed his attention to his physical discomfort and when he thought he might be going to puke he got a box of Mallomars and started munching on them as he stared at the tube and fought the images that seemed to be churning in his gut and flashing across his mind and he kept shoving them down and out or some goddamn fuckin place but his sickness was reaching up to his head and soon every part of his body was sick with, and from, the fight, and he fought as long and as hard as he could but eventually he looked at his watch again and the sonofabitch had stopped and he felt like tearing it off his wrist and throwing it out the fuckin window but then he realized that that was great, that it must be a hell of a lot later than he thought so he dialed the time number and listened to the taped voice and the beep, a terrible sadness flooding his body as he looked at his watch and continued to listen to the voice tell him the time again and again and each time his watch was exactly right and no matter how long he listened to the voice and the tone and stared at those fuckin hands the time wouldnt change and now the sadness was welling up behind his eyes and he felt like a flood of tears was trying to force itself out and his body was bent as he hung up the phone and sat on the couch and stared at the tube while he remained painfully crushed by the hands on his watch and no matter how slowly time moves it is inevitable and now there had been hours that elapsed since she had left and the images and words no longer just vaguely floated around within him, gently pushing against his consciousness, now they would suddenly flash in front of him, almost as if they were outside him thrusting themselves at him and he could see Marion in bed with some big fat fuck who was fuckin the ass off her and he would quickly turn his head and groan and turn and squirm in his seat and he/d curse the fuckin tube and change the channel hoping there would be some fuckin thing on that he could watch and he kept telling himself they were just going to dinner and that you cant just borrow bread and split, but you have to sit and drink wine and bullshit and smile and suck his—what kindda fuckin show is this? and he spun the fuckin dial and he could no longer stop the image of some hulking fuckin guy shovin it in and he quickly tried to clothe them and put them in a restaurant drinking coffee and talking, but he couldnt hold on to the image and even while he did a little voice in the back of his head was mocking him and whispering, *Bullshit, Bullshit, Bullshit,* and he tried closing his eyes tight and shaking his head but that didnt do any good, it only put a spotlight on the bed they were in and even if he could get them at a table she was reaching under the table and Harry went to the bathroom and used one of the bags he was going to save for tomorrow, but fuck it man, I need it now, that last bag was cut too much, the shit just aint too tough and I sure as fuck dont wanta get sick and not be able to get out there and make it, yeah, thats what I/ll do, I/ll get off and see whats happening in the street, maybe theres somethin happenin now and I can cop somethin decent, I cant sit around here all night watchin the fuckin tube, thatll drive me up a fuckin wall, and he suddenly felt sick and he bent over the bowl and dumped the Mallomars he had just eaten and watched the puke, almost hypnotically, as it flowed so easily from his mouth into the bowl, splashing over the sides slightly, the dark chocolate, the white marshmallow and green bile mixing so beautifully that he smiled at the small ocean below him, dotted with small islands and snowcapped mountains, and he smiled and chuckled and flushed it and tossed some cold water on his face and rubbed it with a towel and felt better and sat on the side of the tub enjoying the flush of reassurance that flowed through his body, the calming peace that descended over him and through him, erasing images and obliterating words, then walked slowly back to the living room and finished off the rest of the joint and leaned back and dug the flick and

finished off the rest of the Mallomars, feeling mellow and
cool for a while, and then he started noticing the time, and
now time was registering in hours and that muthafuckin
image was coming back and he tried to squeeze that voice
out of his head but it just mocked him and continued its
insidious whisperings and giggling and soon the restaurant
was well lighted and the walls were down and he couldnt get
them back up no matter how hard he tried and soon he
stopped trying and just watched the games unfold themselves
as Marion and the sonofabitch rolled around in bed and
he was fuckin her every which way and Harrys stomach kept
getting more and more hollow and it seemed to be wide
open and the wintering winds were tearing through him and
at the same time his gut seemed to be alive with twisting and
turning maggots and rats and angry and sad tears moistened
the back of his eyes and his head felt like it was going under
water and the terrible sickness grew and grew within him as
he stared at the images and now he was helping them along
and feeding them energy, energy that came from someplace
within him and drained him even more and the pain increased and the nausea continued to build up but somehow
he knew he wouldnt puke, that he would just hang on to the
nausea, and he unconsciously had a hand on his crotch and
he drew his legs up on the couch and was slowly, but inexor-
ably, folding himself into a fetal position and he kept shoving
the nausea down with cigarettes and the more he watched the
images on the screen inside his head the more his heart
seemed to grow in size and threaten to just push his ribs apart
and ooze out of his chest while some goddamn fuckin thing
swelled in his throat and he had to force the air down and
he suddenly jumped up and changed the fuckin channel
and spun through all the stations a few more times then sat
back on the couch and stretched his eyes open as wide as

possible and tried not to fight or indulge the images, but the sickness persisted and he slowly stopped fighting and just surrendered to that hollow, sick, dead thing inside him and all the pain and dread and anguish became one enveloping veil of despair that was almost a comfort now that the struggle was over, and he just sat back and stared at the tube, almost interested in what was happening, trying to find the ability to believe in that lie so he could believe the one within.

The thought of going out to see if anything was happening floated around Harry during the commercials, but he just couldnt seem to work up the initiative. He entertained the thought briefly, each time it passed by, but he allowed it to continue on its merry way as soon as the movie started again. Eventually Marion got home, the makeup and cold winds putting color in her cheeks. She shook herself out of her coat, O, its cold out there. It took me forever to get a cab. Yeah, its a bitch. She spent so much time hanging up her coat and straightening out the clothes in the closet that she became self-conscious and closed her eyes and tried to think the tension out of her stomach and a sparkle in her eyes before turning around and facing Harry. Well, I got the money—walking over to the couch, trying to appear relaxed and nonchalant, Here. She handed the money to Harry. Good. We should be able to get straight now. He tried to relax and not just ignore but deny the fact that there was a feeling of embarrassment in the room that was so intense it was almost tangible. Marion leaned back against the couch and crossed her legs and tilted her head and smiled, speaking as offhandedly as possible, What movie is this honey? Harry shrugged, Don't know. I just flipped it on. You know. Marion nodded and stared at the screen, fighting, fighting, fighting, but she knew it was not only useless, but senseless to sit here trying to pretend that nothing had happened and that everything was just the same and nothing had changed. That was absurd and she involuntarily shrugged as the word rang through her head, she was far too intelligent and aware to allow herself to fall into the self-delusive trap. She knew she couldnt talk to Harry about it, that that would only make it worse, much worse, but she could not try to deny it to herself. She almost sighed audibly as she reached and accepted the conclusion. What happened happened. She would accept that and just allow it to drift from her mind into some other space and just not say anything to Harry . . . she shrugged inwardly. No, the chances are that he wont ask. She sighed, then smiled at Harry when he looked at her, then rubbed the back of his neck for a moment, I love you Harry. He kissed her, I love you too. She smiled again and then he turned his attention to the tube and she stared at it for a moment, trying to ignore the horrendous knot gnawing at her stomach, then uncrossed her legs and leaned forward, I think I/ll get off. You want to too? I just had a taste. Go ahead. She smiled again, automatically, and went to the bathroom telling herself she was only imagining that Harry was acting funny. After she got off she sat for a moment allowing all the conflicts to dissolve and bathe her in a comforting warmth and she felt a real smile on her face and she went back to the living room. She put an arm around Harry and rubbed the back of his neck again, then kissed his ear and rubbed his chest and he slowly responded and they held each other, desperately, reaching, groping, for many minutes, the television droning on in the background, then they decided to go to bed and Harry grabbed her and squeezed her harder and harder and she clung to him and kissed him and bit him as he kissed her body trying to work up a passion that would force itself though his body but something was missing, something was cutting off the flow of something and no matter how desperately they tried they couldnt get the physical motions to mean any more than motions and the harder they tried the more they withdrew into their own shells of embarrassment until they mutely agreed to stop trying and they sort of exhausted themselves into a semblance of sleep and release.

Sara wore her red dress all
the time. And the gold shoes. Ada still touched up her hair
and if she should suggest that maybe something happened to
the show she should be going on, Sara shook not only her
head but her arms and her whole body. Sometimes some of
the other ladies would come and make a visit and bring a
danish or lox and bagels, but Sara was always not hungry.
She was still thinking *zophtic*. The flesh was hanging from
her upper arms like a hammock, but she was still not eating
and thinking *zophtic*. So be already *zophtic,* but youre needing meat on the bones. But Sara would decline and just drink
her coffee and talk continually about going on the television,
the set always on, Sara studying all the quiz shows so she
would be able to compete no matter what show she went on.
Soon her friends would leave and she would sit in her viewing chair watching, nodding her head and smiling as she
watched herself stand with such poise as she rattled off the
answers, like its nothing, and everyone applauded and she
got the presents and made a little speech and said that she
was not keeping the presents but giving them to somebody
needy, and they applauded even more and theres pictures in
the paper and on the six oclock news and even on the eleven

oclock news she smiled at everybody and when shes on the street people chant, WE LOVE SARA, WE LOVE SARA, WE LOVE SARA, and she sighed and smiled and hugged herself as she watched her television and drank coffee, but every day, in the morning, something happened and she felt strange and she pulled down the shades and closed the drapes and from time to time she got up and peeked out of the side of the drapes to see if she could catch who was watching her and she looked over as large an area as she could without giving herself away to whoever was spying on her and then she/d go back to her viewing chair and glance sometimes at her refrigerator, quickly, and it just stood there, silent, frightened; and then she/d get up and tiptoe very slowly and quietly to the door and listen for long minutes, holding her breath for as long as possible so they wouldnt hear her, and then she would very carefully bend down and take the tape off the keyhole and peek through to see if she could see them but they always managed to get out of sight before she could find them. She would replace the tape, take a few Valium, then go back to her viewing chair and watch her shows, one upon the other, clutching, from time to time, her breast when a mother was worried and she would tell the woman she knew what it was like to miss your son. My only child, my boobala, and I dont even have a phone number. But hes busy you know. His own business. Hes a professional man my Harry, and soon hes making me a grandmother, and Sara consoled her and told her it would all be alright, and then she would take a few more Valium and her eyes would start getting heavy and a shroud like sadness would wind its way around her and tears trickled down her cheeks as she watched the evening and nighttime shows, and even watching herself on the eleven oclock news didnt seem to stop her sadness as she watched everything through a film of tears and she half muttered a prayer to hear from the television what show she

would be on and when; and Harry should come visit and
bring his fiancée with him and they would have a glass tea
and tell her what show and she would wear the red dress, O
Seymour, you remember the red dress? Harrys bar mitzvah?
Seymour, theres something wrong? Youll come on the show
and we/ll win prizes and give them to the poor people and
make nice for them and Harry will be having a grandson for
me and she should watch out for that car . . . O, Im telling
you to watch out, always when a car comes like that and the
man looks around its trouble and I/ll babysit my little boobala and tell her how to make the stuffed fish Harry loves and
why dont you talk to me Seymour? you just stand there looking at me, come, come we/ll go to bed, come, come . . . and
Sara Goldfarb went to bed holding Seymours hand and
Harry and his son and the television swam around in her
tear filled mind and the tears seeped from her eyes and kept
moist the pillow on which she rested her head, trying to
wash out the pain from her chest. . . .

    and then awakening in the morning, turning on the tele-
vision, then starting the coffee and then taking her purple,
red, and orange pills and drinking her coffee and staring
at the drawn drapes and calling the McDick Corp. and
hanging up the phone and shaking her head in confusion
trying to remember what was said and then sitting and
listening to, and feeling, her heart pound so hard and loud
that it felt like it would come right through her chest and
her pulse sounded like drums in her ears and she sat in her
viewing chair, clutching from time to time the arms, as the
pounding of her heart threatened to cut off her breath and
she slowly, then suddenly, realized that someone at that
McDick Corp. was trying to keep her off the television and
they probably tore up her card so they dont know shes supposed to be on the show, she had heard how that happens,
she saw that many times on the television how people do that

and someone gets cheated sometimes out of an inheritance and nobody knows but she would go and find out who and make a new card and she put on stockings and heavy wool socks from Seymour and squeezed her feet into her golden shoes and put on sweaters over her red dress and put on her heavy coat and wrapped a scarf around her neck and one around her head and went out to the street, not slowing down or hesitating in any way as the cold and sleet hit her face, but continuing to the subway, not hearing the people or the cars, but just keeping her head lowered and thrusting herself through the wind, and she continued to mutter to herself as she sat on the subway looking at the ads, recognizing the products that were advertised on television and identifying the show they were associated with and telling the people near about the show and how she was going to be on the television and help the poor and her Harry was going to be with her and the people continued to read their paper or look out the window and ignore her just as completely as if she wasnt there until she got off and then a couple shrugged slightly and watched her for a moment out of the corners of their eyes as she walked across the platform, still muttering, and up the stairs and along the streets holding the babooshka tightly around her head, slipping and sliding on the frozen streets with her golden shoes, but she continued to thrust her way through the wind and sleet to the Madison Avenue building and up the elevator, unaware of the looks and stares of the others, into the reception room of the McDick Corp., and she asked the operator why she wasnt putting through her calls that she wanted to see Lyle Russel and the operator stared at Sara, her switchboard flashing and buzzing, but she was immobilized for a moment as she looked into the haggard face, the sunken eyes, the wet, straggly hair hanging and clinging, the heavy wool socks sticking out through her golden shoes, Sara very wobbly, knocking against a wall from time to time as she continued to talk incoherently and she kept telling her her name and soon the operator recognized the name and asked her to sit down for a minute and she rang the new programs department and told them who was there and what was happening and soon there were a few people trying to soothe Sara and convince her that she should go home and she told them she was staying until she was knowing what show she was going to be on and the water dripped down her face and clothes and her red dress was wrinkled and wet and her babooshka was sliding down the back of her head and Sara Goldfarb looked like a pitiful and soggy bag of misery and despair and she slowly sank into a chair and her tears started to mingle with the melted sleet that was dripping down her face and falling onto the bodice of her red dress, the gown she wore at Harrys bar mitzvah, and someone got her a cup of hot soup and told her to sip it and held it for her so she could get some warmth in her and a couple of the other girls helped her into a small office and tried to soothe her and someone called a doctor and soon an ambulance was on its way and Sara sat crumpled and wet in the chair, sobbing and telling them she/ll give it already to the poor, I dont want the prizes, itll make somebody happy, I just want to be on the show Im waiting so long to be on with Harry and my grandson, and they tried to explain that only a few people are picked and then they tried to soothe her by telling her it takes time, maybe soon, but her sobs continued and from time to time the hot soup was put to her lips and she sipped some and then the two ambulance attendants came and looked at her for a moment and talked to her gently and soothingly, asking her if she could walk, and she told them she was always walking across the stage, they should see her Harry on the six oclock news, and when they

asked her name one of the girls told them it was Sara
Goldfarb and Sara said Little Red Riding Hood and Im going
ipsy pipsy to the announcer, and she sat back down and
sobbed and sobbed and then, in time, quieted slightly and
asked them to call Seymour, he should come get her at the
beauty parlor, and the attendants helped her up and slowly
walked her to the elevator, and down to the ambulance, and
started the ride through the traffic and weather to Bellevue.

Fortunately Sara was unaware of her surroundings, the
crowded corridors and rooms, the rushing people, the cries
of pain, the moans and groans and pleas did not penetrate her
ears and the battered, sickened and bleeding bodies didnt
register on her eyes. Her illness insulated her and she had
all she could bear, being isolated in the cocoon of her pain.
She was put in a wheelchair as forms were filled in and a
medical doctor looked at her briefly and read the report of the
ambulance attendants, then sent her to psycho, and she was
wheeled down corridors and put on another line and after
another hour or so she was wheeled into a room and a doctor
glanced at her briefly, then quickly scanned the forms hanging
from her wheelchair and he asked her her name and she
started to cry and tried to tell him about Harry and the television show and he gave her a new set and she would be on
for the poor people and he nodded and quickly scribbled a
note that she was paranoid schizophrenic and she should be
examined more thoroughly, but shock treatment was definitely indicated. He called the attendant and Sara was
wheeled to another line. After many more hours Sara was
finally wheeled to a bed in the corridor of the locked ward.
Some patients were shuffling around, their expressions blank
from heavy doses of tranquilizers, others roamed around in
straitjackets and others were strapped in their beds alter-
nately screaming, crying and pleading. Sara lay flat on her

back, staring at the ceiling, sobbing from time to time, her own misery protecting her from that of the others. Eventually a young medical resident stood at the foot of her bed. He was tired and yawned as he read her chart. He frowned when he read the comments of the admitting doctors and saw their names. He looked at her for a moment, then spoke to her soothingly as he examined her slowly and carefully. Occasionally Sara responded with an answer and he smiled and patted her hand reassuringly. He listened to her chest, then asked her to sit up and listened to her back and he asked her to raise her arms and bend her fingers and he noticed the flesh hanging from her upper arms and looked again at the hollows around her eyes and her neck and asked her if she had had a heart attack recently. No, its beating very hard. Yes, I noticed, and he continued to smile at her reassuringly. You look like you lost a lot of weight recently momma. She smiled, Yes, Im wearing my red dress on the television. He listened, patted her hand, called her momma, continually smiling and gently and patiently questioned her and eventually she told him about the weight, the doctor, the pills, and many, many times, about Seymour, her Harry and the television. Okay momma, everything will be alright—patting her hand reassuringly— we/ll fix you up in no time. Would you like a glass of tea? grinning at her then chuckling as she smiled and nodded her head, You're a good boy Harry.

The doctor gave the necessary instructions to the charge nurse to have Sara transferred from psycho to medical, and handed her the chart. She smiled, Reynolds again? Who else? He has to be one of the biggest assholes medicine has ever seen. The nurse laughed. According to him everybody needs shock treatment. Paranoid schizophrenic. . . . The only thing wrong with that poor old woman are the diet pills shes been taking.

Tyrone C. Love sat on the edge of the bed rubbing his head, trying to figure out what was happening. He listened to the fuckin wind rattling the windows and it was colderen a mutha fucka out there and soon he be goin out there agin. Sheeit! It seems like such a short time ago it was summer and they was jus easin across town to the morgue and gettin high, and now its cold ass winter an the days an nights jus seem to run all up on each other an each day seem like a thousan years an like summer never was here an will never be here agin. Somethin sure did fuck up somewheres. They was out there wheelin and dealin and takin home the bucks an now theys out there scufflin and scrappin just trying to hustle enough to keep the sick off. Sheeit! An them muthafuckin streets a bitch jim, thats for damn fuckin sure, a mutha fuckin bitch. He turned and looked at Alice all curled up under the covers, jus the top of her haid stickin out an she look so nice an warm an all together, but soon she be wakin up an want a tase. Damn, that bitch sure can sleep. An if she aint sleepin she be noddin. He smiled, but she sure be a fine woman, a natural born fox. He kept rubbing his head, hearing the wind. All that fine shit and them bucks an now ah caint make the mutha fuckin raint. Sheeit. Where all them hassles come from? It used to be so nice an cool an me an Alice would jus be layin up here with the window open and the curtains blowin in the breeze talkin that trash an finger poppin an now it soun like the mutha fuckin win like to tear this god-damn apartment right the fuck down jim. Sheeit. Seem like there be nothin *but* hassles now. Doan understan it. Jus doan understan. Lease we got the braid to cop some stuff tonight. If they be any stuff there. Might be that some dudes jus tryin to get a bunch a cats together with some braid and ripem off.

Doan know what the fuck gonna happen out there jim, them mutha fuckin streets gettin crazier every day . . . every fuckin day. Jus like the big fish eatin the littler fish . . . Sheeit! when you the little fish you in trouble jim . . . serious trouble. An you have nothin *but* hassles. We jus gotta be cool baby an hang tough. Lease we be able to stay cool for a while we cop this shit. An then we doan have to be out there in that mutha fuckin coal scufflin with our tight little asses, goddamn, ah hate hassles. Sheeit! He got up and went to the bathroom and stood over the bowl, leaning against the wall with one hand, holding his joint in the other and sort of looking it over as he shook the final drops, Sheeit, it damn near time for me to get mah ass out there in that mutha fuckin coal agin. Ahm gonna git me some cock before ah freeze the mutha fucka off. He sat on Alices side of the bed and pulled the covers down some and rubbed her neck and pushed her over on her back and kissed her hard on the mouth as he cupped a breast in a hand, Comeon, woman, wake up. If ah want a daid piece ahll git me back to the morgue. Alice blinked her eyes and stared at him dumbly for a minute, Watch you wan? Sheeit, what you think ah want? and he crawled over her onto the bed and pulled her close to him. Ah want me some a that fine thang you got there woman, and he rubbed her stomach and things and kissed her on the neck and Alice started to giggle and try to blink her eyes open, Ah ain even awake yet or had me a tase. Sheeit, your daddy gonna give you your fix woman, and Tyrone C. Love did all he could to store the heat of love in his bones and muscles and his head, and insulate himself from the cold and the possibilities of what might happen this night.

It was the strangest night and the strangest scene the city had ever seen. The captain of the precinct had been advised days in advance of what area was to be used and that everything in that area was to be absolutely controlled and calm. It was like walking through the battlefield of a raging en-

gagement and suddenly turning the corner and finding yourself in a demilitarized zone. The streets were empty. There
werent even any fires in the abandoned buildings. Not even a
bum in a hallway or under a mattress. The emptiness continued for five blocks in each direction from the appointed
area. There were no prowl cars within the area, but they
patrolled the border. The only points of entry were through
one of the various check points where guards with Thompsons
and walkie talkies checked everybody out before letting them
pass. All weapons had to be left behind. When dudes were
told they couldnt carry a piece with them they screamed and
hollered. What the fuck yoe talkin about? Yoe wan me to
go in there with five hundred dollars an git me some fuckin
herron and walk all the fuckin way out here niked, without
mah muthafuckin piece? sheeit, yoe out yoe fuckin mind jim.
Then youre outta ya fuckin dope asshole, and he stuck the
tip of the Thompson in the guys face and the guy turned and
stomped off, muttering and spitting, and came back a few
minutes later, clean. Ahs niked, gawddamn it. They frisked
him very carefully and finally nodded him through, If ah
gets ripped off ahm gonna be on yoe ass mutha. Sue me. The
guy continued grumbling, but continued to join the line that
was blocks long, and it was still only 8/30 and the dude wasnt
supposed to be there until ten.

Harry and Tyrone figured it would be best if they took half
the money each and stashed it all over, taping it to various
parts of their bodies, while they checked the scene out, keeping just a couple of bucks in their pockets in case they did
get jumped they might take just that and split, figuring that
that was all they had. They got checked through easy enough,
and kept looking in every direction at once as they walked
through the DMZ toward the distribution point. Every half
block there was a parked car with a guy on the roof with a
machinegun, and a guy on the ground with a walkie talkie.

Sheeit, you dig that action man? Yeah. I feel like I just
walked into one a those fuckin cartoons man. They both
shrugged deeper into their coats, Ah aint never felt so mutha
fuckin creepy in mah life jim. They walked through the rub-
ble of the blown out buildings, darkly silhouetting their
broken bodies against the sky, the silence weird and strangely
piercing to the ears and eyes. They approached the line
which was hundreds long and the guys were half huddled and
half lined against the crumbling walls trying to keep warm
and not look at the machineguns staring down at them, trying to be cool in their movements so nobody with all that
fuckin heat got the wrong idea, and so they stood as quietly
as possible, shuffling their feet in an attempt to keep them
warm, their hands shoved deep in their pockets, wiping their
running noses with their shoulders, standing with one foot
on top of the other from time to time, the guys with ripped
sneakers wrapping newspaper around them, and their bodies,
to keep warm. Harry and Tyrone dug those dudes and shook
their heads, knowing they would never get that bad, that they
would never get strung out and live just for shit. Every few
minutes someone asked the time and occasionally one of the
guards would tell them and someone would always tell them
to stop askin fa krists sake, Ya make the fuckin time drag
like that man. Cool it, eh? and they went back to trying to
think the time by faster and faster and ignore the ice in
their bones and on their flesh; and the guards just watched
them, saying nothing, warm in their arctic coats and face
masks, looking like something from a science fiction movie
as they moved stiffly, almost invisible with the dark background, the water vapor from their mouths more visible than
their faces, but less visible than the machineguns. A few
minutes after ten a large, black Cadillac pulled up and
stopped and two guys with Thompsons got out, then two
more, and a guy all wrapped up in a fur coat got out carrying

a large suitcase. He walked to what was once a hallway where a portable heater had been set up. It was turned on and he stood on the thick piece of wool rug near the heater. One by one the guys were led up to the hallway and one guy took their money, counted it, put it in a steel box and each guy passed on and was handed his half piece wrapped in plastic, and told to move it. As soon as they left the DMZ the guys tried to melt into the night, the word having gone out that no one would be busted, at least within a mile of the place, but only a fool trusts a cop. Some guys hustled to the dark hallway where they had stashed their gun and then hurried through the streets, one hand clutching their dope the other one their gun; others rushed to parked cars where the dudes who had gone down with them for the stuff were waiting and then they sped away slapping palms and swallowing hard, just thinking about all that fine dope giving them a taste in the back of their throats; and some guys didnt make it out of the cars or past the darkened buildings, getting their heads blown away or bashed in.

The line moved rapidly, but it still took hours for everyone to get their dope, no one about to disagree, in any way, with those machineguns that had everybody locked in a crossfire. Harry and Tyrone taped their stuff to their bodies and when they got back to the streets they picked up a couple of rocks each and walked down the middle of the street, their combined vision taking in a 360-degree area. They clung to the rocks even as they sat in the cab, not letting go of them to smoke, but holding on until they got back to their pad. The first thing they did was to get off, then they cut and bagged the rest of the shit, each guy taking a half piece to take care of their customers. They figured theyd better make the bags a little smaller than double the price. Things were tight and every dope fiend in the city would be willing to pay a dime for a nickel bag, even if it was a little light.

Harry and Marion were sitting back enjoying the warmth and the sense of security of listening to the radiators click and looking at the bags of dope on the table. Are you going to sell all that Harry? Most of it, why? Suppose we cant get any more? What will we do? Theres got to be more. But suppose there isnt, Marions voice was becoming more intense, look how difficult its been lately. But tonight was just a beginning. Marion turned and looked Harry in the eye, very intently, I dont think so. Whatta ya talkin about? Im not sure. Its a feeling. But I dont want to be sick anymore Harry. I dont like waking up and not having anything in the house. Either do I, but its bad business not to put the stuff on the streets. Now that theyve upped the price therell be plenty of stuff around. Marion shook her head, I have a bad feeling about it Harry. Dont sell it, Marions eyes reflected her fear and for the first time there was a pleading tone in her voice, wait and be sure theres going to be more . . . please Harry, please, her body rigid, her eyes staring straight ahead. Dont worry about it, we/ll be able to cop. We/ll be able to get straight.

Dr. Spencer stood in front of Dr. Harwood, the department administrator, his hands clenched in his pockets, his jaw clenched so tightly it ached. Dr. Harwood pushed himself back from his desk and looked at Dr. Spencer for a moment and frowned slightly, You look positively rigid. You had better sit down and relax. He sat and took a deep breath and tried to allow his body to loosen, but it still ached from the rigidity of controlled anger. Dr. Harwood continued to frown, Well, what seems to be your problem doctor? you said it was urgent. Dr. Spencer took another deep breath, closed his eyes for a moment, then exhaled slowly, Its Dr. Reynolds. Dr. Harwood looked sternly at him, I have told you before that if you want to feud with Dr. Reynolds to do it on your own time. This has nothing to do with a feud, it has to do with the proper care and treatment of patients. Dr. Harwood leaned back in his chair, Alright, what is it this time? Dr. Spencer was trying very hard to relax and control himself, but the more he talked about the situation the harder it was to control his anger. He took another deep breath, A Sara Goldfarb was admitted to the hospital in a completely disoriented condition and Dr. Reynolds diagnosed her as a paranoid schizophrenic and sent her to psycho with a recommendation of possible shock treatment, as usual—Dr. Harwood winced slightly, but said nothing—I gave her a routine examination and found that she had been taking diet pills and Valium and had not eaten a decent meal in many months . . . he paused for a moment fighting his rising anger . . . and left orders to have her transferred to medical. This morning I found that my orders had been countermanded by Dr. Reynolds and that the patient is still in psycho and not only that, but he has left a standing order, a *standing* order that all such orders of mine are to be completely and immediately ignored. Dr. Spencer was flushed and sweating slightly as Dr. Harwood watched him fighting to keep control of himself. He has the authority and the right to do that doctor. Im not talking about his right to do anything, Im talking about the patients right to receive the best and the proper medical attention. Are you saying that she is *not* getting exactly *that* at this hospital? Im saying that her problem is medical and not psycho. Give her a little rest, some proper food and clean her body of the stimulants and depressives that she has been taking and she will be completely recovered. Dr. Harwood looked at him coolly for a moment, In your opinion doctor. Its more than my opinion, its my experience. In the past eight months I have taken six of Dr. Reynolds' patients and treated them medically, for just the same symptoms and the same reasons, and they have fully recovered in less than a month, *without*

shock treatment or any psychotropic drugs. Dr. Harwood continued to look at him and to speak slowly, Yes, I know. That
is why he gave those orders. You cannot interfere with another
doctors treatment or— Even when that treatment is not only
incompetent, but dangerous and inimical to the patients
health and well being? Dr. Harwood blinked his eyes slowly,
tolerantly, I do not think you are in a position to judge the
competency of a doctor specializing in a field of medicine to
which you are hostile and who is your superior in rating and
experience. Well I disagree. Completely and vehemently. The
record will bear me out. If someone has a toothache you dont
send him to a chiropodist. And just what exactly is that supposed to mean? It simply means that medical patients should
not be treated as psycho patients, and this woman, as were
the others, is a medical problem not a psychiatric problem.
Dr. Harwood was gently tapping the tips of his fingers together, Again, this is your opinion, which differs from Dr.
Reynolds' opinion. Reynolds is a horses ass. You will not
make insulting remarks about other members of my staff,
doctor, Dr. Harwood was leaning forward in his chair and
looking directly into Dr. Spencers eyes, especially about de-
cisions that have my concurrence. You mean you approved?
Of course. But how could you after reading my remarks on
her chart? There was no need for me to see her chart. No
need to see her chart? You mean you just condemned someone
to shock treatment without even looking at their record? O
really, doctor, condemned is a childish and stupid word to use.
But shock treatments are completely unnecessary in this case.
I tell you I can have her well in just a few weeks with some
rest and nourishment. Dr. Spencer, I am growing a little im-
patient with your anti-Reynolds tirade. Let me remind you,
again, that he is your superior and just on the basis of that fact
you are powerless over his actions. Completely powerless. Do
you understand me? But dont you care about the welfare of

the patient either? Dr. Harwood leaned toward Dr. Spencer, a hard look on his face, My job is to see that this department functions smoothly, with the least amount of trouble and conflict. That is my job and my purpose. I have the responsibility to see that a large department of one of the largest hospitals in the world—in the world—functions to the very best of its ability. I am responsible for thousands of people and that is my responsibility, not one small patient, but the thousands that depend on my ability to keep this department functioning smoothly, and without internecine squabbles. You have antagonized Dr. Reynolds repeatedly, without cause, and I have excused you— Without cause? How can— BE QUIET! I am not interested in your *opinion* about another doctors competency, but in performing my duties to the very best of my ability. But that woman— I have told you I dont care about that woman. Even if you are correct in your diagnosis and assumptions, the worst that can happen is that she will have a few unnecessary shock treatments. The worst— Dr. Harwood was staring hard at Dr. Spencer and leaning closer to him, Thats right. The worst. Whereas even if youre right and I go along with you it will cause so much disruption in the staff and the calm and efficient functioning of this department that far more will be lost than a few months time out of the life of one woman. Dr. Spencer looked hurt and bewildered, I thought your responsibility was to treat the sick. Dr. Harwood looked at him for a moment, Dont be naive doctor. Dr. Spencer just stared, feeling empty and hollow inside, his tongue tasting leaden and his eyes feeling heavy and tear laden. Dr. Harwood continued to stare at him, then breathed deeply and sighed and leaned back in his chair. Of course, if you do not approve of the manner in which this hospital is run you are free to resign your residency. That is your privilege. Dr. Spencer continued to look straight in front of him, Dr. Harwood and everything else in the room becoming a blur. His body was limp. His brain felt soggy. His gut hollow. He closed his eyes for a moment then shook his head. Dr. Harwood continued to tap the tips of his fingers together, Im certain there must be quite a bit for you to do on the wards doctor. Dr. Spencer nodded and stood to leave. And let me remind you of something doctor . . . harmony breeds efficiency. Good morning.

All the radiators clicked, but they were still cold. The panic continued and they were back to the old routine of scuffling the streets, just getting enough to get straight and nothing more. Marion was able to keep a good supply of sleeping pills in the house through her doctors, but she was still hysterical most of the time. Those mornings when they woke up and there was nothing in the house, having used the last the night before when their disease convinced them that it would be alright, that they wouldnt be sick in the morning, she became hysterical and trembled as she shot up a sleeping pill, occasionally blowing a shot and burning her arm so it swelled and turned red and she cried and yelled at Harry that it was his fault they didnt have their morning shot. What the hell you talkin about? Youre the one who was all hot in the fuckin biscuit to get off again last night. Well one bag wasnt enough. Its not my fault it was no good. I needed the other bag. Thats a bunch a bullshit. You couldve made it on that bag. You wouldve nodded out and slept like you always do. I do not nod and sleep, and you know that. And if I could have made it on that bag, why didnt you? You were all for using it last night. Sure, why not? Whatta my gonta do? just sit and watch you get high and not get high myself? Then just dont put all the weight on me, thats all. And leave me alone. You made me blow the first shot and now my arm is all messed up and I dont know where Im going to hit. What the fuck ya mean I made ya blow the shot? And whose the one goin out in this fuckin weather to cop? Youre the only one who can. If I could I would. Theres no joy sitting here alone, waiting. Ah fuck you, eh? Just let me get off and get out there and see whats happenin. Harry shot up a couple of the goof balls and tried to think a bigger and better flash than he got, and tried to think himself higher than he was, but though he didnt succeed, he wasnt sick and would be able to get down some hot chocolate that would help. As his body and mind started to calm slightly he saw Marion trying to get a hit with her left hand and she was trembling so much she was going to blow this fix too, so Harry told her he/d help her. Krist, youll kill yourself. He tied her up and rubbed her arm until a good vein came up then tapped the needle into the vein and they both stared, waiting for the blood to bubble up, and when it did Marion put her hand on the dropper, Let me, let me. Harry shrugged and sat back and Marion squeezed the fluid into her vein, then booted a couple of times, closing her eyes as the hot flush burned her body and a wave of nausea flushed through her and attacked her head momentarily, then when it subsided she opened her eyes and dropped her works in the glass of water. You okay? Marion nodded. Youd better lay off that shit. Youll burn up all your veins. If you get up tight, just drop a couple like you used to and drink the hot chocolate. Marion just looked at him and he shrugged, saying nothing. They both knew that suggestion was absurd, that sticking that needle in their arm was important, and just dropping a couple of pills, no matter how good it made them feel, just wasnt the same. They had to shoot them.

Tyrone called and said he heard there was something hap-

pening so Harry hustled from the house. They pooled their
money because Tyrone would be doing the copping, each one
holding out enough for a few bags, just in case, and not telling
the other. It had been happening so automatically that
neither one thought much of it or even planned it. They
simply held back money, telling the other one that was all
they had. They decided to blow some of the money on a cab
so they could get there faster, not wanting to blow it because
they were too late. It was another scene where it was there,
or at least it seemed to be, but it was also a waiting game,
and so they waited, standing on the street, stamping their
feet, hands buried deep in their jackets, trying to keep their
backs to the bitter cold wind, it being too cold to even smoke
a cigarette, afraid to go into a coffee shop for fear they might
miss the man. And so they waited and shivered hoping ta
krist that someone wasnt running a story down on them.

Marion sat at the kitchen table for a while, drinking hot
chocolate and then coffee, trying to think of some way to not
think, of some way to busy her mind, but all she could do
was just sit there trying not to look at her watch and looking
at it without noticing the time. She almost laughed out loud
as she suddenly remembered, They also serve who only sit
and wait. Wait! God Almighty it seemed like she had spent
her entire life waiting. Waiting for what???? Waiting to live.
Yes, that was it alright, waiting to live. It seemed like she
had become aware of that in therapy sometime, somewhere.
Waiting to live. Thinking of this as a rehearsal for living.
Practice. She knew all that. There was nothing new in that.
If she remembered correctly—did anything correctly—the
shrink she was seeing when she realized this thought that that
was a rather astute observation . . . an astute observation. . . .
She chuckled, I guess that was before I started going to bed
with him. . . . An astute observation. He hadnt heard of
Henry James/A beast from the jungle. Maybe he never heard

of Henry James. He was as exciting in bed as Henry James. Marion stared into her coffee cup. The sides were stained from frequent use and infrequent cleanings. . . . Like a beast from the jungle . . . He told me that with such an awareness, and my intelligence and talents, I should have no trouble coming to terms with my problem and being productive. His favorite word, productive. That and sublimate. Thats all they want you to do . . . sublimate and be productive. She chuckled, Just dont reproduce. Thats the other word! Just. Just do it. You ask them how you do it and they say you *just* do it. Now that you know the problem you *just* stop doing the things that get you into that problem. Thats all there is to it. All of them. The same thing. *Just* do it. Just! She stared at her empty coffee cup, thinking of how she wanted another cup of coffee but somehow couldnt work up the initiative to move, to get the coffee pot and refill the cup and then go through the process of putting in the sugar and cream, and she tried to use her will power—that was it. Now it was complete, Just use your will power. She stared at the empty cup. . . . Eventually she got up and started to pour a cup of coffee and the pot was empty and she just looked at it then went to the living room and turned on the television and tried to allow it to occupy her mind but she continued to look at her watch and wonder if Harry had copped yet and if there really was something out there and hoping he had sense enough to hold something back so we/d be sure to have enough and then she gradually became aware of how dumb the damn show was she was watching and she stared at it, wondering how in the hell they could put anything so absurdly infantile and intellectu- ally and esthetically insulting on television, and she started asking herself over and over how they could do it, what kind of nonsense is this, and she continued to stare and shake her head, more and more of her mind being absorbed by the absurdity she was watching, suddenly leaning back on the couch as a section of the show ended and a commercial came blaringly on and she stared at them too, wondering what sort of cretins watch this garbage and are influenced by it and actually go out and buy those things, and she shook her head, unbelievable, it is simply unbelievable, how can they manage to make so many obnoxious commercials, one right after the other? Its unbelievable, and the show came back on and she leaned forward, face pinched in a frown as she watched the completely predictable events unfold, the time passing by as she waited for something to happen. . . .

Tyrone and Harry damn near froze their asses off. And to make it worse there was plenty of heat on the streets. The man seemed to be everywhere. If youre holding you best be off the streets jim cause the man he out there playin games with every fuckin body an thats no shit. They talked with as many dudes as possible, trying to find out where the action might be, but at the same time they didnt want to spend too much time with anyone, not knowing if the cat might have a set of works onim an the man come an they all get busted for mutha fuckin consortin. They walked around as much as possible and as little as possible. They didnt want to miss Tyrones connection, and they didnt want to freeze to the ground. They found out that there was a dude who was holding a nice taste. Who knows how much, the stories going from a piece to a truckload, but he was holdin, but he wasnt sellin. He only given it up for pussy jim. The only habit that mutha fuck have is pussy. He hooked on that thang. An he only goin for outta sight pussy jim. Ah mean its got to be righteous. Ah toldim ah giveim all he want, but he say ahm not pretty enough forim. Harry and Tyrone chuckled inwardly, but it was so cold they just couldnt seem to crack their faces into a smile, no less a laugh. Eventually Tyrones

man came beboppin down the street and passed them by and
after a few minutes Tyrone followed and after a while Harry
saw Tyrone walking down the block and he followed and
when Tyrone hailed a cab Harrys heart started beating faster
and a surge of hope thrust itself through him and he got a
taste in the back of his throat and his stomach knotted with
anticipation. He jumped in the cab and closed the door.
Tyrone was smiling.

The television was still on, but Marion wasnt still sitting
on the couch. She was in the bathroom, bathing her arms in
hot water, rubbing them hard and then spinning them
around, trying desperately to get a vein up so she could shoot
up another goof ball. She was shaking, crying, and dizzy with
frustration and cursing Harry for not being there with the
dope and she tried to tie up her left arm but couldnt seem to
do that right or anything else and she grabbed her head,
Oooooooooooo, then started hitting herself on the head, and
then tried to sit on the edge of the tub and slid off and ended
up on the floor and beat the floor with her hands, sobbing
with rage. She didnt hear Harry open the door or come in.
Whatta ya doin? She looked for a second, then yanked herself
up, Where have you been? Ive been waiting all day—Where
the hell ya—and I cant stand this any—You cant stand—
more, Marion was trembling and could hardly speak, do you
hear me? and I want something here in the morning—What
the fucks wrong with—do you hear me? DO YOU HEAR
ME? DO YOU HEAR ME? Marions eyes were wide and she
grabbed Harry by the coat and was shaking him, Im not
going to bed until theres a morning shot, I cant stand it, I
cant stand this being sick and waiting— Ya think Im playin
fuckin games for krists sake, grabbing her and holding her
by the arms until she stopped, you want to be sure we have
some extra stuff, we were hipped to a dude thats holding
some weight, but he aint sellin. Marion stared at Harry the

way she stared at the television set, eyes wide, not believing but waiting to hear more, her hysteria keeping her from fainting and giving her the energy needed to stand stiff. Her mouth opened. He likes broads. Marion continued to stare. You worried so goddamn much I/ll fix you up withim. Her mouth closed. You wont have to wait so long . . . and I wont have ta freeze my fuckin ass off in the fuckin streets, Harry spun away and started yanking his coat and sweater off and tossed them on the couch then sat at the table and unwrapped the bundle of stuff. Marion watched for a few seconds, then blinked her eyes and started walking toward him, then stopped as he got up, and went back to the bathroom. Think you can get a hit? She nodded and started to tie up, then Harry shook his head, Krist, are you fucked up, then tied her up and rubbed her arm a few times and a couple of good veins came up, There. He dumped the stuff in the cooker and they both got off. Marion had no idea how frozenly stiff her face and body had been until the dope warmed it and they started to relax. They dropped their works in the glass of water and sat back on the tub for a moment, Harry letting the dope shove out the memory of the frigid streets, and Marion feeling the sense of security coming back that she longed for. She leaned against Harry, I dont know what happened, its just that its getting worse and worse, I dont know whats happening, but I feel like Im going out of my mind. Yeah, I know. Its a bitch. What can I tellya, itll break sooner or later. It cant stay like this forever. She stared ahead and nodded, Its just that I cant stand being like this. But youre not *that* sick. Im not shootin any more stuff than you and— Its different for you. Marion shook her head, I . . . I . . . I dont know why it is but it is. I cant stand not having enough in the house, I just cant, her voice softer, quietly hysterical, Harry rubbing the back of his neck. She moved, still staring straight ahead, and got up, Comeon. Harry stashed the stuff then they sat at the table drinking soda. How much do we have? Enough for a couple of days. Cant we just keep it all? Jesus Marion, we/ve been through this routine a dozen fuckin times. We *have* to *off* some *stuff*. *That* is *how* we *get* the *bread* for *more*. Marion nodded, the panic gone, but the concern still strong. She alternated looking at her glass and at Harry, her expression flat, I understand Harry. I just . . . I just . . . She shrugged and stared at him for a few moments, then lowered her eyes and looked at her glass. Theres a panic and thats the way it is now. What can I tell you. Marion looked at him again and nodded, blinked her eyes a few times and continued to look as understandingly and reassuringly as possible. She studied her cigarette for a moment then looked at her glass as she spoke to Harry, You sure this guy wont sell any? What guy? The guy you said had some but wouldnt sell. Oh the guy thats hooked on broads. Marion nodded still looking at her glass, raising her eyes slightly from time to time. Positive. Why, you have something in mind? Marion continued to look at her cup and toy with her cigarette, I/d like to have more than just a days stuff Harry, I cant make it like this. . . . Suppose what he has doesnt last long???? Harry shrugged, trying to ignore the action in his gut, but even the dope wouldnt allow him to ignore it, but it did allow him to believe whatever he had to believe. He wanted to say something, but couldnt find the means to put the words together even if he could find the words. He just continued to go along with what was happening, go with the flow as Marion would say. With whats happening he could be no where anytime too. Marion rubbed her cigarette around in the ashtray, cleaning off the bottom with her butt and pushing the ashes to the side, Maybe we should look into it right away. Harry took another drag on his cigarette and shrugged, If you want to. She continued with

the butt in the ashtray, nodded her head and murmured. Yes.
A little voice inside Harry said, Thank krist.

Sara went passively to her first shock treatment. She had
no idea where she was going, having only a vague idea where
she was. There were a few times during the day when she
seemed to be on the verge of orienting herself and experiencing a degree of mental and emotional clarity, but then she was
given another dose of Thorazine and the cloud of numbness
once again descended and enshrouded her, and her limbs
became heavy and an unbearable burden, and the pit of her
stomach burned and ached with exhaustion, and her tongue
was so thick and dry it stuck to the roof of her mouth, and
attempting to speak was an unbearably painful ordeal, and she
would strain to try to formulate words, but she couldnt sum-
mon the energy necessary to unglue and move her tongue; and
her eyes felt like two huge thumbs were pressing down on
them and she had to lift her head back to see, and then it was
as if she was looking through a veil that made everything hazy,
and so she would just lie in bed numbed, confused, nodding
off to sleep . . . then waking periodically and sleeping again
. . . constantly feeling sick and, from time to time, struggling to sit up, but unable to, and so they would lift her up
and put some food in her mouth and it would dribble out of
the corners because she just couldnt swallow, and she would
try to tell them to stop, to let her do it, but she couldnt speak
because of drug induced inertia, and so her words came out
groans and they grabbed her and forced the food down her
throat, holding her nose and keeping her mouth closed, forcing her to swallow, Saras eyes being forced open with terror,
mute terror, while inside her heart beat thunderously in her
ears and thudded against her chest, and she was unable to

even mutter a prayer for help and the more she tried to tell them not to do that the more annoyed they became and they shoved the food in her mouth, cutting the corners of her mouth and her gums, them slamming their hands over her mouth and nose and Sara would feel, again and again, like she was suffocating and she tried to swallow as fast as possible but her system just didnt seem to have the energy it needed to swallow, and she fought to get the food down so she could breathe, and the harder she fought the harder they pressed against her, and held her down in the bed until they finally left in disgust, and Sara tried to curl up in a little ball and disappear, and after a couple of days she cringed in abject terror when she heard the food truck approaching.

Dr. Reynolds frowned at her chart as he stood by her bed. You are not cooperating Mrs. Goldfarb. His voice was shrill and his tone threatening, and Sara tried to lift an arm, to raise herself, to tell him, to tell the doctor how she couldnt move, how she couldnt talk, how she felt like maybe she was dying and she was frightened, and she looked at him with eyes that pleaded and begged, her mouth opening, but only inarticulate noises coming out, and he continued to stare at her, You may think that this type of behavior will get you special treatment, but we do not have the time to cater to individuals. He snapped the chart closed and turned sharply and walked away. When he handed the chart to the nurse he told her to schedule Sara for shock treatment the following morning. Sara went passively. She was hoping, in her semi-comatose state, that they were taking her to something better, maybe that nice young doctor that talked to her and got her a glass of tea. Maybe she would see him and he would make it better. She was strapped in the wheelchair and her head kept falling forward as she was pushed along corridors, down in an elevator, along more corridors, from time to time attaining a glimmer of consciousness and remembering that she hadnt had any breakfast that morning and feeling happy that she did not have to go through the ordeal of eating that morning which gave her enough energy to think there might be some hope, that maybe she was going to see that nice young doctor and her head would fall forward again and then she was being lifted on a table and her eyes blinked open but she couldnt recognize anything and she started to tremble and shake with fear as faces passed by her, blurred, and there were lights, and she didnt know where she was but something told her she should not be there, a strong feeling fought through the drugs telling her it was a matter of life and death that she get out of that room and away from those people whose faces seemed to be unformed or hidden behind something and she tried to resist, but was unable to and strong hands stretched her out on the table and strapped her down and she could feel her throat start to close and her heart threaten to explode and something was attached to her head and something jammed between her teeth and people were talking and laughing, but the voices were a blur and it seemed like there were many faces leaning over her and she could feel her eyes opening wider as they looked, peered, and she could hear laughter and then the faces seemed to recede and drift away in a haze and suddenly fire shot through her body and her eyes felt like they were going to burst from their sockets as her body burned then stiffened and felt like it would snap apart and pain shot through her head and stabbed her ears and temples and her body kept jerking and bouncing as the flames seared every cell of her body and her bones felt like they were being twisted and crushed between huge pincers as more and more electricity was forced through her body and her burning body arched and slammed itself down on the table and Sara could feel her bones snapping and smell the burning of her own flesh as barbed hooks were thrust into her eyes yanking them out of their sockets and all she could do was endure and feel the pain and smell the burning flesh unable to yell, to plead, to pray, to make a sound or even die, but stay locked in the torturous pain as her head screamed AAAAAAAAAAAAAAAHHHHHHHHHHHH-HHHHHHHHHHHHHhhhhhhhhhhhhh. . . .

The silence was awkward, and the chatter self-conscious, as they rode to Big Tims. Tyrone had made the arrangements and was thinkin of the dope theyd be havin in a few hours, not thinkin of nothin else much as he wasnt really personally involved in what was comin down. Marion was apprehensive. She was alive with many emotions, but they had gotten off before they left the house so it was all tolerable and everything was possible. She knew she could, and would, do whatever had to be done without any problem. Her only concern was that she didnt get burned, that Big Tim would give her dope like he promised. Sheeit, you doan have to worry about that. Big Tim never cop out. He tough but straight. Marion nodded and continued taking quick pokes on her cigarette thinking of holding that dope in her hand, *her* dope in *her* hand and she wouldnt have to worry about being sick in the morning.

Harry sat in the corner glancing out the window from time to time, and at Marion, trying to figure out what sort of attitude he should adopt, wondering how he should look and sound, what he should say . . . and what he should feel. Shit, he felt relief. They were going to get stuff without having to scuffle those cold ass streets . . . but that didnt sit just right. He didnt like the idea of Marion ballin this dude. Fuck it, whats the big deal. He sure as hell wasnt the first guy she ever balled. If she had to turn a few tricks to— No! No! She aint no fuckin hooker. Shes just getting some shit man. And anyway, what the fucks wrong with a chick ballin some guy?

Thats her business. Shes free. Just like the rest of us. Free to do anything she fuckin wants man. Whats this fuckin Victorian horseshit? A lot of broads fuck their bosses and thats straight. They dont think thats rank. Shit! Fuckem! Right where they eat. They dont like it they can go piss up a fuckin rope. You do what has to be done. Thats all. Harry reached over and started rubbing the back of Marions head, Its alright with me and if they dont dig it thats their fuckin problem, it sure as hell aint mine. Marion turned her head slightly and glanced at Harry, out of the corner of her eye, for a second, then continued to look ahead, looking through the glass partition and the windshield of the cab. She felt Harrys hand and wondered if she was supposed to do or say something. Was she supposed to feel something about Harry? Was she supposed to feel sorry for him? for her? Was she supposed to regret something???? She had vague feelings of regret, but they had nothing to do with going to see Big Tim. She briefly wondered what the feelings were about, but she didnt pursue the thought and it vitiated by itself as she was aware of the feeling of apprehension and the even stronger feeling of impending security.

They went into a coffee shop and Tyrone called Big Tim and when he came out of the booth he gave Marion the address. Its right around the corner. We/ll meet you here. If we not here jus wait. She nodded and turned and walked stiffly from the coffee shop. Harry watched her go, wondering if he should have kissed her before she left. They finished their coffee and Tyrone suggested they take in a movie, Theres one jus a couple blocks. Do we have *that* much time to kill? Tyrone just looked. Harry shrugged and they left.

Marion walked the short distance to the large apartment building, looking straight ahead of her, her back stiff, unaware of the gentle quietness of her surroundings. The building still had a canopy, but the doorman had been dispensed with many years before. She pushed the button and the buzzer sounded and she pushed open the door, and she stood in front of the inner door, unaware of the television camera focused on her. The buzzer sounded again and she pushed the door open and rode the elevator to the twenty second floor. Big Tims smile was from ear to ear as he opened the door and stepped aside to let Marion in. He had to step aside because Big Tim was big, in every sense of the word. He was about six-six, broad, huge, big . . . his body was big, his smile was big, his laugh was big, and even his apartment was big. The living room was huge and endless french doors opened on a balcony that overlooked Central Park and you could see for miles. His view was big. He took her coat and hung it up and told her to sit, indicating the large couch. There was some old Coltrane playing and he moved in time to the music as he went to the bar and poured himself a large glass of bourbon. What would you like? Marion shook her head, Nothing. O, you strictly a dope fien? Marion was startled by his question. She had never thought of herself as a dope fiend. She shook her head and felt a need to buy some time, but she wasnt sure why. Eventually she asked for some chartreuse. Yellow or green? Again she was surprised and muttered yellow while she tried to compose herself and recover from the rapid series of surprises. Her surroundings were starting to register and somehow they were diametrically opposed to what she had expected though she hadnt been aware of expecting anything. She looked over her shoulder at the incredible expanse of sky and skyline and then around the room. Big Tim brought the drinks, and bottles, over and put them on the table, then opened a drawer and took out a hash pipe and put a nice size piece of hash in the bowl. He lit it and took a long poke then handed it to Marion. She accepted it automatically and took a couple of pokes then handed it back to Tim. They handed it back and forth until the hash was gone and Tim turned the pipe over an ashtray and let the ashes fall out. Whats your name? Marion. His laugh was loud and deep and happy . . . very happy and relaxing, What you know, Maid Marion, hahaha, Im Little John. Marion sipped her chartreuse and smoked her cigarette feeling the combination of dope, hash and alcohol dissolving all concerns. She finished her drink and as Tim refilled the glass Marion leaned back and closed her eyes and felt the warmth flow through her as her body and mind relaxed and she smiled and then chuckled as she thought of what her family would do if they could see her making it with a *schvartzer*. What's so funny? Marion shook her head, laughed for a moment, Nothing. Its a family joke. You outta sight fox, why you want to get all fucked up behind scag? Again Marion was surprised by the reference to her being an addict and she shook her head and took another drag of her cigarette, buy more time. I like a little taste once in a while. Sheeit, you aint sittin here with me cause you like a little tase baby, uh *huh*. Marion shrugged and sipped her drink and tried to say something, but continued sipping her drink instead. Sheeit, that dont mean nothin to me. Jus so long as ah doan get into mah own shit. Ah aint even horned any an ah aint goin to neither, uh *uh*. He took a drink, A little juice and little smoke make it for me real nice. He refilled the hash pipe and lit it, took a long poke and handed it to Marion, Ah jus like to sit back an be cool and dig mah man Trane—sheeit, ah shore wish that mutha fucka was still alive. Damn he could blow. He refilled his glass and Marions and took the pipe when she handed it to him and took a couple of hits and gave it back to her, speaking to her while still holding his breath, Better make it quick baby, its bout gone. Marion dumped the ashes in the ashtray and drank some chartreuse and Tim put an arm around her and pulled her next to him. He put his legs up on the table and stretched out and Marion put hers up on

the couch. You dig mah man Trane? Marion nodded, I have
every record he ever cut. All the old Miles quintet, Monk,
all of them. No shit? Thas nice. Ah likes a chick that knows
how to listen to music. You know most broads jus dont know
how to listen. Women arent the only ones. Maybe. But most
brothers know how to listen. Ah mean really listen. He took
another drink, licked his lips and leaned back with his eyes
closed for a minute, listening. Marion closed her eyes and just
leaned against his chest, feeling the weight and security of
his arm around her, moving her toes slightly in time to the
music. That last hash and the chartreuse really did it. She felt
fine. She felt warm. She felt at home. Trane had just finished
a chorus and the piano player came in and Marion muttered
a soft, Yeah. Tim opened his eyes and smiled and looked at
her. You know what ah likes best about patty chicks? They
give good haid. Nigga broads—Marion felt something in her
stir, she felt her eyes pop open, but remained immobile. Tims
huge hand was fondling her right breast—doan know nothin
about givin haid. Ah dont know why. Might be it has somethin to do with some ancient tribal custom. Marion heard
his laugh and wondered why it reminded her of Santa Claus,
but it was true, he sounded like a commercial for jolly old
St. Nick. He put his other arm around her and pulled her
up to him and kissed her as his hands seemed to cover her
entire body at once. She put her arms around his neck and
kissed him as hard as she could, clinging even tighter to his
neck. After a minute he backed off slightly, Better save some
a that energy. His laugh made her smile. Her hands slowly
slid from around his neck and she was resting on his stomach
when he gently turned her head around and took out his
joint. All of Marions reactions were slowed from the dope and
alcohol and so she just looked, stared, but inside she felt
startled, as if she should say and do something besides just
look at his joint. There was a terrible battle going on within

her. She knew what she was supposed to do, but her entire
being was suddenly repulsed by the reality of it. Her insides
trembled and knotted. Ah know its purty baby, but ah didnt
take it out for air. He nudged her slightly. Marion responded
and grabbed it with her right hand and started kissing it and
rubbing it with her lips when she became aware that she was
getting sick. She sat up, her eyes wide, her hand over her
mouth. Tim looked for a second, then laughed and pointed to
a door, That way, and continued to laugh, still sounding
like jolly old St. Nick. When Marion finished throwing up
she bathed her face with cold water then sat on the side of
the tub trembling with fright. For a second a panic froze her
body and mind. She breathed deeply and closed her eyes. The
nausea was gone. But she was sweating. Trembling. What
would he do? She had to get that dope. She breathed deeply
again. Put some more cold water on her face and patted it
dry and tried to fix her hair as best she could. She almost
prayed that he wasnt bugged. Please God, dont let him be
bugged. Im alright now. *Its all the same. All the same.* She
went back into the living room and did her best to smile.
Guess it was the chartreuse. He smiled and laughed. Im
alright now, her smile turning into an eager grin. He spread
his legs as she knelt in front of him and closed her eyes and
pulled his pants off and caressed his ass as she sucked his
joint with all the enthusiasm the thought of the dope generated, glancing up at him from time to time and smiling. Big
Tim leaned back and took a drink and laughed, Yeah, Little
Bo Beep done foun her sheep. . . .

Harry fidgeted in the movie. He continually squirmed,
trying to find a comfortable position, but each time he
thought he had his back would start hurting, or his ass got
sore or his legs started cramping and so he continually

adjusted his position, smoking one cigarette after the other. He couldnt stay in one position more than a few minutes so he got up to get some candy, Want somethin man? Yeah, Snickers. He got a couple of candy bars and came back and started the routine all over again. One movie wasnt too bad, an old Randy Scott shootim up, but the other one was a fuckin drag, a real fuckin drag. A would be romantic comedy that musta had a budget of a dollar ninety eight. Jesus, what a bunch a shit. From time to time he would glance at Tyrone, from the corner of his eye, and he was just staring at the screen, diggin what was goin on. He tried to concentrate on the dumb ass flick but his head kept fighting him and telling him he was an asshole for even waiting for the broad, that she was there for a while man and forget it. Shes up there with a heavy weight dude with a pile of shit and youre going to sit and wait in a funky ass coffee shop for her? Shit, youre outta ya fuckin mind. Shes up there fuckin the ass off that dude man and youre here chewing them fuckin Chuckles until theyre all stuck all over your fuckin teeth and watchin some dumb ass flick made by a bunch of fuckin assholes. He moved around again and grunted out loud. Tyrone continued to stare at the screen, but reached over and patted him on the back, Its cool man. Everything cool. He turned and smiled a big, white toothed smile and patted him again. Harry nodded and shoved a few more Chuckles in his mouth.

Big Tim was leaning against the doorjamb, naked, rubbing his chest, smiling, and feeling gooooood all over, as he watched Marion brush her hair. He was bouncing the package of ten bags in his hand. You know, you cut this shit loose an I can turn you out an make you some real braid baby. Marion smiled into the mirror and continued brushing her hair, Not today. And Im not *really* hooked. Big Tim laughed his jolly

old St. Nick laugh, Yeah, ah know, and tossed the package to
her when she finished brushing her hair. Marion clutched it
for a moment, then put it in her pocketbook. What the fuck
you doin? Marion was startled and stared at him for a moment, then shook her head, Nothing. Im— Damn! he laughed
and laughed, the sound so happy that Marion started smiling
and chuckling without the slightest idea why, Damn! hahahaha, ah got me some kind a fuckin virgin. Now you got to
be kiddin ol Tim, you just got to be. Marion was still smiling
and shaking her head. I dont kn— You mean you not goin
to count whats there but you jus going to be puttin it in your
pocketbook an jus walk out in the street???? Damn! You sure
aint been aroun long, have you baby? and his smile broadened
and his expression and tone were amused and gentle. Marion
flushed and shrugged, and started to protest, Im not exactly
a naive school girl, she fidgeted with her pocketbook as Big
Tim continued to smile down on her, I . . . I . . . her head
and shoulders jerking about, Ive been all through Europe,
an . . . an . . . and Im just not— Big Tim was nodding and
smiling, Sheeit, aint nothing to be ashamed of baby, we all
gotta git down with it for the firs time. Ah aint bad rappin
ya. Ah jus want to set you straight so you doan get ripped
off. Sheeit, you earned that baby—Marion flushed slightly
and blinked—an you sure as hell doan want to donate it to
some purse snatcher. He laughed again and Marion smiled,
You Tyrones bitch? the smile still in his voice and on his
face. Marion shook her head. Then there be a couple a dudes
waitin for you? Yes. I do— Well, lookit here, there be one
place you can stash ol doogie without you worryin about it
be accidently getting in the wrong hands, you dig? Aint no
purse snatcher or mugger goin to rip you off there baby.
Marion flushed, then smiled and shook her head. When she
realized how dumb she must look to Tim, she flushed even
more. An if you smart you make two packages, you dig? and

you keep one for yourself. He laughed again and walked back
to the living room and poured himself another glass of
bourbon. Marion opened the package and put two bags in a
separate package and put that up her snatch first, then put
the other package in too. When Marion went back to the
living room Big Tim was still naked and standing near the
stereo, his glass in one hand, a cigarette hanging from his
mouth, looking cool and nodding in time to the music. He
glanced at her then smiled, Jus a minute, I want to dig this.
He listened until the sax faded then he started walking
to the door, I/ll hear from you soon. Well . . . I dont . . . I . . .
Marion shrugged and blinked involuntarily— Big Tim just
kept smiling, opened the door, Catch you later baby.

   Tyrone and Harry were sitting in the rear booth of the coffee
shop when Marion got there. The movie was bad enough,
but this past hour or so, or however fuckin long it was, was a
real fuckin drag. Somehow the movie took care of some of
the action in him, but sittin in a fuckin coffee shop, waitin,
made his fuckin crotch squirm. Jesus, it was drivin him
fuckin bananas. He kept adjusting himself and rubbing and
scratching until Tyrone started to giggle, Watch you doin
to your thang jim. You look like you fixin to take the mutha
fucka out and whip the table with it. I/ll beatya over the
fuckin head with it, and Harry smiled in spite of himself and
put his hands on the table, Hows that, and continued fidgeting until Marion walked into the shop. She and Harry looked
at each other for a moment, each frantically searching for
some way to start a conversation without saying what was on
their minds. Then Tyrone asked how it went. Marion
nodded. He gave me eight bags. Harry gave a silent and inner
sigh of relief. That aint a bad tase. How mah man Tim?

Marion nodded. Yeah, he be a cool mutha jim. Ah mean cooooooool. Harry stood, Lets split. Crazy. Good. Im dying to get home.

Marion stashed her two bags just as soon as she could, and when Harry left to sell some dope and cop some more she sat with them in her hand, fondling them, caressing them, closing her eyes from time to time and sighing, rubbing the bags of dope between the tips of her fingers, securely nestled on her couch listening to Mahlers Resurrection Symphony.

Sara trembled with such terror when she heard the food cart in the distance, even with the massive doses of tranquilizers she was being given, that they stopped trying to get her to eat and force fed her. They strapped her in a wheelchair and shoved a rubber hose up her nose and down into her stomach, Sara retching and gagging, then taped the end to her head. Her feeble attempts to defend herself and try to speak were quickly overcome as they simply slammed her against the back of the chair and tightened the straps. When they finished she reached up to tug at the hose and they told her to get her hands off that hose, and tied her hands to the arms of the chair, Weve had enough trouble from you. Youre just going to stay tied in that chair until you learn to cooperate and stop thinking that youre some kind of a queen. She continued to retch until her stomach felt like it was torn apart and she exhausted herself and no longer had enough energy to retch and she sat in her mute and immobile terror, staring at the world around her through her tear filled eyes, struggling to break through the haze of tears and drugs and understand what was happening. She tried to keep her head up, but it continually fell forward and she struggled to get it erect, but the energy was not there and it would hang like a gourd for a few moments, then fall back on her chest, each movement a monumental effort, each failure a death knell. With each breath the tears seemed to build up within her and she could feel and hear them swishing around, feeling them threaten to drown her as her lungs seem to hang limp in her chest. She wanted to cry out, at least to herself, but she forgot that there was someone, something to call out to. There seemed to be a vague sense of recollection in the back of her mind and when she tried to dig it out she once again fell exhausted, and if she hadnt, the drugs and shock treatment would not have allowed her to recognize the word God.

The straps seemed to be tighter, but there was nothing she could do. They were cutting into her wrists and were pressing so hard against her chest they were restricting her breathing, but she could say and do nothing. She wanted desperately to go to the bathroom, but when she tried to call for someone to help her she gagged on the hose and only spittle dribbled down her chin as she fought to withstand the pain the hose caused in her throat. For hours she fought against her bladder and bowels, and when someone came by she looked, hoping they would look at her and see she needed help, but when they saw her they just walked on by and her head would fall once again on her chest and then she would start the long, long struggle of trying to raise it to get help, but they continued to simply walk on by, and still she fought, harder and harder, but eventually nature won, as always, and her bladder and bowels relieved themselves and she felt the warmth and moisture and her last semblance of dignity fled from her, along with her tears, as her mind called out for help . . . called, begged, pleaded, and then a nurse walked by and stopped, looked at her for a minute, came over, looked, twisted her face in disgust, You ought to be ashamed of yourself. Even animals dont do that. Well, you can just sit in it. Maybe that will teach you a lesson. Two days later Sara was

still sitting in it, no longer attempting to lift her head, allowing it to hang in her shame, her tears streaking her face,
blotting her gown, and filling her soul. Two days later she
was still strapped in the chair and chained to her indignity
until they came to prepare her for her next shock treatment.

Marion called Big Tim and went to see him again. Harry
was out when she called and was watching TV when she got
back. Harry didnt ask where she had been and she said
nothing. He had copped a bundle, offd some for a lot of
bread, and was holding out dope and bread from her. She
stashed her two bags with the others and felt a warm glow as
she looked at them and couldnt wait until she was alone so
she could take them out and hold them and caress them. She
gave Harry the other eight bags, then took one of them and
got off. She joined him on the couch, Howd it go tonight?
Pretty good. Lucked out. Ran into something almost right
away. Good. She pulled her legs up on the couch. Thats
really good stuff, isnt it? Yeah. Dont find that out on the
streets. Lets not sell that, alright Harry? Just the other. You
dont see me passing it out, do you? No, but I . . . you know
what I mean. Yeah. Dont sweat it. Im not going to part with
the good shit. Marion stared at the television for a few
minutes, not knowing what she was looking at, not caring, not
trying, just biding time and waiting for the words . . . Harry?
Yeah? Do we have to tell Tyrone about these bags? He looked
at her, a voice inside saying, fuck no. Me and him are tight.
He set the whole thing up. I know, I know, Marion looked
up into Harrys eyes, but Im the one who went up there. Harry
could feel the burning flush seeping out from his inner being
somewhere and was hoping to krist he didnt turn red. He
nodded his head, Okay. I guess what he dont know wont
killim.

Tyrone was stretched out on the couch, alone, watching television. Alice had split, gone back to her family in some jerk town in Georgia. Couldnt take the cold or the heat. She was a fine fox, but Tyrone was happy and relieved not to have another vein to feed. She sure didnt dig bein sick. Like to scare her to death. Sheeit, ah sure doan dig it. Dont dig the hassles either. But it aint so bad. Las night we cop right away and get back some heavy braid. Things going to be better soon enough. There doan seem to be too much hassle now. Tyrone C. Love watched the television for a while, wondering, anticipating, chuckling, using the images and sounds from the set, along with the heroin in his system, to quiet a little gnawing of questioning confusion that seemed to be scratching him from time to time. He/d been spending many hours of each day and night scufflin and hustlin in those streets an man its a cold mutha fuckin bitch out there an this panics a bitch jim, a mutha fuckin bitch. Yeah . . . a bitch baby, an hes all caught up in the mutha. Ol Ty was caught up in it for so long it didnt seem so bad anymore. It seemed less and less like a hassle. But what the fuck, a habit aint no real hassle. A habit you do in your sleep. You caint think about it. You jus do it. An a habit create its own habits. And he lay on his couch, staring at the set, getting his kicks, and when he wondered why he was happy to be alone, he just stopped wondering and got back in the spoon and turned the channel. These things sort of itched Tyrone, but he soothed them away from his consciousness with his habit and the tube and jus didnt worry about not havin the energy—the desire—to get himself another bitch. No, he jus take care of his own self till things gets a little cooler. Right now he/ll jus hang tough and take care of the little jones he had goin. Later for the bitches man. Yeah, mah names Tyrone C.

Love and ah loves nobody but Tyrone C., an ahm goin to take
good care o you baby.

Sara was tied in her wheelchair each morning and she sat
mutely and docilely watching the people coming, going,
giving medication, caring for patients, making beds, mopping
floors, going about their daily and various chores, her mind
and eyes moist with tears. Voices and noises mingled and
clanged through the ward unnoticed by Sara. She sat mutely.
They continued to pass her by as she waited . . . waited for
someone to come to her, to talk to her . . . to help her. They
did come to her. They came to prepare her for another shock
treatment. Sara wept.

Harry and Tyrone were holding out a little more on each
other each day. If one guy somehow got caught short and his
nose and eyes were running and his body shivering as they
scuffled and hustled the street trying to cop, and asked the
other one to give him a taste, the guy swore up and down
he had nothing, that he had just done in his cottons, and he
would start shaking, trying to fake his friend out.

They roamed the streets in the snow, the sleet, fighting the
freezing winds, sometimes hustling from one spot to another
all night, always just missing the connection, and other times
they were able to cop within a couple of hours. Everywhere
they went there were thousands of sick junkies trying to cop
or get cop money, and when they did get their hands on
some shit they split to get off, but they didn't always make it
and dying and dead bodies littered the hallways and debris
of abandoned buildings. Like the others, Harry and Tyrone
ignored the bodies and remained huddled in their jackets
and their needs, saying nothing to each other, saving their

energies to find someone who was holding. Then they would get off and cut the bags as much as possible and off as much as they could and start the search all over again.

When Marion was home alone, she would take out her stash and look at the bags, enjoying the feeling of power and security she felt. She was seeing Big Tim a couple of times a week. Now she told Harry she was only getting six bags, that was why she was going so often. Harry didnt even bother wondering if he believed her or not, he just took three of the bags, not telling Tyrone about it, and whenever he copped he always held back a few bags on Marion, and when the pangs of conscience started to disturb him they were readily dissolved by the heroin.

Occasionally Marion would notice her sketch pads and pencils and the memory of the plans for the coffee house and some other vague memories started to work their way to her consciousness, but she just pushed them aside and stared at the tube, thinking about her stash. A few times the pangs of remorse would start to unnerve her as she stared at a scene of sunny Italy in a Cinzano ad, but she just reminded herself that she had been, and a bag of good stuff was a hell of a lot better than a mob of garlic smelling italians.

Harry and Tyrone were standing in the wet snow, freezin their asses off, waiting for the connection, again, and listening to the other dudes talk about how all the big time connections were in Florida sittin on their mutha fuckin asses in the sun while they were up here ass deep in the mutha fuckin snow. Yeah, an those mutha fuckas sitting on all that dope too jus to git the fuckin price up jim and thats the onlyest reason they doin it. Sheeit, they be a bunch a stoned mutha fuckas man, ah mean they be some stooooooned pricks jim. Harry and Tyrone had heard the same old bullshit a million times just like the rest of them, but they never tired of listening and nodding their heads, just like everyone else, cursing the bastards for starting the panic just so they could make more money when they were fuckin millionaires a dozen fuckin times over already. The intensity of their anger not only helped pass the time, but helped create a little much needed inner warmth. By the time they finally did cop that night they were numb with the cold and had a difficult time walking. Harry stopped off at Tyrones to get off before continuing to Marions. They sat around smoking and relaxing when Harry started thinking about those pricks who were sittin in the sun and wondered what would happen if someone went down *there* to cop. Tyrone looked at him with droopy eyes, What you talkin about? Whatta my talking about? just what I said. Everybodys up here scufflin just to stay alive and still gettin ripped off or knocked off, and nobodys thought about goin right to the fuckin source man. What the fuck you talkin about? goin up to the mutha fuckin room clerk at some hotel an askin for a connection? Sheeit. Comeon Ty, get with, eh? You tellin me you cant nose out some dope when its around? Thas here man. The Apples mah neighborhood. What the fuck ah know about Miami? Them mutha fuckin *eye*talians aint sitting aroun jus waitin for me to show up jim. I/ll take care of that. I know how those bastards operate. Thats no sweat. Tyrone looked at him for a few seconds, Thas a long ass walk jim. Not if youre drivin. Look man, its coleran hell and those streets are hotteran a bitch. Guys are gettin knocked off like theyre giving blue chip stamps with every dead dope fiend. Man, we got nothing to lose, Harrys enthusiasm increasing the more he talked about it. Tyrone was scratching his head, If its such a good idea then why aint somebody else thought of it? Because theyre assholes. Harry was sitting on the edge of his chair, his face glazed with sweat. And thats just it, nobody else *has* thought of it. Its wide open. Tyrone continued scratching and nodding, an if we can get there before anyone else we can name our own price and sit back an be cool and have those fools scufflin the streets for us. Tyrone continued scratching, Las summer was a ball jim, he suddenly frowned and tilted his head, seem like a thousan years since las summer. Sheeit. Itll be back like that after we get some weight. Why doan we fly down there? We be there an back in one mutha fuckin day. Harry was shaking his head, No man. No fuckin good. We/ll need a fuckin short when we get there, right? Tyrone nodded. An we can get there in a day easy. We got enough shit to last an we can get some uppers from Marion. No problem. Tyrone had been scratching and looking up at the ceiling. Gogit could probably get us a short easy enough we promise him some dynamite scag. That mutha fucka can dig up anythin, even the daid. Harry laughed and continued nodding energetically, their desperation making everything seem so simple, An its warm in Florida man.

Harry told Marion that they had heard where there was some dynamite shit and asked her for some money. The more we get the better off we are. Where you getting it? Harry shrugged, Cant really say, but its out of state. Be a few days or so, you know. Marion thought for a few seconds, I dont know Harry, Im just about out of the rent money now. Dont sweat it. In a couple a days we/ll have a sack full a shit and plenty of bread. Marion thought for another moment, knowing she could spare a hundred dollars without any trouble and thinking it would be great to have even more dope than she had. And too, she would be completely free for a few days and she could keep all the stuff she got from Tim, and if she saw him every day she would have a nice taste stashed. Okay, Harry, I can give you a hundred dollars, but I have to have it back before the end of the month, I need it for my rent. Harry dismissed her concern with a wave of the hand, We/re gonta be doing some driving so youd better lay some of those uppers on me. We want to make this a fast trip.

Marion called Big Tim after Harry left and in a short time she was on her way downtown, thinking of how many bags she would have by the time Harry got back, feeling independent of Harry.

Gogit had no trouble getting them a car. It wasn't much of a car, but it ran. A cousin was doing some time on Rikers and he conned his aunt out of the car, telling her he would take care of it so the tires wouldnt rot, and the battery get run down, or the kids strip it to the frame some night.

Harry and Tyrone got their shit together and got off just before leaving, about nine oclock at night. They figured they would miss all the heavy traffic then and with the uppers they could drive through the night without any trouble and get into Miami at a good time. Harry was having more and more trouble finding a vein, having to go into his fingers, but they were proving to be no good too, and he sure as krist didnt want to blow a fix now. A bag of shit was too precious these days. So, from time to time, he would be forced to go back into a spot in his arm that had been festering occasionally and was now a hole. He always made up his mind he would stay away from it, but when he was getting off he just couldnt go through the hassle of trying to find another spot so sooner or later he would just drop the needle in the hole in his arm and squeeze the shit in. Tyrone would shake his head, Thats a nasty mutha fucka jim, you should learn to get some ropes like me. Thas the trouble with you honkys, you too sof. Thats okay man, just as long as the shit gets where its goin . . . an just as long as we get where we/re goin.

It was cold and windy when they left, but dry. Ah sure hope this mutha fuckin heater works jim. Harry was driving, Tyrone staring at the heater controls, turning the heater on every few seconds, then turning it off as cold air whirled around his feet. They were almost on the Jersey Turnpike before the air from the heater was warm, Sheeit, there it goes. I guess this aint goin to be such a bad trip.

The radio wasnt too bad and so for the first few hours they finger popped, dug the sounds, and drove as rapidly as possible along the turnpike, keeping their eyes open for the cops, not wanting to be stopped for anything. The night was soothing and comforting. And it felt still. The lights from the occasional car passing made them feel warm and secure in their well heated car. The lights from distant houses or nearby power towers and factories twinkled in the cold air, but their attention was on the road and the distance between them and Miami. From time to time Harry would become aware of the ache in his arm, then straighten it slowly and adjust it on the arm rest. Every now and then Tyrone would check the odometer and announce how much closer they were to Miami and all that warm sun and fine shit. Yeah man, an when we get back with all that stuff we/re gonta be cool. Right on baby. We/re not gonta let anybody know we got weight, we/re just gonta cut that stuff and slip out a few bundles a night to those dudes like we just copped it ourselves. You damn right jim. Ah dont want all those runny nosed dope fiens bangin down mah door. Tyrone rubbed his head and looked out the window at the snow and frozen slush that was gray and spotted with black, the lights picking out a rare spot of white where the surface snow had been ripped away. How much you figure we get? I dont know man, maybe two pieces. You really think we get that much? the mutha fuckin price is gone crazy jim. Yeah, yeah, I know, but I figure a grans gotta get us two pieces even with this panic. We/re *schleppin* the stuff and takin all the heat. Thats gotta be worth somethin. Yeah, Tyrone was smiling and leaning

back in his seat, an we be cool till this mutha fuckin panic
and winter is gone jim. Maybe I/ll get me a sun lamp an jus
lay back like you honkys, Tyrone let his teeth hang out in a
wide grin. Harry glanced at him and started laughing, then
snorting as he fought to control himself and keep his eye on
the road. Hey baby, be cool, we got a long way to go.

After driving for a few hours they stopped at a Howard
Johnsons and bundled their clothes around them as they
hustled from the car. They ordered soda and pie then went
to the mens room. Harry very gently took his jacket off and
rolled up his shirt sleeve. The hole in his arm was hurting
so bad now that he wasnt laughing and talking about all the
dope they would have soon. He and Tyrone looked at it for
a moment and Tyrone shook his head, Thats lookin bad jim.
Yeah, it sure as hell aint pretty. Harry shrugged, O well,
fuck it, I/ll take care of it when we get back. Yeah, but you
best not use that anymore. You best be getting off somewhere
else. Yeah. They each went into a separate stall to get off
and Harry tried to work up a usable vein in his right hand
but no matter how hard he tried he couldnt get anything
close to what he wanted so he just went back into the old
reliable hole in his left arm rather than taking the chance of
blowing a fix. It hurt like hell for a minute, but it was worth
it, and soon it was just a dull ache again. They drank a few
glasses of soda after eating their pie and grooved behind the
dope and the waitress and giggled and scratched for a while,
then dropped another dexie, got a couple of containers of
coffee, and split and continued toward Miami and the connections. They were quiet for a while, listening to the music
and feeling warm and secure with the dope and the future,
each smiling inwardly thinking about the end of their problems and the panic, at least for them. Then the dexies
loosened their tongues and they started nodding in time to

the music, singing, finger poppin and rapping endlessly,
Tyrone announcing how much closer they were to Miami,
from time to time, and the connections.

Harry was still driving when the sun started to come up.
Damn, we been ridin all night an there still be snow on the
mutha fuckin groun jim. How far south you got to go
before they be no snow? Very far man. This panic and cold
spell goes right down to Florida. They stopped for coffee
and dropped a couple more uppers, then went to the mens
room, one at a time, and got off, got a couple of containers of
coffee and split. Tyrone got behind the wheel and Harry
stretched out in his seat, trying to rest his arm and get the
son of a bitch to stop hurting. It wasnt so bad now that he
had just gotten off, but it still throbbed.

Tyrone still looked at the odometer, announcing how much
closer they were to Miami, when all of a sudden it dawned on
him how far away they were from New York. They dropped
some more uppers and drank more coffee, and thought about
the distance between them and home. They had driven all
night and they realized they couldnt just jump on the subway or grab a cab and get to where they wanted to go. However they may have felt when they left they were now
committed, they had passed the point of no return.

The radio continued to play, but the car was quiet, Harry
continually rubbing his arm trying to soothe it. Tyrone
leaned the elbow of his left arm against the door and stroked
his chin with his hand. Neither one of them had ever left
the state of New York before, and the only time Harry had
left the city was when he was a kid and he went to the Boy
Scout camp. They were becoming more and more overwhelmed by the strangeness of the countryside. They became
increasingly quiet. The uppers and the heroin fought for
control. The area around the highway seemed to be getting
closer somehow. They squirmed, trying to find a comfortable

spot in their seats. They stared through the windshield. They tried to numb their minds with the uppers and heroin, but still the desperateness of the situation forced itself upon them. Separately they each felt increasingly aware of the fact that what they were doing was insane. They were half a world away from the neighborhood. They were strung out, a fact that they pussy footed around for a long time, but now it thrust itself right in their guts. They were strung out and they were driving through some asshole fuckin state trying to get to Miami and find the big connections. They could smell them. They knew they were following the connections. But what the fuck were they going to do when they got there? What the fuck was goin on? They squirmed. Adjusted. Harry soothed his arm. The fuckin pain was suddenly so bad he was goin blind. They were scared shitless. But they were just as scared to cop out in front of the other one. They both wanted to turn around and go back. Scufflin those fuckin streets in this mutha fuckin panic was like death man, but it was better than this. Where the fuck were they goin fa krists sake? What was comin down? Suppose they run outta shit before they got back? Suppose they got busted down here in the fuckin South? Each almost prayed, or came as close to praying as they knew how, that the other one would suggest turning around and going back, but they just continued to stare through the windshield and squirm as the car continued going straight ahead. Tyrone stopped looking at the odometer. Harry was unable to sit still for more than a few minutes. From time to time he was almost doubled over with pain. He rubbed his arm, trying to soothe the pain away. I dont think Im gonta make it man. This fuckin arm is killin me. He squirmed out of his jacket and rolled up his sleeve and blinked a few times as he looked at his arm. Tyrone glanced at it from time to time, frowning, Sheeit, that really looks bad baby. Around the hole in Harrys arm a

huge greenish white lump had formed with red streaks spreading out toward his shoulder and wrist. I can hardly move the
son of a bitch. Im gonta have ta do somethin man.

Big Tim told Marion he would arrange for her to pick up
a nice taste for a few hours work, Though its more like play
baby. What do you mean by a nice taste? Big Tim laughed his
Santa laugh, Damn, you sure is greedy for scag. Marion
smiled and shrugged. They be six of you cutting up a piece.
An its good, and he smiled as Marions eyes widened and
sparkled. When? His smile broadened, Tomorrow night. He
waited for a moment, wondering if she would ask what she
had to do but he was sure she wouldnt. Its a little party for
some people ah know. Ahll take you there. Who will be cutting
up the piece with me? Five other bitches. Youll be the entertainment . . . you know, kind of enjoy each others company,
you dig? and he smiled then laughed his Santa laugh as he
saw what he meant register on Marions face. And the men?
They come later, and Tim laughed so hard Marion started
chuckling. What time? You be here by eight. Marion smiled
and nodded and Big Tim laughed his Santa Claus laugh.

Harry and Tyrone pulled into a small gas station and
got out of the car and stretched. The attendant was in the
back talking to the mechanic. They looked at Harry and
Tyrone for a moment, then the attendant put down his bottle
of Coke and strolled out to them. Harry was leaning against
the car holding and soothing his left arm, Fill it up with
regular, eh? An wheres the mens room? We/re fresh out of
gas. O shit. Thas alright jim, we got enough for a while.
Harry nodded at Tyrone, May just as well use the mens
room. The attendant stared at Harry, Its out of order. Harry

looked at him for a moment and noticed the hostile expression on the guys face. A car pulled up to the other pump and the attendant went over to it, Good morning Fred, filler up? Yup. The attendant started pumping gas into the car and the mechanic came out from the back and leaned against the wall and stared into Harrys face provokingly and spit. Harrys pain and confusion started to turn to rage and Tyrone opened the door, Lets cool it baby. Harry looked at Tyrone for a moment, then got into the car. The mechanic continued to stare at them, and spit, as they drove away. What the fuck was that shit, man? Thas the solid South baby. Jesus krist, its like a bad fuckin movie. I thought the fuckin Civil War was over. Sheeit, not to these muthas. They both looked at the gas gauge. What the fuck we gonta do man? How the fuck ah know jim? We jus be cool an get us some mutha fuckin gas, what the fuck else we gonna do? Harry nodded his head and clutched his arm closer to him and they drove in silence, each holding on tight, not wanting to blow his cool and wishing to krist they were somewhere else. The time seemed to drag as they stared ahead, not noticing the trees and poles rushing by. They kept glancing at the fuel gauge and then ahead at the horizon where the sides of the road pinched together and remained unreachably ahead of them. Harry rubbed his arm and, from time to time, Tyrone reached up and rubbed and scratched his head, then leaned his left arm against the door and rested his chin in his hand. Theres one. Yeah. They became increasingly aware of the sweat running down their backs and sides as they pulled into the station. They stayed in the car and Harry leaned out slightly and told the guy to fill it up. Regular. The guy leaned against the pump, ignoring them, as the gas was pumped into the car. When it was full Harry paid him and they drove off, the silence unbroken for many long minutes until Tyrone turned on the radio. The tension started to ease from their bodies along with the sweat. Damn, I could sure use a tase. Yeah, you aint shittin. Theres gotta be a diner pretty soon.

They stopped at a small roadside place and went into the mens room one at a time, the other one sitting at the counter watching carefully. After getting off they relaxed and thought theyd get something to eat, as well as coffee, and Harry called to the waitress who was standing at the other end of the counter talking to a customer, but she ignored him. He called again and the cook jammed his head out and told him to shut up. Harry closed his eyes for a moment, breathed deeply, exhaled slowly, then looked at Tyrone, shaking his head. Tyrone shrugged and they got up and left.

Sara finished her series of shock treatments. She sat on the side of her bed and stared out the window, through the gray glass at the gray sky, the gray ground and bare trees. From time to time she would twist off the bed and shuffle, in her paper slippers, to the nurses office and lean against the wall opposite the door and stare. Do you want something? Sara blinked and stared. Do you want something Mrs. Goldfarb? Saras face twisted slightly and she almost smiled, then she blinked a few times before resuming her staring. The nurse shrugged and went back to her work. Sara slid down the wall and crouched on the floor, still trying to get, and keep, a smile on her face. Her cheek muscles twitched, the corners of her mouth trembled. Eventually she stretched her mouth in a tight, torturous looking wide-eyed grin. She fumbled to her feet and shuffled across to the door of the nurses office and stood grinning until the nurse looked at her. Thats very good, now go back to your bed, and she once more turned her back on Sara and continued working. Sara turned and shuffled back to her bed and sat on the side and stared through the gray windows.

Sara was put in a wheelchair and taken from the ward, down an elevator, through a long, gray tunnel to a waiting room where other patients docilely sat, their attendants in a corner smoking, joking, keeping an eye on their patient. Sara looked at those in front of her and blinked a few times, squinted, then stared. From time to time someone would open a door and call a name and one of the attendants would wheel the patient through the door, and they seemed to disappear, yet there always seemed to be just as many people in front of Sara. Time continued to be time and Saras name was called. Her attendant wheeled her through the door and Sara tried to smile. In front of her a man sat behind a desk. There were others in the room. The man behind the desk was called your honor. Someone stood up and opened a folder and read some things to the judge. He looked at Sara. She tried to smile and her face started to stretch in her wide-eyed grin as little bits of spittle dribbled down her chin. He signed his name to a piece of paper and handed it back to the man. She was committed to a State Mental Hospital.

Sara was awakened early and hustled out of bed and taken to the basement of the hospital where she was put on a bench to wait. And wait. She asked if she could have something to eat and was told it was too early. When she asked again they said it was too late. Eventually she was checked through one line, then she waited. She sat on the bench and stared. She went to the next line. And waited. She was given her clothes. She looked at them a long time. They told her to dress. She stared. They put some clothes on her. She struggled into the rest. They led her to another bench. She waited. They put her on a bus and she sat and stared ahead as the others were placed in their seats. They drove through the streets with a lifetime of familiar sights and sounds and Sara stared in front of her.

They were led off the bus and their names were checked

off a list and then they were led through a gray, moist and freezing tunnel that connected with other tunnels and eventually to a building on the remote part of the grounds and locked in a ward jammed with others shuffling, sitting, squatting, standing, staring. Sara stood still and stared at the gray walls.

Ada and Rae made a visit. They sat in a corner of the visiting room and stared at Sara as she shuffled toward them. They knew it was Sara, yet they didnt recognize her. Bones stuck out everywhere. Her hair hung dead from her head. Her eyes were clouded and didnt see. Her skin was gray. Sara sat and Ada started taking food out of a large shopping bag. We got some lox and cream cheese and bagels and blintz with sour cream and some danishes and pastrami and chopped liver on rye with mustard and onions and a container hot tea and. . . . How are you dolly?

Sara continued to stare, Yes, and tried to smile and took a big bite out of the sandwich and made a grunting clacking sound as she chewed, the mustard oozing out of the corners of her mouth. Ada blinked and Rae gently wiped the mustard, and spittle, away. They looked at their friend of so many years, trying hard to understand. They stayed for an endless hour then reluctantly, but with a sigh of relief, left. They stared at the gray walls and lifeless trees and grounds as they sat waiting for a bus, tears flowing from their eyes. They hugged each other.

Harry and Tyrone stared silently through the windshield, their fear and apprehension increasing with each mile. Harry was almost doubled in a fetal position. The pain and panic had almost cut off his breath. The closer they got to Miami the more deeply the distance between them and the neighborhood was drilled into their minds. They still had plenty of stuff and uppers, but the fear was so intense that it was a tangible substance in the car. Harry would try to close his eyes and forget everything except the fact that the connections were in Miami, but as soon as he did he saw his arm, a flaming red, then green, and he could hear someone sawing his arm off and he jerked himself up in his seat and grabbed his arm and tried rocking back and forth as much as he could. Man, I cant cut it. I gotta get some penicillin, or somethin, for this fuckin arm.

They parked the car around the corner from a small medical building and went into the first office they saw. There were a few people in the waiting room and Tyrone went over to the nurse to tell her about Harry. Yawl have an appointment? Tyrone just shook his head, No. Its an emergency. Why dont yawl go to the hospital? Ah doan know where it is an he— Harry came over, I got a bad infection in my arm and Im afraid I/ll lose it. Cant the doctor see me? Please. Harry shoved his arm forward and she glanced at it for a moment, then at them, Sit down. After a few minutes the nurse came back and opened the door to the examination room and called Harry, This way.

Harry paced back and forth, holding his arm, trying, from time to time, to sit, but couldnt stay still for more than a minute. Eventually the doctor came and looked at Harry for a minute, Whats your problem? My arm, its killin me. The doctor grabbed Harrys arm roughly, Harry wincing with the pain, and glanced at it then dropped it. I/ll be back in a minute. The doctor left the room and went to his office, closed the door, and called the police. Hello, this is Doctor Waltham. Over to Russell Street? Ive got a young man here I think you should see. Hes got an infection in his arm that looks to me like it came from a needle, and his pupils are dilated. I think hes a drug addict. He sounds like a gawddamn New Yawk bum and hes with a nigga. He hung up then buzzed his nurse and told her the police would be there in a few minutes, so just keep your eye on that New Yawk nigga. The doctor waited a few more minutes before going back to Harry. He roughly grabbed Harrys arm again and twisted it, Harry gaggin and his knees bending from the pain. This is going to take time to clean out. Ah have one more patient to treat, then ahll be able to take care of you. He left before Harry could say a word, or even catch his breath.

Tyrone tried to look at a magazine, but he kept feeling like getting up and running out of the office. There was something wrong, but he didnt know what it was. He glanced at the nurse out of the corner of his eye from time to time, and she always seemed to be staring at him, and looking like he had just killed her moms or something. It made him feel creepy. He went back to the magazine and turned his head so he couldnt see her and just stared at the pictures, occasionally glancing at the words and wishing he was back in the neighborhood, panic or no panic, cold or no cold. It was too mutha fuckin hot here an he didnt like it. He wondered what was happening with Harry. He felt Harry had passed through that door into something else. He sure as hell didnt like the way he was feeling or the way that bitch was lookin atim. Damn, he wished he was back in the Apple. He/d be happy to jus lay down in the mutha fuckin snow if he were back there right now. What was he doin here anyway. Sheeit, he never wanted to be in no mutha fuckin South. Gahddamn, he wish Harry would hurry up an get his arm fix so they could get their asses outta here and back—he suddenly became aware that somebody was standing beside him and something in his stomach dropped to his knees. Before he turned his head he knew it was the man. What you doin here, *boy?* Tyrone slowly turned his head and looked up into the face of a cop.

His partner walked into the room where Harry was waiting. As he heard the footsteps and then the door starting to open a feeling of relief started to flow through Harry and he almost smiled as the door started to open—the cop stood staring at him, then moved into the room. Harry died. Where you from? Harry blinked, his head shaking uncontrollably, Huh? Uhhh a what???? Whats the matter with yawl? caint you talk? and he grabbed Harry by the chin and stared into his eyes for a minute, then shoved Harry from him, Ah said where you from? The Bronx . . . a, New York. New Yawk, eh? He pounded Harry in the chest with his finger, knocking him against the examination table, Yawl want to know something? we don't like no New Yawk dope fiens aroun here. Especially white nigga dope fiens. Harry started to say something and the cop hit him hard, on the side of the head, with his open hand, knocking him down, Harry falling on his arm. He grabbed his arm and moaned with pain, trying desperately to catch his breath and hold back the tears that the pain had brought to his eyes. Ah dont want to hear one fucking word from you, *nigga lova*. The cop grabbed Harry by the bad arm and dragged him, half fainting, to the car, cuffed his hands behind his back, and shoved him in. Tyrone was already sitting there, his hands cuffed behind his back.

When they got to the station Harry asked the booking officer if he could see a doctor and he laughed, Yawl want room service? My arm. I gotta get it fixed. Plenty time. Yawl wont have no use for that arm anyways for a while. There most probably will be a doctor here on Monday. Maybe he might be up to seeing you.

Tyrone sat in the corner of the cell watching Harry pace and thinking of the old time dope fien he was locked up with, who cooked up his shoulder pads. They didnt have nothin. Just themselves and their habits. A million miles away from the neighborhood. What the fuck was he doin here? It was that goddamn Harry. Him and his mutha fuckin ideas. Lets follow the fuckin connections. Lets go to Miami. Cop a nice tase and cool it until the weather gets warm. Even if they giveim a phone call, who he goin to call? Mutha fuck that Harry! Got me all fucked up down here in some funky ass town. Sheeit! He watched Harry holding his arm and trying to sit. A couple of drunks were sprawled on the floor. The shitter in the corner was covered with puke. It stank. Sheeit! Friday. Wont be shit before Monday. We/ll fuckin die before then. Tyrone hung his head between his knees and wrapped his arms around it. What happened man? What the fuck happened?

Harry rocked back and forth with his pain. It had been a couple of hours since their last fix and that was it. If only he had known that was going to be his last fix. He wouldve dumped a couple of bags in the cooker and got wasted. If he just had a fuckin cotton. Balls! His body strained from the more than twenty four hours without sleep and the combination of uppers and dope and the overwhelming pain in his arm. Now that he knew he couldnt get any more dope the junk sick descended rapidly. He stared at the steel walls until his eyes burned and started to close, but they quickly opened as nightmares started even before he was asleep. His head burned. His tongue was so dry it stuck to the roof of his mouth. He tried to stand to keep pacing, but his head was woozy and his knees buckled. He leaned against the side of the cell and slowly slid to the floor and sat with his head between his knees, rolling back and forth, his eyes burning and closing and opening, closing and opening, his gangrenish arm swinging in front of him like a pendulum.

From time to time a drunk was thrown in the tank, but Harry and Tyrone stayed alone in the small cell, wrapped in their separateness and pain, Harry slowly, but progressively, going deeper and deeper into delirium, Tyrone trying to warm the coldness within him with his anger. A couple of drunks fought over the toilet, one hanging his head in the bowl, puking, the other one puking all over him, the both of them eventually passing out and lying in their own and each others puke. The stench filled the cell. Harry and Tyrone stayed wrapped in their separateness and pain. Tyrone started to get stomach cramps and diarrhea and he tried to clean up the gahddamn shitter enough to use it, but as he wiped the fuckin thang with toilet paper the stench got him so sick he started puking and as soon as he stopped he had to turn around, almost sliding in the slimy puke on the floor, and stand over the fuckin bowl and let the foul smelling liquid pour out of his cramping body, and even as he stood, bent, he started to feel the nausea rising and he had to clamp his mouth closed as his body contorted with spasm. Eventually he finished for a while and he staggered back to his spot on the floor and leaned against the cold steel, bone cracking chills going through his body, and then he would double with cramps and sweat oozed then poured from his pore,, burning his nose with the smell that comes only from long use of dope, a sick smell that clouded his head with the feeling of death.

Harry tried to huddle within himself, clutching his legs, but he could only hug himself with one arm and as the sweat from the dope and his fever poured from his body he shivered and shook with uncontrollable chills and agonizing pain. From time to time the pain became so bad that he passed out for a while and then his body and mind would drag him, reluctantly, back to consciousness and he would huddle in a ball, trying to force some warmth into his body, desperately trying to find something to do with his arm so the pain would stop, and the fever would burn and chill him and he would go into the relief of deliriums.

Sometime Monday morning the cell was cleaned out. The

drunks went first, Harry and Tyrone last. Harrys arm was
starting to turn green and smell. The guard grabbed him by
his bad arm and spun him around to cuff him and Harry
screamed out with pain and passed out and slumped to his
knees, the guard continuing to twist his arm until he had
cuffed Harrys hands behind his back. When Harry screamed
Tyrone reached to grab him and one of the other guards hit
him on the head with a small club then kicked him in the
ribs and stomach as he lay on the floor, Dont you ever raise
yoe hands to me, *nigga*. They cuffed his hands behind his
back and dragged him to his feet and stuck a patch on his head
before they took him and Harry to the court. They were
shoved into chairs and Harry continued to moan and fall
forward and the cop told him to shut up and slammed him
back in the chair. A guy dressed in a suit sat next to Tyrone
and started to explain that he was appointed by the court to
represent them and read off the numbers of the charges and
Tyrones body continued to spasm with pain and nausea and
cramps and the sweat stung his eyes and he tried to wipe the
sweat from his eyes with his shoulder, but every time he
moved the guard smacked him on the side of the head and
Tyrones vision blurred and his head hung forward and this
guy told him if he would plead guilty to vagrancy that he
would only have to serve a few weeks on the work gang.
When you get out theyll give you a bus ticket back to New
York. Where our money? Did you have any? Tyrone looked
at him for a moment, blinking his eyes, trying to see him
clearly, We had over a thousan dollars jim. Not according to
this report. Tyrone stared for another moment then inwardly
shrugged. What about Harry? He sick. O, youll both be examined by the doctor before you are sent to the camp. O
sheeit, how he wished it was las summer. No fuckin hassles.
Things be goin smooth an every day be like a holiday. **Sheeit!**

Marion sat on her couch, alone, watching television. When the entertainment had finally finished and she was on her way home she had to fight hard to deny what she was feeling. She had been naive. She had no idea what she was supposed to do with the other girls. She knew what she was supposed to do with the men, but the girls came as a shock. She almost puked. But she knew why she was doing what she was doing and it made everything possible. It wasnt until after it had started that she remembered the little books she had read, and the photographs she had giggled over. It wasnt only what she had done that was disturbing her, but the ease with which she had done it. And when she got her share of the piece she knew it was all worth it. When she got home she got off and any disquieting feelings were immediately dissolved by the heroin and she didnt even bother bathing, that could wait until morning. She just stretched out on her couch, in front of her television, ignoring the smell from her body and lips, thinking over and over that Big Tim was right, this is good stuff. That taste will last a long time. She smiled to herself. And theres more where that came from, and no one to share it with. I can always have as much as I want. She hugged herself and smiled, I can always feel like this.

Harry and Tyrone were waiting on line with a dozen others in a back room of the jail. They had been given three months on the work gang instead of a few weeks. The bus to the work camp was parked outside the open door. The prisoners shuffled, one at a time, up to the guard, standing next to the doctor, holding a clipboard with a typewritten sheet of names. The doctor and the guards kidded each other and laughed and drank Coke as the prisoners shuffled along in their chains. They gave their name and number to the guard and he checked their name on the list and the doctor looked at them and asked them all the same question, Can you hear me? Can you see me? They nodded and the doctor slapped them on the back and okayed them for the work camp. As usual, Harry and Tyrone were last. Harry was in an almost constant state of delirium and kept stumbling and whenever Tyrone tried to support him he was hit or shoved. When Tyrone stood in front of the doctor the doctor looked at the bandage on his head, the lumps and discolorations, and smiled, Have a little trouble, *boy?* The guards laughed. Can you hear me, *boy?* Can you see me, *boy?* Tyrone nodded and the doctor slammed him on the face as a guard jabbed his stick in the small of his back, Say sir, nigga. These here New Yawk dope fien niggas aint got no manners. They laughed, We/ll learn him some soon enough. Tyrones body twisted with rage, frustration, as well as his junk sickness as he shuffled out to the waiting bus. He wanted to smash their mutha fuckin haids in, but he knew they were just waitin for him to try so they could hang his ass, an he didnt want to make it any worse than it was, wantin to do his time and get on home, and his junk sick made it easier to try nothin . . . he could hardly move.

Harry was held up in front of the doctor. This heres another New Yawk dope fien. Hes a nigga lover, ain yoe *boy?* Harry moaned and his legs started to buckle and the guard yanked him up, Say hes got somethin wrong with his arm. Yeah? The doctor yanked the sleeve of Harrys shirt up and Harry yelled and collapsed and they yanked him up again, Cant yawl at lease act lack a man an stan up? The doctor glanced at his arm then chuckled, Ah dont think yoe goin to be puttin any more dope in that arm, boy. He nodded toward the other guards, Looky here, aint that somethin? The guards looked and twisted their faces in disgust, Damn, it smell worse than he does. Yeah, he smell worse than a nigga, and they all laughed. Yawl better get him over to the hospital before he stink up your jail. More laughter. Ah dont expect he/ll live out the week. Any more? No, thats it doc. Good. Ah have to get ovah to mah office. See yawl next week.

Sara shuffled along the medication line with the others. She stood still for a moment, then shuffled forward a little, stood still for another moment, then shuffled forward again until she stood in front of the attendant who put the Thorazine in her mouth and watched her swallow it before letting her leave. She stood in the corner, her arms wrapped around her, watching the others shuffle up and get their tranquilizers. Then the area was cleared. Empty. She continued to stare in front of her, then slowly turned her head and looked in various directions, then she, too, left. She kept her arms wrapped around herself as she shuffled, in her paper slippers, into the television room. Some of the others were sitting with their chin on their chest, already feeling the effects of the medication. Some were laughing, some were crying. Sara stared at the screen.

Harry was unconscious when they wheeled him into the operating room. They amputated his arm at the shoulder and immediately started anti-infection therapy in an attempt to save his life. He was being fed intravenously in his right arm and both ankles, and was strapped to the bed so the needles wouldnt rip his veins if he started to convulse. A tube was in his nose so a steady supply of oxygen could be fed to his lungs. There were two drains in his side connected to a small pump under the bed in an effort to pump the poisonous fluid from his body. From time to time Harry stirred and groaned as he struggled to free himself from the claws of a nightmare and the nurse sitting by his side wiped his head with a cool, damp cloth, and spoke to him soothingly, and Harry would calm and once more be motionless, seeming almost to be dead, as he was absorbed by a dream and a feeling of weightlessness . . . then light surrounded him, light so complete and intense he experienced it in every part of his being, making him feel like he had never felt in his life, like he was something special, something really special. Harry felt the light/s warmth and he smiled so widely that he almost laughed as he felt joy flowing through his entire being. It was like the light was saying, I love you, and Harry knew that it was alright, that everything was alright, and he started walking without knowing why. Then it slowly dawned on him that he was looking for the source of the light. He knew it just couldnt be everywhere. It had to come from somewhere, and so he started searching for the source because he knew that the closer he got to the source the better he would feel, so he walked and walked, but the light didnt change. It stayed the same. No brighter, no dimmer, and so he stopped and tried to think, but he couldnt seem to think . . . not really. He could feel his face trying to work itself into a frown, but the smile was immovable and the joy continued to flow through all of his being. Then he had a vague sense of discomfort and he suddenly became aware of the fact that he was frowning and that the light was getting dimmer and though he couldnt see it he could feel some hideous monster coming toward him from some dark cloud that was forming somewhere behind him, but no matter how he moved he couldnt find the cloud. He tried desperately to find its location so he could run from it and try to stay in the light, but the more he turned and ran the more he stayed in one place, and he tried to catch his breath to put forth a burst of speed and run and run and run . . . but still he remained in one place and now the ground under him seemed to become increasingly amorphous and he started to sink deeper and deeper and his struggle only seemed to increase the speed of his descent and now he became frighteningly aware that the light was receding and though he still could not see that black cloud he knew without doubt that he was sinking deeper and deeper into it and closer and closer to the hideous monster that made him try to cry out in terror but no sound came out of his mouth. He could feel, and somehow even see, his mouth move but no sound came out and now he could taste the blackness it was so intense, and feel the claws of the still unseen monster as he squirmed and struggled to find a voice to his terror, but only silence followed his contortions and he knew that if he did not scream soon he would be ripped apart, his flesh and bones shredded by the monster, so he forced his mouth open even wider and could feel his lips being twisted and stretched and then he finally heard a slight sound and the blackness was partially penetrated with grayness and he became aware that he was struggling to open his eyes as he fought for endless lifetimes to open them before the claws of the monster ripped them out . . . then light was suddenly there, not the same light, but light, and he tried to move, but couldnt, tried to speak, but only incomprehensible sounds dribbled from his mouth. The nurse saw the fear and panic in his eyes and smiled at him. Its alright son, youre in a hospital. It took time for the information to register. . . . Endless time. . . . Harry tried moving his lips. Everything seemed so heavy. He couldnt move anything. The nurse rubbed his lips, gently, with an ice cube. Does that feel better? Harry tried to nod, but couldnt. He blinked his eyes. She wiped his head and face with the cool, damp cloth. She could see the fear and panic subsiding. She smiled gently as she rubbed his lips again with the ice cube. Youre in a hospital son. Everythings alright. Slowly, painfully, the reality of his situation registered in Harrys mind and he nodded his head to let her know he understood. Then he winced, My arm, my arm—he was almost crying—it hurts like hell. I cant even move it. The nurse continued to wipe his face with the cool, damp cloth, Try to relax son, the pain will go away soon. Harry looked at her for a moment, feeling the cool cloth on his head, then felt his eyes closing and fought with everything in him to escape the blackness and the claws of its monster and get back to the dream of light as he descended into unconsciousness.

For weeks Tyrone thought he was going to die any minute, and there were also times when he was afraid he wasnt going to die. He shivered through the cold nights, his bones brittle and aching, his muscles cramping, the pain doubling him up, the ache in his legs dragging him almost immediately from the short and pitiful moments of sleep, and he would lie huddled and twisted in his bunk, teeth chattering, begging in his mind for some warmth while he hoped five oclock would never come so he wouldnt have to get up and spend twelve hours with the work gang out on that highway. The guard always looked at him, shivering, for a moment, then laughed as he dumped Tyrone on the floor, Git yoe ass movin, *boy,* yawl got work to do, and he started laughing again as he walked through the barracks yelling the prisoners awake.

Tyrone spent most of the first week doubled with cramps and weakened from diarrhea and the constant spasms of retching, nothing coming up but driblets of bitter bile. When he fell over from exhaustion and cramps the guard would laugh, Whats the matta, *boy,* caint yoe take it? These here otha niggas is doin just fine, *boy*, what be wrong with yawl? and he laughed as he pushed Tyrones chin back with his foot, finishing his bottle of Coke and tossing the empty bottle into the ditch, then yanking Tyrone up on his feet and grabbing him under the chin and almost lifting him off his feet, Yoe know somethin, *boy*, we dont like yoe smart ass New Yawk niggas, yoe know that, *boy*, uh? yoe know that? Tyrone hanging from his hands, his body jerking with spasms. Aint no one ast yawl to come down chere, did they, *boy?* uh? did they? We dont like your kine, an if you ever git back to New Yawk yoe tell the rest a them niggas that we dont like your kine. Yoe hear me *boy?* Huh? Yoe hear me? We take care a our own niggas, aint that right—glancing at the prisoners around him —we takes care a them jus fine, but we doan like your kine comin down chere an startin no trouble. Yoe hear me *boy?* huh? Yoe hear me? He threw Tyrone down and spit, sneered, then laughed, Bet youd like to kill me, wouldnt you, *boy*, huh? Like to bury that shovel in mah haid, wouldnt you, *boy*, huh? He spit and laughed louder, Tell yoe what ahll do, *boy*. I/ll turn mah back an give yoe a chance. Like that, *boy?* huh? Comeon, *boy*, doan lay there like some snivelin, yella livered nigga, git yoe ass up an hit me right chere—pointing to the back of his head—this your chance, *boy*, and he turned around and watched his long shadow on the ground, and the lack of one beside it, then laughed and started walking away, Comeon, comeon, git your black asses to work, this ain no fuckin sideshow. Tyrone was still lying in the ditch, struggling to his knees, his head raging, wanting to yank that mutha fuckas tongue right the fuck out of his mouth and shove it down his throat, but unable to move as he knelt, holding on to his shovel, his head hanging and body convulsing with dry heaves. Another prisoner came over and helped him, Take it easy brother. Tyrone was panting as he cursed the honky mutha fucka, but the words were sucked back into his mouth with his convulsions. The other prisoner helped him to his feet when the convulsions stopped, Dont git no ideas brother, he blow your haid off with that shotgun. Jus be cool an he lighten up ventually. Tyrone struggled through the day, with the help of a few of the other prisoners, then fell into bed when they got back to camp after sunset. From time to time he fell into an exhausted sleep and even then his body continued to torment him, then quieted as he dreamed he was a little boy back with his moms, an he was sick with a tummy ache an the moms was holding him so nice he could feel her warm breath on his face, an it felt so good an sof an it kinda tickle his nose jus a little bit an almost make him forgit his tummy ache, an she give him a spoon a some nasty tastin medicine an he shake his head no, no, no, an turn his face, but she talk so nice and soothing an tell him hes mommas big boy, an she so proud a him, an she smile so big an wide an bright like all the sun be in her eyes, an he closed his eyes and swallowed the medicine an the moms smile even more an now her face all bright an shiny too an she hug her boy to her breas an rock him and hum, an he put his arms aroun her as far as they go an she sing so quiet her voice be like the angels she tole him about an it felt so good there, listenin to the moms sing and feelin so warm and safe, an he could feel himself drifting to sleep an all of a sudden his tummy hurt bad, real bad, an he started to cry again, mommy, mommy, an the moms hold him even tighter as her dress blotted her babys tears an Tyrone jerked and twisted involuntarily as he was dragged from his sleep and dream by his pain and tears. He opened his eyes almost wishing . . . hoping . . . but there was only blackness. For a brief second his mind was still aglow with the picture of the moms hugging him and singing, then the blackness devoured that too and all he heard were his tears as they wet his cheeks.

Eventually the spasms and retching passed and he was able to struggle through a days work with the help of other prisoners, and soon he was just another black ass to the guards and they left him alone to do his work and his time, and at night Tyrone would lie on his bunk thinking of his moms and the warm sweetness of her breath.